PRETTY CITY MURDER

ROBERT E DUNN

Pretty City Murder
Robert E Dunn
Email: robert@robertedunn.com

Published by Robert E Dunn Publishing
First published in the United States of America
Copyright © Robert E Dunn, 2018
All rights reserved
978-1-7323793-1-2
Cover art by Milan Jovanovic.
Cover photography by CanStockPhoto 19234241.

Dedicated to

Heather Wilder
Michael Routery
Joe Gartrell
Ben Gibson
Mark Malatesta
Kevin Martin
Sara Pineda
Zora Knauf
Lily Knauf

*There is nothing concealed that will not be revealed,
nothing hidden that will not be known. Everything you
have said in the dark will be heard in the daylight;
what you have whispered in locked rooms will be
proclaimed from the rooftops.*

Luke 12:2-3

Chapter 1

Thursday, July 4

Larry Leahy sat at the kitchen table and lifted a spoonful of oatmeal mush. He grabbed a granola bar and smelled its nuttiness. The previous week, his doctor had said, "Your skin is smooth and pink. You are five feet nine inches and weigh 180 lbs. Lose five." He heard the hall clock chime six times as if time were running out, and in between bongs his cell phone beeped and vibrated.

"Leahy."

"Larry?"

"James, what's wrong?"

"My security people tell me an ex-employee was seen on the twelfth floor. They told him to leave. Now, he's reentered the building and is in the garage."

"Call the police."

"I've tried that before, and it hasn't worked. This guy keeps coming back."

James sounds worried.

"What's his name?"

"Gerald Smith."

"When did you fire him?"

"Three days ago."

"What's he look like?"

"Big. I think he's thirty-five, dirty blond hair, pony tail."

"What's he wearing?"

"They didn't say."

"All right. Tell them to keep an eye on him. I'll be in there in fifteen minutes."

"Thanks. You remember our lunch date at noon today? Are we still on?"

"Sure. Have security meet me . . . what floor are your people on?"

"First floor."

"Are there cameras in the garage?"

"Yes."

"All right. Have them watch me and Smith on camera. If there's trouble, tell them to back me up. I'll call Inspector Trang and have him meet me there."

"Is he close?"

"Trang lives in North Beach, near Chinatown. He may get there before I do, but I'll fill him in on the details, and don't worry about it, James, we'll help Smith see the light, or else."

"Thanks."

He quickly stuffed the granola bar into his black jacket. Lauren was still upstairs and would be annoyed to find his unwashed mush bowl sitting on the table, but he didn't have time to worry about cleaning up. With the agility of a much younger man, he jumped down the inside staircase to the basement. The police radio sputtered to life as he grabbed the flashing red light off the rubber mat and slapped it on the roof.

He punched the number three while driving. His police badge bounced on his sternum when his red Chevy Tahoe hit cracks and potholes.

"Hieu, can you meet at the Greenwich on Mason across from the Hilton? The Greenwich owner wants an ex-employee out of the hotel. He's in the garage, so park out in front in the white zone, and don't forget the parking placard. His name is Gerald Smith, and we'll make sure he's not in the hotel lobby or anywhere else but the garage. As I recall, the stairs to the garage are near the elevators. Just follow me. How are you?"

"Ready to go, chief."

"Very good. Let's do some good today."

Larry passed St. Ignatius Catholic Church, the University of San Francisco's Italianate chapel, sitting majestically on the hill, its twin towers obscured by invading fog.

No Mass today.

Hieu's black Toyota Forerunner left just enough space for Larry to park.

"Where to?"

"Follow me."

The lobby was eerily quiet. Larry looked at his watch: 6:30 a.m. They walked past the front desk and down the hall. He found the stairs next to the elevator, right where he remembered they'd be, and felt the sponginess of new Venetian red carpet on the treads.

At the far end of the garage stood three men, one of them facing the other two. Larry looked over at Hieu, whose gray, pin-striped suit was buttoned up.

One of the Hispanic men had his hand on the chest of the man who fit the description. They were arguing. The third man was tall and muscular and stood behind his partner. They were dressed in the same colors – green, white, and red. The ceiling was low, making Larry's perspective tunnel-like, but it expanded as they got nearer to the convocation.

He heard the muscular one say, "It's a trade, your debt for a gun."

"I don't have a gun, doofus."

3

When the short one saw Larry and Hieu, he dropped his hand, reached under his bright green shirt, and extracted a shiny semi-automatic from behind a belt.

Any hope for friendly relations had ceased.

Larry charged forward just as the Caucasian man grabbed the short one around his neck. He broke free, swung his fist, and felled Larry. Hieu axed the tough guy's wrist, and the gun hit the pavement and bounced like a firecracker. Larry reached for the gun, which was a foot away, and grabbed it.

Hieu turned his man around and shoved him against a parked car. From his belt he carefully unhinged handcuffs and snapped them shut.

Larry got on his feet and growled, "You two, stand on either side of the car. No, come forward. Stand a foot from the rear end."

Hieu told his man, "You're under arrest for assaulting a police officer."

He protested, "Dude, I didn't know you was the police."

"You, what's your name?" Larry asked.

"Gerald Smith."

"You?"

"Pablo."

"Pablo what?"

"Morales."

"What's your business here?"

"I work here."

"What about the guy with the charm bracelets on? Know him?"

"Yeah, he's my friend, but I didn't know he had a gun."

"What about you? You work here, too, Smith?"

"No."

"All right. Inspector Trang, read your man his rights. You two, come with me."

Hieu recited the magic words.

"You and you, get out in front of me and start walking toward the stairs at the end of the garage. Morales, what were you doing in the garage? Don't you belong inside?"

"No, man, I don't have to be at work until three."

"Then why were you here?"

No response.

"All right, Smith, why were you here?"

Smith and his pony tail turned.

"Keep facing forward and keep walking."

With only his face turned around, Smith said, "Look, officer, I live in the neighborhood and happened to walk into the garage and saw these two guys and we started talking."

"That's bullshit. This is the last time you come into the Greenwich. Understand?"

"Yes, sir," Smith responded, in a Southern drawl.

"Morales, Smith, I'll be walking you to the front door. Don't turn around to talk to me or anyone else."

"What about my homie?"

"What about him? He's been arrested, and you won't be seeing him for the rest of the day."

Larry kept his hand on his service revolver as they walked back through the hotel.

The lobby is still quiet – normal?

Larry waved his pair toward the door. "Don't want to hear or see you for the rest of your lives." They stepped outside. "And Smith, if I see your mangy shoes and you attached to them inside this building again, I'll be ringing your doorbell." Smith made a funny, crooked sort of smile, and then both men disappeared quickly.

Larry reached for his back and massaged a sore spot.

In the lobby, Hieu was marching his man out in front.

"What's his name, Inspector?"

5

"Carlos Ortiz."

"All right. Call Central and wait here. I'll be talking to O'Hara."

Larry saw a sleepy clerk looking surprised.

"Is Mr. O'Hara's office on the second floor?"

"Yes, sir. What's happened?"

"Nothing."

Larry took the elevator to the second floor, turned right, and pulled on the double doors. The doors were locked. His cell phone beeped and vibrated again.

"Leahy."

"It's Father Ralph."

"What's wrong, Ralph?"

"It's about Cornelius."

"What's happened?"

"He got a phone call saying his life is in danger."

"Who was it?"

"He didn't know. What should we do?"

"You want me to talk to him?"

"Yes, if you could. Is it too much trouble? Am I worrying too much?"

"No, not at all, Ralph. I'm already here at the Greenwich. Remind me of his room number."

"1212."

"All right. Sit tight. I'll see what it's all about."

"God bless."

"Thank you."

After rechecking his service revolver, he rode the elevator up and checked his watch: 7:05 a.m.

Cornelius greeted him at the door.

"Hi, Cornelius. May I come in?"

"Oh, yes, sir." Cornelius looked startled.

Inside the entry hall, Larry said, "Your brother tells me you had an anonymous phone caller say that your life is in danger. Is that right?"

"My brother told you?"

"Yes, he did." Larry saw that the apartment was large and well-furnished. "Can we sit somewhere?"

"Please come this way."

They entered the living room. Cornelius sat down on a black silk Orient Express chesterfield, one of a matching set, and Larry took a seat on the opposite one. Cornelius looked at Larry without a smile or any sign of emotion, and only a port-wine birthmark below the right eye marred skin as immaculate as the casing of a peach. A fan on the side table puffed air, and tendrils of gray hair floated on his head.

"Do you know who called and said your life is in danger?"

On the coffee table lay an opened Chronicle, a pair of reading glasses, a yellow highlighter, and a bowl of oatmeal mush sitting on a tea towel. Cornelius hurriedly picked up a page of the newspaper that had fallen on the floor. The redness in his face slowly disappeared after he had reassembled the pages. Headlines had been highlighted. He seemed to have forgotten the question or lost his concentration.

Questions with a simple "yes" or "no" as an answer would be better.

"What time was the call?"

"About twenty minutes ago."

Larry once heard Father Ralph discuss his brother's disabilities with another priest. "Cornelius couldn't achieve grade-level on state tests. The school district formed a plan and discussed it with my parents." Larry could still see Cornelius' Mission High School yearbook picture and his linen complexion in the picture. A program for others like him and coaching from his mother, the ex-nun, got him through.

7

Larry began to suspect that Cornelius was having difficulty answering questions, even the simplest ones. He couldn't predict how much Cornelius would be able to grasp. The degree to which Father Ralph had overprotected Cornelius was about to be revealed.

Let's start again.

Larry took out a small notepad and pen from his jacket's inside pocket.

"Was it a male caller?"

"Yes . . . yes, I think so."

There it is.

The shyness in his manner remained. He avoided direct eye contact. It didn't suggest dislike or resistance, just shyness.

"Did the voice sound old or young?"

"I don't know . . . I don't know." Cornelius wrung his hands.

"All right. Don't worry."

"Did I answer all your questions?"

"You did fine."

They sat in silence.

Larry wanted to help Cornelius understand what kind of information they should be after, and he searched his reservoir of interview experiences. An old memory popped up, and he could hear Father Ralph retelling the story. Cornelius got lost one day on public transit and struggled to explain where he wanted to go when he was on the Muni bus, and where he had been once he got off. Had he not been seen by a family friend, Cornelius might not have arrived back home to explain his three-hour absence.

A worried mother had asked her other son, Father Ralph, for advice. He had called Larry.

I suggested transportation for the handicapped. It was nixed. Cornelius could do better.

"Did you ask his name?"

"Yes."

8

"What did the man say?"

"He hung up."

Cornelius picked up the bowl of mush and headed for the kitchen.

Larry looked at his watch. A quarter after seven. Cornelius' docile nature made Larry think about himself and how hardened he had become. It happened whenever he encountered innocence or confusion. He sat there, staring at Cornelius, and rolled his shoulders. They felt sore, exacerbated by the fall in the garage and the blues that had started after breakfast. Cornelius' simplicity caused Larry more discomfort; he knew that Cornelius would have a tough time sensing threat.

"Thank you, Cornelius. I'll show myself out."

Running water at the kitchen sink blotted out Larry's voice.

Suddenly, Cornelius turned and said, "I go to Mass at noon every day at St. Patrick's Church. I walk there. Ralph says the fresh air is good for me." He dried a dish with a small white towel. "Will you see Ralph today?"

Larry ripped out a page of his notepad and scribbled his phone number. He walked to the edge of a half-wall separating the kitchen from the living room and handed Cornelius the note. "Call me if you get another bad phone call. Okay?"

"Yes, I will. Thank you for coming."

"You have a good day." They shook hands. Though his grip was firm, in an instant, Cornelius appeared as innocent as a bird who'd lost all its feathers, or a man for whom a cop would lie or destroy evidence.

In the hall outside the door, Larry called Father Ralph.

"If there's another one, tell him to keep the caller on the line and use his landline to reach me. Do you have any ideas who this caller could be?"

"No, none."

"Okay. How is he doing, Ralph?"

"He plans to retire next month and live up at Topaz Lake. How did he seem to you?"

"Oh, fine."

"You don't sound like yourself."

"Well, the letter from Mark still bothers me . . . you told me to meet his girlfriend. Isn't that encouraging them to keep living in sin?"

Father Ralph chuckled. "Well, maybe, it's better to have simple problems like Cornelius. We'll talk again about Mark."

"Ralph, Cornelius made your parents proud, didn't he?"

"Yes, but mother wanted him to live at home and not move into the Greenwich."

"All right. I'll see what I can do."

"God bless, Larry."

"Thanks."

Larry walked to the elevators and thought about the MacKenzie parents, and about Father Ralph, Cornelius, and their sister, Anne. They lived at Number 10, Fifth Avenue, right next door to the O'Hara family. James O'Hara had contact with Cornelius, and much more after he came to work at the Greenwich and became O'Hara's concern. Larry wondered if O'Hara would be any help giving Cornelius one night of extra protection.

Over time, Larry had picked up colorless bread crumbs of information about Cornelius. He was supervisor of bellhops, lived alone, and could take care of himself. Cook? Love a woman? Larry didn't know.

At the elevator, he began planning the next phone call, pulled out a 3X5 booklet with Mary in rose and blue on the cover, and read the prayer to the Holy Spirit.

Let my weakness be penetrated with Your Strength this very day that I may fulfill all the duties of my state conscientiously, that I may do what is right and just.

Larry punched in some numbers.

"What do you want, Leahy? I'm at city hall with the mayor. Make it fast."

"I'm concerned about the brother of a friend of mine – Cornelius Mackenzie. He oversees bellhops at the Greenwich Grand Hotel. He got a phone call saying his life's in danger. I think we should post an officer at the Greenwich for a couple of days. That's my request."

Larry heard his own appeal ringing in his ears. The captain didn't expect too much precision, and he wasn't the kind of man who'd listen to a proposal, say he'd think about, and then fire off a rejection letter the next day.

"Do you know who made the call?" Dempsey snapped.

"No, but it's a credible warning that should be taken seriously."

"Request denied. I need more to go on than that."

"But, sir, I think . . ."

"Denied. Talk to me tomorrow when I'm not busy and when you've got something more to go on."

Click.

Larry searched for an alternative.

It's a bad moment, not a bad future.

The phone beeped and vibrated a third time.

"Leahy."

"Larry, Ortiz is at Central."

Another arrest will help my chances for the promotion.

"Good. I wasn't expecting three men in the garage. O'Hara said Smith was by himself."

"Did you ask O'Hara about that?" Hieu inquired.

"He wasn't in his office."

Without knowing why, Larry thought of a story in the Journal of the Police Officers Association. "Yesterday, I saw something about the murder rate. It's doubled over the last year."

"Not the results we've been working for."

"Before you became an inspector, I investigated the murder of a Catholic priest by a religious fanatic who claimed the priest molested him. Some of these claims are bogus, and this one was."

Larry shifted on the front seat.

"Notice how balmy it is? It never rains in summer."

"I know. It's dark, very dark outside," Hieu responded.

Larry saw a crow feeding on some scraps.

It flew off as his vehicle approached.

Chapter 2

Thursday, July 4

"You look gorgeous."

A Gucci handbag with tiger-head clasp allowed one hand to rest on the braided chain stretching from one end of the purse to the other. Inside a lipstick-red, silk-georgette dress was the body of a former ballerina. The high collar couldn't hide a neck that was long enough to reach the canopy of a rainforest.

Clare O'Hara smiled delicately and glided over to the nineteenth-century French gilt mantle clock.

"Good. It keeps time." She turned to face her husband of twenty-seven years. "I have a luncheon date at the Olympic Club. Three ladies and me."

O'Hara squinted to see the hands on the dial. "Enjoy yourself. I'm having lunch with Larry Leahy."

"Good. I meant to ask you how he's doing. Why don't we see him more often?"

"I don't know."

He walked her to second set of doors, where they kissed, and she said, "I love your long eyelashes. I want to lick them." She turned toward the elevators and was gone.

O'Hara faced his busty blond secretary, Anita Keck. Her smile was bright white, her ocean-green eyes politely dopey.

"Mr. Fletcher called."

"What did he want?"

"He said he has a report."

"Get him in here." O'Hara plopped down in his executive chair and swung around to get a look at the improving weather.

Fletcher entered the office.

"Well?" O'Hara said, still looking out his window.

"Mr. O'Hara, I saw Maureen Daley enter the building about thirty minutes ago."

O'Hara swung around. "What!"

"Sir, I'm just doing what you told me to do."

"Where is she?"

"Twelfth floor."

"Forget you saw her."

O'Hara waited for Fletcher to exit before he got up.

What is she doing in Cornelius' apartment?

He lifted the master key off a hook inside a deep drawer and squinted.

Eleven thirty.

"Keck, I'll be back in twenty minutes. Call me on my cell phone if you need me."

At Cornelius' door he pushed the key in quietly and stood motionless in the entry hall.

Voices came from the kitchen.

"Thank you for this and everything."

"The Solano Adop . . . Adoption Agency did everything. I think they're great."

"And make sure you thank your sister for me. Her five children are growing up so fast," Maureen added.

O'Hara looked for a place to put his cigar and stuffed it inside his pants pocket.

"I spend mornings with them, but not today, because a po . . . police officer visited me. The other children, you know, the three who aren't adopted, they are . . . are gone already. I'm glad I made it out of parents' house. I have Mr. O'Hara to thank for that."

Yes, you do.

"No, you earned this apartment, Cornelius! Oh, you have a spot on your shirt. Let me get a sponge."

Water began running.

"There. The spot came out."

As she emerged from the kitchen, O'Hara stepped out of the entry hall.

"What are you doing here?"

"James!"

"Outside."

Maureen followed James out the door.

"James, I can explain."

"I don't want to hear an explanation. You went behind my back. You've got to be more discreet. Clare was here minutes ago. What's that?"

In an open Gump's box with a silver ribbon hanging off was a glittering female figurine, the color of hoar frost touched by blue sky.

"Just something Cornelius gave me. Limoges. Don't I get a kiss?"

"I smell vermouth on your breath."

"Cornelius and I had a little drink. I feel bloated."

Her hand came out from a blue fox bomber jacket and massaged her stomach.

"I'll talk to you later. Larry Leahy and I are having lunch in the bar. You make sure you're out of the hotel before he arrives." O'Hara turned, trooped to the elevators, and didn't look back.

O'Hara found a bar stool next to a girl with long, wavy, yam-colored hair. From where he was sitting, he had a view of the door and a sign on the door window announcing the bar was open every day from ten in the morning to ten at night.

When he saw Larry, he told the girl to scoot. Larry wore a black jacket, white shirt, and tie.

O'Hara smiled and pointed at the hipster boxes lined up on one side of the bar beneath medicine-bottle blue stain glass, which kept the bar appropriately dim for a private seminar and liquid lunch. "Got a row of them. Apple computers impress the younger crowd. You wouldn't know about that."

He signaled the bartender and then wrapped his big arms around Larry, whose arms hung at his side. "What would you like to drink?"

Larry looked around O'Hara and said, "Just a coke, young lady."

O'Hara let go and said, "He's on the clock, Doogan."

She said, "Whom do I have the pleasure of serving?"

O'Hara spoke to Larry's round face, "This is Inspector Leahy, illustrious member of the San Francisco Police Department. When he's around, don't say cops."

Larry stepped back as if he were assessing a criminal.

"Have a seat, Larry."

He pointed his cigar at the stools. They stood there briefly, waiting for each other to make the first move.

Doogan filled Larry's glass with ice. A beverage dispensing gun and maraschino cherry finished it off. O'Hara noticed her eyes looking keenly at Larry. "She's the only broad around here who can speak to me without peeing in her pants – surprising because she's in here all day. Now get your eyes off Inspector Leahy. He's happily married."

"I'm just being friendly, the way I am with all the cops who come in here."

"What?" Larry asked.

O'Hara turned his big head back toward Larry and said, "Cops come in here all the time to relax . . . after work. Sometimes, I think you've got blinders on. Doogan, someone wants a drink down at the other end of the bar."

"Nice to meet you, Ms. Doogan."

She headed for two three-piece suits.

"We've got a few things to discuss," Larry said.

He sat down on a bar stool, and O'Hara sat on his.

"Do we? Let's not get too detailed. I'll order lunch." O'Hara pulled out his cell phone and called the restaurant, which was behind the bar.

"Two New York steaks."

"I found Smith in the garage and two others, one Morales and one Ortiz. Ortiz was arrested."

"What happened?"

"What I want to know is why you forgot to mention Morales and Ortiz."

"Nobody said anything about the other two."

"I find that hard to believe."

"Well, believe it. It's good to see you, Larry. Clare asked about you."

"How is she?"

"Fine. Aren't you going to ask about me?"

"How are you, James?"

"I'm getting enough. What about you?"

"You're so charming."

"I am, they say."

They sipped.

O'Hara savored the smell of his cognac and picked up his Padrone Maduro cigar.

"So, I'm hearing Harry Duncan is retiring," Larry said.

"Can you believe the balls on that guy? His father expands his dental practice just for Harry, only to lose him to Wall Street six months after the office remodel is complete. Smart move, though. Harry made more money in the week before retirement than his old man ever found in forty years of fitting his five fingers into some jerk's mouth."

He felt his belly shaking with laughter and patted Larry on his head. "Your head looks like a snowball."

Larry was silent.

"Speaking of retiring rich, Quigley played doubles with a widow who was wealthy enough for him to quit his job as a tennis pro. Of course, that meant that he had to quit the first wife, too."

No reaction from Larry.

Jazz music from a sound system installed when the bar was remodeled filled the silence. Eight micro ceiling speakers spread the sound evenly throughout the bar, and he was pleased. The voices of patrons mixed it up.

O'Hara smelled his own husky scent, and he liked that, too.

Behind them, small tables began filling up under a low ceiling that was lit with the same medicine-bottle blue color as the windows. He liked that even more.

He grabbed Larry's arm. Larry pulled away, lifting his coke in an automatic reaction. Some splashed out on his harlequin tie.

Larry turned towards the door and asked, "What's that for?"

An opaque, plastic covering hung from the lobby ceiling to the floor.

"That monstrosity. It'll be down in a day or two. I think the workmen sip coffee all day long."

"I'm sure they're working hard."

"Like city employees?"

O'Hara could see Larry's eyes quietly and carefully focused on him from above the rim of his glass. "You know, the Jesuits taught me one thing. Get to the top."

"I doubt that."

"Larry, we've had different careers. Yours is to catch the guilty. Mine is to give them a place to hide or sleep it off."

"Your hotel isn't that sort of place. I doubt there are any broken window shades or radiators or bathrooms with pink and green tile."

Although the Greenwich was built not long after the 1906 earthquake, it had been updated frequently and had a modern feel. To O'Hara, it was dark and comfortable.

O'Hara grabbed a napkin and said, "Sign it."

"What?"

"Put your signature on it."

Larry pulled a pen from his black jacket and signed the napkin as it slid around and began to tear.

"Just as I remember it. Girlish penmanship."

But O'Hara had something important to discuss with his friend of fifty-three years.

They had met in first grade of Star of the Sea Catholic School. Both had lived on Fifth Avenue, but O'Hara wasn't about to point out that he had lived on the correct side of Lake Street, where hired gardeners maintained long-branched trees only found in the better neighborhoods.

"Did you see the newspaper and the obituary?"

"I did," Larry answered.

"Ever meet this guy?"

"No. Every few years, I'd go to the police archives and read the report.

"What did he look like?" O'Hara asked out of the corner of his eye as he lifted his glass.

"The mugshot was taken by the FBI. Martin Flaherty was twenty-three years old and a high school drop-out. The record showed that my dad planned the bank robbery, and Flaherty and your dad went along. Flaherty was a big fellow, six feet five inches, brown hair, small forehead, blue-gray eyes, clean-shaven, single. They got to know each other at a bar way out in the avenues. Flaherty was no schoolboy."

"Say that again."

Larry raised his voice and said, "From the ears, he looked like he'd been in the ring more times than he should have."

"Did he work somewhere?"

"Unemployed and died in prison."

"Well, dad stopped drinking after he got out of San Quentin."

"Mine, too"

Larry raised his glass. Ms. Doogan was quick, and her sway from the other end of the bar made him chuckle. "Fifty-four years ago. A lot has happened since then."

O'Hara tapped the slick wood. "Count them as they ticked by?"

O'Hara grabbed a glass and told Doogan to fill it with crushed ice and Gatorade. A swig chilled his throat like limey gin slush.

"No, I didn't count them out. I just know."

They looked at each other.

"It wasn't my dad or yours who killed the cop."

"I know that," O'Hara said and looked away.

"Ralph's father, good old Henry, was good to us."

O'Hara faced Larry again. "Ralph's family and the Tobin's, even Angus, my grand uncle, wrote out affidavits of support for my parents. My adoption came just weeks before the robbery, and there was doubt about Mom and Dad keeping me. The affidavits, especially the one from Angus, the bank president, made the adoption stick."

"Good old Henry did a lot for us."

"You're referring to my bachelor's from USF and masters from Berkeley in the new field of computers. When my Dad got out, he said, 'go into the computer business', and you remember how good I was at math, so I switched majors."

"First, you went to IBM, then Xerox, then you opened your own copier company."

O'Hara interrupted, "Xerox had their technicians in the field day and night because their printers were breaking down all the time, but as you know, or maybe not, their name became synonymous with copiers." He swallowed. "Fantastic bit of marketing. I wish I could get the Greenwich to be another Xerox . . . in the hotel industry."

"You sold the business and . . ."

"No. Before that. The burger joints were springing up next door to each other, and it gave me an idea. Fight the big guys. So, I captured the rights to patents in the copying process. Bought them up and kept the raiders away. Henry's lawyers came in handy. The rest is too complicated for you to understand."

"Your pride is deserved. I had to get a job to marry the wife."

"Well, never mind." O'Hara gripped both sides of his glass. "You got a good wife."

O'Hara heard concealment in Larry's laughter and said, "My dad redeemed himself."

"Sure. He got rich selling real estate."

"Nope. It's true that Henry hired him, but it was dad who had the get up and go." O'Hara looked into the dimmest corner of the room. "That's our only family resemblance. He's dead and not missed. Never mind. We were never in danger of losing the house when he went to prison. The Tobin money and the O'Shaughnessy money prevented that."

"Mm. I forgot your mom's name was O'Shaughnessy. What an engineer her father was. City employee, too." Larry beamed.

"Uh-huh. When your dad went to the pokey, the Dolores Heights home was sold."

"So, what. Henry searched and finally found the house on Fifth Avenue."

"Your mom had to go to work."

Both sipped.

"I saw Ralph at Mass this morning."

"You still go every day?"

"Of course."

Larry thinks he's a saint.

"Father Ralph, now there's a success story. Dean of Arts and Sciences at USF. Henry would have been proud of that."

"I don't know. How's Cornelius?"

"He's fine. One thing old Henry failed to do was get my dad into the Bohemian Club or the Olympic Club. He didn't try very hard. My dad was back in the good graces of the Tobins and MacKenzies, so there was no reason for that failure. Right before dad died, I took him to dinner one last time at the Bohemian, and we ignored the Tobin's."

"Back to Cornelius. Did you know he got a phone call saying his life was in danger?"

"No," said O'Hara, rolling the liquid at the bottom of his glass with unconcern. "But I'm not surprised."

"Why do you say that?"

"You think you meet a lot of crazy people in your line of work? Try a couple of shifts at the Greenwich. Some guests come here to meet someone else, and they don't want to be found out." O'Hara leaned in a little closer. "Sometimes, they want to *be* somebody else, and the time spent here is their only chance to play pretend. Sheets tell the story. Language changes so fast now-a-days I can't keep up, but you probably know what each letter of these sexual acronyms represents."

"Yes, I know most of that."

O'Hara continued. "I've trained my staff to be discreet and avoid conversations with these weirdos, but they probably end up as imaginary characters in some guy's weird fantasies, and 'baby' isn't what you think it is. Someone has to do this job." O'Hara paused and gave Larry a grin that felt sly. "Don't tell me that no one ever calls in threats to Central because they're tired of sitting around in underwear and bored out of their minds."

"We still have to make sure the warning isn't credible. And Ralph made it sound serious."

"Was Ralph on the line as well?" O'Hara asked. "How would he know?"

"Cornelius told Ralph that he didn't recognize the caller, but, whoever called, the warning may be real."

"Larry, you know I've been looking after Cornelius for years. I'd rate his threat assessment skills somewhere between a smoke detector without batteries and a broad passed out in a bar. Whenever he interviews new bellhops, I keep a special 'assistant' on hand to make sure Cornelius isn't accidentally helping an applicant case the joint."

"Then why put him in charge of the bellhops?" Larry asked.

"Because for twenty-five years he worked harder than anybody else here. And it makes him happy to do the interviews. So, I gave him the promotion. It's not like I can't afford paying his helper. With the kind of money I make and the debt I owe Henry, which is zero, I could pay for a whole fake staff for his son if Henry were still alive and wanted it."

O'Hara swilled what remained. "By the way, you know he gave me half of this hotel? His partner had the other half, I bought him out, and now this baby is all mine. Look what I've done . . . and, what makes you think I forgot the promise we made to Henry to watch out for Cornelius?"

"No, but I haven't forgotten either. That's why I'm here."

"Sure, sure," O'Hara said. "The hotel is a pretty cesspool, but I'm telling you, Cornelius' living here is for the best. He can stick to his little routines and not have to worry about things like paying utility bills, and he's perfectly fine. Every now and then, something will come up, like a small pain in his leg or a jury duty summons, and he will call his brother in a panic, but it never amounts to anything. The last person to lay a hand on Cornelius was Jimmy McCullough in fifth grade, and Jimmy's nose is still pointing in the same direction it was when he was born. His wifey told Clare he had an operation on the nose a few years ago, but he still snores like a Harley."

O'Hara had both hands on the counter and looked at Larry's. Despite years of police work, Larry's hands were no rougher than his own.

He put his arm around Larry's shoulders and said, "Look, Larry, I know you're a nice guy . . . basically . . . and you've had some accomplishments . . ."

Larry interrupted. "Advancements need the helping hand of God, and at the end of a long day, I try to give Him the credit."

He's kidding me.

"Trust me. I know what to do with my employees."

"I'm up for a promotion," Larry said in a surly voice.

"Good for you. Every little success is a good thing. Who's the opposition?"

"Inspector Joe Varton."

"I saw his name in the Business Times recently. He solved some sort of white-collar crime. I thought you guys investigated murders and suicides."

"The most common causes of murder are money, revenge, and jealousy."

O'Hara stared at him. "What made you say that?"

"The phone call to Cornelius."

"I wish you'd stop thinking you have to check up on everyone."

"I want you to put a man on Cornelius tonight. We can't give him police protection."

"No. I have one man on duty. If this request had come a day or two ago, I could have helped you out, but not now."

"Call your man. I want to talk to him."

"I run this hotel. It's a safe place. He's in no danger."

"Call him."

This interferes with plans.

He picked up his cell phone. "Keck, get ahold of Fletcher. Tell him to meet me in the bar."

"How's Clare?" Larry asked.

"She doesn't have to worry about paying utility bills either. We've been married twenty-seven good years. She doesn't give me any reason to complain, and I made sure she knows her future is taken care of."

"And Maureen Daley?"

"She's fine, too" O'Hara said, removing his arm from around Larry's shoulder and abruptly losing his amiability. "I know how to handle my business, Larry."

There was a moment of silence before O'Hara continued. "But if you do want to talk to Cornelius, you'd better run along up to his room. He gets anxious if he thinks he's going to be late for his shift. He's in 1212, just in case you've forgotten."

"I already talked to him. I heard Maureen is pregnant."

"Who said that?" O'Hara shifted in his seat.

"Just a rumor. I ignore rumors."

"Best to ignore that one, buddy."

"Whatever you say."

"Yeah, big guy," O'Hara said in a steely voice. "Ignore that one if you know what's good for you."

"Threaten and threaten some more. Just keep your nose clean. No matter how loaded you are, or how much pull you have at city hall, you're an ordinary citizen – one, fine American I might have fun with some day – at the right time."

O'Hara slapped the counter. The bartender sashayed to their end. "We're done. The inspector's drink is on the house. All right, Leahy, let me take you to the lobby. You can find the front door."

"Just a minute. What about Morales and Ortiz?"

"No knowledge of them. Glad you came today. It may not look that way, but I appreciate it. I don't want Smith in the hotel again."

Fletcher walked in.

O'Hara sighed. "Leahy wants to talk to you."

"Mr. Fletcher, I'm Inspector Leahy. What time are you off duty?"

"One o'clock in the morning."

"Tonight, I want you to escort Cornelius to his apartment when he goes off duty. Check each room. Make sure the apartment is empty. Tell Cornelius to call 911 if he sees or hears anything out of the ordinary. Same for you, call 911. Do you understand?"

"May I ask what this is about?"

O'Hara said, "No. Just do what you're told."

"Yes, sir."

Fletcher backed out of the bar.

O'Hara and Larry followed him, and they shook hands beside the plastic covering.

O'Hara headed for his office.

The slow learner in 1212 is my problem.

•••

Pepper Chase stood behind the front desk in the Greenwich's lobby. In the middle of helping guests, the operator popped out from her room and told Pepper she had a call waiting. She finished checking in an elderly couple and picked up the desk phone.

"Hello."

"Hi, darling."

"Is that you dad?"

"Don't you recognize your daddy's voice anymore?"

He sounded drunk.

Her thoughts bunched up. The dead-beat dad. Out of work most of the time, abusive to her mother and brothers, at the bar drinking himself into a stupor so he could get to sleep at night. She looked at her watch: half past one.

"Yes, what do you want?"

"I need a little money, but that's not the real reason I called."

"What is?"

"Your brother is in jail again. He got arrested for selling weed."

"I'm busy. I have an important job and can't take personal phone calls. I'll call Michael later."

"So, your big job in the big city makes you too good to talk to your daddy?"

"I've bettered myself without any help from you or Mom or anyone else. I've even got a 401K plan, but I live from paycheck to paycheck and have no extra money. Ask Aunt Gertrude to help Michael. She's your sister!"

"You make me sorry I called."

"You make me sick."

"Is that any way to talk to your own father?"

"I'm going to hang up."

"Your brother will call when he finds out."

Pepper felt scared and threatened. Michael was even meaner than her father, but she couldn't hate him.

The beatings he took are too horrible to think about.

There was only pity and a feeling of helplessness in her heart.

A guest stood waiting. Pepper hung up the phone without saying good-bye.

The man in front of her was older and balding, on the short side and alone. She thought of Cornelius. Unlike her father, Cornelius was kind and dependable.

Right. I'll deliver Cornelius' dinner to him.

•••

After a couple of hours of work, O'Hara strained to see the gilt clock.

27

Half past three. Inspection time.

He rode the elevator from the second floor to the first and headed for the doorman. Ever ready, he tilted his cap. The brunette clerk was giving directions from the front desk to a middle-aged couple wearing matching khaki shorts. Knowing they would regret their clothing choices when the weather cooled, he offered a skillful smile that gave way to a sneer once the couple was outside.

Behind the desk, he landed a quick slap on the brunette's posterior. Lawyers be damned, the hotel was his to do with as he wanted, and what were employees but hotel chattel. Not caring what her reaction was, he looked over at a bellhop and said, "I hope you're all ready for a busy night." He didn't wait for an answer and didn't expect one. His employees were in such awe of him that they couldn't put a sentence together.

Guests stood in twos and fours, preparing to leave and looking eager. O'Hara judged they had correctly made restaurant reservations. He weaved in and out of colorless conversations, red, white, and blue paper lanterns dangling from chandeliers, and miniature flags sticking out of wall sconces.

The lobby was undergoing remodeling, and it didn't look good. "When's that damn covering coming down?" He looked around for the workmen and motioned to the doorman. "Have this monstrosity removed. Thanks."

The review was almost complete. The brunette stood alone at her station. He lowered his eyeglasses down his nose and took them off. "Where's Chase?"

"She's up in Mr. MacKenzie's room, sir."

"What's she doing there?"

The clerk pulled herself up against the desk counter and answered, "I'm not sure, sir. She said she needed to talk to him."

"I'll see about that. Don't you have anything to do?"

"No, sir, we're waiting for the arrival of guests. They went on a tour and . . . and should be back in about an hour."

"Fine. Look busy. Give me the master key."

O'Hara put his eyeglasses back on, marched down the long hallway, and passed a framed picture of his pale gold 1964 Rolls-Royce Silver Cloud, driven every day to the hotel. His hands could almost feel the hardness of its real chrome grill.

Another vehicle remained at home in a garage with its own air filtration system. It was an orange 1972 Chevrolet Corvette Stingray, the first automobile he had purchased with his own money, with an odometer reading of 135,000 miles, racked up on trips to Southern California beaches and now only driven to car shows to get him what he wanted most: a trophy.

Maureen Daley swayed back and forth in his head. He hoped she would be dressed in something red for the evening that was fast approaching.

"Chase will be sorry she's in Cornelius' room," he remarked. Two sunbaked ladies, each with a flower tucked behind an ear, exited the elevator and looked at the man who was talking to himself. Gardenia scent trailed him onto the twelfth floor. As the elevator doors closed, he exhaled loudly, stormed the hallway, turned the master key, and pushed the door open. He had more ballast than was needed to launch a battleship.

"Pepper, a kitchen helper usually brings me dinner. Why you?"

"Oh, I saw him with the tray and said I would bring it to you and I've brought your dinner before. Don't you remember? Would you like a glass of milk?"

"Yes, please."

O'Hara kept silent, but the sound of glass landing on a glass table felt like grit in his shoe.

After I kick them out, let that milk sour.

"Who's at the front desk?" Cornelius asked.

"Doris."

"Shouldn't you be there?"

"It's not busy. This will only take a few minutes. I'll get back to the front desk." A moment later, she said, "The music is lovely. What is it?"

"*Madame Butterfly.*"

"What's that?"

"Opera."

O'Hara whispered, "How stupid she is."

"How is it?" she asked.

"It's good. I had an argument wi . . . with Mr. O'Hara today."

"What about?"

O'Hara's lips tightened.

"Gerald Smith." O'Hara heard three sucking sounds in a row. "Mr. O'Hara hasn't made an announcement, yet, but it'll get around. He . . . he fired Gerald."

Pepper gasped. "Why?"

"Gerald was late three times and didn't call."

"I haven't seen Gerald for a few days. That explains why. Gerald's a good guy. That's unfair."

O'Hara pulled on the lapels of his suit jacket as he prepared to charge.

"Gerald is staying at Topaz Lake. Pepper, you should return to the front desk now."

"Yes, sir," she said, then stammered out the words, "Mr. MacKenzie, can I ask you something?"

"What?"

"Have you ever been in love?"

"No."

"I know someone who's interested in you."

"I'm too old to be in love."

"You don't really mean that, do you? I'm twenty-four, and I don't think you're old. Oh, I meant to thank you again for the dozen red roses you gave me on my fourth anniversary last week. You know how much I love roses and working here, but I was so surprised."

What made him do that?

O'Hara pulled the cigar out of his mouth. He looked for a napkin or a place to toss it and stuck it in his pants pocket.

"Mr. O'Hara called me an old man, and I told him he's four years older."

Pepper giggled. "You shouldn't have said that. You need someone to look after you."

"I pl . . . plan to keep working and not retire like Ralph said I should. Tomorrow I'll be with people I really like. We volunteer to help people with disabilities. When I'm not doing that, I like to spend time with my sisters' children."

"Oh, that's nice. You're still young, Cornelius, about the same age as my father."

"I nev . . . never heard you talk about your father."

"I don't like him, I mean, I don't like to talk about him. So, are you in love with someone?"

Is she after him?

Cornelius didn't answer.

"Why was Mrs. Daley here?"

"I gave her a present."

Why?

O'Hara scratched his head.

"She's beautiful."

"Yes," Cornelius said.

"You think my hair is pretty?"

"Yes."

"You think I'm as pretty as she is?"

"Yes."

"Why don't you think you could fall in love?"

O'Hara watched as Pepper entered the living room and looked around. He stepped back into the darkness of the entry hall. On top of an end table next to the black chesterfield she found gold cufflinks and pocketed them. She saw his suit jacket lying on the back of the chesterfield, lifted it, and examined the tag inside the collar. She skillfully re-laid the jacket and returned to the kitchen.

"You never told me you shopped at Wilkes Bashford. Where is that?" Pepper said.

"I . . . the tailor comes here. Father Ralph orders my suits. He says that's where Mr. O'Hara shops. I don't know much about that."

"Don't you think you could fall in love, Cornelius?"

There was no answer.

She asked again, "Don't you think you could be in love?"

The apartment was quiet.

Suddenly, she blurted, "I love you, Cornelius," and flew out of the kitchen.

O'Hara took a position between her and the front door and yelled, "What are you doing here?"

Pepper pushed past O'Hara and threw open the door.

O'Hara spoke loudly to her back. "If I find you in here again, I'll fire you." He followed her out into the hall and saw her entering the elevator. "I'll fire you!" He turned around and saw Cornelius coming out of the kitchen. "This is the *last* time she comes inside your apartment. She's on duty and has no business here. Do you understand?"

With a starched white bib still attached, he answered, "Yes, sir. I apologize for our . . ."

Before Cornelius could finish, O'Hara was on the elevator and riding it to the second floor.

As he entered his office, his secretary said, "Mr. Fletcher called."

"What did he want?"

"He said he has a report."

"What about?"

"I didn't ask, sir."

"Get him in here."

Three minutes later Bud Fletcher walked into the inner sanctum.

O'Hara faced the window and said, "What have you got, Fletcher?" He swung around in his desk chair and flicked his cigar in a lead-glass ashtray.

"Mr. O'Hara, Gerald Smith was in the hotel this morning."

"And?"

"I asked him to leave. You told me he had been fired."

"Did Smith leave?"

"Oh, yes. Security escorted him out the front door."

"Fix the report. Larry Leahy took him out. I've warned you before about lying."

"But I'm part of security."

"You're my investigator! If Smith enters again, send for security. Do you understand?"

"Yes . . . yes, sir, but I'm the only man on duty tonight."

"Exactly. Now, as for tonight, keep doing what you do and forget about Leahy's request to escort Cornelius to his apartment." O'Hara turned around and said, "Go back to work."

"Yes, sir."

O'Hara buzzed Keck and demanded Smith's cell phone number.

A minute passed while he waited.

"Mr. O'Hara, what's his name?"

"Gerald Smith! I'm surprised you know your own name."

"Oh, yes. I see it."

She recited the numbers slowly, and he became impatient. "Thank you." He put down the receiver, snuffed the cigar in the ashtray, and took out his cell phone. He did not want the call to appear in the hotel's phone records.

The voice that said "hello" sounded hoarse.

"Smith?"

"Yeah."

"O'Hara here."

"Mr. O'Hara." There was a pause. "I'm at Topaz Lake."

"What're you doing there?" O'Hara was worried. As if he were picking up Maureen's black lace panty, he plucked the cigar from the ashtray and dumped it into the golden spittoon.

"I've been on vacation . . . ever since you fired me." Gerald laughed.

"I don't want you to step inside the Greenwich ever again. Understood? Your association with Cornelius has ended. And I'll be speaking to his brother about you being up at Topaz Lake. He should know that you are no longer welcome at the Greenwich and why."

"Hold up, man. You can't stop me from coming up here."

"You wait," O'Hara screamed, and ended the call.

Chapter 3

Thursday, July 4

Lights radiated abundance from every window at O'Hara's Sea Cliff mansion as the Jesuit community's black Buick entered the semi-circular driveway and Father Ralph stepped out. Blue-coated attendants moved arriving cars to the parking area, and a shuttle shepherded guests from the China Beach parking lot, where a canvas tent had been set up with security. Confetti-colored flowers filled giant Thai bamboo baskets that hung from the rough-hewn balconies, and exterior accent lamps displayed a bankroll sustaining every inch of the Spanish colonial.

The heavy oak door swung open.

Clare O'Hara was dressed in a mauve silk evening gown and offered her warm, bone-white hand. "Nice to see you again, Ralph." Still holding his hand, she kissed him on the cheek and said, "James is somewhere. You'll have to go looking for him if you want to talk." She motioned with the other hand and an easy laugh followed.

The cocoa aroma of Padron Maduro floating inside the portico entrance tickled Father Ralph's hooked nose and gave him relief from a dull pain in his stomach that began on the way to O'Hara's.

"You don't look so well, Ralph. I can take you into the kitchen and fix you a drink myself. Maybe, a ginger ale?"

"No, no. I'm fine."

The ache came whenever he contemplated leaving the priesthood and having to explain his reasons to his mother and Cornelius. A mission trip to Mexico or farther south, where the sun burns the dust and the roads are without real sidewalks, would burn away his desire for happy domesticity.

"You're looking as beautiful as ever. I hope I'm not late." Father Ralph let go of her hand.

"No, more guests to come. Make yourself comfortable." She turned and with her left hand motioned again in the direction of the great room. He caught a glimpse of the cut-out on the back of the gown and the chestnut hair wrapped on top of her head like twisted pastry. A quick scan left little doubt that, even at age fifty-two, she continued to toil at the ballet bar.

He looked up at the full-length portrait hung at the landing where two sets of stairs came together from opposing directions. Pastel brushstrokes perfectly captured her essence and the chiffon-like softness of her skin.

She escorted him to the party room. Walking by the side of the poor and unwashed might cure him of this desire for a wife, but not require as much faith as Lourdes. A pilgrimage of the kind that is done slowly in a country where bad politics makes heroes out of nuns might cure him, but the possibility that he might be offered a college presidency would mean enough income to support a wife.

Before returning to the front door to greet more guests, Clare bowed her head at several friends. Father Ralph's lasting loyalty to her had begun when her father sponsored Father Ralph's father, Henry, for membership in the Bohemian Club. Tonight, others would be in attendance for sundry purposes, both social and business.

Father Ralph spotted Maureen Daley out on the balcony and directly thought of Clare's predicament. Years ago, she had confided in a counseling session that she was barren. He wanted to cover her eyes, but she abruptly turned around and left his side. A favorite passage extolling the beauty of womanhood came to mind:

To the steeds of Pharaoh's chariots would I liken you, my beloved: Your cheeks lovely in pendants, your neck in jewels. Song of Songs 1:9-10.

He charted a way around the grand room and found a tony, young couple he didn't recognize and said hello. Not far from them he noticed an older couple who knew his mother. He told them that she was as stylish as ever, even after eighty-nine years of triumphs and defeats, but didn't disclose the fact that she needed help dressing. He saw Maureen's eldest daughter, Megan, and wondered if she knew about her mother's affair with James.

Where was James?

Standing near a window overlooking the Golden Gate, the District Attorney and the Public Defender enjoyed a drink but didn't say much to each other. Amused that they were in the same room, Father Ralph shook hands with each and delighted in the intimacy he had with the man who was responsible for bringing them together. James O'Hara supported all reasonable Democrats, and politicians who did not ask James for too much were deemed reasonable.

He was closer to Maureen now. Wrapped in a silver and blonde, full-length, natural lynx coat over a blood red dress, she gazed out over the iron railing of the balcony. A tiger-orange ball floating above the horizon gave her face a hot glow and allowed her to be seen easily through the double doors, and in the cool night air, the lynx and glass of blush wine were keeping her warm.

"Hello, Maureen, happy Fourth of July."

"Ralph, I was hoping you would be here." She shook his hand and pulled him closer, his roman collar coming within inches of soft lips that kissed his cheek and exuded lilac, helping him to forget about the ache.

Swirling eighty feet below was the stench of sea water.

Out came Joyce Contorado and her husband.

The balcony was suddenly overcrowded.

Rather than look at Joyce, the woman who had obtained his affection, he focused on the fiery ball, now sunk a quarter of the way

37

below the horizon, and on the shards of blue-violet and red light shooting across the water and over the house.

"It's getting cold. I think I'll go inside." His black sleeve brushed lightly against Joyce's uncovered arm. Joyce reached for Father Ralph's hand, but Mr. Contorado put his hand on top of hers and spanked it once.

"Ralph, wonderful party, isn't it?" Joyce's voice trailed after him through the door.

A bourbon and soda absolved Father Ralph of an affair of the heart, but only for a minute. He rotated on his heels and was off-balance when he saw two women approaching, followed by Joyce, in a gallop, without Mr. Contorado. Each one of the women nudged out the other to be nearer to the most distinguished and urbane priest in San Francisco.

"Did something embarrass you, Father, outside on the balcony?" one woman asked.

"Nothing surprises Father Ralph. Just imagine all the juicy things he's heard in confession. Why, when I told him . . ." Joyce broke off in a state of alarm, her cheeks turning dark as mulberry.

He gulped down his bourbon and soda and said to another passing waiter, "Please give me a refill."

As the color in Joyce's cheeks returned to normal, Father Ralph wondered if she knew about Maureen's affair with James.

He drank a mouthful and looked above the liquid at Joyce's lips, pink as plumeria and shimmering in the light of a sparkling, diamond clip pinning down a side-curl. It was as though a spotlight had cast Joyce's face in shades of cantaloupe.

She moved, and his gaze descended.

A thin black belt firmly cinched a sleeveless, coconut-colored dress, and the perfume reminded him of their favorite flower, Hawaiian pikake. The divine scent of a pikake lei was said to be a prelude to marriage. She wasn't wearing one. He felt woozy, and an apparition materialized. He saw a man and woman walking hand-in-hand over sand. A light breeze was blowing, and they drifted to the intoxicating beat of distant drums, washing away all other sounds.

An ice cube sealed in bourbon bumped against the side of his glass, and the tinkling snapped him back to reality. The glass tipped, causing the ice cube to fall out. He bent over to pick it up, felt light-headed and, on his return to a more soldierly position, was giddy enough to tell a joke to the women.

"There were three professors on a skydiving adventure. The pilot informed them the airplane was going to crash and that there was only one parachute. The first professor said, 'I deserve the parachute; I have seniority.' The second professor said, 'I deserve the parachute; I have three children.' The third professor, a priest, said, 'Seniority and children count for nothing when you've got God on your side and the parachute in your hands. So long!'"

They all laughed and continued laughing. "Excuse me. I'd better greet our host." James stood in the middle of male admirers. Father Ralph knew he had more in common with his host than most people could, or would, ever understand. James had turned the Greenwich into a modern money pot, and throughout, they had remained ardent devotees of one another.

"Ralph, you look downhearted," James said, placing his hand on Father Ralph's shoulder and steadying him. "Cheer up. It's the Fourth of July."

"Just thinking about something," Father Ralph answered, not wanting to let on. Spend the rest of his life alone or marry that woman, Joyce.

"Ralph, there's something I want to talk about . . . privately." James guided Father Ralph to a corner of the room. "Cornelius told me he's not retiring. That means he won't be vacating the apartment. I'm not concerned about that, but I know you'd want to know. As head of the family, you should."

O'Hara's mouth was twisted in a weird way, but Father Ralph felt tired and moody, and his eyes began to lose focus, keeping people, problems, and Joyce away. "What? He is all set to retire. I better call him."

"Upstairs, in the hallway. No one will be up there."

"Thanks. I'll be back."

The call went straight to the message recorder. He paced and punched one again. The recorder answered a second time.

What to do?

The party entered its third hour. Father Ralph stood near the balcony's open door when James excused himself from his group and stepped onto the balcony.

His hand touched Maureen's elbow. She was chatting with her daughter.

Father Ralph listened near the open door and looked for a waiter.

"Maureen, would you mind stepping inside for a minute?"

"Yes, of course."

At six feet and 180 lbs., it wasn't easy for Father Ralph to stand behind a narrow drape. They walked past. He heard James say, "Ralph's upstairs calling his brother. Clare asked me to be discreet. She's right. Do you think you should leave?"

Father Ralph felt like an interloper and thought he should announce himself.

"James? I've always been welcome in your house. I don't believe Clare would ever say that. Is it you? Do you want me to go?" Maureen said, with a hand resting on James' shoulder.

James wrenched his shoulder away from her hand. "For Christ sake, be careful."

She slowly closed the blonde lynx around her herself. With a finger wagging at him like that of a school teacher, she said, "Don't be so unforgiving." The finger flattened as she stroked his face.

"Ouch."

She withdrew her hand and backed away.

Father Ralph witnessed the reaction on James' face.

"That color on your nails. What's it called?"

"Pleasurable Pink," she answered.

"Get rid of it."

The slap that followed shocked Father Ralph. He experienced the sensation of falling and looked around the room to see if anyone else had seen her hit James.

"I'll talk to you after the fireworks are over. Clare will want me by her side."

Maureen fell back against one of the chairs and steadied herself on its arm. "It's hot in here."

Father Ralph moved away, unnoticed.

•••

At five minutes past eight, merrymakers filled the hotel lobby. Pepper Chase and her front desk partner, Doris, were nearing the middle of their shift.

Pepper was still upset that Mr. O'Hara had yelled at her in Cornelius' apartment.

The advice columns telling her to be more assertive came to mind.

Talk to Cornelius.

"Doris, I'm going to talk to Cornelius."

"Okay, sweetie."

From her purse she pulled out a brush and bent over, and her long, curly, red hair flew forward. She stroked it repeatedly from the nape of her neck forward. She stood up and inhaled. No one staying at this hotel boarded public transportation, and the last customer had paid his bill with hundred-dollar bills. She felt proud to be working at such an establishment, but unanswered love was tenaciously summoning.

"Hello, miss, we'd like to know if it gets cold at night here in San Francisco."

"Yes, I recommend dressing in layers."

"Thank you."

Pepper looked at Cornelius and down at her fingernails, painted a special color just for this night. Conversations bubbled with excitement and faded down the hallway to the elevators. The warm air in the lobby was still saturated with the sugary fragrance of a vineyard during an afternoon harvest, but the problem remained.

If I tell him again, I might be rejected.

She stepped back from the counter, pulled out a compact and lip-gloss from her purse, reapplied strawberry balm, and boldly took a step toward Cornelius. He pulled on a loaded baggage trolley and disappeared down the hallway. Pepper's hopes sunk.

"Hello, can you order a cab?"

"If you stand outside, one will pull up shortly."

"But it's so cold outside."

She smiled and repeated the advice given to a different couple earlier.

Fifteen minutes passed. She had no one to talk to about Cornelius. That morning on the way to work, she had window-shopped Saks. The last Greenwich customer looked like the type who could shop there, and Pepper longed for the day when she could enter and be served by a brand ambassador. Tiffany's silver-lined casement windows had only stimulated terrible longings within.

Doris asked, "Pepper, we're not busy, so can we talk?"

"Uh-huh."

"Did you see Mr. O'Hara earlier today? He was asking about you."

"Oh . . . I don't want to talk about that now."

"I need to go on another diet."

"Have you gained weight? It doesn't show," Pepper said.

"Well, I weighed myself today, and the answer is no, but I don't like my flabby stomach. I look like an old man with a pot belly."

Pepper laughed.

"You want to know who I have a crush on?"

Pepper felt stressed and managed to say, "Who?"

"Ready, the boy in housekeeping. Lindsey says he looks kind of thuggish out of uniform, but she probably hasn't done anything exciting in her whole life. Maybe, he is kind of thuggish, and maybe, I don't care. Do you think I'm making a mistake if I flirt with him?"

"If it's a mistake, you've made it about a thousand times already, so I'm not sure why you're asking me now."

"I didn't know it was so obvious. No . . . you're making that up."

"Let's talk about something else," Pepper said to her junior clerk.

"What can we talk about?"

Pepper didn't answer.

Five more minutes passed.

"You want to get married and have children, right, Pepper?"

"Of course." Pepper felt warm again.

"I just love Maureen Daley's hairstyle. I'd like to get my hair done that way. I wonder why she's here so often. Have you heard any rumors about her?" Doris asked.

"No, and you shouldn't be listening to gossip."

Both laughed.

"I need to have my hair straightened. It's getting out of control. What do you think?" Pepper asked.

"You have gorgeous red hair. Just get it styled."

"Thanks, Doris. Do you think Maureen's pretty?"

"Very."

Pepper felt sick.

"She is, but she's too old to have another baby." Her eyes searched for Cornelius.

How do I get hold of him?

Doris turned to help a guest. Pepper relaxed and opened her e-mail. Amazement filled her heart when Cornelius' name appeared. He had sent her an e-mail! The first try at expressing love didn't go well, but now there was another chance.

Success on the second try would be amazing.

She crossed her fingers. Raw feelings twisted them tighter as she read:

Dear Pepper,

I have a big favor to ask. I have a gambling debt. Please bring $50,000 to my apartment. The money is in the vault. I'll pay it back. A loan shark is demanding the money by tomorrow. Delete this right after you read it.

Cornelius MacKenzie

A shudder rippled through her. Pepper quickly closed the e-mail, looked over at Doris, who was still giving directions, signed off, and closed the screen.

Cornelius is an honest man.

He goes to church every Sunday.

His brother is a priest.

So, how could he have a gambling debt? She thought she knew him, but maybe, not.

The e-mail frightened her, even more than when she was forced to get an unwanted abortion at age nineteen because the sperm donor offered no support and said their encounters were about having fun and nothing more.

She felt sure Cornelius and Maureen Daley were having an affair, and if she said no to his request, any chance of winning him would end.

Inside her purse was a compact lying face-up, and she turned it over to hide a weak chin. Cornelius was talking to a bellhop.

Interrupt and discuss the e-mail.

Drag him to the employee break room and pelt him with questions.

Force him to his apartment and wrench from him a promise of love.

E-mail him back and wait until tomorrow.

None of these options looked good. He said he needed the money immediately. Politely asking to see him in the counting room outside the vault would seem suspicious.

This is my chance to prove I love him, and I may not get another.

The difficulty of comprehending what would come next began to extinguish her will, but, marveling at a semblance of resolve, and not knowing why, she picked up the front desk phone and called Gerald Smith, her only real friend, then left a message devoid of any mention of the dilemma.

There was still time to consider the choices and weigh the risk.

Doris was giving directions again. Pepper's hand reached for the metal lock box under the front desk. An unsteady forefinger punched buttons on the four corners of the lock box. The hotel master key hung on a tiny hook inside. Her free hand pushed the hair out of her eyes. She shut the lock box, pushed the small button down to confirm it was secured, and clutched the master key as if it were a solid gold coin.

"Doris, I'll be right back."

Doris stepped back and whispered, "No problem, Pepper. I'll take care of things."

Pepper started fast, then braked.

I don't want to give any clues about what I'm doing.

She nodded casually at a man in Doris's line and said, "Now there's a handsome man." She squeezed her lips together so tightly she could taste the balm. With a single stroke from the hand holding the master key, her hair flew back.

Once in the employee hall, she looked in both directions. No one was close by.

Inside the counting room her teeth began chattering at the sight of the great, gleaming vault. As she turned back and faced the shut counting room door, second thoughts surfaced, but there was no time.

45

She steadied herself, dumped the master key into her purse, and placed the purse on a table. Her right hand turned the dial back and forth. The other rested on the vault's brushed, sleek face. The room smelled of new money.

The first try failed.

On the second try, with a sound that was deafening in the closed room, the locking mechanism released, and the heavy door sprung open a fraction of an inch.

With one foot in front and one foot behind, she pulled on the five spoke handle. This time it seemed heavier. Hands pushed the door to the wall and dropped to her side. Her foot got caught, and she stumbled on the vault precipice. When she regained her balance, she stood face-to-face with the first row of silver cash trays, their luster lost forever in the face of the task that had brought her there. This time, she was a cat in water.

Her heart pounded wildly as she stepped out of the vault and scooped the purse over one arm.

She scanned the five shelves. A finger lifted the lid of the first tray on top to reveal bundled stacks of bills. Both top trays contained five stacks of one hundred-dollar bills. Each stack had one hundred bills apiece. The tray she had lifted contained $50,000. Below were other trays for fifties, tens, fives, and ones. She looked in the second top tray, and the bills were still in their bank straps, just like the first tray. Perfect.

The first stack of hundreds dropped into the purse. Suddenly, a tray tipped over and plummeted to the steel floor. As it slid and turned over, a blue strap broke, and one-dollar bills spilled out. She bent over and hastily put the tray back on the bottom shelf. After gathering the dollar bills and carefully placing them in the tray, and still terrified that any one of the trays might fall again, Pepper pushed them back as far as they would go.

All the stacks she needed filled up her purse.

She turned the five spoke handle again until the mighty locking mechanism clicked shut.

Where's the master key? I need to get in his room.

It was where it was supposed to be, inside the purse, buried under the money. Snapping the purse shut reignited the panic and propelled her out of the counting room and down the hall to the elevators.

Pepper punched the dimly lit button several times until the elevator door opened.

Empty.

Exiting on Cornelius' floor got her closer to the end of her mission, and the realization that no one was in the hall slowed her footsteps. She found the keyhole, and with a short twist, entered and placed the bills on a black coffee table. The fingers of one hand interlocked the fingers of the other. The purse dangled from her arm.

The phone rang.

It might be Cornelius.

"Hello."

"Who is this?"

"Who is calling?"

"Father Ralph. Where's my brother?"

She hung up, but panic strangely helped her remember the first time she spoke to Cornelius. He needed help reading a city map. He tried so hard, and she ended up asking Doris for help. Afterward, she attempted to pry information from coworkers and got only vague scraps of information. Later, employees whispered that they had been told not to talk about him.

Why does love have to be so complicated?

She picked up Cornelius' phone.

"Doris, is everything okay?"

"Well, yes, of course, everything is fine."

"Did anyone call? Anyone asking about Cornelius?"

"No. Where are you?"

"I'm outside in the back. I needed some fresh air. I'll be right back in a few minutes."

"Hurry up. The line is getting longer."

On the wall was a photograph of Cornelius kissing a fluffy white bunny. It conjured his cuddly head. A sterling silver coffee and tea set on a side-board conjured his shiny face, a beacon of light, leading, moving, inspecting. Next to the bunny hung a snapshot of Mr. O'Hara handing Cornelius a twenty-fifth anniversary watch at a luncheon in the hotel restaurant. This picture evoked an even more powerful memory, the day Cornelius had invited her to lunch in the restaurant and had offered to pay for the most expensive item on the menu.

She had few friends. No one to play matchmaker. No text messages to read. No voice messages to replay. Still, here she was, in *his* apartment, alone, but surrounded by his calming presence and filled with the power of feelings that had brought her there in the first place.

A small habit forced a glance at her watch's pink mother of pearl dial.

Five past nine.

No exit could have been faster than that of leaving the forbidden apartment.

Paper-white legs vaulted down the hall to the elevator. Straightening her uniform jacket became more difficult to do as guests boarded. Looking dumpy might make her appear frazzled and expose her deception. When the door opened, she rushed forward into the employee hall. The sight of the counting room door made her legs buckle.

A little boy came running down the hall, and a woman in a red coat was chasing him.

How did they get in here?

One last breath filled her lungs with enough strength to get behind the front desk, and the activity on the other side helped her feel she was blending in.

"What took you so long?"

"I'm sorry, Doris, you can take your break now."

Doris left, and Pepper handled a guest checking in. She remembered to return the master key to the lockbox. Half an hour later, Doris returned and startled Pepper, who flinched and hit her hand on the counter.

"What's the matter?" Doris asked.

"Oh, nothing." Pepper shrugged her shoulders, rubbed her hand, and glanced at the lobby clock. "It's only 9:40 p.m. How are we going to get through the rest of the shift? I'm already pooped."

"Why so tired, pumpkin?"

"Oh, just stress, Doris." Pepper pulled her chair forward and propped her chin on wet palms. Her elbows were hard-pressed on the counter.

"You need some time off, and the man you said was handsome . . . he's a bachelor. The woman behind him was his sister."

Pepper grew sluggish and used what energy was left to pull a one-ounce tube of buttery hand cream from deep inside the purse, the secret place where it was protected from sharing. The blend of almond and coconut wafted upward. The swipe of a hand over beads of perspiration to loosen her sticky white blouse from the back of her neck released an odd odor.

When no one was looking, she wiped her hand on her pants. A smell like that of dirty aquarium water floated upward.

Midnight approached. Doris listened to a guest complain about the lobby heat and another about her sore feet. A tipsy couple entered the lobby from outside. The girl said, "Tarzan, lead the way." Colorful holiday streamers swathed her virtue.

Cornelius looked at Pepper, said good-night, and walked off as if it had been a normal evening. Pepper pulled back her shoulders and watched. Suddenly, before she realized what she was doing, she left the front counter and darted into the elevator hallway, pushed her way past Tarzan, and intercepted Cornelius before he could reach the elevators.

"Cornelius!"

He held onto her arm.

She wanted to stroke his face but felt a shove back. His mystified look muted her voice until courage gathered and the toes in her shoes began to curl like claws.

"Cornelius, I just wanted to tell you I did exactly what you told me to do. You don't have to say anything. I . . . love you."

His hand dropped, freeing Pepper to move forward and caress a button on his jacket. She moved closer and pleaded, "Just tell me you have feelings for me. I'm not asking for anything more. Just tell me . . . so I know." Taking the money to his apartment was on her mind.

"Pepper, I'm tired. Can we talk about this tomorrow?"

She stood back, glared at him, and said more stridently, "I need to know now!"

He took a step toward the elevators.

She blocked him. "Is it that woman, Maureen Daley?"

"Leave me alone." With a hand on the wall, Cornelius stepped around her.

For the first time, Pepper felt the impact of Cornelius' frailty. Up to now, she had been certain he was a prospect. Was she completely wrong? No one had encouraged her flirting. No one had discouraged it. There was no change in his demeanor whenever she came near. The more she thought about it, the more she doubted.

Maybe, he found out I had an abortion.

Maybe, I flirt with hotel guests too much and he thinks I'm a floozy.

Maybe, one pricy lunch in the hotel restaurant was not the start of a romance.

Maybe, I'm too ambitious.

Maybe he does love someone else. . .

Suddenly, she felt as if Maureen were choking her. Remorse followed her back to the front desk.

"Doris, stop surfing the internet and get back to work."

But there's nothing to do," Doris complained.

"Just look busy!"

•••

O'Hara moved among his guests, and black water eighty feet below drowned out noise from the grand room. The fireworks had ended two hours ago, but the bridge still glowed like a campfire. Guests were regrouping.

Father Ralph kept his distance and looked at his watch. "Thanks for the evening, James. I need to see Cornelius. Please give my thanks to Clare."

"No problem, Ralph. You have a good night."

While an attendant retrieved the Buick, Father Ralph thought about what had been revealed. As he closed the car door, an image of the Topaz Lake vacation home appeared. It was a place for hunting and fishing. Cornelius had friends who liked the sporting life and invited him on expeditions into the mountains, something that was foreign to Father Ralph. The friends had found the cottage and had raved about it. As executor of the family trust fund, he had reluctantly agreed to its purchase. The location was remote, one Father Ralph didn't care for, and so his emotions were torn between wanting Cornelius to retire but wanting him to stay in San Francisco.

He looked at his cell phone. The time was fifteen minutes to twelve, and he would arrive at the Greenwich sometime after midnight.

He was on the verge of a decision. The sick feeling that he had whenever he was driving began to intensify, and it was time to decide, remain a priest or marry Joyce Contorado.

When the Greenwich came into view, he had a strange and vague sensation that something sinister was afoot, and it had nothing to do with Joyce.

•••

Cornelius turned the knob. The tangerine-colored swivel chair comfortably accepted his tired limbs. Off came the shoes. A glance at the clock told him it was fifteen minutes until midnight. The room was neat as usual. However, a stack of bills sitting on the coffee table caught his attention.

•••

At the back door used by tradesmen and employees, Pablo Morales, one of the bellhops on duty, was meeting up with a friend. "You have it?"

He bumped fists with Ready from housekeeping.

Ready looked away and said, "How come I have to bring it, bro?"

"I'm a little short on cash, but I know where to get more."

They walked thirty feet down the sidewalk, over a homeless man sleeping against the hotel wall, and escaped into the doorway of another building. A dull ceiling bulb threw their shadows on the sidewalk.

"Spark up, man."

Ready drew the lighter and confetti-colored, glass pipe close to his mouth. As the smoke poured out of his nostrils, he asked, "Hey, man, what happened to you? Ortiz got arrested, and your ass was gone."

"I'm not gettin' my ass locked up." Pablo took the pipe.

Fifteen minutes later Pablo killed his cigarette and lit one more to cover the smell of the weed. Beneath the entrance overhang, he back-handed the Marlboro into the street. On the way to the front desk, his mouth opened for a peppermint tic-tac to cover what lingered of marijuana. He felt dizzy from inhaling a hidden stash of linen-scented glade in the Envoy Suite, but not so much as to trip and fall.

He saw Pepper enter the counting room and followed. Pepper turned and said, "What are you doing? I can take care of this. Please stay here while I go in the vault."

He hid his resentment. "Yeah, whatever." He watched Pepper's backside disappear into the vault and shook his head. "Bossy, skinny-ass bitch. She don't know what I know."

Pepper pushed the vault door shut and twirled the spoke handle.

He followed her out of the counting room but decided to take the elevator hall back to the lobby. He looked around for admiring glances. Passing twins watched his tattooed fingers stroke long, shining hair the color of dark syrup. He patted his zero-cropped side cuts for added affect.

White girls.

Back in the lobby, Pablo scanned Pepper's face and caught a glimpse of her left eye looking at him from behind snarled, red hair. Now he would get a chance to do what he needed to do, and she would cave into his request for another break because she found the half-Filipino, half-Mexican muscleman irresistible, just like all the other white girls.

He stood in front of the grandfather clock and looked himself over, and though he preferred his gang's colors, no matter how he was dressed, he looked better than anyone else at the Greenwich. The West-Point-gray-blue uniform, black cuffs, one-inch black collar, and white shirt underneath put girls into a trance. He noticed it was half past eleven.

Without looking at him, Pepper said, "Pablo, can you take that obnoxious green purse on the baggage trolley to Lost & Found?"

He watched Doris step toward Pepper and whisper in her ear.

"What's wrong with asking him?"

After helping another customer, Pepper snatched a quick glance at him.

"I saw you."

Pepper stared back and said, "What?"

"I saw you earlier."

Pepper ran around the counter and pulled on Pablo's arm. "What do you mean?"

"I saw you go up Cornelius' apartment."

"Did you follow me?"

"I saw the elevator go all the way to the top."

"Be quiet. Don't tell anyone. I was just doing him a small favor."

"The hell you were. You took him money, didn't you?"

"No. I was putting the money in the vault from my cash drawer."

"Give me another break."

"Aren't you still on one?" Pepper asked.

"Another break or I'll tell the boss what you did."

"I didn't do anything."

Pepper pushed the swinging gate and returned to her station.

Pablo watched Gerald Smith walk up to the front counter. While Pepper was distracted, Pablo walked away, laughing loudly enough to cause panic in the little brains of mama mouse and papa mouse and send their family of five to a different hole in the hotel kitchen.

•••

"Gerald, what're you doing here?"

"Where's Cornelius?"

She looked at her cell phone. Eleven-thirty. "Do you want me to page him? Is it urgent?"

"Yeah, I need to talk to him right away."

He looked exhausted.

Pepper paged Cornelius.

"Cornelius isn't answering, and you don't look too good, Gerald."

"Can I go up to his room?"

"You know I can't let you do that."

Gerald's phone rang.

Pepper couldn't hear what he said, but she could smell him. He looked as if he had been rolled in mud and beer. She couldn't put his needs ahead of her own when it came to Cornelius, and knowing that Gerald was in AA, she didn't feel that much sympathy. That was just enough for her to stand firm and keep him from Cornelius. She was glad Cornelius hadn't answered.

"What was the phone call about, Gerald?"

"Nothing. I need to see Cornelius. Now."

"What about? Can I help?"

"No." He walked over to an Edwardian three-seater and sat down. Pepper was not pleased at the prospect of an untidy ex-employee sitting on the fine white and gold fabric, and when he pulled up his socks and it looked as if he might put his feet on the seater, she prepared a reprimand. He folded his hands in his lap and crossed his legs at the ankles. She was relieved.

"Doris, can you handle the counter for a few minutes?"

"Sure. You want to talk to Gerald, don't you?"

"Look after the customers."

Pepper carried the cell phone over to the three-seater, as if another incoming call would make her appear to be occupied. She stood to the side and bent over. "Gerald, can we talk?"

He looked up. With half a smile, he said, "What about?"

"Can we go outside?"

He followed her to the sidewalk. The bitter wind blew up inside her black skirt.

"Over here."

They stood at the edge of the white zone.

The noise is good.

"I have to tell you something about Cornelius."

"Why I can't see him?"

"You just can't. Besides, you don't want to see him."

"What do you mean? He's my friend."

"Would you listen to me if I tell you something?"

"I want to see Cornelius. It's important."

Gerald paced and shivered. A street-cleaning truck entered the white zone, and its heavy forward brush whirred. They stepped back.

She took his arm and pulled him closer.

He let her.

"Cornelius asked me to bring him something. I can't tell you what it was."

"Why not?"

"Because. But, it's bad. And I don't think you should be seeing him."

He turned away and stepped toward the front door.

She lifted her right hand. Her fingers touched the goosebumps on the back of his neck.

He turned back.

"If he's such a bad guy, then why are you helping him?"

"I don't know. . . I just. . . "

"Why?" demanded Gerald.

"Don't be mad at me. I'm in love with Cornelius."

"What? How can you be? Does he know?"

His face turned beet-red.

"Please understand. I've got to tell someone."

"Why me?"

"I don't know. I can't tell Doris. She's my junior, and she will think I'm crazy. I told Cornelius I love him, but he pretended he didn't understand."

"He doesn't. You know his situation."

"The only thing I know is he's a little slow. What else do you know?"

"Really? Really?" he said angrily. "All he can do is the job given to him. Beyond that, he's . . . limited. I don't know if he's ever been in love. Do you?"

"He says he's too old."

"Then believe what he says and leave him alone."

"I can't."

"Why?"

"Haven't you ever been in love? Something inside me is telling me he just needs a woman in his life and it will be complete."

"You read too many romance novels."

"I do not." She didn't feel the need to lower her voice, and she daren't now with cars and people thrumming by.

"Do you think I'm pretty?"

Gerald looked perplexed. "Yes."

"Then why wouldn't Cornelius?"

"Maybe he does, but that's not the point. He does his job, family visits him, he goes to bed and gets up the next morning. Why not ask him to take you to church? He goes almost every day. That would be a better way to get to know him and what he is capable of, but, honestly, I think you should look for someone else."

"Like you?"

Gerald teetered on the sides of his feet. "You need a man your own age."

Pepper scoffed. "You really don't know men like you think you do. Cornelius doesn't drink or smoke, and he comes from a wealthy, educated, and sophisticated family. If he's religious, that's a good thing, something I could learn from. I want children, and he can give me that."

Gerald shook her and said, "Leave him alone," and with that he pushed the front door open and left her standing in the unfriendly airstream of his wake. Her lip balm had become suddenly bitter.

She followed him as he walked over to an Edwardian three-seater and sat down.

Back behind the front desk, Pepper answered a call.

"O'Hara here. Is Cornelius on duty?"

"No, sir, he's gone up to his apartment."

"What about Morales?"

"He's on his break."

Pepper heard a click. Puzzled by the phone call, she nervously busied herself and looked at Gerald again. Minutes passed. She glanced at the clock: five minutes after twelve. When she looked for Gerald, he was gone.

•••

The door buzzer awakened Cornelius. A giant, pyramidal light on the roof of a building across the street threw its beams on the blue and green tartan sweater he placed an arm into as he shuffled out of the bedroom into the kitchen. Not a single dish or utensil lay on the kitchen table. He passed into the living room. Not a single piece of clothing lay about, and the newspaper was neatly folded on the black chesterfield. He crossed the entry hall rug in his slippers and, from the other side of the door, he heard a voice say, "It's all right." The door knob turned. It stopped. He placed his hand on the knob and rested his head against the door when there was a click and the sound of someone stepping back.

Cornelius flicked on the entry hall light and opened the door.

"Oh, it's you. What are you doing here? Come on in." In the living room, Cornelius turned around. "No. No!" he shouted. "Ralphy, Ralphy, come help me."

A single shot was fired.

Cornelius was dead.

•••

Father Ralph cupped a hand in front of his mouth.

A pistol shot aimed at the temple would be better than being stopped for a DUI.

He opened the window for some fresh air and saw the Corinthian pillars of the Academy of Art University building at Post and Mason.

At half-past midnight, Father Ralph walked into the lobby.

"Pepper, I've come to see my brother. Is he in his room?"

"Yes, Father, he went off duty an hour ago."

Father Ralph passed a limping woman and felt her eyes fasten on his collar in an accusatory way. Could she sense his eagerness to reach Cornelius' apartment for another drink, something to dispel the visions of domestic bliss cohabiting with priestly duties and the demands put upon a university dean? She wasn't in view long enough to know.

The chatter of the party needed to put it to bed, but he couldn't help wondering what it would be like to come home to Joyce's companionship, rather than stealing away from it. Her face was all pink and white. With a start, he realized that he had been staring vacantly at the elevator doors like a ghost about to be sucked in and hurled down the shaft. He hadn't even pressed the button.

When the limping woman joined him at the elevators, the overpowering strength of her perfume brought the taste of booze-coated hors d'oeuvres up into his mouth. Her floral dress was tired and worn, like drooping plastic flowers.

Even though the chime announced the doors were about to open, she jabbed the button again and again. He found the idea of sharing the same space with her unbearable. "Aren't you coming?" she asked. "You were in a rush before."

"I'll take the next one," he said with a weak smile, unable to find a plausible excuse in the eternity it took for the doors to close again. He boarded the next elevator and listened to the elevator's beep and a honeyed female voice say, "Twelfth floor."

Maybe, he didn't need a drink. Maybe, all he needed was the quiet company of his brother. Cornelius might need help caring for himself, but he knew how to make a place feel like home. The apartment had offered him the chance to labor over a place, like a garden, away from a hovering parent.

"Are you in bed?" With fondness he recalled the story of the first night Cornelius was a bellhop, fell asleep on a luggage cart, and stayed too long because no one thought to tell him his shift was over.

"Cornelius? Are you in bed?" he called, as he entered his brother's apartment.

Troubled by the lamp on the living room floor, he left the door resting against the frame and moved forward. The black lacquered coffee table was clean and clear of drinking glasses.

Something felt wrong.

Abruptly, the awfulness of the scene became apparent, and he jumped back. Just enough light revealed a molten, reddish-purple pool spreading out on the white carpet.

Father Ralph waved the sign of the cross in Cornelius' direction and brought his hands together over his eyes in the vain hope that the scene might change.

Time started coming in fragmented, jittery sections. Was it possible that the brother he had spent hours training to pass as a man without a disability, the brother who never harmed anyone, never told a lie, and never forgot his morning and evening prayers, was gone?

Father Ralph reached for the ache in his stomach and forced down the bile in his mouth. He looked around the impeccable apartment for a bucket or a dish to vomit in and swallowed. The smell of iron hit him, and his legs shook. He knew the smell from hours spent waiting outside emergency rooms.

Closing his eyes did not discharge the impending specter, a conspicuous scene imagined in all its gaudiness, employees grouping, guests straining, and strangers gawking. Medics would arrive and pull the white sheet over his brother's face, as if departure from this life and reception into the next could be dispensed in such a pragmatic way.

Then there was nothing.

•••

He came to.

"Leahy."

"Larry, it's me."

"Ralph?"

Father Ralph heard concern beginning to course through his friend's voice. "Larry," he said, "Larry, you've got to get over here right away. I'm in Cornelius' apartment. He's dead."

"What? What did you say? Repeat it, Ralph."

Father Ralph summoned his fortitude. "Larry, I'm in Cornelius' apartment. He's dead. There's blood."

Larry's voice turned sharp. "Stay where you are. Don't touch anything. Understand?"

"Yes, I think so."

"All right. I'll be there in fifteen minutes."

Father Ralph pushed the phone back in his pants pocket and rose to his feet. From across the room, air seeping out of an iron wall grate warmed the smell of gunpowder. As the oldest of three, it was his duty to look after his brother and sister. Now there were just two. He got on his knees with barely enough power to begin the Sacrament of the Sick ritual, though his brother was already dead.

May the Lord who frees you from sin save you and raise you up.

It took a long time. It seemed important to say each word with exactness and deliberation. Once his rhythm got going, his mind drifted. There was Cornelius staring down in fascination at horses, camels, foot soldiers, and gyrating women crossing the stage of his favorite opera, *Aida*, and then, there he was, perched like a pigeon on a long tree branch in their Fifth Avenue backyard, waving his heels in the air.

For almost his entire life, Father Ralph had undertaken the obligation to protect Cornelius, and ever since becoming a priest, and

61

most especially with the decline in his mother's health, the burden had intensified. What he never imagined was failure so abject.

Chapter 4

Friday, July 5

Larry threw on his white shirt and black jacket, struggled to get pants on pajamas, ran down two flights of stairs, and backed out of his garage. His siren blared across shiny streets, and the flashing lights cleared a way. He started to punch 911 when the hotel's marquee and lobby lights appeared.

He rushed the front desk and lifted his badge. "Inspector Leahy. Here to see . . . the MacKenzies. What's your name, miss?"

"Pepper."

He was breathing hard. "Thank you, Pepper." Larry saw her begin to shake and asked, "Is there something wrong?"

She didn't answer.

He looked at the other clerk and asked, "What's your name?"

"Doris Harris."

"All right, Doris. Here's my phone number. Call me if you need me." Larry scribbled his number on a notepad, ripped out the page, and handed it over.

The elevator binged. In his notebook, he jotted down his arrival time: 1:15 a.m. When the elevator door opened, he bumped into a man and apologized.

He wiped his brow with a handkerchief and wondered what Father Ralph's condition would be. Outside Cornelius' apartment he listened with his ear against the door, drew his service revolver, and pushed.

"Ralph, are you hurt?"

"No, I'm okay." Father Ralph was hunched over. The entry hall light was on. Larry saw one side of his face and its high cheek bone. Hearing Father Ralph's voice was a relief, and now Larry really began noticing details.

"Is anyone else in the apartment?"

"Just the two of us, but I didn't . . ."

"Shush." In his head, he heard an admonition. Go in twos. Two detectives, or one detective and one cop, was best.

But best wasn't always possible, or even right.

"Stand still, Ralph." With the service revolver in his right hand, Larry carefully walked on the edge of an oval rug and brushed up against a framed picture. "All right, Ralph, get behind me and stay there."

"Larry?"

"Shush."

Go in twos. Go in twos.

Father Ralph did as he was told.

Larry reached his left hand around the door frame and slid his fingers over the switch. The room lit up. A fine crystal chandelier hung over a broken lamp and end table lying on the floor. A gun lay abandoned like a piece of garbage two steps to the right. Cornelius' eyes were open and clouded. Even if he were upright, his eyes could no longer see what Larry tried to deconstruct, the fine, dark woodwork of the windows and doors, the chesterfields upholstered in shiny black material with green, purple, pink, and yellow crisscrossing stripes, and the hearth insert.

He had been there less than twenty-four hours ago, but now everything had to be considered in a different light. Anything was possible. Larry stared at a scene, but what he saw was a eulogy, Father

President praising Cornelius to an overflowing audience, professors sitting up front, and members of the Board of Supervisors, recipients of O'Hara's largesse, squirming in reserved seats.

The back of a swivel chair touched a sofa arm and faced Larry. Cornelius must have fallen backward against the swivel chair and knocked over the lamp and end table. Blood spatter on the chair and lamp led Larry to estimate that the gun was fired at some distance, possibly from where he stood.

No other furniture was upended or out of place, and no clothes or other objects lay strewn about. Windows were closed. Room temperature was normal. The place smelled like the inside of an orange crate. He skirted the entry hall carpet and quietly pushed the front door shut with his elbow. There were no signs of forced entry, but Father Ralph's fingerprints would be on the doorknob.

"What's the smell?" Larry whispered.

"Gunpowder."

"No, the other smell."

"Cornelius liked room freshener."

Go in twos. Go in twos.

A floor board creaked when Larry entered the living room. A repellant smell, like a rusty sink, infused the air. Five stacks of money were on the table.

He looked back at Father Ralph, put his finger to his lips, and said, "Stay put."

Larry stepped around Cornelius and surveyed the kitchen.

Go in twos. Go in twos.

Larry passed through the kitchen with the barrel of his service revolver pointed straight ahead.

An open door on the right summoned, but danger might be lurking in the dark. Crouched a few feet back, a big man with an iron bar might take a swing. Stumbling over a second dead body was another possibility.

He took one hand from his gun and felt for a light switch. A mazarine-blue lamp on a side table lit a bed draped with a white comforter. The top sheet was open, and one of two white pillows bore the indentation of a head.

As he stood there, a bead of sweat the size of a small jelly opal rolled out of his scalp and lodged inside the pajama top.

Go in twos. Go in twos.

He could see nothing through the space between door and frame and rolled his eyeballs up and down, left and right, and stepped in. A crow sat outside a closed window. Its smooth head and sharp beak showed like a disembodied menace above the window sash. The roost was a ledge lit like a miniature stage. Diaphanous eyelids were frozen. The crow's demeanor was unemotional, and its presence imitated the room's peace.

Did the weapon have a silencer?

Larry flipped up the purple bed skirt but feared a hissing cat would swipe his face or a man might lurch forward and land on his back.

He traced his steps back to the window and looked out one more time. The bird didn't move.

Oily, black vagrant sitting there like it's part of the architecture.

Larry's gaze over the ledge assured him that no one could have entered the apartment that way. He felt dizzy looking.

A twelve-story nose-dive would hurt.

With the instincts of a coyote sniffing out a chicken coop, the forty-year veteran advanced toward an armoire on the opposite side of the room. He opened the doors. Should he shake the suits or be happy no villain was inside? He bent a collar back.

A door on the right was next.

Go in twos. Go in twos.

He yanked it open. Pulling on the ceiling chain wasn't necessary. The shelves were white.

An open door on the other side of the armoire was next.

Go in twos. Go in twos.

His hand found the switch and turned on the ceiling light. There was only one more hiding place, and this was it. Was there a perpetrator behind the frosted glass door of the shower? Tile dry. No footprints. Mirror free of condensation. A sticky trigger forced him to free his finger. Natural gas had warmed the bathroom.

Larry felt liberated.

He retraced his steps to Cornelius and knelt, but not too close. The size of the hole in the forehead matched the handgun's small caliber. Drawing himself away, he looked around for the casing, which would be an easy spot on white carpet.

"Where did your brother get the money lying on the coffee table?"

"I have no idea. I didn't see it."

Larry noticed drops of blood on the money wrappers.

"What about the gun?"

"There's a gun?"

"Does Cornelius own a gun?"

"He has some guns up at the lake, but none here. Can we handle this as quietly as possible? I don't want people pawing over Cornelius and gossiping about what happened."

"Ralph, first we have to determine *what* has happened. How did you enter the apartment?" Larry kept looking for the casing.

"With my key."

"When did you last talk to Cornelius?"

"I tried calling him during the night from O'Hara's, and the only person who answered was a woman. I don't know who it was. It was probably nine o'clock."

"What were you doing at O'Hara's?" Larry saw the casing lying next to a baseboard in the living room and left it there.

"Fourth of July party. I'm ashamed to say it after what has happened." Father Ralph looked like a man standing over a suicide, unsure of who was at fault but willing to take the blame.

"Who else has a key?"

"I don't know."

"Is there a way up to this apartment besides the elevators?"

"Yes, there's a stairwell on the other side of the hall."

Larry walked to the front door and counted out the steps from the front door to the living room entrance and from there to the body – about ten steps for each. Father Ralph's visage had turned gray. "Okay. Wait outside in the hallway. You'll make a formal statement. Write down the time you arrived, how you came into the apartment, and what you saw."

"What will happen to Cornelius?"

"Leave that to me."

Larry put his hand on Father Ralph's shoulder.

"God bless you, Larry."

"Thank you, Ralph."

Larry withdrew his white handkerchief, placed it on the glass door knob, and let Father Ralph exit first. Once outside, he decided not to close the door. He turned around and punched number two for Central Station.

"Take a few paces down the hallway. I don't want you to hear what I'm about to say."

"Of course."

Larry explained the situation to the desk sergeant and asked for immediate notification of the Captain, Homicide Unit, and Situation Investigation Team.

He began rehearsing an answer to the question why he didn't call 911.

He saw no blood on the mocha-colored carpet where he stood and pressed his handkerchief down on the lever of the stairwell door. Small gold stars sprinkled Venetian red carpet covering the short treads of a cavernous, unpainted stairwell. It would be possible to see blood on the carpet only if he got on his knees, as he did almost every day in church. He leaned his face to the side about an inch from the nap. Nothing glistened.

I didn't call 911 because Father Ralph and Cornelius are like family.

Larry scanned Cornelius' front door. Lauren had turned over when Father Ralph's phone call came in, and he was glad for that, but why did Father Ralph ask for secrecy? Larry hoped that no one else would appear on the twelfth floor, but a plan of action was taking shape.

Despite the shock and search, he had seen and recognized the framed picture in the entry hall. The original was a J Englehart "Yosemite Valley" painting which hung over the fireplace in the old Leahy family home in Dolores Heights. What a coincidence that Cornelius had a print of the same picture. Larry looked down at the floor.

The MacKenzie Name! Name! Name! Protect it!

Father Ralph's intention was now clear. He wanted to protect his family and its reputation. Larry wholly understood Father Ralph's reaction. Later in life, Larry had come to realize that he had become a cop to redeem his own family and its repute.

"What are you thinking?"

Larry licked his lips. "Did Cornelius have any enemies?"

"You know him. He wouldn't hurt a fly."

Larry wanted to act, but stale air was depleting his energy, and this tragedy required a clear and calming presence. It was bigger than the problem that had been bothering him for more than a year, which was returning, and it did whenever there was pressure and confusion at work. He could hear his wife say, "Why don't you do something about Mark? What kind of a father are you? Act." Lauren knew nothing of Mark's letter. Larry hid it in between the mattress and box spring on his side of the bed. The letter warned that things were coming to an end. Larry was planning to reread it and hadn't.

Fixtures spaced far apart down the hallway gave the same amount of light as flickering candles.

A wraithlike image slowly formed. He saw himself at age five walking up the steep sidewalk of Twenty-First Street beneath black trees, white sky, and ropes of hanging gray moss. He heard his mother's voice warning him not to venture near the corner house on Sanchez Street, the house once owned by a San Francisco mayor who had repeatedly rejected assertions that it was a whorehouse.

"Would you like to say a prayer with me?"

"Yes."

Father Ralph began.

Hail Mary. . .

Larry reached into his pocket.

That's right. Mark's letter is now in the drawer at home. She won't see it.

Police protocols began circulating in his head.

Dammit. What's taking them so long?

He took stock of Father Ralph, whose stamina now seemed to have taken over. He always had Larry's admiration. Over the years, they had spoken about the bank robbery his father had committed. From counseling sessions with Father Ralph came the recognition of why Larry chose the same career as his own father. Lauren said that Larry idolized his father, but Father Ralph said that Larry wanted the past to be erased and idolizing his father was a way to paper it over. Father Ralph told Larry again and again that he needed to forgive his father.

Larry's head touched the front door.

"How are you doing, Larry?"

Only Ralph would worry about someone else in this situation.

"I'm fine." Larry knew the quiet and late hour were conspiring to dull his senses. It had happened before, on previous midnight-mad investigations, and so he let his mind wander a little more, but he was beginning to feel small and inconsequential. He knew a writer once who had gotten mixed up with the wrong woman. During the writing phase, he said that he knew there was something important to say, but afterward, all of it seemed trivial and inadequate.

Larry recognized the feeling, and yet, there in the apartment . . .

Suddenly, the elevator doors opened and out came the Situation Investigation Team. Larry looked at his watch: 1:45 a.m.

"This way, gentlemen. Where's Captain Dempsey?"

"On the way. We informed the front desk clerks of the death. They are to remain at their posts. We'd like you to handle the lobby."

Larry and Father Ralph rode the elevator to the first floor.

"Ralph, stay here. I'm going to talk to the front desk people."

He nodded at one of the clerks, and she directed a short line people over to the other.

"You're Inspector . . .?"

"Leahy, and you're?"

"Pepper."

"You've been told what has happened?"

"Well, yes, sort of, but it's all so hard to believe. Exactly what happened?"

"Mr. MacKenzie has died. The circumstances are under investigation. We know nothing at this time, and you are to say nothing."

As he was finishing, she fell backward.

"Pepper, Pepper?" the other clerk said, looking frightened.

"I'm okay." Pepper righted herself by pulling on the counter. "It's so shocking."

A brush against the front counter opened Larry's jacket and exposed the service revolver on his hip.

Pepper stuttered, "Is that your gun?"

"Yes," he answered and closed the jacket.

"Doris, look busy."

Doris tried and failed to hide her umbrage.

"Inspector Leahy, is there anything I can do? Anything?"

Larry scanned the lobby. Flashing lights streamed through the windows and cast the white and gold drapery in ghoulish colors. The front door was like a sieve filtering exhaust and the sounds of cars slowing and people grinding against each other. One couldn't see across the street for the number of faces whose collective pressure against the windows seemed to have flattened the rippling in the old plate-glass. Two cops stood outside, balance-shifting, talking to keep themselves looking officially occupied.

"Just stay calm," Larry said to Pepper and Doris.

Larry's feet hurt. Leaning on the front counter gave him a new friend. "Pepper, a crowd may start filling up the lobby, and they'll want to know what's happened. You're to say nothing. Understood?"

"Yes, sir. Doris, you are to say nothing about what's happened. Is that understood?"

"I know."

Pepper clicked her tongue.

Sleepy, giddy hotel guests were filling the lobby, and some kissed total strangers and some of those who were kissed pulled away and some didn't.

"Let me come around to your side of the counter and speak to you privately."

Pepper opened the swinging door.

"Is there a place for Father MacKenzie to have some privacy?"

"The employee lunch room. This time of night, it's practically empty."

"He'll need a blank sheet of paper."

Pepper grabbed some paper from the shelf near the lock box and visibly shook.

"And we need a place to talk."

"The counting room. Is that okay?"

"Fine."

They walked down the hall to Father Ralph, and once he was in the lunch room, she reversed direction and slowed.

"This is it."

On the window across from the door where Pepper stopped was a big, round decal with the word, "Security", printed in green and white. It was dark inside.

They entered the other room. It had a long table.

"Let's begin with your full name."

"Pepper Darlene Chase."

"What is this room used for?" he asked, looking around.

"Brinks picks up money and delivers small bills and change for us to use."

"Can you tell me who has a key to Mr. MacKenzie's room?"

She looked up at the ceiling.

"His brother. The master key is kept in a lock box."

"Is the master key in the lock box now?"

"Yes."

"Where is the lock box?"

"Under the front desk counter."

Other employees might have access to it.

The vault's five spoke handle had a dull spark, like cowboy spurs.

The money in the vault might have found its way onto Cornelius' table.

"Is something wrong?" Pepper asked.

"It's warmer in here than Furnace Creek."

"Do you want me to open the door?" she asked.

"No. Is all the cash kept in the vault?" Larry's blue eyes began to water.

"Yes, sir, except for the money in our cash drawers."

"How much do you keep in your cash drawers?"

"Well . . . we keep $500 in small bills and change. When the amount is over $500, we take the excess to the vault. Two clerks count the money, the senior clerk brings it here, places the money in the trays, fills out a receipt, and places the receipt in the cash drawer."

"How many clerks and bellhops were on duty this evening?"

Larry noticed her thumb touching the tops of her fingers as if she were counting how many gnats could be mashed in ten seconds.

"We have overlapping shifts, two are on duty, myself and Doris, and we are about to be replaced by two more."

"Number of bellhops?"

"Two, and they will be replaced by two more."

"Is the vault always locked during the evening?"

"Yes. Should I check?"

"No. Don't touch the handle. Do you have the combination?"

"Yes. Only the senior clerk has the combination."

"Does it change every day?"

"Yes."

"Who else knows the combination?"

"Mr. O'Hara, the chief accountant, and the Security office manager."

"Did you see anything unusual tonight?"

"I . . . I . . . don't think so."

"Did you see anyone . . . other than guests . . . did you see anyone you didn't recognize?"

"No. I don't think so."

"Are the bar and restaurant open?"

"No, they close at ten o'clock."

"All right, those are all the questions I have for now. Do not discuss our conversation with anyone. Thanks."

He watched her exit, the back of her white blouse covered by a tangled mess of red hair.

I'm not any closer to what really had happened.

Father Ralph was writing his statement in the lunch room.

Larry quietly backed out to call O'Hara.

"It's Larry. Cornelius has died. I need you here at the Greenwich."

"What happened? Does Ralph know?"

Except for voices and music in the distance on the other end of the phone, there was silence.

O'Hara's assessing the situation.

"Where's my security man?"

"I don't know, and Ralph is here."

"All right. I'll do whatever is necessary. I should be there in thirty minutes. How bad is it? What about the other employees? Do they know?"

"The front desk clerks have been informed. Don't run any red lights. We have things under control. Just get here."

Larry stepped back into the lunch room and said, "Go home, Ralph."

Father Ralph embraced Larry, something they had not done in a long time. Still holding onto him, Larry said, "Don't worry, Ralph. I'll do my best."

They parted in the hallway, and Father Ralph descended the stairs to the garage.

At that moment, it all came crashing down. A man of utmost integrity and innocence had died. Feelings both immediate and remote forced him back into the lunch room. He sat down and wanted to weep. Father Ralph's statement on plain, white paper lay on the table What could be worse, the actual event or the piece of paper, a soundless testimonial to a brother's life and death? He dared not read it.

He felt himself entering the darkest shade of blue, the kind that cannot be blotted out by florescent light.

What's wrong with me?

He needed to escape the emptiness of the room and lifted the statement by one of its corners. Hopeful that faces would raise his spirits, he left the room and reentered the lobby. Its buzz softened the impact of all that had happened, and the faces of people he might have disliked at a party gave him what was needed, purpose.

At 2:00 a.m., two unmarked police cars parked in front of the Greenwich, and four men stepped out. Larry told a sidewalk loafer sitting against the flower boxes and trying to get a look up skirts to beat it. He huffed away.

"Captain, the team is on the twelfth floor."

"We can find the way."

The body snatcher arrived two minutes later and asked where he should go.

A young man and another girl passed the front desk. Two bellhops looked fresh and ready to go to work. The girl said, "Pepper, what's happened?"

One of the bellhops chimed in, "Everyone wants to know what's going on."

"Yeah," the shorter one said.

"People, I'm Inspector Leahy. I understand that you want answers. There has been a death in the hotel. Unfortunately, we can't give out any other information at this time."

The lobby got quiet except for the noise outside.

"My name is Larissa Rey. I'm the switchboard operator. Can't you tell us anything?"

"Larissa, don't ask the inspector," Pepper answered. "It's a police secret."

Larry swallowed a grunt.

The young man with Larissa bobbed from side to side, keeping his distance from Larry, and yelled over the noise. "Larissa, let's go."

Pepper leaned in and whispered, "Inspector, that's Pablo. Larissa and Pablo live together." She had apparently deputized herself.

"Okay," Larry replied, thinking about Mark and his girlfriend and trying not to be intolerant.

Larissa turned and said something to Pablo about going home.

The bellhops got busy. Guests milled about.

Larry stayed close to Pepper, and Doris and Pepper leaned on each other.

Two men, one with a bulky camera balanced on his shoulder, approached the front desk. Guests moved out of the way. "Hello, John Roberts from Channel 5 News. Can you tell me who was shot?"

Roberts had TV hair, the coif a funeral home director designs.

Pepper looked annoyed and said, "No, I'm sorry, I can't say anything."

"Why not?"

"You have to speak to the hotel owner. He hasn't arrived."

"When do you expect him? Where did it happen?"

Larry stepped in front the reporter. "Please stand back, out of the way."

The cameraman looked around Larry and asked, "What's the owner's name?" Like a creature from outer space, the camera bobbed and floated and zoomed in and out, following Pepper's movements as she tried to get an unobstructed view. The lobby was in a slow frenzy as more and more guests assembled.

"Inspector, we seem to be losing control."

"Pepper, just carry on. We can expect some interest. I'll keep them away from the front desk. O'Hara will be arriving soon." He retold the reporter to step away from the counter.

Someone dropped a glass bottle on the lobby carpet and out poured a currant-colored liquid. Pepper grabbed a rag and ran over to wipe it dry. A lady bent over, trying to clean up the mess. "Oh, dear, so sorry," she said.

"No problem. It spilled on the red part, not the black." Pepper's eyes were forgiving. The lady adjusted the bra strap beneath her worn flowered dress and looked around. Pepper wiped her nose to clear away the lady's perfume.

"Inspector Leahy, can you come over here?" Pepper looked as if she were praying. "I can't get Cornelius out of my head. I saw the anniversary pin on his lapel today." She dabbed the red liquid with the rag and suddenly pressed with all her might.

"Leave that alone. Let me help you get up."

"Mr. Leahy, can't we just order everyone out?" She looked around Larry and said, "Where did Doris go?"

"The officers at the front door won't allow anyone else into the lobby."

Larry noticed that the spilled liquid affected Pepper, whose face bore a likeness to a photograph of something that shouldn't be there.

"Pepper, are all the rooms on the twelfth floor occupied?"

"Yes, the hotel is booked solid."

"Thanks." He started down the hall. At the elevator, he recognized O'Hara's footsteps on the stairs. Larry looked at his cell phone: 2:30 a.m.

"I'm so glad to see you, Mr. O'Hara." Pepper came running from behind Larry and tripped into O'Hara's arms. His chest covered her face. She looked up. He whispered something, and she nodded. Larry couldn't hear what was said.

O'Hara stepped back and said loudly, "Just be gracious and keep on working until 3:00 a.m. . . . and tell Doris to keep working."

He didn't have to push. She seemed in synch with the pressure to retreat.

"Yes, sir." She started down the hall and looked back. "What about the girls coming on shift?"

"Inspector Leahy will tell them what's going on." He looked at Larry. "Just work alongside them . . . and Pepper, you are senior clerk until you leave."

He brushed off his jacket.

"Yes, sir." She rearranged her blouse, pulled down on her skirt, and walked with added verve.

O'Hara exhaled loudly.

Larry scrutinized O'Hara.

"Glad you're here," O'Hara said. He looked at the officer guarding the elevators. "I'm the one in charge in my own hotel, and it looks as if I'm not."

"Let's go to the vault."

"See what I mean."

"Just follow me."

Larry led him into the counting room. "Cornelius has been killed by a gunshot to the forehead. We don't have a cause or a suspect. Ralph found him in his apartment. I saw a pile of money on Cornelius' coffee table. I think the money might have come from the vault. How much cash do you keep in there?"

"Let me open it."

"I brought some gloves for the occasion." Larry pulled them out of his pocket. "Here, put them on."

O'Hara entered the combination, and the heavy door sprung open an inch. An automatic light switched on as he entered. Larry smelled booze when O'Hara's mouth fell open.

"The one-hundred-dollar tray is empty. $50,000 is gone. What the hell has happened?"

He yelled for Pepper and kept roaring her name across the counting room and down the hall. Around the corner she came, sifting fingers through tangles in her hair.

"Yes, sir? What is it?"

O'Hara grabbed her arm and pulled. Her serenity and his conduct surprised Larry. He moved between them and pulled O'Hara's grip loose.

"Let me do the asking. Pepper, please walk to the counting room."

She got out in front of them. The counting room door was still open, and they walked in.

"The top tray is empty. Has anyone else had access to the vault during the evening?"

"No, Mr. Leahy, just me."

"When was the last time you were in the vault?"

"Probably before midnight."

Larry entered the vault, focused on the steel ceiling, and backed out.

"James, do you have cameras in here?"

O'Hara pointed at the black globe attached to the ceiling's decorative molding.

"Where are the other cameras?"

"There's one outside. It's pointed down at the entrance to this room. There are more on both sides of the front desk."

"Where can we watch the video?"

"My office."

"Pepper, is there any way that money could have been removed during the night, maybe, when you weren't looking?"

"No, I don't think so."

O'Hara interrupted. "Cornelius took the money."

"Mr. O'Hara!" Pepper exclaimed.

Larry stared at him. "What makes you say that?"

O'Hara took off his monogrammed glasses. "Can we talk alone?"

"No, say what you have to say now."

"Pepper took the money to Cornelius. She's in love with him."

Pepper's face turned yellow-green, and she collapsed into a chair.

Larry looked at her and said, "Is this true?"

"No. No."

O'Hara put his glasses back on and rubbed the back of his neck.

Larry studied James for a moment and began to feel as if they were all in a surgical theater. The walls were white-hot, and he felt as if he needed to get out. "Pepper, I will be looking at the video, so you had better be telling the truth. Go back to the front desk."

She hobbled out of the room.

"James, this is a serious accusation you've just made. Is it true?"

O'Hara rubbed the back of his neck. "She was in his apartment today. She's in love with him. She knows more than she's saying."

"The videotape will be picked up, and I'll be viewing it tomorrow. Let's get out of here. Stay in your office. The police will question you."

O'Hara groused and aimed for his office. He waved on a man passing by.

The man limped and was wearing black earphones. He snatched a soggy toothpick out of his mouth when he saw Larry and said, "Hello, Inspector . . .?"

"Inspector Leahy."

One hand stuck the toothpick in his suit pocket, and the other hand pulled the earphones out of his ears.

"Did you escort Mr. MacKenzie to his apartment tonight?"

"No."

"Mr. MacKenzie died. An investigation is underway. Did someone else escort Mr. MacKenzie to his apartment?"

"No."

"What? No one?"

"That's right."

"I asked you to escort Mr. MacKenzie to his apartment. Don't you remember?"

"Yes, but that was earlier, I mean, and then he said, 'Don't bother.'"

"What? Repeat that."

"O'Hara told me not to escort Cornelius to his room tonight."

Dumbfounding. Absolutely dumbfounding.

"Where did you come from?"

"The basement. I was doing my rounds."

"Were you on the twelfth floor this evening?"

"No. I stick to the first and second floors and the basement."

"When did your shift begin?"

"I'm working swing shift, but it can change, depending on what O'Hara wants."

"Did you see anything unusual tonight?"

"No."

"Do you keep a log?"

"Yes."

Yes's and no's is all I will get out of him.

"Where is the log?"

"In Mr. O'Hara's office."

"Do you have the combination to the vault?"

"No."

"Are you armed?"

"No."

"Are you present when money is brought from the front desk to the vault?"

"No. Is there anything else?" Fletcher asked. He moved heavy black glasses up his nose and pawed at his five o'clock shadow.

"I would stay a while longer, in case the police want to question you."

"No problem, I can stay as late as they need me, but I really didn't see anything tonight."

"Good-night."

Larry had seen enough of him.

The Situation Investigation Team would be in the Greenwich for several more hours. He returned to the lobby and got on Pepper's side of the front desk when he noticed two broken fingernails.

"What happened?"

"Oh, nothing. When the lady dropped the red liquid and I bent down to clean it up, I must have pressed too hard." The baroque smell of the stain lingered, even on the employee side of the counter.

She beamed at Larry as if he were catnip and smiled at a couple approaching the front desk.

Larry heard them ask, "What is happening here? Is this normal?" Larry saw a blue and yellow Lufthansa tag on their luggage.

Pepper answered, "Oh, nothing to worry about. You're late, but we held the reservation just for you."

The front door was wide open, and the air in the lobby had cooled. Two middle-aged women hanging onto each other's arms ogled the two newsmen. The Channel 5 camera man dropped his equipment on the three-seater.

Larry followed Pepper as she strode over to him and boldly ordered the equipment on the floor.

"Miss, you might get in the news. Can't you tell me something?"

Larry shook his head back and forth.

Back behind the desk, she said, "I haven't seen Gerald Smith since he came in."

"Who is he?"

"He's an ex-employee."

"He will be questioned."

"Doris, I need a break. I'm not feeling well."

"You've been gone from the desk most of the night, Pepper."

"I'm sorry. I had to answer lots of questions."

"Let's go to the lunch room, Pepper." She walked very close to Larry's side when they passed the counting room door.

Once they were inside the lunch room, she expired loudly and said, "I feel as stubborn as a mule."

Larry patted her on the shoulder and said, "It's the effects of all that's happened tonight."

She looked at her nails. "I feel like lying down. Maybe, I should call my aunt."

They sat down.

A spider crawled along the edge of the table. Two sets of eyes stared at it. Pepper backed her chair away. With a half-turn and quick survey of the counter behind, she grabbed a bottled water. One crunch would have debilitated the bug, but two more whacks sent it to bug heaven. Larry laughed and so did Pepper.

At three o'clock, Pepper and Doris ended their shifts and said their good-byes.

"Pepper, do you live close by?" Larry asked.

"Just three blocks."

"I'll walk you home."

"Oh goodness, you're so sweet. I've only got my red cardigan, so I walk fast."

After Doris exited the front door and Pepper reached for the handle, Larry whispered, "Did you take the money out of the vault?"

"No. I didn't."

They stepped around stragglers. The police had stopped redirecting traffic. One hooker stood on a corner, and a homeless man howled about personal possessions he had laid out in front of a shop's black scissor gate.

Before parting at the front door of Pepper's apartment building, she asked, "Do you think Gerald has something to do with the murder?"

What made her say that?

84

"Good night, Pepper."

"Good night and thank you."

Larry returned to the Greenwich. Ten minutes later, he was driving home and repeated what she had said, "Do you think Gerald has something to do with the murder?"

Chapter 5

Friday, July 5

Father Ralph leaned against the cold sink, grabbed a comb, and pushed it through thick black hair. A gray streak ran from his forehead, up and over the top, and down to his neck. Once, he heard someone say that it made him look as if he were marked by God, so Father Ralph left it untouched. He stepped out of the bathroom and straightened a black and white photograph of a snowfall on Lone Mountain hill, dated March 3, 1896, the site of Loyola House, the Jesuit residence, his home.

"Hi Ralph. How are you?"

"I'm okay. How are you, Larry?"

"Didn't get much sleep. Lauren sends her condolences."

"It's still a shock. I'm not sure if my Jesuit brothers know."

"Does your sister know?"

"Yes. She couldn't stop crying. Morning Mass is for Cornelius."

"All right. I'm on my way. We'll talk later."

"God bless."

Father Ralph looked around the room. Above his bed was another rare, original photograph with a brass plate at the bottom, inscribed, *San Francisco Waterfront 1864*. He donned a black sweater and closed an electronic tablet holding an impressive collection of his favorite mystery novels, which he read almost every night after dinner, but not last night. Framed in blue and gray was an MA in Philosophy from Gonzaga University, and beside it, in mahogany and glass, hung a Doctorate in Biblical Theology from the Pontifical Gregorian University in Rome.

He sat on the edge of his bed and thought about his friends, Larry and James, whose lives might be ineffably linked to his forever because of what had happened.

The last step at the bottom of the stairs took him into the foyer and the sound of a door bell. The porter greeted Josh Hawkins and turned to Father Ralph. A tear clung to the porter's lower eyelash. Father Ralph squeezed his hands. "I'm okay. Josh, let's go."

On the way down the Lone Mountain steps to St. Ignatius Church, Josh's black and orange baseball cap blew off. Father Ralph kept descending while Josh scrambled, grabbed the hat, and returned to Father Ralph's side.

Three days a week, Josh hiked a half mile from his home in the Laurel Village neighborhood. He lived with his mother, Larry's divorced sister.

"I hear you're doing a fine job at the Greenwich."

"Yes, Father, bell hopping and running cross country during summer keep me in shape."

I ran at St. Ignatius, but how do I tell Josh the news?

"Did you have a good holiday?" he asked.

"My friends and I watched the fireworks at Aquatic Park."

The hazy sunshine took Father Ralph's mind off the present moment and buoyed him up under feelings that had kept him awake all night.

The sunny miasma evoked a memory. He saw James and himself meeting at Larry's house and lining up in the schoolyard on a day just like this, barely half-a-mile away. Chubby white seagulls searched for scraps, and little blackbirds danced on their toes. He heard the snap-snap of black clackers as each one of the sixteen, habited, black and white nuns straightened her line.

Cornelius' last joke came to mind.

"A boy asks his father how to catch a fish. The man says, 'Wait a minute. I'll be right back.' He goes into the house, comes out with a fish, and says, 'Son stand back thirty feet.' The boy backs up, and his dad says, 'Okay, catch this.'"

The memory brought Father Ralph back to the Greenwich and the awful scene the night before.

Waiting for a consolation, Lord.

Instead, he got a distraction, a vision of James standing out in front of the hotel like a reigning president.

Josh stopped whistling at the bottom of the steps. Once more, he reminded Father Ralph of himself when he was young, and another consolation arrived: James, Larry, and Father Ralph had remained in the city that had claimed their love.

I hope Josh stays.

He crossed the street against a red light. A car screeched to a halt. The driver made an obscene gesture and cursed out the window. Father Ralph's black sweater slid up his forearm when he raised his hand and waved the sign of the cross at the back of the vehicle.

"C'mon, Josh."

"Yes, Father. That was kinda close."

Father Ralph's sleeve bunched up as he withdrew a starched handkerchief monogrammed *RHM*. His middle name was his father's first name. Henry expressed resignation when his eldest child chose religious life over leading the family real estate brokerage. "Well, you won't do any real harm," he had said. Father Ralph's becoming president of a university might have impressed him. A cool line of sweat on Father Ralph's forehead left him wondering if he should quit drinking coffee in the morning.

He saw a child playing in a driveway that he passed every day on the way to church. She looked up at him as if she had never seen a priest before. He wavered on whether he should say hello.

If he did, she might ask, "What does God look like?"

You were created in His image, so you know what He looks like. Look for him in the faces of the rejected, poor, unborn, and voiceless, but not in mine.

Father Ralph's imaginary conversation was broken by the sound of Josh's footsteps as they approached the sacristy. The cell phone in Josh's hands had the full attention of this sixteen-year-old charge, and as soon as they were inside the sacristy, Father Ralph was glad Josh made it safely through two doors without tripping.

"Take off your hat, Josh."

Josh stifled a burp. "Sorry, Father, pizza from last night."

Father Ralph picked up his chasuble and stole laid out by the sacristan and turned the morning Chronicle over.

"I might be going up to Uncle Larry's cabin this month. How come you never go?"

"I have other things on my mind."

"Oh yeah, you have your annual retreat at the end of this month."

"That, and other things to take care of." As Josh lifted the black cassock and white surplice over his head, Father Ralph pushed the Chronicle against the yellow window. On its Sunday society pages were families like the MacKenzies and O'Haras, families that were emblematic dynasties representing one face of San Francisco. They were the former newspaper owners, bank founders, old-order politicians, and squire class of funeral directors. They were Catholic, Protestant, and Jewish, and all hid their influence on society under the protection of athletic and social clubs that concealed membership and purposes.

Now, high-tech, new arrivals were replacing these families, and people like his mother were disappearing into assisted living facilities.

"Shoes polished. I'm ready."

"Good. After Mass, I'll explain what happened last night. Do you know?"

"Yes, I know. Mom saw it on her phone. I didn't know if I should bring it up."

Father Ralph placed his hand on Josh's shoulder and leaned more heavily on him than ever before. "Cornelius' death is being investigated."

"What happened?" Josh asked.

"We'll talk about it after Mass."

Josh rang the bell, signaling their entrance to the sanctuary.

As he bent his knee in front of the altar, Father Ralph wondered how Cornelius' death might affect his chances at becoming a university president, or his standing at school or the other Jesuit universities around the country. He worried over how the death might affect the reputation and profitability of the centerpiece of the family's wealth, the MacKenzie Real Estate Company. He worried about the man now leading the firm, Leonard Morton, his brother-in-law. All of it was base, and he asked God for forgiveness.

A loving fog horn bellowed as he lifted the consecrated bread. Josh held the gold plate under his uncle's chin, and Larry's fatherly smile belied the stocky build of a hard-hitting cop. After Mass, Father Ralph felt on edge as he spoke to Larry at the back of the church. They noticed Josh moving closer. Larry nodded, turned, and went back into the church.

"What did Uncle Larry mean when he said, 'not to pursue the MacKenzie case too aggressively'?"

"Josh, let's go back to the sacristy. I'll explain."

In the sacristy, Father Ralph sat down opposite Josh. "You know Cornelius had a disability, and you were so polite and, in your own special way, let him know that he could talk about anything, including his disability, if he wanted to. Someone shot Cornelius." Father Ralph saw Josh tearing up. "Cornelius taught my family about unselfish love. I know Cornelius was ready for heaven, and God is taking care of him now. Uncle Larry will do his best to find out what happened."

Josh listened to Father Ralph's every word. "I'm so sorry, Father."

"Thank you, Josh. Now, you take care of yourself and don't do anything I wouldn't do and let God take care of the rest. Okay?"

"Yes, of course!"

Josh wiped his eyes with Father Ralph's handkerchief and said good-bye.

Father Ralph searched for a story on Cornelius. Finding none, he thought, "Honest, incorruptible, trustworthy, Larry is a good example for Josh."

The smell of gardenias caused him to turn around abruptly. A bright yellow scarf circled her neck and trailed down the back of a buttoned-up black trench coat. She had the pallor of a vampire. He had forgotten plans made two days ago. They were set to go sailing. They would drive to the Marina, board his Chris-Craft, and return before noon.

Before he could say anything, Joyce laid her cheek on his chest. He stood stiff as a pillar. The ten-year, unconsummated love affair was intruding at the worst moment. How would he break the news that Cornelius was dead, or did she know?

"I waited until Mass was over. I saw a young man leaving. I was thinking, why don't we meet tomorrow for lunch?"

He let her relax in his arms.

She needs me.

The softness of her black curls touched his chin and made him feel guilty for allowing her to talk sweetly, but he wanted to hear the melodic notes of her voice, and he allowed his thoughts to drift back to the party and the apparition he had of a man and woman walking along a beech and holding hands.

How inexcusable, considering what has happened.

Joyce hugged him, and he hugged her back.

"Remember the joke, Ralph?"

Oh no! Not now.

"There were three professors on a skydiving adventure. . ."

"Joyce . . . I have a lot going on."

Her smoky-gray eyes twinkled stardust.

"My brother died last night."

"Oh my God. I'm so sorry, dear."

Her tremolo was high. She caressed the razor-sharp edge of his jaw.

"I found him in his apartment."

She moved slightly but didn't let go. Suddenly, he was gripped by an overpowering emotion and kissed her passionately.

There was a knock on the door and no time to break.

"Father, I forgot my Giants baseball cap."

Father Ralph saw the shock on Josh's face. He seized Joyce's arms and pushed them down to her side. Josh found the crucifix under his t-shirt and rubbed the white cotton covering it. He watched Josh look down at the baseball cap, its center crushed under Joyce's foot.

Father Ralph saw Joyce's face change colors, from amber to salt. "She was just comforting me." He wanted the world to begin again and saw something in Josh's eyes.

Is it more than suspicion? Is Josh possessive of me and protective, too?

She collapsed. He caught her and set her carefully on a red velvet chair. He looked up at Josh. Man and boy heard her gasping for air. She looked fragile and overburdened in the light filtered by the symbol of hospitality, the pineapple, which was etched into the yellow, pebbled sacristy windows.

Joyce's breathing and the faint sounds of vehicles on the street filled the void.

Father Ralph picked up the cap and handed it to Josh. "It's not what it looks like."

"Yeah, right. I'll see you later." Josh turned and walked out the door.

Father Ralph's attentions turned back to Joyce.

"Are you okay?" he asked.

"I'm fine."

She rose, and they maneuvered around each other.

"How can I can leave you at a time like this?" she asked.

"How can you stay?"

"Will you be all right, Ralph?"

"I have to get back to Loyola House."

"Can I kiss you?"

"No."

•••

The spotlight on the crucified Christ above the high altar drew Larry's attention to the oil paintings below the clerestory walls. The pictures dripped with sacrifice and were a reminder of the high-gloss pages in the Latin/English Missal now obsoleted by Vatican II. He looked down at the daily missal, whose pages were printed on paper any daily rag could use.

The bouquet of paraffin melting in votive bottles drifted his way.

Out of the corner of his eye he could see the facsimile of St. Aloysius Gonzaga, stretched out under a side-altar with glass front.

Thank God for Josh's devotion to Father Ralph.

He felt a tap on his shoulder and turned around.

"Hi, Dad. I'd like to introduce you to Joan."

Mark's voice was shaky. She stuck out her hand. Black hair pulled back in a pony-tail and a white cardigan unbuttoned at the top demonstrated her modesty, and she stood tall as Mark but without his self-importance. Her lips rose like a crescent moon when she said, "Mark has told me so much about you. I'm happy to meet you at last."

"Nice to meet you, Joan." He turned to Mark. "Why did you come here? I have to go to work. Cornelius MacKenzie, Father Ralph's brother, died last night."

"Dad, I came here because you won't meet us."

"That's correct, and it will stay that way as long as you are living with her outside the marriage bond. Good-day."

Larry didn't know what to do but staying with them wasn't an option. They followed him out the side door, and under cloudy skies, Mark took hold of his arm.

"Dad, you can't ignore us."

"Fine. You want to argue, then let's see Father Ralph. Did you go to communion?"

"No."

"Good."

Larry entered the door in the back of the church. A woman in a black trench coat came out of the Sacristy. He was too upset to say hello and wondered why Joan wanted Mark. There must be plenty of Jewish men at the right age. Would she know that a Catholic has certain obligations, which, if not fulfilled, could bar entry into heaven, and how would her parents react to the Leahy family?

Father Ralph's eyes were bloodshot, and he looked as if he had seen the devil.

Starting a conversation with them present will be harder than climbing a mountain.

"Ralph, good morning. This is Mark's girlfriend, Joan. We need to talk."

"Hello, Mark. I haven't seen you in ages." He shook hands with Mark and then Joan. "Did you come to Mass?"

Larry answered for him. "Yes, but the real reason for coming was to see me, and that's what we need to talk about. Mark and Joan are living together and not married. His mother and I have expressed our disapproval, but Mark has chosen to do what he pleases."

Larry waited for Father Ralph's reaction.

"Mark, you teach at Riordan High School, isn't that right?" Father Ralph asked.

"That's right."

"And you, Joan, what do you do?"

"Mark has told me so much about you and the influence you've had on the whole Leahy family, and I'm so happy to meet you." She looked relaxed. "To answer your question, I teach at Lowell High School."

"She teaches calculus. You could teach calculus. Right, Mark?" Larry asked bitterly.

"Well, it's more of a challenge than geometry."

Larry stared. "You went to Stanford. Calculus should be a breeze." Mark shrugged off the remark.

"Bah."

Joan looked at Mark. Mark looked at Father Ralph.

"Please, let's all sit down. We can discuss what is going on and what your plans are. Children?"

Right question, and he said it with a sincere smile.

Joan quickly answered, "Yes, definitely."

"Then you will be getting married soon?"

"We haven't . . . we haven't looked that far ahead," Mark said.

Father Ralph directed Joan to the red velvet chair and said, "Please have a seat."

His voice is as calm as a doctor's.

"Mark, are all of the teachers at Riordan Catholic?"

"I don't know. Probably."

"Well, it's very important that they set a good example for the boys. Wouldn't you agree?"

"I'm not a religion teacher, but I'm sure they get the faith presented in a favorable way."

Joan said, "I teach character education. You know, respect for oneself, respect for others and their differences, diversity, doing your best, and kindness and helpfulness."

Larry looked at Mark with a scowl and said, "Is that what they teach at Riordan? Diversity?"

"Yes, I suppose so."

Father Ralph sat down in an antique chair with a black leather seat and leaned against the back of the chair. "Well, Joan, Mark, that's wonderful, emphasizing character education. A much better job than in my day, and, Mark, I think what your dad wants to know is if Catholic character education is being taught."

Larry looked at his watch. "I want to know when they are going to start living apart."

"Mark, does Riordan require that you live according to the teachings of the Catholic Church?"

Larry looked at Mark and waited.

Joan reached for Mark's hand. His shoulders relaxed, and he answered, "Father, if you are referring to a mandatum, the answer is no."

"Mark, just answer Ralph." Larry's leg began twitching.

"I did!"

"What's a mandatum? What's it got to do with the question?" Larry asked. His eyes shrunk into a glare.

Father Ralph broke in, saying, "It doesn't matter. Mark is a fine teacher, and I'm sure he knows his responsibilities and the need to set a good example." After a few moments of silence, Father Ralph added, "Mark. It's something for you to consider. The future rests with children, and yours would benefit from a father who lives his life the way your father does."

Exactly.

Joan said, "I agree, Father Ralph. Mark and I have talked about this."

Mark said angrily, "About what?"

Larry raised his hands in hopelessness.

Joan looked at Larry and said, "The Catholic faith, Mark. We've talked about my coming into the Church. I'm Jewish and leaving that behind is not an easy thing."

Father Ralph started to say, "Joan, you can become a Catholic and still retain your Jewish identity. There is a wonderful organization called the . . ."

Larry interrupted, "You didn't answer the question. Does Riordan require you to live according to the teachings of the Church?" Larry smelled something foul, and it wasn't the fragrance in the room.

"We're leaving."

Joan pled, "Mark, I urged you to talk to your father. Please stay where you are. I have more to say." She tugged on Mark's hand. "Father, my mother was born in Cairo. She was sent to a convent school because it was the best. She has fond memories of her friends and the nuns." After a pause, she said, "I'm thinking about what all this may mean."

Father Ralph gently touched the top of Joan's hand. "When you decide to have children, you wouldn't want them to be ignorant of God, would you? Of course not. You will want to give them the advantage over others who don't have the language to talk about God. I hope you don't mind my speaking so frankly." She smiled. "Would your parents be terribly upset if you were received into the Catholic Church?" Father Ralph asked.

"They would be, but they know I love Mark."

"Here's something George Bernard Shaw said." Mark's voice sounded sardonic. "He said, 'Because the medieval doctors of divinity couldn't settle the question of how many angels could dance on the point of a needle, they cut a poor figure next to physicists who've settled to the billionth of a millimeter every movement in the dance of electrons.'"

Father Ralph responded, "Ah, but could George Bernard Shaw dance on the point of a needle? Even he was subject to the laws of God."

"Including his electrons!" Joan said. She and Father Ralph laughed.

Larry said, "Father, I've got to get back to work."

Father Ralph answered, "I'm sure we'll meet again, Joan."

Mark pulled on Joan.

Larry looked at the door and said, "You go. I want to talk to Father Ralph, privately."

As they exited, Joan turned back and gave them the same crescent-like smile.

"Ralph, it went about as well as it could."

"She's a nice girl. Living together is their decision. Marriage will solve the problem. Of course, they must live apart for some time before marriage. Let's not put pressure on them. Joan has to be thinking about what comes next. Whatever Mark says or does, Joan is the one we can count on."

"I want them to separate. The rest is up to them." Larry rubbed his hands.

"Why don't you come up to Loyola House?"

"I've only got a few minutes."

"We can talk over a cup of coffee. Don't you think you need to?"

•••

Sweat was pouring down Father Ralph's neck by the time they reached the top of the stairs and faced Loyola House. "I've got a slight pain in my hip. Probably from tossing and turning."

The dining room smelled of mascarpone, strawberries, and syrup.

"Would you like some breakfast?"

Larry sat down opposite Father Ralph.

"You look dejected."

"Ralph, there's something more I want to say. About the phone call to Cornelius yesterday. I met with him and later with O'Hara. I got a promise that his security man would escort Cornelius to his apartment. It never happened."

"I see." Father Ralph pushed his scrambled eggs around. "Not good. Not good. What can we do now? Who's to blame?"

"Ralph, I talked to Captain Dempsey, and he refused to send an officer . . ."

"I'm calling O'Hara." Father Ralph stared at his cell phone. It was 8:30 a.m.

"Hello, it's Ralph." He pressed the speaker button and said, "Larry told me you failed to give Cornelius protection last night. How could this have happened?"

"I told my man to look after Cornelius. I will talk to him later today and find out what went wrong. My plan is to work closely with Larry. Ralph, you are the best man I know, heads above Larry, but I'll give him whatever help he needs. If questions come up, I'll call you first before I call anyone else."

"I see."

"I had only one man on duty. Larry has a whole cadre of police officers that could have been assigned to the Greenwich. He's the one with all the experience, and he's a cop. Why didn't he give Cornelius protection? Why?"

"He's here. Do you want to talk to him?"

"No. You talk to him. Ask him. Clare offers her condolences and says she will talk to your sister. I plan to contact Leonard and give him whatever help he needs. I will call my contacts and make sure the brokerage is not affected. You have my promise."

"Thank you, James. Mom will be brokenhearted when she hears the news."

"I know. I'm so sorry. Clare can visit your mother if needed."

"God bless you, James."

Larry saw Father Ralph staring.

"You heard him. The blame is yours, Larry." He pressed down on his fork, and it snapped at the base. "How do I begin to tell the others about Cornelius? Do you have the words I need? I'll be watching everything you do from now on."

"I'm very sorry, Ralph."

Larry got up from the table.

"Wait."

Larry looked down at Father Ralph.

"There's something I want to tell you. I got a phone call yesterday. It was Gerald Smith, the bellhop who was fired. My brother had given him the keys to the Topaz Lake house. He was up there when I talked to him." He paused. "Cornelius asked me to talk to him. I didn't want to. I don't know what's going on. Smith and my brother fished up there at the lake. Smith still has a key. I think he should return the key. Can't you demand he return the key?"

"Are you Cornelius' executor? If you are, can't you ask for the key back?"

"You're a cop. Tell me what to do."

Larry could feel the heat of Father Ralph's smoldering anger.

"Are you suspicious of Smith?"

"I don't know." Father Ralph left his half-eaten, dried-up eggs on the plate. "Please don't call me today. I have too much to do, and you need to figure out what has happened . . . if you can. Good-bye."

Father Ralph got up from the table and stormed out of the dining room.

Chapter 6

Friday, July 5

A glance in the rear-view mirror at a stoplight on Van Ness Avenue reminded Larry that constantly looking in the mirror, though it was necessary to drive safely, was also a sign of vanity. His thoughts turned to his son. Mark looked more like his mother, or maybe, it was just the fact that both had escaped the toxicity of a police beat and the hours of midnight investigations. All Mark had achieved was a credential and teaching high school boys. Another peek in the mirror – his eyes had a drained look.

When he ran over speed bumps at the entrance to Central's garage, his eyes blinked, trying to adjust to the darkness, and his cell phone bounced in the cup holder. He was reminded of a phone call the week prior. A vagrant had been taken to the sobering center and had asked for Larry's help. The homeless shelter attendant's answer, "You need a reservation, Inspector," drew a quick response. "What for? A continental breakfast in the morning?"

The agreeable smell of musk in the garage drew him nearer to the card reader. The smell of a bakery had the same effect. As he swiped his badge, his thoughts turned from the meeting with Mark and from his letter, which was now pressed inside a jacket pocket, to the work ahead, and a plan on how to investigate Cornelius' death began taking shape.

The door sprang open, giving access to a long hall and officers chewing over the previous night's storylines. The police services aide stopped tapping. "Good Morning, Inspector Leahy."

"Morning, Christy."

"Have a good day, sir," she replied and turned back to the screen.

Rich, mahogany skin lit up, and her lips were full and wet.

He walked past the line-up room on the right and a sergeant handing out instructions only a pharmacist could understand.

"Morning, Inspector Leahy. How are you?" Hieu asked.

"All right. You beat me here."

"Live down the street, Larry."

"All right, let's head for Dempsey's office."

Larry looked at his watch as they walked down the hallway. Ten after nine.

Standing at attention were three members of the Situation Investigation Team and Inspector Joe Varton.

Being addressed by Dempsey is one of several unpleasant ways to die.

"Good morning, dream boy," Varton said in Larry's direction.

"Knock it off, Inspector," Dempsey said.

"I have some information on the case. May I proceed?" Larry asked.

"Go ahead. Keep in mind what I said to you on the phone this morning about not pursuing the MacKenzie case too aggressively. I'll have more to say about that."

Something doesn't feel right.

"Last night I questioned James O'Hara and hotel employees Pepper Chase and Bud Fletcher." Larry scanned the room. Everyone looked as if payday had been cancelled. Dempsey gazed at his blotter, and his fingers acted as a fulcrum for a yellow pencil, or a poison dart, depending on the circumstances.

Larry continued. "Mr. O'Hara was at home when I rang him after finding MacKenzie's body. It was Father Ralph MacKenzie who called me to the scene. I noticed the money sitting on the coffee table and asked O'Hara if the money came from in the vault. He told me there was $50,000 missing."

Dempsey interrupted, "Leahy, I brought everyone here so that we all know how the investigation will proceed." He looked up at Larry. "I'm turning the case over to Inspector Varton. You know the people involved. You're too close to the MacKenzie family."

"Captain, was the money in Cornelius' apartment in the amount of $50,000? O'Hara's office has the videotape of the counting room. Has anyone reviewed the videotape?"

"We are processing all the evidence, Leahy, including the gun, money, and videotape. We fingerprinted the vault door handle and the door handle of Mr. MacKenzie's apartment. The rest of the apartment was dusted. The gun is being examined for fingerprints. We found the shell casing. We don't know if the gun lying in the apartment was the weapon that killed MacKenzie. The money was counted, and the total was $49,500, leaving $500 unaccounted for."

"What did the videotape show? Chase said she was the only one to enter the vault up to the time Cornelius was found."

"Inspector Varton is looking at videotape from noon yesterday up to one o'clock this morning. Is that right, Varton?"

"Yes, sir. That's right, sir." His obsequious manner irritated Larry.

"Captain, Cornelius received a call yesterday. The caller said his life was in danger. I was at the hotel and asked O'Hara to provide extra security, and his man, Bud Fletcher, failed to do so."

"Why didn't you tell me?"

Did he forget about the phone call I made asking that a police officer be stationed there?

"I thought I could take care of it."

You need to figure out what happened . . . if you can.

"Leahy, what we know for sure is that the bullet entered the forehead, but, from what the team observed, it appears the gun was fired from a distance, perhaps outside the living room."

"Why am I not leading the investigation? The fact that I know the people involved is the reason I should be leading the investigation."

The dimples on both sides of Joe Varton's smile deepened.

"I've assigned the case to Inspector Varton. That's an end to the question."

Larry expected a show of support and shared astonishment over the case being wrongly assigned to another, but all eyes, even Hieu's, were on Varton.

"We'll catch the God damn idiot," Varton said, feet wide apart, hands on the lapels of his green and gray checkered suit jacket. "This case has it all, even if we don't know the particulars. Moneyed people, prominent families. It'll be front page riff for a few days and then blow over."

"What makes you say that?" Larry asked.

"I can smell it," he answered, putting his right index finger to this nose. "I can smell it," he proudly reiterated. "These things don't go unnoticed, while important crap does." His eyes circled the ceiling and the walls as if they were feeding him inspiration.

He's looking for an argument.

While Larry was thinking of something to say, he heard a door shut outside. "Well, I'd better get back to my office. I've got several cases to work on. I'll be keeping an eye on everything you do, Joe. You can count on that."

"Fine. Meet me at the Police Academy. I'm there every morning, and I jog five miles around the track. I can give you some pointers. Seven o'clock?"

Dempsey interrupted, "I want this case solved in ten days."

"I will do that, Captain," Varton resolutely said.

•••

Larry had enough unopened letters on his desk to make him want to get drunker than a skid-row lush. Plans made the day before pushed him across the threshold, but cold paper pled for a withdrawal. The blinds were closed and begged to stay that way. He ignored their protest, twirled a rod, and pulled down on one blind to get a look at the neighbors' back windows, but glass dirty with droppings persuaded him to turn away. His desk chair welcomed him on its leather seat sliced open in several places by time.

What's done is done.

He thought about Varton's six foot two, 200 lb. frame.

Size doesn't matter. Otherwise, the Eucharist would be a hundred times bigger.

Larry felt the urge to keep a tidy office and pushed the chair back. It ran over rippled cracks in the linoleum. Inside the top drawer, he guided one of several prayer cards to the bottom. Push-pins poked at this finger, and gray-brown dust rose in tiny plumes and floated away as the card came to a stop.

The latest memo from Human Resources was stuffed inside the drawer. It stated, "Using the expression 'God bless' is prohibited."

They're so dumb they don't know "Good-bye" is an abbreviated form of "God be with you," same as "God bless."

He crumpled the memo and threw it into the waste basket.

There was a knock on his open door.

Hieu walked in as if nothing had happened, but his eyes said otherwise. He carried the morning Chronicle in his left hand and an SFPD training manual tucked under the other arm. His medium gray suit fit a short, tight body, making him look like a banker, which left Larry feeling as if he'd been strong-armed by a pretty boy, but that wasn't true. Hieu had just completed an online bachelor's degree in criminal justice, which made his parents proud.

Larry heard thumps on the roof.

"Have a seat." Larry's grins were usually measured out at work, especially now.

"Hey, Larry, sorry about the reassignment."

"He's an ass. I've got a tin badge I could slap on." He waved his official badge around. "You know Joe and I are up for the Chief Inspector job? I finished number one on the written, and Joe was second. Next is the interview with Dempsey."

"You're the best man for the job."

Larry smiled.

"What's on for today?" Hieu asked and looked up at the ceiling.

Larry's first impression of Hieu was changing. He wasn't a cocky SOB.

"Poor Father Ralph had to tell my nephew about Cornelius. His name is Josh, and he works at the Greenwich on the weekends." More thumps. "Just some seagulls up there."

Larry couldn't fix the location of Hieu's reaction to any news, the lips and cheeks, or eyebrows and forehead? This was only his third day as an inspector trainee. They spent part of the first day looking at the black and white photographs hung around Larry's office, pictures of department history, pictures of him building his Russian River summer home, and pictures Ansel Adams might have snapped but didn't. Larry's thoughts drifted to his end-of-day walk along the seawall, seven blocks from home.

His cell phone rang.

"Oh. Hi. Fine. Hang on." He held the phone away from his ear and said, "Hieu, would you mind stepping out for a minute? This shouldn't take long."

"Of course. I hear Inspector Varton – I'll visit with him while you're busy."

Varton's office was the last place Larry wanted Hieu to go.

"Are you there?"

"Did you read my letter, Dad?"

"Yes." Larry cupped the phone with his hand as if it were a feather pillow.

"Did you talk to Mom about the letter?"

"No, I haven't spoken to Mom." Larry pictured Lauren sitting up in bed and smoking a cigarette, its filter tip smelling of tincture of whiskey.

"Well, did you show her the letter?"

He raised his voice to quell opposition. "Yes, I showed her the letter, and she didn't say anything." He lied and now had a reason to go to confession. "Are you contracepting?"

"Yes."

"Next, you're going to tell me she had an abortion!"

"So, what if she did? Dad, I plan to move out of the Bay Area. I see no reason to stay."

"Good-bye, Mark." Larry's nostrils flared, the phone dropped, the chair leaned back, and he rubbed his face.

How do I tell Lauren Mark is threatening to move?

Hieu walked back in.

"I'm going to stay on top of the case regardless of what happens."

"I'm not sure what you mean, Larry."

Larry's cell phone rang again.

"Leahy."

"Stay away from the Greenwich." The caller hung up.

"Wow. I just got a call telling me to stay away from the Greenwich."

"Who was it?"

Larry logged into his computer. "I don't know. It was a man. Sounded middle-aged. I'll add an addendum to my report on what happened last night. I'm not worried about the call. We'll find out who made it."

"Did you come back to the office to write the report?"

"No, I filed it last night from home. Hieu, Varton doesn't know these people like I do. I need to be involved, and Dempsey doesn't have to know everything."

"Maybe I can help?"

"Absolutely not. I don't want your feet in quicksand. If I need help, I'll ask."

Larry was glad about his decision recommending that Hieu be promoted from patrol officer to inspector. He had all the qualities of a politician, well-bred, fit, amiable, stylish, and ambitious, everything Mark lacked, and Hieu was married.

Larry pulled the letter out of his jacket pocket.

"Hieu, close the door. I have something I want to read to you."

Larry pressed down on the letter's edges and breathed deeply:

Dear Dad,

I know you are disappointed with me. There are so many things I would like to say, but you won't listen. The choices I make are mine, but I need your support. Joan is a wonderful girl and makes me feel like a man. I'm happier than ever before. She's my best friend, and I couldn't ask for more. Please give her a chance. If you cannot do that, I don't know how we can continue any kind of relationship.

Mark

Larry watched Hieu thinking. He had passed the civil service exam and pointless interviews. His middle name was "Clement," the same as Larry's father. Larry had told Hieu nothing of his father's past, and while waiting for a response, he was reminded of a story that Hieu had told two nights ago at dinner. His parents had fled Vietnam with the help of their grandfathers. They had arranged for certain government officials to be bribed and, even though the money was accepted, both men were sent to "re-education" camp as punishment.

Hieu's story is so much more uplifting and serious than a family spat, or is it?

"What did Varton have to say?" Larry asked, not really interested in the answer.

"He asked me if I run every day."

"And?"

"I said that's where I get my tan."

Larry laughed, "Well, you know, most people think he can't tell the difference between one Chinese and another, but his wife is Japanese. It's his hard exterior. Former Marine."

"I gathered that from his haircut. High and tight."

"Mm. Nothing flusters him."

Hieu looked at the letter now folded over in Larry's hands and said, "Varton said the workhouse should be reopened and the homeless invited to spend some of their free time there." Hieu said it without comment, as if he had heard it before.

"What do you do in your spare time, Hieu?"

"I have too many adult toys, according to my wife."

"What was that?"

"Not what you're thinking. Four skateboards, a snowboard, a bike, and motorcycle."

"When do you have time for all that?"

"My wife asks me that all the time. She tells me to quit spending."

"My wife talks like a drill sergeant." A rakish smile on Larry's lips dissipated when the thumping of the seagulls resumed.

"Okay, do you want my opinion about your son's letter?"

"That's why I read it."

"Mark isn't seeing multiple women while claiming to be monogamous. So, if they're happy, shouldn't you be?"

"Like O'Hara and all his fooling around? No, Mark's problem is that he's spending his time pleasing others."

"What do you mean?"

"He's been influenced by his own vanity and the world, except that he doesn't have the kind of ambition the world proscribes, the lust for money, power, and sex. A Catholic must gain control of

111

himself and reject lust of any kind. The world didn't spend the time building his life or giving him an example of self-discipline. His mother and I did, and Lauren agrees with me. The phone call that sent you to Varton's office was from Mark. He said he's planning to move out of the Bay Area."

Hieu pulled his seat forward. "Larry, my father says that happiness comes with sadness. If you know love, you will know sorrow."

Hieu's advice hit hard. Larry recalled the words of a Jesuit retreat master.

We know how to enjoy food if we know what hunger is.

As the seconds ticked by, Hieu's advice began to feel like the stomping-on he got when he tried to break up a fight outside a bar on Columbus Avenue and a six-foot-eight drunk with a bright red face and extra-large hands got the best of him.

Hieu sat there with a bronzed face and fixed stare like that of a Hollywood statuette.

Larry shook his head, indicating that the matter was closed.

"I met with Father Ralph this morning. He believes wholeheartedly in O'Hara and said I failed to protect Cornelius. Henry MacKenzie, Cornelius' father, paid for my education and O'Hara's college education and made us promise to look out for Cornelius. It looks like neither one of us kept the promise."

Larry moved over to the window and slid it open. The building next door beckoned Larry's evaluation of its parts. "For now, Varton is leading the investigation, so let's do some good with the other files piled high on my desk before their owners get the impression I'm their whipping boy, too."

An hour of work passed, and Hieu closed Larry's door on the way out.

No more phone calls came in, no paperwork arrived, and no susurrus passed under the door. Larry closed his eyes and entered a deep sleep.

A car leaves a Greyhound bus stop for Napa.
"Why didn't you ask me to drive you there?"
"I'm just visiting someone."
A lie. Larry wonders why his father rolled down the window.
Doesn't he know, after twenty years, that his son has allergies? Why
are they going to Napa together? Getting away from him was the
whole point.
"Who are you going to visit?"
"No one."
"Then we'll go home."
"Fine."

Larry awoke and bolted for Varton's office. An open window allowed cool air to lift the edges of paper held down by one elbow. Joe's face was buried in his own paper mound. On one wall was a clock. It was fifteen minutes before twelve. On another wall hung a 1983 honorable discharge. A black cord draped against ruddy cheeks and was attached to eyeglasses sitting on his Nordic nose.

Sunset Magazine's *The Western Garden Book* lay on the only other chair in the room.

Larry placed the magazine on a corner of Joe's desk and sat down without a fuss. He knew Joe to be a non-smoker and light drinker, and the only stout odor that lingered after a tough morning work-out was body lotion liberally massaged everywhere except his teeth. On his left, a picture of his wife, Aioki, was turned in such a way that anyone could see her upon entering the office. Larry averted his eyes from a large wall picture of a crate branded Hula Apples, which featured a sun-bronzed, bare-breasted woman sitting under a palm tree.

"Ahem, Joe, I want to talk with Pepper Chase. Has she been called in for more questioning?"

Joe looked up. "Larry, you heard what Dempsey said. I'll be making the decisions from now on. I'll keep you informed when necessary. As a matter of fact, she is coming in today at one o'clock. Do you want to be present?"

"Yes, of course."

"All right. Get some lunch and, when you return, you can sit in on the interview."

Larry went to Chinatown, this time alone, still smarting from the early-morning show of disloyalty and needing a place to feel proud and useful again. Merchants stopped talking to each other and smiled when he walked by. One of them chatted with Larry for a minute. On Stockton Street, yellow and green vegetables rested in tilted crates placed in neat rows. He sat down at a sidewalk table belonging to Tony of Tony's Pizza Napoletana's. The building was elaborately painted olive green and yellow. He ordered meat balls.

At precisely one o'clock, Larry and Hieu walked into Joe's office.

"I got a call telling me to stay away from the Greenwich."

Joe looked up. "Who was it?"

"I don't know."

"Let's head to Interview Room #2."

The men entered a plain, white room with a city desk that had a chair on each side. A voice recorder was inside a wall niche next to the desk. The desk and chairs were bolted to the floor, and the recorder was locked behind a transparent acrylic cover. Two more chairs were shoved up against the opposite wall and touched the bottom edge of a two-way, observation mirror set into the wall. A giant, phony daisy camouflaged a hidden camera.

Dressed in a sky-blue jacket and sitting straight, Pepper Chase fiddled with an orange clip on the back of her head. She smiled at Larry. A red patent-leather purse sat in her lap, and a paper cup filled with water was in her right hand.

Larry leaned against the wall with his hands behind his back, and Hieu took the wall chair next to Larry.

Varton extracted a pencil from his pocket and placed it on the desk next to a piece of paper, yanked a key from his other pocket, unlocked the recorder cover, pulled it down, and hit the record button. "Ms. Chase, the interview will be recorded. Do you understand?"

"Yes, sir."

Her eyes flickered at Larry until he said, "Please listen carefully to Inspector Varton and answer the questions truthfully."

"Ms. Chase, my name is Inspector Varton."

She looked down at his pencil.

He looked at the piece of paper. "Your name is Pepper Darlene Chase, you work at the Greenwich, and you live in San Francisco. Let's see. You come from Chowchilla, California. Is that right?"

"Yes, sir," she answered cheerfully.

Larry asked, "Do you have brothers and sisters?"

The skin covering the area above her cheeks rippled like water, possibly signifying the gnashing of teeth. Both hands trembled slightly. "I have two brothers, but I don't like talking about them."

"Okay," Larry said, "We won't talk about them." Larry remembered the old kidnapping case in Chowchilla and avoided any further mention of her hometown. "Are you happy here in San Francisco?"

"Oh yes, I love the city."

"Are you happy with your job?"

"It's my first job, and it's the best. The guests are extremely nice to me. I couldn't ask for more. I'm making friends. The employees are wonderful. I'm able to buy clothes I never could afford. I have an ideal apartment for one. The weather is sunny and mild. I get my nails done every week at the Greenwich. The rooms are elegantly decorated, and the hallways are vacuumed every day. So, yes, I'm happy. Really."

She likes being the center of attention, but not being questioned.

Varton lowered his voice. "Do you know how money got into Cornelius' room?"

"No, sir. I have no idea. I brought him his lunch at three thirty. He is so precise. Always wants his meals at the same time every day. He can be a problem . . . oh, you know what I mean, don't you Mr. Leahy?" She scanned Larry as if he would provide an answer. "I brought him pot roast from the hotel kitchen. That's something I would like to learn how to prepare when I get married, but it is so difficult to find a good man. Mr. MacKenzie was a very good man, wouldn't you agree?" She looked at each one of them.

Her voice is no different from the twang of a rubber-band.

Larry prepared to probe Pepper about her relationship with Cornelius.

Was O'Hara right about a romantic relationship?

"Ms. Chase, when was the last time you were in Mr. MacKenzie's room?"

Her attention shifted to Larry. "Four o'clock."

"Is something wrong, Ms. Chase?" Varton asked.

Larry pulled out his notepad and quickly wrote, "Last time Pepper was in 1212 was at four in the afternoon." He added an exclamation point, his way of noting the shock questions caused.

"No need, Inspector Leahy. The interview is being recorded."

Larry held firmly to his notepad and noticed Hieu quickly stuffing his in his suit pocket.

Pepper pulled a red compact from her purse and said, "I look terrible."

"Are you feeling okay?" Varton asked.

"Yes. I'm fine."

"And what did you mean when you said, 'Mr. MacKenzie can be a problem'?"

Larry saw a torn poster announcing May's Officer of the Month lying on the floor in a corner of the room. Dust balls covered a picture of his face.

Varton said, "So, what did you mean?"

Pepper wriggled like a kindergartener. "Well, he told me that he had an argument with Mr. O'Hara about someone who had been fired. I liked looking after him. He is . . . oh, I mean, he was . . . a fine man . . . and a religious man, too. I don't know much about religion. My family never went to church. You understand, Mr. Leahy?"

"Miss Chase, just answer the questions," Varton said without emotion.

Larry asked, "Pepper, do you want another drink of water?"

"Yes, please."

"Inspector Trang, get her water," Varton ordered.

As Hieu walked out of the office, Larry sat down and slid his chair over ruts to be closer to her. "Just be calm. The questioning shouldn't take too long. Take your time."

"Okay, thank you."

"Ms. Chase, the last time you were in Mr. MacKenzie's room, you say, was about four. Did you leave after that?" Varton asked in a flat voice, as if he were a lounge singer sitting on a grand piano and not caring who was there.

"About twenty minutes later."

"Where did you go?"

"Back to the front desk."

"Did you return to his room later in the night?"

"No, of course not. It was the Fourth of July, and we were getting busy."

"Did anyone else go to Mr. MacKenzie's room . . . to the best of your knowledge?"

"No."

Hieu walked in with a paper cup and handed it to Pepper. She drank deeply and, with the other hand still clutching the compact, pulled the purse up her lap, which drew her black skirt up. Not knowing where or how to get rid of the paper cup, she pulled the skirt down and studied Larry.

"Let me take that," Larry said.

"I can get rid of the paper cup," Hieu said.

"Give it to me." Varton threw it in the waste paper basket.

Hieu leaned over and whispered into Larry's ear.

"Excuse me, Inspector Varton. I need to talk to Inspector Trang outside."

"All right. We'll wait until you return and begin the questioning again."

They stepped out. As if speaking to the dead, Larry said, "Okay, great. We'll wait five minutes and go back in, just enough time for Pepper to wonder what's going on. That might get her to relax and talk." Hieu took out his cell phone. Five minutes passed, and they nodded at each other.

"Thanks, Inspector Varton. Pepper, tell us more about your job and what it's like to be a front desk clerk."

Pepper asked, "What's wrong?"

"Nothing. We received a report from the Greenwich."

"A report, Mr. Leahy?"

"Accounting records, phone calls, e-mails. . ."

"E-mails?" Pepper lifted the compact, looked at herself, and said, "Sometimes, I have to work with security. They will ask me questions, and they've taught me to be on the look-out for dishonest people and people with motives. I notice things, and if I'm asked, I always report what I've heard or seen. It's my duty, and I always do my duty. Really."

"And how does that work out? Have you ever been commended for what you've reported? Has Mr. O'Hara ever given you a raise for a good report?" Larry asked.

"No, he hasn't, but I got a letter of commendation from the accounting office one time for catching an employee who was stealing. He wasn't putting his tips into the tip pool, which is a large jar under the front counter."

"Who was that?"

"I . . . I don't know if I should say his name?"

"Pepper, you don't have to, but it helps us gather information during this phase of the investigation," Hieu said.

"Well, all right, his name is Gerald Smith, but don't tell him I said that."

Larry asked, "How do you know?"

"I saw him put a tip into his wallet."

"Maybe, he intended to put it into the tip jar," Larry said.

"No, because I saw him buy a bottle of gin from the hotel bar with his tip money. We are prohibited from entering the bar or buying anything there."

"Did the bartender get in trouble?"

"All right. Enough of that," Varton said. "Last night you said you were in the vault some time before midnight. Is that right?"

"Yes." Pepper looked at the recorder and said, "I really don't know anything more about this."

"Pepper, it's very, very important that you answer truthfully and completely. Did you take money to the late Mr. MacKenzie's room?"

She looked at Larry and said, "He needed money."

The red purse came up against the desk and lodged there.

Larry spoke in a gentle voice, "Pepper?"

"Yes?"

"Did you take money to Cornelius' room?"

"He sent me an e-mail." She inspected the ceiling as if she preferred it to answering any more questions.

"What did it say?"

"He said he needed money."

"Ms. Chase, this is a serious matter. A man is dead, and you say he asked you for money. From now on you will tell us everything. Is that understood?" Pepper's compact fell out of her hand and the sound of shattering glass broke the calm. "Leave it there. Now tell us what you did," Varton bellowed. His pencil snapped.

Hieu jumped up, lifted the compact, broken glass still wrapped by the frame, and placed it back in her hand. "Inspector Varton wants to know if you brought Cornelius money. That's all. You are being recorded."

"Cornelius is not your supervisor. What business do you have with him?" asked Varton, digging into the drawer to find another pencil.

"Like I told you, I brought him dinner."

Varton broke another pencil. "Dinner or lunch?"

"Dinner," she said sheepishly. "Yes, yes. I brought him the money."

There it is.

Varton took charge.

"How much?"

Her answer didn't come soon enough.

"Answer my question."

"$50,000."

"Did he say why he needed the money?" Hieu asked.

She whispered, "He said he had a gambling debt."

Varton exhaled loudly. "So, you brought him $50,000 to help him out . . . so he could pay off his debt . . . correct?"

"Yes."

Hieu asked, "Did you know he gambled?"

"No."

Larry asked, "You said he sent an e-mail. We'll need to see it."

Her chair slipped. It could have come off a linoleum crack, and when she stuffed the compact in the purse, the purse slid out of her lap, and the compact jumped out of her purse like a hot potato. Pieces of glass fell out of the frame. She reached for it, and her shoe ground the glass into the floor. She left it there and slouched back in the chair.

"Take your time, Pepper, and we'll get the compact after the interview." Larry felt sorry for Pepper and picked up the compact. "When did you bring him the money?"

"About eight o'clock."

Hieu snuck a peek at Larry. "Who else was on duty with you last night besides Doris?"

Hieu knows her name, so he must have read the report.

"Pablo and another bellhop."

"Did Pablo visit MacKenzie?"

Pepper rolled her eyes at Varton and said, "I don't know."

Larry moved closer. "Did anyone else visit Mr. MacKenzie?"

Pepper cast a frightened gaze around the room as if she were in an enclosure of panthers. "Umm, yes, Gerald Smith. The guy that was fired. He came to visit Cornelius around midnight, but I don't know if he did, because he disappeared, and I didn't see him for the rest of the night. Honestly, I don't know much more about all of this."

"What was the real reason Smith was fired?"

Varton is fishing.

"I don't know."

Varton laughed. "No, not you."

"I'm getting tired. Are there a lot more questions, Mr. Leahy?"

"Just a few more. Hang in there."

Varton said, "Tell me about Smith."

"Well, everyone knows that Cornelius has a vacation home at Topaz Lake and goes up there, sometimes by himself and sometimes with Mr. Smith. Cornelius spent the Fourth of July holiday with his sister. Gerald called many times asking for Cornelius, and he asked me to page Cornelius around midnight."

"Mr. MacKenzie spent most of the day with his sister?" Larry asked.

"Yes, he did. He's so sweet."

I spoke to him in the morning. She might be lying.

"Did you see Cornelius returning to the hotel after seeing his sister? Try to remember," Larry said.

"No."

She looked troubled.

"The interviews make me so . . . well, Mr. Leahy, I know this may sound odd, but I was going to ask if I could get a phone number from you. That police officer taking everyone's finger prints – I didn't get his name. He's the one with the honest eyes. I suppose that's why he is so good at his job. People trust him to hold their hands and hearts," she added, "or at least their thumbs. I made a joke about how he had my digits, but I didn't have his, and he said that was a shame. Then, I asked him if it was true that twins have the same fingerprints, and he never was able to give me his phone number. I feel silly asking you, but they say that if you feel that spark, you shouldn't worry about being foolish. Just a phone number."

"No. Now, back to what we are talking about. Did anyone report hearing a gun shot?"

"No. Cornelius lives on the top floor on the corner of the building, no one above and no neighbors on either side. On one side of his apartment is a utility room. Across the hall is a housekeeping room. He liked the apartment because it gave him so much privacy."

Larry saw Varton's lips miming the words, "Nine-eighteen."

Larry mouthed a reply, "No, she's not crazy."

"So, Ms. Chase, one more question. Did Mr. MacKenzie answer when you paged him for Smith?" Varton asked.

"No. He must have been asleep."

"How do you know that?"

"Well, I just assumed he was asleep."

"Did you go to his room and ring the doorbell?"

"No. No." Pepper sank into her seat.

"I hope you have told us the complete truth." Varton looked at Larry.

"Yes. That's the truth," she answered, and with one last breath, she exhaled, "I've told you everything I know, honestly."

"Thank you, Pepper. Inspector Varton, is there anything else you would like to know from Ms. Chase?" Larry asked.

"No. Be available for further questioning. Do you understand?"

"Yes, sir."

Larry tendered her the red compact.

Hieu said, "Let me show you out."

After she stepped outside the room, Varton told Larry to put off charging her with grand theft until the medical examiner had determined the cause of death.

Outside, Larry told Pepper, "You did the right thing, telling us you took the money to Cornelius. I appreciate . . ."

"You took the money! You're fired."

Larry turned around and saw eyes glaring behind monogrammed glasses.

"Mr. O'Hara!" She pulled out a pair of gold cufflinks, hid behind Larry, and passed the links into O'Hara's hands.

"I don't want those." O'Hara handed them back. "Your final paycheck and the contents of your employee locker will be delivered to your residence later today." The cigar in his mouth appeared grotesquely large.

"I just wanted something of his to keep."

"I don't care. Now leave."

"Please, Mr. O'Hara, my job is all I have. I just did what Cornelius told me to do."

Larry placed his right hand on O'Hara's upper arm and said, "James, this is an investigation, and we're gathering facts."

O'Hara looked around Larry and yelled at her, "Do as I say."

She ran, dribbling her emotions down the hall.

O'Hara calmly pulled out his cell phone and punched in some numbers. He looked at Leahy. "Let go of me. Stay out of this, Larry. I'm a master at what I do." O'Hara took two steps away from Larry and spoke into his phone. When he turned around, his broad shoulders gave him the appearance of a buffalo.

"James, there is more to this story."

"It's simple. She brought him the money from the vault. What employees do affects the hotel. I don't give a damn what they do with their personal lives, but when it affects the hotel, I move on it. I've been a rat too long to be screwed by a mouse."

Varton came out of the interview room. "What's going on out here?"

O'Hara shouted, "Chase should be arrested. Why did you let her go?"

Larry said, "We gather all the facts before any action is taken. It's standard police procedure."

"Where's the interview? It's supposed to be for two o'clock" He looked at Varton and said, "Are you Varton?" He faced Larry again and said, "Glad I came. Found out what that foolish girl did." He looked around for something to spit in, walked over to the water fountain, and coughed.

When Larry reached his office, he realized he had left Hieu behind. He returned to the interview room and found Hieu just before he entered. "Are you staying for the interview?"

"Is that all right?"

"Sure, why not."

Half an hour later, Varton walked into Larry's office. "Didn't learn much from O'Hara. Does he have any children?"

"No."

Varton peered out the window and said, "That's my only regret, not having children. Parents divorced when I was fifteen and never saw much of the family. Didn't care. Too busy with football and baseball."

"Well, you may not have missed much, not having children."

"Anyway, the wife takes care of my mother. What a bargain I got with Aioki, not like the first wife. Hmm. Suppose you're thinking about retirement. How's that Russian River home?"

Varton admired the two rings on his fingers. The rings sparkled like sugar under Larry's florescent light.

"When did you join the Marines?" Larry asked, but he knew the answer.

"Twenty."

"Didn't you think about college?"

"Two years in junior college. The most gullible people in the world are college graduates."

"Some people would describe them as idealistic."

"Gullible."

"Where's Hieu?" Larry asked.

"I sent him back to his office."

"I need him in here. We have a lot of work to do, and I'm not thinking about retirement, Joe."

"Oh, don't worry about the investigation. I've got things under control. Just sit tight. I'll be looking at the video to confirm Chase's story."

"Joe, I think I know who it was that called telling me to stay away from the Greenwich."

"Who?"

"Bud Fletcher."

"How do you know?"

"He's O'Hara's flunky."

"He's scheduled for an interview. We can interrogate him about that. While I'm here, I have some questions about Cornelius."

"What do you want to know?"

"You have this special relationship with the MacKenzie clan. Tell me why Cornelius had an apartment at the Greenwich. Isn't that an odd arrangement?"

"No. You have to understand a few things about Cornelius. He needed a lot of help. He only graduated from high school because he was in a special program and had private tutors."

"What was wrong with him?"

"He managed. Father Ralph, O'Hara, they all protected him."

"So, he had the IQ of a turnip, and they all protected him, up until he got himself killed. Someone wanted him dead. What else can you tell me about Father Ralph and his relationship with Cornelius?"

"Father Ralph looked after him. Phone calls, visits . . . that's why he found the body."

"Wasn't a bit late for a priest to be visiting his brother?"

Larry stood up abruptly. "Not if you knew the family and their love for Cornelius!"

"All right. Calm down Larry. What was the priest doing there? Was he soused?"

Larry pulled out his white handkerchief and wiped his face.

Joe sat back and said, "We need clear heads and a calm approach."

Larry was aggravated. "Let me try this again. Cornelius got the apartment when he was promoted. He learned the job and worked his way up. Henry MacKenzie, Cornelius' father, made O'Hara and me promise to protect Cornelius." Larry sat down. "It's my opinion that Father Ralph and O'Hara were well-meaning, but they left Cornelius vulnerable."

"What do you mean?"

"A few years ago, Cornelius recommended a man for a bellhop position. The hotel did a background check and discovered the man's arrest record. Cornelius told O'Hara that the priest in charge of St. Anthony's Dining Room had said that all the man needed was a fresh start. O'Hara reluctantly agreed, and the man was hired.

126

"Six months later, he found his way into Cornelius' apartment and stole his childhood collection of baseball cards. The police investigated, and the man was fired. Father Ralph spoke to O'Hara, and they took Cornelius aside and had a talk with him about helping others."

"Sounds like he was a child."

"Not long after, maybe, a couple of months, Father Ralph confided to me that Fletcher had asked O'Hara why Father Ralph visited Cornelius so often. O'Hara's answer was, 'They are brothers.' The Topaz Lake home was purchased and Cornelius . . ."

"What's that got to do with anything? The murder occurred in San Francisco."

"You asked me for background."

"Just stick to the facts surrounding what happened at the hotel. Why does O'Hara keep so much money on hand? His hotel is a two-bit joint." He picked up a pencil from Larry's desk. "I wonder what he's doing with all that money." The tip of the pencil disappeared into his mouth. Joe leaned forward. "All right. Keep your ears to the ground and keep me informed."

"If you're lucky," Larry murmured.

"What's that?"

"Nothing."

Joe gave Larry the pencil out of his mouth.

"Ask Fletcher why he failed to escort Cornelius to his apartment."

"I will."

"When's his interview?" Larry asked.

"I'm working on that. By the way, I asked O'Hara if there was any other trouble at the Greenwich. He asked me what I meant. I asked if there were any pending lawsuits against the Greenwich. He said there was one in Sonoma County involving an adoption agency. It's all in his statement. Have a look."

That was a smart question.

He heard the rapping sound of Varton's cowboy boots moving down the hall and thought there were more hornets in this nest, but for now it was time to take a snooze.

It's tiring explaining things to someone who doesn't listen.

Better read O'Hara's statement first.

Larry found the spot. It read:

"The agency had some land to sell. I made an offer, and everything seemed to be going fine. During the negotiating phase, information came to me that the adoption agency had some dealings with Cornelius MacKenzie and Maureen Daley. I determined that the agency was not dealing honestly and had kept the information from me. I sued the agency for nondisclosure of all relevant matters affecting the sale. At this time, I cannot provide more information, because the lawsuit is pending."

Before closing his eyes, he thought about getting lunch and about Mark and heard the squeals of baby seagulls on the roof.

Maybe, one of them is a male bird about to fly away from the nest, for good.

Varton's boots were on the move again.

He's number two, not far behind me, and has won Dempsey's favor. What if I don't get that promotion? How will Lauren react?

Chapter 7

Friday, July 5

Leaning over an eighteenth-century rosewood desk, a platinum-blond woman hastily withdrew a pencil from her mouth, leaving orange lipstick on the end she was chewing.

O'Hara swung around in his chair.

Mm.

He liked the picture, stacked, curvy, and clueless, just the image he wanted outside the double doors to his office. The inner sanctum was weighted with Blue Oak and Coast Live Oak, paneling usually reserved for ships.

She has a hellava lot more than ten fingers and ten toes.

"How long have you been my secretary?"

"This is my fourth week."

"Good. You're a keeper. Hang up the smoking jacket. It's over there." O'Hara pointed to a black leather sofa in a corner of the room. In front of two matching black leather chairs, a brown and white English bull dog lay on a red Persian Heriz rug with a medallion design. "Don't be afraid of him. If he howls, give him a tidbit. They're in my bottom drawer."

O'Hara lifted a fresh cigar from the humidor. "Know what that is?" He pointed. She looked confused. "Just stand there and answer my question."

"It's where you keep your cigars?"

High, broad windows behind his desk gave the oak walls luster, and the same streams of light shone on Ms. Keck's fuchsia-pink high-heels.

Smelled, fondled, and rolled over, the dark wrapper of a Padrone Maduro lightened as it was lifted from its tight resting spot.

He heard the outer doors open and shut. "Get out there and see who came in." He watched her cross the floor in a straight line with notepad and pencil swinging beside her rear-end, and, as she left his office, he thought he recognized the voice in the outer office.

Ms. Keck asked a question, and the familiar voice answered, "I'd like to see Mr. O'Hara."

"Do you have an appointment, sir?"

"I'm Inspector Leahy and this is Inspector Trang. It's important we see him."

O'Hara sat still and enjoyed listening to Leahy plead. His intercom buzzed. "Tell them I'm busy."

He heard Leahy say, "Miss, let me take care of this."

His intercom buzzed again, and O'Hara pressed down on the lever. "Through the doors in front of you, Larry." Larry's round face appeared.

O'Hara stood up. "Who's that?"

"This is Inspector Trang. I want to talk to you about Cornelius."

Ms. Keck shut the door behind them.

O'Hara extended an arm and said, "All right, but I thought we said all we needed to say yesterday." He raised his eyebrows. "Sit down, sit down."

Their suits looked rack bought, but he cast another gander at Trang.

Nice looking Chinese. He's stepped on scraps in the back of a shop.

O'Hara was amused by the look on their faces and wanted to say, "No, there aren't any trapdoors in my office – under your chairs or anywhere else." Instead, he said, "Care for a cigar, Leahy, Trang, or are you on the clock?"

"No thanks."

Larry looked at Hieu.

"No thanks."

"No problem. Good-looking secretary I've got, huh? She's new and expands office appeal with that rack." He lifted the San Francisco Business Times, walked over to the leather couch in the corner, and threw the newspaper onto its smooth seat. The bull dog raised his fat head a millimeter off his paw.

My dog looks almost as good as I do in the light from the window.

He observed them looking at him from their chairs. From the corner, he bellowed, "So, Larry, before you start, I have something for you."

He walked back to his desk and opened the top drawer. Lying on top of a contract for the hotel's seismic retrofitting was a thick, seafoam-green envelope. He handed Larry the envelope and waited for a reaction. When Larry smiled, O'Hara said, "Twelve days in Ireland. Airfare, transfers, and hotel in Dublin are paid for."

Larry ran a hand over his bald head and had a peculiar look on his face. He stood up and offered O'Hara his hand. O'Hara stood up, his thighs shoving the drawer shut, and accepted Larry's hand.

"So . . . whadda you think?"

"Um, I'm not sure what to say? I'd like to take a trip to Ireland, but . . ."

"It's not a bribe, Larry, just something I've planned on doing for a very long time. I've never really treated you to anything, and you need something rewarding in your life, seeing as how little you get."

The peculiar look on Larry's face reappeared. "Thanks."

"Enjoy yourself!"

The two men sat back down.

Silence followed.

"How's Maureen Daley?"

"I'm having a late business lunch with her in a few minutes. We have to make this quick."

"Your man said he never walked Cornelius to his apartment. What happened?"

"He did." He buzzed Ms. Keck and said, "Get Fletcher up here."

He stood up, studied Larry and Hieu, placed a hand on his chest, turned, and looked out the window. Then he sat down again.

They waited.

O'Hara lifted his heavy, black-framed eyeglasses and placed them back on his nose. "Let me get a closer look at you, Trang."

Hieu shifted in his seat.

O'Hara wondered where their guns were. The cigar shifted from one side of his mouth to the other. His observations drifted downward, and he wondered what stuff Hieu was made of. He might be impressed by the surroundings, but he didn't move a muscle and seemed to possess the belligerent face of a raccoon, as if to say, "Got a problem?" Larry looked more human.

The humidor has more substance than most men.

O'Hara adjusted his eyeglasses to get a better look at Larry. "You promised a round of golf, Larry, so when will it be? I've been waiting two years."

"You've got plenty of partners. Where's your security man?"

"Dammit, Larry, you're not up to a challenge. My man will be here." His Rolex caught some beams from the green hurricane lamp and gave O'Hara the urge to tip the light onto Larry's face and have a closer look.

The trip will renew our rapport.

Smoke drifted toward the ornate crystal chandelier above his desk.

The intercom buzzed.

O'Hara leaned forward and pressed down.

"Mr. Fletcher is here."

"All right."

"Should I send him in, sir."

"Yes, of course, woman!"

"I heard your car dealership failed," Larry said.

O'Hara looked at the double doors. "It was an investment. Not one of the managers knew what the hell he was doing." The doors opened. "Fletcher, get in here."

"So sorry, sir, for being late."

"Never mind. Now, answer some questions from Officer Leahy."

"You told me you did not escort Cornelius MacKenzie to his room the night he died. Is that correct?" Larry asked.

"That's right," Fletcher said, his gaze transfixed.

O'Hara was enjoying the look of fear.

Fletcher's waist, which had grown moderately in middle age, shifted back and forth beneath his biscuit-colored shirt and dull brown suit jacket, and one trembling finger rubbed a bulbous nose covered by creeks of broken capillaries.

Larry glanced over at O'Hara and lowered his voice. "You said to me that Mr. O'Hara told you not to escort Cornelius. Correct?"

Silence.

"Didn't I give you specific instructions to check in with me?" Larry grabbed his notepad from the pocket inside his jacket and waved it in front of Fletcher.

O'Hara sat forward and stared at Fletcher.

"May I ask what is going on?" Fletcher asked.

"No, you may not," O'Hara shouted.

"Well . . .." Larry said.

Hieu spoke up. "Mr. Fletcher, did your plan for Cornelius change during the night?"

Fletcher said, "Yes!"

"Get out."

"Yes, sir, Mr. O'Hara." Fletcher backed all the way to the double doors and bumped into them. O'Hara laughed, and Fletcher quickly shut the doors behind himself.

O'Hara readjusted himself in his chair and looked around the room.

"James, do I have to remind you of the promise we made years ago? We promised to look out for Cornelius."

"I'm the sole owner of this hotel now, and I'll do what's best for the hotel, and that means I can handle all employees the way I want. It's your job to find the guilty, whoever they are. If you ask me, you should look at Pepper Chase. I told you I caught her in Cornelius' room the day he died. I heard her express undying love for him. I forbade her from entering his room again. Did she comply? It doesn't look that way."

"I think you should reconsider your decision to fire her."

"Why should I? She stole $50,000."

"I did some research. She has no criminal record, and she was in love with Cornelius. You said so yourself. I saw the e-mail from Cornelius telling her to bring the money."

"Only a criminal would do what she did. I can't trust her."

"How long has she been at the Greenwich?"

"What difference does that make?"

"Doesn't she have a spotless record?"

"I can find out. I'll call HR."

"Hasn't she had regular pay increases?"

"All my employees do. I'm a very generous employer."

"And you're a very understanding employer. No one else knows she took the money and hiring her back would have no impact on the operations of the hotel. In fact, if you don't change your mind, you'll have to hire a replacement."

What's Larry after?

"I like what you said. I *am* generous, and I *am* fair. Her aunt called me this morning and begged me to take her back. I already called Pepper and told her she can return. However, Larry, do not interfere anymore with my hotel and its employees. I don't know what you're thinking, but the hotel is going to be run the way I see it, and nothing, including this investigation, will interfere."

"Right decision. As for the investigation, interference will come only from your side. I have a job to do, James. Don't stand in my way."

O'Hara looked around the room again. "You told me at the last reunion that you would join me at the Olympic Club. I'm waiting. Don't tell me you've crawfished a way out?" His head bent forward as he looked out over his eyeglasses at Hieu, and said, "You look like an educated boy. Isn't that what you call it when you renege on a commitment?"

Larry answered, "I'm busy."

"Busier than I am? I doubt it."

Larry thinks he's outsmarted me.

O'Hara started to speak, but Larry interrupted, saying. "Let's do it. You bring one of your buddies, and I'll bring one of my buddies, and we'll have a foursome."

O'Hara felt his core engine getting hotter and faster. He stood up, offered his hand to Larry, and lowered his voice, saying, "You're on. Set the date. Next Wednesday?"

Larry and Hieu stood up.

"What time?" Larry asked.

"Tee time, ten o'clock. Are we agreed?"

"Sure."

They shook hands. O'Hara leaned over and drooled into a golden spittoon on the floor. "I'm looking forward to this. You'd better get in a round before we meet. Otherwise, you and your buddy will be forced to pay the tee fees."

Larry let go of his hand quickly and said, "Fine. Trang, let's go."

"What about your wife? She will *love* the trip to Ireland. How is she?"

O'Hara watched Larry's body twist in place. "She keeps me respectable."

"The leash around your neck is growing tighter every year, Larry."

"You should have one. And not around your neck."

O'Hara belly-laughed. It was a good day. He followed Hieu who followed Larry. All three of them filed past O'Hara's secretary, and Hieu said good-bye to her. O'Hara couldn't see the expression on Larry's face but imagined that he wanted to reprimand Hieu on the spot for the courtesy.

As Hieu and Larry left the outer office, O'Hara overheard Hieu ask, "Who's Maureen Daley?"

"His girlfriend."

O'Hara smiled and shut the door quietly.

O'Hara smiled again when he faced Ms. Keck and walked past her into his office.

He sat down and pressed on the buzzer. "Get in here."

Ms. Keck opened the door and looked in.

His voice softened. "Don't be shy."

She pulled down on her skirt and advanced.

"Make sure the humidor is filled with cigars. You're doing pretty well so far." He lifted the lid and said, "That's the filter. Your shorthand is good, and you know how to answer calls. Where do you come from?" The velvet-lined lid dropped without a sound.

"Long Beach."

"Where did you go to school?"

"Charter College."

"What did you do before that?" he asked.

"I started working as a model when I was sixteen."

"Oh, yes, I remember that from your application. Very good, very good. Do you live in San Francisco?" He didn't have high regard for claims on an application, but this one stood out. Now he was about to capitalize on it.

"Yes. I have a studio on lower Nob Hill," she answered.

"When did you move here?"

"Two months ago."

"Any friends?" O'Hara asked.

"No, not yet."

She sounded sad.

"Well, if you do your best here, you may make some new friends. Are you good at that?" He stroked his cleft chin.

"Well, sir, sometimes women say mean things about me. At my last job, one girl accused me of having . . . breast implants." Ms. Keck looked down at the floor. "It's untrue."

She's got nothing to lose. She's young, alone, and will take whatever she gets.

"I don't want to eat my lunch in the break room. Where should I go?"

"Are you afraid of the female employees . . . or the men? My employees are good and hard-working. If one of them bothers you, tell me and I'll put an end to it. As for lunch, you can eat over at Union Square. There are plenty of benches and lots of people to watch."

"How far is it?"

"Two blocks."

"I bring my running shoes, so I can walk there."

"Good." O'Hara leaned back in his chair. "I know all about women, but you're different. You're the sensitive type, aren't you?"

Her pale pink face turned the color of her fuchsia shoes. "You look like a girl who loves animals. Is that right?"

"Yes. How did you know? I love cats. I had a cat when I was growing up, but my landlord doesn't allow cats."

"Would you like to keep a cat here?" he asked in a deep, low-pitched voice.

She had a pitiable look on her face. "Is that possible? Would you allow it? I'm afraid of the dog. How could I keep a cat here?"

"Duke sleeps all day and is harmless. He might even like a kitty cat. Housekeeping takes care of him, so he's not one or your duties. Stand back."

She took a few steps back, standing straight as a toy rocket.

"Very good. Where do you shop?"

She opened a mouthful of teeth, as white as a brand-new picket fence and said, "Macys."

"Upgrade."

"I'm sorry?"

"Take yourself to Neiman Marcus tomorrow, your day off, and ask for Tobias, the manager of the women's section and my wife's personal stylist. I'm going to call him and make an appointment just for you. He will pick out a collection of clothes that are more suitable for your position in this office as my girl Friday. Do you think you can be that kind of girl?" he asked in the same deep, low-pitched voice.

"Oh, yes."

"That's what I like to hear." The back of the chair straightened as he leaned forward. *"His Girl Friday* is the name of a movie from Hollywood's Golden Age."

"Oh, I love that movie. My mother wanted to be an actress, but she never made it."

"Too bad. What about you? Did you want to be an actress?"

"I did, but I wasn't any good at it, and I wanted to move away from my family."

All he could see was a candy counter of red-hots and Valentine hearts, and he mugged for an invisible camera. "When you get to the appointment, tell Tobias I want more mini-skirts and silk stockings." O'Hara grasped the edge of his desk and pulled himself forward. Out of the drawer came his personal check book.

When she saw the amount on the check, her eyes grew to the size of sunflowers. "$2,000?"

"That's right. I want you looking good for me. Do you understand?"

"I . . . think so."

"Good. If you need more, tell me and I'll review. Your perfume smells good. Keep wearing it."

"Yes, sir."

His voice got louder than he anticipated, but he liked what came out. "I don't like people who complain or whine . . . and get the gum out of your mouth. I don't want any unprofessionalism in my office."

"Yes, sir."

"Now, get back to your desk and wait for my buzz."

She hurried to the door, dropped a pencil, and bent over. In seconds, she recovered and closed the doors quietly. Her leaving was like an antidote to delicious venom. He called Duke, who lifted his head. It took him several minutes to get up, and O'Hara made sure that cigar smoke did not reach the lazy superstar.

Five minutes passed. O'Hara's intercom buzzed.

"Mrs. Daley is here, sir."

He met her inside his office. They kissed, but this time the doors to his inner sanctum had not closed all the way. At the elevator, he said, "In the future, Maureen, make sure you close the doors."

"Yes, dear. Where are we going?"

"I reserved a table at The Rotunda for three thirty. Mind walking?"

"No, I don't mind walking. There's lots of sunshine. We can do some shopping after."

"Which will make me sweat."

"I'll carry your jacket, and it's good for you to get some sun. You tan so beautifully."

"I can't go shopping with you. I have to be back at the office."

"What for? It's the end of the week."

"I told you I couldn't see you for a few days, but you called ten times this morning. Fortunately, my secretary is new. She's a dumb-bunny but will do, and she's not one to tell . . ."

"James, be nice today."

She hung onto his arm on the way down the elevator, but on the first floor, he shook free. They passed by the front desk, close enough to hear the switchboard operator practicing her phone pitch.

James ordered a scotch and water from The Rotunda bar and guzzled it down. He pulled out a white handkerchief and wiped the condensation off the glass.

"You know, I had nothing to do with Cornelius' death."

"Yes, I know that."

James looked up at the glass ceiling, and his eyes stayed focused there for a time.

The waiter made James think Mexican. He might pull out a switch blade as soon as put a plate on the table.

"Two lobsters."

He felt warm under the glass canopy. The constant droning of female shoppers put him on edge, and the buttery fragrance of the lobster failed to alleviate his worry.

"Get me another napkin. You should know that. What's your name?"

"Jose."

The waiter returned with two and handed the first one to James, who grabbed it. Maureen thanked the waiter.

James stopped his foot from tapping.

"All right. Let's go."

"No dessert?"

"No. I've got to get back."

He left a hundred-dollar bill in the waiter's folder.

They arrived back at the Greenwich lobby, and he let go of her hand.

Her light pink Pashmina wrap opened. "Let me give you a kiss good-bye."

James turned his face away, and her kiss landed on his ear.

Pepper's head popped up from below the counter.

"I told Smith to return the keys," he said, loud enough for Pepper to hear.

"Who's Smith? What keys?" Maureen whispered with a hand resting on James' shoulder.

"Bellhop I fired," he said loudly. "Smith was set to be Cornelius' replacement. Not now."

James wrenched his shoulder away and whispered, "For Christ sake, be careful."

She closed her wrap and said, "This feels good on a warm day. You always know what to buy a lady. I wore it just for you."

O'Hara pulled Maureen over to the three-seater and said, "I've told you before to be careful, and why were you in Cornelius' room the day he died?"

Maureen steadied herself against the furniture. "He gave me a little gift . . . for his troubles. Anyway, he's dead now, and it doesn't matter."

"In the future, let me know what you're doing. You could get us in trouble."

James turned and headed for the elevators.

When he opened the door of the second-floor accounting office, conversations ceased.

He walked to the office in the rear and said, "Let me see the report for June."

A middle-aged Chinese lady with a plump face smiled, lifted the report off a file cabinet next to her desk, and passed it to him without a word.

Despite ongoing building improvements, the cash flow from operating activities was just over $30,000.

"Did you certify the report?"

"Yes, sir, we did."

"Very good."

"Is Fletcher still bothering you?"

"No. He finally stopped coming in here after I told him you had barred him from the office permanently."

"Buy some flowers for yourself." He handed her a one-hundred bill.

"I'll buy them for the office."

"Suit yourself. Just keep up the clever work."

Ms. Keck stood up when he entered his office.

"You're doing fine, Keck. You can sit down."

He shut the double doors; he didn't want Ms. Keck to overhear him.

"What a good boy you are. Want some treats?" He stroked Duke's ears. Duke raised his heavy head, and James scratched the dog's jowls. James stood up and walked over to the wash basin, pulled out a Persian white towel from a drawer, and began cleaning the fleshy rope above the nose of Duke's face. "There, now you're all cleaned up."

Duke's sad eyes made him feel better. He lifted Duke up and put him on the floor, and the sight of Duke's wide stance reminded him of himself, broad shoulders, formidable features, people-oriented, exertive, gentle, and protective of family.

I can face anything, bigger worries, bigger obstacles, bigger everything.

He pulled out his cell phone and checked the stock market. He clicked on another app and made a fast donation to his favorite charity, the American Red Cross. He took a picture of Duke and sent it to Clare with the caption, "Your honey taking care of his boy." Moments later, she texted back, "I heard my honey is nominated for the Bohemian Club Jinks Committee. It is true?"

"Your honey is a popular SOB, and hijinks are my specialty."

"I love you," she texted.

"I love you more than anything."

"Will you be home for dinner?"

"Yes. Tell Bessie to have two Porterhouses on the grill and her dark gravy. Oh, and there's a surprise waiting for you at home!"

"What is it?"

"It's a surprise. Just remember, you are always safe with me."

"I know. You're my hero. Bye."

He could imagine the look on her face when she opened the box with a dozen black roses from Podesta Balcocchi.

He punched in another number.

"Hello."

"Doll."

"James!"

"You have a surprise waiting at home, Maureen."

"What is it? I love surprises."

I sent her a dozen black roses, too.

"It's not a surprise if I tell you."

"Okay. I'm rushing home. Thank you for lunch."

"You're welcome. You know you're more special to me than anyone in the universe."

"Even more than Clare?'

He stuck out his chin.

Why does she have to ask that question every time we're on the phone?

"Uh-huh."

"Talk to you when I get home, lovey."

James rushed his words together. "Okay. Bye."

He felt good, and the future was looking bright. Could anything interfere with his plans?

No, nothing.

Chapter 8

Friday, July 5

Larry slipped into the Chevy and bumped his head on the door frame. The jarring motion was a painful reminder that Varton had been appointed lead investigator. Questions about how to proceed nagged at him like an agnostic throwing water on every supposition.

Traffic was light.

Hieu asked, "Larry, why did you accept that trip to Ireland?"

"Do you think it's a bribe? Why did he say it wasn't a bribe? Does he want to influence the outcome of the investigation?"

"Sounds like it."

"And he's not owning up to the fact Fletcher failed to escort Cornelius."

With a glimmering eye, Hieu said, "Why would he leave Cornelius unprotected?"

"We have more work to do. I'll let Varton know about the tickets."

The screen on Larry's phone lit up.

"Leahy."

"Inspector, this is Sergeant Flynn. I have some information from Greenwich Security."

"Go ahead." Larry punched the speaker button.

"They reported that the front door to the Security office was found damaged the morning after the murder, and two nine-millimeter guns are missing from the gun locker."

"Thank you. Has Inspector Varton been informed?"

"Yes, he has."

"Thanks."

Larry looked over at Hieu and said, "We're headed back to the Greenwich."

His cell phone hit the floor.

Hieu picked it up and said, "Larry, you have a missed call."

"I didn't hear it ring."

"It's a call from Lauren. It might be on silent."

Hieu turned the phone it on its side. "The silence button is in the 'on' position. Here, look at this." Hieu showed him the tiny bar. "When you see red, it's on silent. Just push the bar up. Green means the silence button is turned off. See?"

"Yes. I'll call her later. What time is it?"

"3:20 p.m."

Larry shoved the cell phone in his pocket.

On Columbus Avenue, near Hieu's home and Central Station, they made a quick U-turn, leaving behind a narrow strip of horizon sandwiched between gray and blue.

Larry caught Hieu looking out the window. His fresh-faced appearance stimulated an urge in Larry to protect Hieu and give him a city that would be less depressing than a rained-out ballgame. That meant getting rid of the meat and flies of society and their homeless coalition taint at every street corner, even greasy-sweet North Beach. Work tethered Larry and Hieu to the city, but only one of them plotted making a run for Russian River, the resort where he had built an all-year cabin, and it wasn't Hieu.

A car backfired, sending a flock of pigeons across Columbus. A man sprinted across, and Larry had to apply the brakes to avoid hitting him.

"Was that Gerald Smith?" Hieu asked.

"How did you know?"

"I think I saw his picture in the file."

"Nice. Hieu, let's do some good today."

Larry smiled at the graduating rows of purple and white alyssum, white phlox, and blue hydrangea that filled long boxes and were bravely resisting spit and blowing litter in front of the Greenwich. An awning striped in green and white sheltered the boxes from the San Francisco damp that welds most bits of paper to the pavement.

Sounds of hammers and voices came from one corner of the lobby. Brass fittings sprinkled the red and black carpet. Suspended near the barrier was the smooth, scorching smell of copper soldering. Ghost-like workers spoke muffled blue-collar axioms. The soldering smelled almost as good as fiery tar bubbling in a roofing bucket.

Bunches of red daylilies in white, oversized vases stood in the corners, and a black and white drawing of an oversized wagon wheel in the foreground of a line of covered wagons hung on a wall.

They walked down the steps to the parking garage.

"Why the garage, Larry? I thought we would be going to the Security office."

"I just want to check it out and see what we can see."

A porky parking associate stuffed into a white military-style uniform with gold buttons said hello. Larry saw the Rolls, which let him know that O'Hara was still on the premises.

It was quarter to four according to his watch when they slipped into the employee hall and passed an employee coming out of the breakroom. He kept his head down. On the tan carpet outside the darkened Security office, a shiny object flashed. Thinking it was trash, he picked it up and watched if anyone else besides Hieu was around. A sharp edge made him look again.

"What is it?"

"Looks like a broken fingernail, Hieu." He looked around more carefully. "I wouldn't have seen it except for the tan carpet. I'm not sure what it means, but I better turn it into evidence."

"Those are acrylic nails. My wife wears some like that."

When a Filipina came walking down the hall, Larry turned and continued to walk out in front of her. Hieu followed him to the back entrance. They exited, walked down the alleyway, and slowly rounded the corner. After passing the doorman, Larry realized that there was no doorman on duty on the night of the murder.

"Hieu, without a doorman on duty, it would be easy for anyone to enter and find Cornelius' apartment."

"Do you think he knew the person and let him in?"

"I do."

"Did you see Larissa Rey?"

"Was that who we saw?" Larry asked.

"It sure was."

"I wonder if it was her fingernail."

"Are we going to talk to O'Hara again?"

"No. We won't get much more out of him . . . for now."

•••

Larry dropped Hieu off at home and returned to his office. He sent an e-mail informing Captain Dempsey, Inspector Varton, and the rest of the team of the gift from O'Hara. He passed Varton's office, caught sight of Pepper sitting there, and stopped long enough to hear Varton ask if she knew about the missing $500.

She's been called back, and I wasn't invited.

"No. I didn't count the money. I picked up the stacks of money and threw them into my purse."

Larry stuck his head in, cleared his throat, and was delighted to see the furrow between Varton's eyebrows deepen.

"May I come in?" Larry smiled at Pepper, walked through the door, and shut it firmly.

"Well, you're already in. Take a seat, Leahy."

Pepper's shoulders relaxed. Her face was as flushed as a purple rose.

"I repeat. What do you know about the missing $500?"

"I just took everything there. I've been rehired, and I need to get to work. May I go?"

Pepper lifted herself up, tugged on her white blouse, and smoothed the black skirt.

"All right, Chase, you can go."

Pepper hurried out the door.

"You have something on your mind, Larry?"

"I sent you an e-mail about O'Hara. He gave me a gift."

"I read it. Keep the gift but don't use it."

"What do you mean?"

"I don't see a problem, for now, but he's your personal friend, and you wouldn't want a little gift to jeopardize your career."

Larry returned to his office and decided to call the elusive Gerald Smith.

Varton and Dempsey are splashing about like trained seals.

He sat back.

Only I can get this case moving. I know people.

"Mr. Gerald Smith, this is Inspector Leahy, SFPD. How are you?"

"Fine."

"Mr. Smith, I'd like to ask you some questions in connection with the recent death of Cornelius MacKenzie. I understand you were a friend of his?"

"Yeah. Am I in some sort of trouble?"

"No. I'd like to see you and talk."

"I got home from Topaz Lake an hour ago, and I'm tired."

Larry looked at his cell phone: 4:32 p.m.

Hieu and I just saw him and hour ago. Is he telling the truth?

"Where do you live?"

"220 Ellis Street, apartment 202."

"All right. I'll be there . . . in thirty minutes. Don't go anywhere."

•••

At five minutes past five, Larry found himself in a dingy apartment building's dingy, empty lobby. He listened at the door of Smith's apartment and could hear the television and whistling. He knocked loudly, and the whistling stopped.

Smith opened the door.

Tall drink of water.

Larry estimated that he was six feet tall, 190 lbs.

"I'm Inspector Leahy. May I come in?"

Smith sported a gray sweat shirt, gray sweat pants, and white socks. Larry had a peachy view of the studio when Smith turned and headed for an open box of Cheerios on a small, metal kitchen table. A cereal bowl sat on the floor in front of the television, and an open tackle box lay next to a fishing pole whose tip touched cracked molding.

"Yeah, come on in."

Larry saw long dirty-blond hair pulled back.

Probably played basketball.

Smith turned around.

He needs an operation for that kinked nose.

Larry saw the scar above his upper lip.

He's a man who talks with his fists.

"Where are you from, Mr. Smith?"

"Waco. What's this all about?"

"May I sit down?"

Smith pushed a kitchen chair toward Larry.

"How old are you?"

"Thirty-five."

"Do you have children?"

Larry sat down in the chair, a few feet from Smith, and looked up at him.

"What? Why are you asking me personal questions? I thought this was about Mr. MacKenzie," he said from the sofa in a slow drawl.

He reached down and lifted the cereal bowl. The fishing pole rested upright against the sofa.

A single, neatly made bed lay against the wall with the only window, which was covered by a white sheet. Behind Larry was a partially open closet door. Larry got up and looked inside. The closet was sparse but in order. A mirror on the inside of the door made him jump.

No, that's just me – just a reflection.

He walked to the window and slowly pulled the white sheet back. He could feel Smith staring, swung around, and said, "I have a son, about your age. I think he wishes he had brothers or sisters. Do you?"

"Yeah. I have two brothers and two sisters. I'm the oldest."

Smith lifted a spoonful of Cheerios. "Oh, sorry, would you like something to eat?"

"No thanks. May I call you Gerald?"

Smith rubbed his chin and said. "Yeah, sure."

Larry watched him finish eating his cereal. Smith's elbow left the dingy brown couch, and he put the bowl in the sink. The studio smelled moldy and needed paint.

"Gerald. I'm told you were fired by the Greenwich. Can you explain why?"

Gerald dropped into the sofa, leaned forward, and picked up a fly. At the end of the curved hook dangled a shiny face with blue and red fringe, a transparent tail, and wings springing out from a light brown body with evenly spaced gold threads.

Larry sat down and was annoyed by television static. "Can you turn off the TV?"

Gerald looked for a remote control to lower the sound.

"Yeah, so what? O'Hara fired me a few days ago. I don't have to tell you why." He started tying the fly and said, "This is a crystal dip midge. You see the tail and wings. That's aurora borealis." His face seemed to brighten.

The scar might be from a brawl.

"Are you drinking again?"

"Whatta ya mean?" Larry watched Smith's eyes scan one side of the fly, which gave Larry a reason to stand by the fly tying box.

"This is beautiful work. How long have you been tying flies?"

He could tie a fly with the D.T.'s.

Gerald looked up and said, "I started when I was a kid. I used to fish at Lake Waco."

"Did your dad teach you?"

He glanced up at Larry, then down at his fly. "No, he didn't teach me nothing."

We have something in common, Gerald, maybe, the only thing.

"I understand. Did you ever buy alcohol from the Greenwich bar?"

"I don't know what you're talking about. I thought you were investigating Cornelius' murder."

"Is it a murder?"

Larry felt a sweat bead trickle from his arm pit.

Gerald got up and grabbed a toothpick from the kitchen, then sat down and began picking his teeth. The remote dropped on the sofa after he turned off static as loud as Niagara Falls.

"You know what I'm talking about, Mr. Smith."

He tucked the toothpick behind his ear, sucked in deeply, took up his fly, and said, "No, I don't know what you mean. Cornelius let me use his vacation house, and he helped me once. He brought me to AA and the Gambler's group. Look around. There ain't a bottle in sight."

"Did Mr. MacKenzie ever loan you money?"

After waiting for an answer that was late in coming, Larry repeated, "Did you get a loan?"

"Yeah."

There it is.

"When did you get a loan?"

"A week ago."

Gerald looked to his right. A book stuffed in between the cushions of the brown couch fell onto the floor. Gerald dropped the fly, quickly grabbed the book, and shoved it back between the cushions.

"What are you reading?"

"Novel I picked up at the Main Library." He pulled it out and said, "See."

Larry saw the pink jacket cover and picture of a muscular man and buxom woman seated on a rock. "I think you visited Mr. MacKenzie the night he died and came asking for money. I think he said no, you got angry, and killed him. Isn't that right? Isn't it?"

Larry's heartbeats shifted to his mouth.

"Yes, no, I mean I went there to borrow a little extra to pay rent. Is that a crime? O'Hara fired me couple days before Cornelius was killed. O'Hara is a big, important man and a louse. You need to talk to him." Gerald's weight pressed the book out from between the cushions. He pushed it back in.

"Why were you fired?"

"Late to work." Gerald kept working on the fly without looking up.

"Were you fired for buying a bottle from the bar?"

"Who said that?"

"Not important. Do you own a car?"

"No."

"How do you get to Mr. MacKenzie's cabin?"

"I rent a car."

He's lying.

"Did Mr. Mackenzie know you got fired?"

"Yes."

"Were you going to talk to him about that?"

"I was plannin' on it."

"I think he had something to do with your being fired. He was your supervisor. Did you see him that night and kill him?"

Gerald's brow line rose. "No."

"No to which question?"

"Both. I didn't see him. When I knocked on the door, he didn't answer. I heard someone comin', so I ducked into the stairwell."

There it is.

"Why were you hiding?"

"I didn't want anybody besides Pepper or Pablo, that half-Mexican, to know I was in the building."

"How long did you stay there, in the stairwell?"

"Until I heard his door shut. Then I left."

"What time was that?"

"I don't know. Twelve thirty."

"Did anyone see you leave the building?"

"No, I went out the back door, which is the way I come in and out, Inspector. Got the picture?" He grabbed his fishing pole with his right hand and slammed the bottom end down once on the bare floor. The book sprung out of the cushion, and he back-kicked it under the couch.

"Except that you were fired and didn't belong in the hotel. Did you hear a shot fired?"

"No."

"Where did you go after that?"

"Home."

"Does anyone else live here?"

"No."

"Did anyone see you arrive?"

"No. Are you done?" Gerald started ripping bits of the fringe from the fly. Tiny bits of a blue and red hackle dotted the floor beneath his feet, and some littered the topside of his white socks. With one foot on top of the other, he tried removing the colored bits off the socks and said, "It was late."

"There's a night attendant and people going in and out of your apartment building all night and hanging out in front of the building. Your window is closed to keep the noise out. Someone saw you coming and going. Answer the question."

"Okay, so I stopped off at the store to buy some milk and Cheerios. Then I came home and watched TV. Is this over?"

"You were pretty cool that night, even after you knew Mr. MacKenzie was dead."

"I didn't know he was dead."

"Do you own a gun?"

"No."

"Do you possess a gun?"

"No."

"You're from Texas. Do you own a gun?"

"I said no. What you got against Texans?"

"Have you ever been arrested?"

"No."

"I will run a background check on you." Larry stood up. "All right, Mr. Smith. Stay around. I may have more questions for you later."

Gerald dropped the fly on the sofa, got up, and spoke in a low, steady tone. "Cornelius was a gentleman and one of my best friends. He did more for me than anyone I know. I would never do him harm. That's the truth. Whether you want to believe that or not, I don't care."

"You are part of an investigation, whether you like it or not. Have a good evening."

He's afraid of something or just doesn't like the law.

Larry waited outside the building to see if Smith would leave. Dressed in a white wind breaker over gray sweat pants and holding a small satchel, he passed through the front door. Larry followed him on foot at a distance. Gerald walked on the sides of his feet with a definite purpose. Three blocks from the apartment, Gerald got into a day rental. Larry jotted down the license plate number, wrote some notes, and after the last period asked himself, "Quo Vadis? To a connection?"

Chapter 9

Friday, July 5

At half past five in the afternoon, Maureen Daley put down one of her favorite Hay Publisher's self-help books and answered a phone call.

"Mrs. Daley, this is Inspector Leahy. I'm working on the case surrounding the unfortunate death of Cornelius MacKenzie. I'd like to ask you some questions. Can we meet at your home tonight? Shouldn't take more than thirty minutes."

"Larry, how are you?"

"I'm doing fine. How are you, Mrs. Daley?"

"Oh, don't be so formal, Larry. You can call me Maureen."

"Okay, then. I'll cut to the chase. You have a close relationship with James O'Hara. The untimely death of Mr. MacKenzie requires that I follow up and find out what anyone might know about what happened."

Not wanting to talk with Larry and trying to be considerate of James and her own needs, she decided that informality was the best way to deal with Larry. "Larry, dear, I really don't have anything to tell you. Of course, I knew Cornelius. He was James' employee, but James hardly ever talked about him."

"I see. I'd like to meet with you personally and discuss these matters. Can I visit you tonight?"

"Well, no."

"Why not?"

"I'm busy, Larry. Can we make it another night? I don't have anything to do with this."

"I'm sorry, Mrs. Daley, but either I see you this evening or you can come into the station. It's your choice."

Maureen took another sip of her early white wine and felt it go tasteless against the roof of her mouth. She let her arm slip down to her side, the receiver in her hand, then raised the receiver back up to her ear and said, "Would you mind calling me tomorrow?"

"I'll see you at six, Mrs. Daley."

A click left her staring at the phone. When it began to beep an urgent reminder to return the receiver to its cradle, she banged it down.

Maureen was dressing in her bedroom when outside her window she could see Larry parking in the driveway, blocking the Escalade. She stepped away from the white hurricane shutters and heard his footsteps on the front stairs. The last chime of the hall clock was off-key, sounding like a clang.

She spotted a wine glass on the entry hall bench seat and left it there. One last look in the mirror restored her composure. A sterling silver hair clip with diamond solitaire, a twenty-fifth wedding anniversary gift, pulled her hair to one side. After securing the top button of her blouse, she turned her indigo-blue, indicolite tourmaline and diamond wedding ring around several times.

She ever-so-slightly pushed aside one of the sheers covering the right-side window panel, quickly let go, and swung open the heavy, dark-stained oak door.

"Hello, Mrs. Daley. Thank you so much for meeting with me."

"Come in, Larry." She turned left and under the frame of the living room entry turned again and said, "Remember, Larry, you can call me Maureen, and I would prefer that."

"Oh, yes, Maureen." She watched him take off his black jacket.

"Here, let me take it." Careful not to knock over the wine glass, she hung his jacket on a peg, picked up the glass, and led the way.

"Please have a seat on the chesterfield."

He's staring at me. What is he thinking?

"Larry, what would you like to drink?" The liquor cabinet was at the other end of the living room.

"Just a soft drink, Maureen."

"Certainly." She pulled a lemon-lime drink out of the cabinet with her right hand and with her left hand grabbed one of the cut-glass crystal cocktail glasses sitting on a mirrored silver plate.

"Is lemon-lime okay?" She held up the can of soda.

"Sure."

She opened the ice bucket and pulled out two ice cubes with silver tongs, plopped them into the glass, and poured out the lemon-lime. It splashed on the mirror, and she wiped it off with her bare hand, turned with a flourish, and looked over her nose at Larry.

He's a skilled listener, not a trained Pomeranian. Say as little as possible.

"If you don't mind, I'd like to begin the interview right away."

Maureen handed him the glass of lemon-lime and turned the way she always did, to fanfare, and sat down in a chair of a matching set, close to the front window, which was large and framed by yellow, champagne, and white striped satin panels over sheers, lightening her hair and almost blinding seated onlookers.

"You have a beautiful home, Maureen."

"Oh, it's just something I've thrown together over the years."

Maureen took a sip and watched Larry place his soft drink on the coffee table. She jumped up and grabbed a coaster. "If you don't mind, Larry," and placed it under his glass. Back in her chair, she waited, wine glass carefully balanced.

She guessed Larry to be about five feet nine inches tall and 180 lbs. She liked his white eyebrows, trimmed so neatly.

"Maureen, do you possess a gun?"

"Oh, well, no, of course not." The wine glass wobbled. The skin on her arms tingled as if stung by a horde of mosquitos.

"Does James?"

"Well, yes, but you must know that."

"What kind?"

"I don't know. I know nothing about guns. I've never handled one," Maureen replied, raising and dropping her shoulders. With her free hand, she smoothed the lap of her gray pants, which felt tight, and thought about switching to plain ice water.

"Were you at James' house on the Fourth of July?"

"Yes."

"The whole night?"

"No. I left at two."

"Where was James?"

They heard glass shatter in the kitchen.

"What was that?" Maureen asked.

"Is anyone else at home?"

"No. Should we check the kitchen?"

"Let me do that." Larry got up quickly and passed into the dining room. Maureen followed. "Let me go first. Stay back." Larry pushed the swinging door open and looked into the kitchen. "It looks empty. One of your glasses fell off the counter."

"Can I follow you?"

"All right but stay a few paces behind me." Larry walked to the back door.

"It's locked."

Maureen looked out the kitchen window and saw James' Rolls parked on the street.

They heard a noise.

"What was that?" Larry rushed to the pantry door and opened it. "Nothing inside. Where does the other door lead?"

"The hallway, but the door's locked."

"I saw a cat in your breakfast room. Maybe, the cat knocked over the glass."

"Thank God. Thank you, Larry."

"Let's go back to the living room and finish up."

Maureen lifted her glass of wine, and Larry sat down on the chesterfield.

"We were talking about O'Hara's 4th of July party. You were present. Was Mrs. O'Hara?'

Maureen hid her face behind her glass, took another gulp, and garbled, "Clare was entertaining the guests . . . of course."

"Are you willing to make a formal statement to that effect?"

The wine glass came down. "Of course. Why do you need a formal statement from me?" She lost focus for a moment, trying to glimpse the dark wood beams of her Mediterranean style home, until she felt she'd regained some composure, set her drink on the bare glass end table, and covered her wedding ring with the other hand.

"A formality, that's all. A few more questions. Are you seeing James romantically?"

"No."

"Were you dating Cornelius?"

"No." The question felt like an itch in an unusual spot. Maureen looked at her diamond watch, stood up, and felt herself tremble. With hips leading the way, she glided to the entry hall and turned.

You haven't gotten anything from me and never will.

She smiled. "Are you finished, dear?"

"Yes. Be available for more questions."

"Oh, I'm around. Two of my girls are keeping me busy this summer. I have the usual social engagements that claim attention, too."

"Good-bye."

She handed him his coat and said, "I have a busy day tomorrow, organizing a fund-raiser for the Junior League."

"Mm. Thank you again for meeting with me."

"I don't expect we will meet again. We move in different circles." She shut the front door, leaned against it, and breathed deeply, knowing full well they would meet again.

Moments later, Maureen heard the door to the basement open.

"I'm here, James."

James walked down the hall to Maureen. "What was he doing here?"

"Don't I get a kiss first?"

"I asked you what he was doing here."

"What are *you* doing here?" With a heap of hurt pulsing through her veins and looking for some ointment to soothe her feelings, she walked over to the liquor cabinet. She bent over to pick up the silver tongs and felt dizzy. She fantasized about throwing wine in his face. Her heart was racing. The Hay book said to put anger in a letter. Her legs stiffened instead.

"How can you just stand there after what's happened?"

"What? What happened?" James asked.

Maureen turned around fitfully. "Larry asked me questions about the gun! You should have been here to answer the questions. I have no idea what's happening. Explain all of this to me now!"

James cocked his head to the left, opened his arms, and displayed his bowling pin teeth.

"Maureen, come here. Let me hold you."

"No." She felt restless.

"Why are you drinking wine?"

"Why do you smoke cigars around me?"

"All right. I won't. You should stop drinking alcohol, Maureen. Now come to me."

"No. I want answers." She stood perfectly straight.

As he got closer, the potent Padrone Maduro odor filled up some part of her emptiness. Hands on his chest added support. He gently caressed her hair. The curled fingers of her hands, still pulsating from the surprise visit, touched the lapels of his jacket and robotically smoothed the fabric.

James pulled her into a warmer embrace, and his belly lay against hers. "You feel good, even in your condition." His eyes were listening. "That was a close call. I thought you would be alone. While I was in the pantry, I knocked over a can of cat food, so I went out the other door and snuck down the stairs. I'm sorry about the mess in the kitchen. I'll clean it up."

"He asked me if I had a gun. I said, 'Of course not.' What should we do?"

"Nothing. He knows nothing. Where is it?"

"Behind me. In the liquor cabinet."

Maureen kissed him long on the lips, then reluctantly tore herself away from the powerful emotional release his welcoming arms had triggered and walked into the kitchen to look for a broom to sweep up the glass.

He followed.

"Why don't you fix all this mess?"

He reached for her broom.

"No, James, I mean the mess we're in."

He left the kitchen and returned to the liquor cabinet. She leaned the broom against the kitchen counter and followed. "I can't stand this much longer."

"Let me see the gun."

She moved to the cabinet. The sound of a gentle click in the key hole freed her pent-up emotion.

James sprang forward, pushing Maureen against the cabinet and causing her to gasp when her knee hit the mirrored front. She squirmed under his weight.

"What's the matter with you?" she said as he nudged her aside.

He opened the door and lifted his monogrammed frames to look inside. Resting on a plush gray hand towel was a gun, the color of oil, the length of a hand.

"Keep it here, safe."

"I don't want that gun. I don't want that thing in my house," she said to his backside.

James took a few steps away from her, his broad shoulders forming a square silhouette, blocking the afternoon light streaming through the sheers. His barrel chest heaved. A sweetened scent filled the room.

Calmly but firmly, he stated, "I have been taking care of you for some time and, for that reason, and many more, I expect you to do what I ask. As for the mess you speak of, you need to do what I do. Push negative thoughts out." With the eyeglasses at the tip of his nose, he said sternly, "I won't face your problems for you. You need to face them head-on."

"What about Clare?" The mention of his wife lit a spark between them.

With this new provocation, Maureen saw O'Hara's back stiffen.

"What about her? I take care of her. She has nothing to complain about. She's a damn sight better at keeping her mouth shut than you are."

Maureen stepped forward and shouted, "Your wife puts up with all this. You're seeing me, and you got me in this mess. I can't believe what I've done to Clare. She invites me to her house and is gracious to a fault. If my father knew about this, he would be furious."

O'Hara stood silent, as if the machinery in a deep mine had been turned off. His eyes looked dark and bottomless.

"I care about my father's opinion. Look what he did to my sister when she married one of the Crew's," Maureen said in a loud voice.

"Your father is a prejudiced man. Everyone knows by now that he should have accepted his son-in-law. He has three grandchildren, for God's sake. Having children of mixed race is nothing to be ashamed of."

"How dare you speak about my father that way? My sister got pregnant and had no choice, and here I am, in the same position, and all you can do is criticize the man who loves me the most."

She looked down at her wedding ring, now a quiet reminder that she was a widow. Something had chipped the pink nail polish on her left forefinger. One foot tried to take a step forward.

She said, "If I were married to you, I would get a divorce."

"If I were married to you, I would give you one."

"My father would know what to do. I'll call him and tell him the whole story. You better know this, James . . . I've had a lot of family turmoil, but I've survived." She hesitated, then said, "Now, what are you going to do about this?"

Maureen could see James was speechless at hearing resolve in her voice and was struggling at the mention of her father, the great undertaker who had buried thousands of San Franciscans, good or bad. Something had been worked loose, which was her intention. She was relieved for the small shift in the balance of power.

He took off his eyeglasses and said, "The gun belonged to Cornelius."

"How did you get it?"

"Maureen," O'Hara warned, his voice quickly cooling as he put his glasses back on and leveled a gaze at her.

"James." His name fell from her lips in a soft admonishment. Maureen took a cautious step forward, extending her hand toward him as if he were a dangerous animal. When it didn't look like he would bite, she laid a hand on his chest.

A row of pink nails lay at the base of a full neck under a heavy jaw.

James looked away from her pleading eyes. He shrugged off her touch and walked across the room.

"Take it to the police," she said.

"No. My fingerprints are on the gun."

"So are mine. Just take it."

"No. I can't do that."

Just as he answered, there was a low-pitched rumble that rattled the front window. A car alarm started blaring. They looked at one another.

"What was that?" she asked.

James walked to the front window with a martial cadence. Maureen followed on his heels. "Stay back . . . away from the window. We just had an earthquake."

They heard a second rumble, and the air whistled as if it were being expelled through the back door. Maureen's fear grew on hearing the Great Dane howling next door and the fine china bouncing in her dining room. Another rumble. Neither said a word. A minute passed.

"Do you think it's over, James?"

James looked down at his gold wedding band. "I'd better go home. Keep the gun. I'll think about what to do with it." James started in the direction of the front door but quickly changed his mind, turned, and kissed Maureen on the cheek. She grabbed him tightly.

"I'm sorry for getting so upset. I'll stop drinking."

"And I'll stop smoking cigars around you."

"But I don't want that gun here. You can go out the front door." She followed him and waited for an answer in the entry hall.

"I'll think about it."

When he swung the front door open, the world suddenly intruded. Across the street, a lady in a gingerbread-colored bathrobe stood resolutely, her arms folded, looking up and down the exterior of her house and its side-by-side, shingled turrets, the top halves of which shone in the sun setting behind the houses on Maureen's side of the street.

Feeling as if she were caught in the spokes of a wheel that wouldn't stop turning, she said to his back, "Do more than think about it. I'm bringing your child into the world."

"I can't." He looked up and down the street, hurriedly stepped off the last riser, and left her standing outside in the fading light.

In the quiet of the entry hall, Maureen pulled out the hair pin, allowing her hair to cascade over shoulders and caress the skin that only James appreciated. Against the solid surface of the front door she leaned back and looked straight ahead. In her mind's eye was the full-length portrait hanging at the landing where two sets of stairs joined. The picture of Clare O'Hara in her Sea Cliff mansion couldn't be ignored.

She could compete with anyone.

Maureen walked down the long hall to the landing outside the back door, and there, standing alone, she listened to the back-yard fountain regale her with the sound of dancing water.

"Dad, it's Maureen."

"Hi, bonbon. I was thinking about you."

"Dad, there's something I want to talk to you about. Can I come see you?"

"Of course. Come over now. Did you feel the earthquake?"

Maureen hung up without answering. She drove to Magellan Avenue and looked up Path Street, the public stairway-walk that led to her father's gray, two-story mansard. The twenty-seven stairs and a turn to the right brought her once again to the front door, and once again, she worried. Her recently-widowed father was seventy-nine years old.

They embraced at the front door.

"You look wonderful, Dad. How's the gout?"

"Never mind about that. Come on in and sit down." From the direction of the kitchen, he asked, "Tea?"

"Let me get that." Her father shuffled to his favorite chair in the living room, and she picked up his newspaper, which lay scattered about. She straightened the kitchen's old coocoo clock. It was quarter past seven. He retired every night at eight o'clock.

While the water boiled, she rinsed some dishes and placed them in an already full dishwasher. She poured the water into two tea cups, let the tea bags steam, and started the dishwasher on its first cycle.

"Dad, here's your tea. I have a little problem."

"Thank you."

She looked at his bushy gray eyebrows and the hearing aids in both ears. The purpose of the visit soon became obvious. Fifteen minutes later, she tucked him into his favorite chair with his favorite throw, watched him fall asleep, emptied the dishwasher, and drove home.

Standing at the back door and looking at the fountain, its water not dancing so dazzlingly as before, she felt like Mary, standing at the foot of the cross.

•••

On the way home from Maureen's, Larry deliberated over the kind of relationship she had with James. The aroma of her home lingered like the rosy fragrance of burning votive wax in the chapel across from St. Ignatius, where on most Saturday mornings Lauren sought advice from a Cristo Rey nun sitting behind a grill while he waited for an hour in the white zone.

The habit of making quick assessments of people, which had developed over time, had fallen away in Maureen's presence. He turned the police radio off and drove past the Seventh Avenue reservoir, and in three more blocks entered Golden Gate Park.

The setting sun caused him to avert his eyes in the direction of memorial groves peopled by trees with the mournful look of wooden figures. After the black Redwood Memorial Grove came the Heroes Grove. Larry's grandfather, John Leahy, survived World War I, unlike the fallen heroes honored by silent trees whose significance was lost on most San Franciscans. Heroes Grove deserved a salute and got one.

The Hibernia Bank robbery engineered by his father came in 1958, the year after his grandfather died.

The engine hummed after it changed gears and reminded Larry that he had waited until he turned twenty to learn to drive.

"Your father wants to teach you," his mother had said.

"I've learned everything else on my own!"

"Didn't I teach you anything?"

"That's different."

At Twenty-Fifth Avenue there was a bump. Two light poles on either side of the street swayed, and electric lines slackened and tightened. He pulled over, stopped in front of a driveway, turned on the radio, and searched for a news station. Over the static, he heard the announcer say, "Earthquake."

Lauren will be worried.

He wondered if this was a portent and sped through a red light.

She was sitting with a cigarette poised in one hand and the phone in the other hand.

"I think it was an earthquake, Maude. Larry's home. Good-bye."

He placed his keys on the counter next to the Jack Daniels.

Lauren talked to the next-door neighbor every day. He spotted the drink on the table and looked back at the bottle. The words on the label were blinking at him. He squeezed into the breakfast nook's bench seat and felt the small nick in the table's Formica edge.

"Pot roast." She grabbed the drink and walked over to the oven. "You're hungry, aren't you?"

"Uh-huh."

She left the drink on the counter, walked back to the table, and set a plate before him.

Larry looked out the window and addressed silent words to the shed whose door he had spoken to on many nights. The door's frame was painted park green and could not be obscured by the hypnotic, cool, white, drizzly air filling the back yard, floodlit by the kitchen light. Their house was seven blocks from Ocean Beach, and, depending on the night, the incoming breezes were salty or fishy or odorless, but always left the neck feeling good. He could barely see the shed at the far end of the back yard, the shed he had built when he worked midnights and needed sleep. Inside was a single bed ready to embrace his warm body. Banishment from the bedchamber could happen on any night, and taking orders was easier than arguing. He had memorized the number of steps from the house to the door. Thirty-three steps would take him past a barely visible, single orange calendula, last in a long row, not needing his fatherly love for another day or two.

After he said grace and Lauren listened, he asked, "Did you take your medicine today?"

"Went up to St. Thomas and said a rosary for Mom and Dad." She stood by the side of the table near his elbows.

"God is taking care of your mother. Why don't we take a trip to Ireland and visit Kevin in . . . September or October . . . before winter?"

"No."

He pulled out the green envelope and said, "Here."

While she opened the envelope, he looked out the window again and back at Lauren. He hoped a smile would appear. It didn't.

"Who gave you these tickets?"

"O'Hara."

"Well, I'm not going."

She handed him the envelope, its contents shoved back inside.

He heard scratching on the roof gutter.

Same two doves getting cozy with each other.

Lauren's rants against the side effects of the medication never stopped. Telling her that she was not responsible for her mother's choking to death went nowhere. According to Lauren, the meat she was feeding her mother the night she died was not cut in small portions.

She sliced the lemon meringue. "What did you want to tell me? Is it about Mark?"

The slice slid into sauce left by the scalloped potatoes.

"Yes. He asked me to meet Joan. Can you get me another plate?"

"And?"

"It didn't go well."

She sat down on the other side of the table, lit a cigarette, and snuffed it out in the pink ashtray. Her eyes were blank. "Call him. You're his father."

Larry reached over and turned on the radio.

She got up and turned it off. "Joan isn't . . .."

"Don't bring her up." Larry looked down at the plate and lifted a fork.

"I told you when you built that home up at Russian River I wouldn't go. It's unfinished, and that corner store never has what I need. All I do there is talk to the neighbors on the phone. I could stay at home and do that. I wouldn't know what to do in Ireland, and I can send letters to the relatives, which I do, when I'm not busy. I think I'm going to die soon."

She was not going to die.

Lauren rubbed her dull-white forearm scar as if it could be removed and said, "When's Cornelius' funeral?"

"Monday."

"Are you going?" she asked.

"Yes. Father Ralph will say the funeral Mass." He tasted the lemon and butter. "Do you want to go?"

"No."

"Why not?"

"I won't be feeling well on Monday." She stood up and moved a few feet away.

The ceiling light, a white bowl with a point and gold paint lining the edge, made him squint. He knew the frailty of existence. He stood quickly, moved forward, and lightly grabbed her shoulders.

Lauren pulled back and complained, "My feet hurt. Watch out you don't step on them. They hurt all day. For Christ sake, call Mark and tell him you love him and . . .."

Larry leaned in and kissed her on the cheek.

"What was that for?" she asked.

"You."

"I'll be upstairs."

For the next hour in the living room, Larry read his *History of the Roman Empire*. A fragile page on the rule of Diocletian drifted back and forth, and he thought about what it would be like to be prevented from going to Mass or confession for an entire year, and which one of Diocletian's descendants would have warned him to stay away from the Greenwich? Pity crowded out empathy for those with an impediment to the faith.

I'm going to solve this case in one week or else.

Or else what?

Chapter 10

Saturday, July 6

"Can you buy some baby formula? Do you need some money?" Larissa Rey asked.

"No, I got money. I'll be back later."

Pablo Morales got off the Muni bus and found a good spot at Eighteenth and Castro while locals patronized restaurant patios and bars. The corner was busy on a Saturday.

Ortiz got arrested at the Greenwich, and Larissa knows.

Hiding essential details was a habit, except on Saturdays outside the corner bank. He looked at his reflection in the window. White wife-beater straps rose and fell as corded trapezius muscles rolled, giving him a private thrill and the idea that what was needed was something to go around his neck.

With tips from the Greenwich in his pocket, he swung the baseball cap around down over his forehead and walked into a leather shop next to the bank. Inside a glass display case was a black cord and a German iron cross. He had seen it before. Where the black-enameled horizontal and vertical pieces intersected, the words, "Cowboy Up," crowed its first wearer's status in gold leaf. Barbed wire facsimiles around the top and bottom of the cross matched the barbed wire tats wrapped around his upper arms.

Without looking at the clerk, he handed over thirty-five dollars. The mirror on top of the display case showed two enlarged muscles squeezing the new cross.

The bank's prominence gave maximum exposure. He took off his baseball cap and saw someone staring at his reflection. Pablo pivoted around and said, "What are you looking at?" The short man hurried across the street, and Pablo felt good that so little effort from him could intimidate a grown man.

Pablo was in front of the bank for a reason.

Across the street, two police officers, one male and one butch-looking female, strode toward the corner. Their relative closeness convinced him to turn back to the window. He pulled the baseball cap from his back pocket and placed it on his head and pulled down. It was better there than riding piggy-back on one of his best assets.

Standing so close to the bank window was like roasting marshmallows. He risked a look upward to assess the weather situation. Fog was failing to get over Twin Peaks.

The neon-red, polarized sun goggles stayed in place as he pulled the wife beater over his head and stuffed it an inch down his back pocket. Black, tight-fitting twill pants, black high-top shoes, and a black leather wrist band were earning him a predatory reputation to those men who knew. Grooming was a specialty. He liked the worshipping glances of passersby, male or female, and shifted his weight from one foot to the other, hoping to catch a man.

"Are you gay or straight?" a woman asked. Without waiting for an answer, she inquired further, "Can I touch?" Her two female companions giggled as the hand of the thirty-something reached his right pec. Pablo felt pinned to the wall like a poster idol and responded with a pec flex. Standing with both feet wide apart, just as her hand landed on its target, he leaned back on the heels of his running shoes, and, slightly off-balance, tilted his head up and grinned. She got closer and another flex got another squeeze.

"That was nice," she said. "C'mon girls. Have a go at it."

Pablo side-stepped the women and started walking. Light footsteps from behind made him stop and then speed up.

After some minutes had passed, he was back at the bank window. Looking over his sunglasses afforded a better view of who was watching. The butch cop stood directly across the street and was chatting to a store owner. Pablo pulled the wife beater out of his back pocket and scrambled to get it over his head. He knew it was better over his torso than adding cargo to what was already displayed in back. He readjusted the baseball cap to the correct angle, turned back to the window, lit a Marlboro with a cupped hand, and exhaled at the red and white no-smoking sign glued to the wall between the windows.

A few feet away, a dirty-blond, long haired man squatting on the sidewalk with his back up against the bank panhandled passersby.

Damn hippies. They belong on Haight.

He wanted to kick the man into the gutter.

A young Hispanic woman and an older lady, who could be her mother, passed by. He thought briefly about Larissa. Before turning away, a peek let him know they were strangers. Moving the baseball cap from the right side of his head to the left side gave him a better view of the young Hispanic woman's rear end, which forced him to think about how he was spending his Saturdays.

Jesus, come get me.

Moving around the corner into the shade allowed him to see his reflection in a different bank window. A hand slicked down his hair, and the other hand placed the baseball cap in his other back pocket.

The handsome face looking back made him think, without knowing why, about the MacKenzie affair, which took him around the corner again into the bright sun at the edge of the sidewalk. He cracked his knuckles and inhaled another cigarette with a snap. Glossy whites showed inside a jaw squared by a chin strap beard.

Can't believe they haven't connected me with what went down at the Greenwich.

A middle-aged white guy with a paper bag in his hand walked by Pablo and gave him a knowing look.

Cracker. Fatso.

Pablo watched the man jaywalk, stop in front of a bar, and continue a slow walk to an empty spot where he could get a clear view of Pablo. Pablo looked around for the two cops and argued with himself on whether to cross the street.

More men passed by. The cracker seemed to lose interest, and Pablo lost interest.

A man in leather gear, smooth and soft to the touch, stopped. Pablo quickly turned his head and stared. This was the man who had tried to put Pablo in restraints. Pablo remembered that he enjoyed the bondage at first, and he was the first dude Pablo had ever kissed. They had smoked marijuana to get warmed up for the session, and just as the first wrist handcuff snapped shut, Pablo ordered him to stop.

The man's masculine face reminded Pablo of what was said. "What's wrong little man? Scared I might rape you?"

Pablo hated being called "little man." He remembered being a little high, knocking the man off his bed, demanding the handcuff be released, and getting the startled man to submit.

I grabbed his wallet, and his license let me know the bitch was forty-five.

"You're the one who stole twenty dollars out of my wallet. I want it back, asshole."

"I gave you the finger then and you're gettin' it now."

The leather man was intimidated, one more time.

Pablo cooled down. Suddenly, he felt lonely, threw the cigarette into the street, pulled out a tic-tac container, and popped some in his mouth. The plastic candy container pinched his thigh, and a fake ID in his money-clip that would get him into any bar rubbed against his butt.

There got to be a better way to make money than this.

The leather man was now across the street talking to a group of other leather men. None of them were seeing Pablo.

They look hot.

If I hook up with that rich man, it would mean an end to prostitution.

If I do, what about the gang, my Mom, my bro?

Pablo's big brown eyes had failed to regulate the entire street. The middle-aged, white man he had scared away had crossed to Pablo's side. Pablo hogged the curb and ignored the stares and sounds of displeasure from old and young waiting to cross.

He thought he heard someone say, "Tip slip." Holes in his pants earned him the nickname in elementary school, but there were no holes in his pants and nothing sticking out, and straight-up confidence incited a desire to thump the first person who scorned his existence.

The middle-aged man approached.

Pablo looked away.

"Hey, stud. How are you?"

What a lame-ass, dumb-shit way to greet me.

Pablo said, "Okay. How are you?"

"Great. Um, can we walk somewhere?"

"Where you wanna go?"

"My car is parked a couple blocks away."

"You got a place?"

"No, I thought we could do it . . . it will be real quick."

"In the car?"

"Yeah, is that okay?"

Pablo looked away. He looked back and said, "Yeah, whateva." They started walking. "Where's your car?"

"On Diamond, next to the rec center."

"Damn, dude, you wanna do it there?

"Just a few minutes . . . I swear."

"One hundred dollars, nothing less."

"Sure. Not a problem. How old are you?"

"Why you asking?" but Pablo didn't want to lose his pick-up and answered, "Twenty."

Pablo's sunglasses shielded him from the bright midday sun baring down on sidewalks and windshields they passed. Moving cooled his sweat. He tried putting his hands into his pockets, but they wouldn't fit. The money-clip poked at his butt.

The pitter-patter of the man next to him was annoying and comical.

"You got any poppers?"

"No." He wished he had. The smell was going to be sour no matter how brief.

His heart pounded even though the pace was steady. He lifted the baseball cap and placed it facing backward.

"Give it to me now," Pablo ordered.

The man pulled out his wallet. He handed Pablo five twenty-dollar bills. The bills crumpled as Pablo pushed them into his pocket. His heartbeat increased. The man's short legs moved quickly and with every step he tried to stay at Pablo's side. Pablo didn't feel a need to change his long strides as they moved him away from his buyer.

"You married?" Pablo asked, looking back at the man.

"Divorced."

"Got kids?"

"Yes."

"Sons?"

"Yes."

"Ever fool around with them?"

"God, no!"

"My uncle used to fool around with me."

"Did he?"

"No, just wanted to see what you'd say."

Pablo looked at the black Cadillac SRX parked on the street next to the rec center. Un-tinted glass made the whole idea risky.

"What's the tattoo on your fingers?"

"Bang."

"What's the dice tattoo on your arm mean?"

"Life's a crapshoot. Now, shut up."

Twenty minutes later, Pablo looked in the rear-view mirror, slicked his hair into place, wiped his lips, then wiped his hands on his pants.

"Can I kiss you?"

"What? Hell, no, I don't kiss dudes."

"Well, thanks."

Pablo felt for the baseball cap in his back pocket, leaned over, touched the rubbery ridges of the floor mat, and found it. It wouldn't look good to be driven anywhere. The man yelled, but Pablo didn't look back.

The J Church streetcar was five blocks away. Fog whipped down the street. He pulled down hard on the baseball cap until it rested on his sunglasses as he ran and wiped his sweaty armpits midblock with the wife beater.

Just before a more calculated sprint to the Muni platform, the kid bellhop stepped out of a shop on Eighteenth, three blocks from the Castro corner. Josh Hawkins was alone. Pablo nearly ran into him. When they were face-to-face, Pablo hoped he might be mistaken for someone else and raised a hand to the bill of the cap. It seemed possible. Josh acted as if he hadn't seen him.

Images of the Greenwich flooded Pablo's brain, and he swore, wishing it was his day off. He had twenty minutes to get to work.

•••

Pepper watched Josh Hawkins approaching the front desk. He was a boy and knew nothing of what had left her feeling as if she needed to see a doctor. Her feminine needs and being fired and told to come back left her head achy.

Josh dropped a bag at the counter, which elevated her unease.

"Pepper, I heard you were fired."

She drew her hand to her mouth and coughed. "A misunderstanding."

"Can I take my dinner break?"

"I guess. I'm your boss until a replacement is found . . . for Mr. MacKenzie."

"Oh. No one's said anything to me about that. Only Father Ralph."

"What time did you start today, Josh?"

"Three thirty."

"It's seven, so that's fine."

She was glad to be back and now it seemed she had another duty, supervising the bellhops. She felt good about that, mostly.

I wonder who will replace Cornelius. I hope it's someone other than a Greenwich employee. They're too young and inexperienced.

"I'm glad to be back at work," she whispered.

"Me, too. I'll be in the break room. Oh! I saw Larissa there, and she asked about some cufflinks. Do you know who they belong to?"

Her body shook. She had taken the eighteen carat cufflinks out of her purse and placed them on the table to admire.

She offered an explanation. "I saw them, too, but when I looked at my cell phone, I realized I had gone past my break time by five minutes and forgot to take them to Lost & Found."

After patting her white blouse into place under the medium-wide, black belt, she said, "Doris, I'll be back in a few minutes."

Pepper got out in front of Josh as he walked down the main hallway.

A young man passing by winked, and Pepper noticed that Josh got closer to her.

She had a strange premonition just before opening the door and said, "Stay here."

Pablo sat at the table, but she entered anyway, hoping to overcome her anxiety. He looked delirious, his forearm lying on the table. When he saw her, he hurriedly pulled his uniform jacket sleeve to his wrist.

"Chase, I want $200. Give it to me."

He shimmied and shuddered in his seat.

Pepper didn't understand, and she raised her hands.

"I saw you take money out of the vault the night MacKenzie was killed. I want $200."

"What are you talking about? I don't have any money."

"I know about you and MacKenzie, always talking, up in his room. Give me the money or I'll let O'Hara know."

"Please, I don't have any money."

A click drew her attention to a switchblade in Pablo's right hand. It flashed like a mirror under the long florescent light above, which blinked unrhythmically.

Josh entered the room.

"What the hell are you doing here? You s'posed to be carrying bags, you stupid shit."

Josh answered meekly, "Pepper said I could take my dinner break."

"Get outta here, faggot," Pablo yelled in a hoarse voice.

"Josh, go back to the lobby. I can take care of this."

"Do what she says, cocksucker." Suddenly, Pablo stood up, knocking his chair backward, and lunged at Pepper, and, with the full weight of his body, he pressed her up against the counter and laid the knife on her neck. "Don't move, or I'll kill you."

She felt powerless, bent backward, the small of her back lodged against the counter's edge. She smelled his pungent scent, felt the cold blade, and didn't dare speak for fear it would cut. Out of the corner of her eye she could see Josh trying hard to look as if he was going to do something, mouth open and cheeks looking as gaunt as a man on his death bed.

Pablo let go and dove at Josh. Another blue chair flipped over. Josh grabbed the door handle. She saw the door hit Josh's foot and rattle. Pablo's hand struck the door and pushed it back against the wall. The knife lay on the floor.

Pablo yanked Josh forward, tossed him to the right, and, with one hand, forced the door shut.

Pepper hoped someone heard the door slam and would come running. She looked straight ahead and heard Josh's head hit the wall. Pablo's hand was on top, and Josh's forehead made a chafing sound as it scraped the wall, the movement sending her eyes downward to the knife, which was inches from Pablo's foot.

She screamed.

Pablo turned Josh around, so they were facing each other, reached behind and pulled his hair. She gasped when Josh's cross popped out from under his t-shirt. Pablo moved and blocked her view, but she heard air escaping from Josh's mouth.

Pablo looked back at Pepper. She noticed droplets dotting his forehead like the white string of beads that had burst out of his uniform. Josh came into view again, and his white cross matched the beads.

He turned back to Josh, pulled harder, and in a low voice grumbled, "What're you hanging around her for, faggot?"

Josh's words were garbled, distorted by the extreme angle of his neck and by the cross, which had flipped up into his mouth.

"Josh, please let me take care of it," Pepper begged. She could see his slender white fingers extended, stiff from the pressure of Pablo's hold.

She smelled cigarette smoke and onions.

"That's it, tell him." He held tightly, and Josh's neck was fully exposed.

Pablo let go. "Aight. I'll kill you, fag, if you try something."

Josh stepped over the knife.

Pablo picked up the knife and pointed it at him.

The cross dangled over Josh's uniform. He quickly buried it inside.

"Okay, okay, but, but I'm going to stay outside the door." Josh opened the door and started to back out.

"I saw you in the Castro. What if I spread the news around the hotel, huh, then what?" Pablo raised his voice. "How'd you feel, everyone knowing you're a faggot?"

"I'll tell Mr. O'Hara and my uncle you pulled a knife on us."

"You do that, and I'll kill you."

Josh opened the door and began walking out.

With the side of his shoe, Pablo kicked the door, which bounced against the wall and shuttered. He stood back, looking stunned, turned his head around, and yelled at Pepper, "Bitch. Go back to the front desk with him. I'll see you later. Forget you saw me, or I'll fix your little boy here."

The switchblade retracted, and the blade was swallowed.

Pepper slunk past the hand holding it. He grabbed Pepper, held her still, and put his mouth against hers. "If you say anything, you'll see me again. Understand?" Pablo bit into his upper lip and swiped his tongue lewdly across her lips. He pocketed the knife, nudged Josh out of the way, and casually walked out.

Pepper collapsed.

Josh rushed to her side.

She feared Pablo would return. "Don't worry about me." In between sobs, she comforted Josh. "I'm okay. He's just angry. I don't know what he was talking about. Can you get me up?"

"Sure." He fumbled trying to lift her up.

"Here, put your arms under mine."

Now Josh was face-to-face with her and blushed.

She stopped sobbing.

"I must look a fright. Help me over to the table." She sat down and asked for water.

Josh lifted the upturned chair, rearranged a few magazines, and said, "I can't forget seeing the knife."

"Some water."

He snatched a paper cup from the wall holder and turned on the faucet. Water overran the cup. With his left hand, he passed the cup, and with his dry hand, he felt for the crucifix under his uniform.

"Thank you so much, Josh. You're my hero."

"But . . . he threatened you. Aren't you going to tell?"

"No, Josh, I just want the whole thing to go away."

"Why? He's a total gangbanger!"

"I know, but we're at work, and I need my job. I can't have any more problems."

"What are you talking about?" Josh asked. "My uncle is a police inspector. I can tell him what happened."

"No. Absolutely not." She stamped her foot. "Go back to work, Josh. I'll be back at the front desk in a few minutes. Please don't say anything. Please?"

"All right, but I don't get it. If you see Pablo, just stay out of his way. I will, that's for sure." Josh headed for the door with a slight limp and a shoulder drooping to one side. He looked down the hall in both directions and said, "He's gone."

Waiting customers packed the lobby, and a large bus blocked a view of the street. Tiny wheels landing on top of baggage trolleys punctuated the racket.

Pepper got behind the desk.

Josh helped customers despite his pain.

Pablo acted as if nothing had happened.

Pepper grabbed her hair with both hands and tugged it to fit into a hairclip.

Except for yes's and no's, the threesome exchanged no words for the next few hours.

"Doris, can you handle the counter for the next couple of minutes?"

"What's wrong?"

"I left something behind in the break room."

"Cufflinks?"

"How did you know?"

"I have them right here."

"Who brought them to you?"

"Mr. Fletcher. He said they belonged to Mr. MacKenzie and wanted to know how they got there."

"I don't know. Put them in Lost & Found. I don't want to see them ever again."

"Why?"

"They're . . . they're ugly."

"Gold, ugly?"

Pepper couldn't answer.

She was worried.

Chapter 11

Monday, July 8

On his way to Cornelius' funeral, Larry picked up a call at quarter after eight.

"Inspector Leahy, this is Sergeant Mulligan. Inspector Varton asked me to give you information about the Cornelius MacKenzie autopsy, and we have the ballistics test."

"What did the medical examiner say?"

"He listed the death as a homicide."

"And the ballistics test?"

"The gun found next to the body and the bullet found in Mr. MacKenzie's body are not a match."

"That means the gun that killed MacKenzie is missing?"

"Yes, sir."

"Fingerprints?"

"No fingerprints were lifted from the gun next to the body, but even if there were fingerprints, the gun is not the murder weapon."

"But fingerprint evidence would have helped us identify who was in the room."

"Sorry, Inspector, that's all we have for now."

"Thanks."

No closer to solving this crime.

A great crowd crammed the pews for Cornelius MacKenzie's eight thirty funeral Mass at St. Ignatius. In the left pews were family and friends, and USF professors and members of the Board of Supervisors occupied the right side.

Larry took his place in the seventh pew on the left.

Minutes later, in walked James and Clare O'Hara. They sat in front of Larry. Clare wore a charcoal, double-breasted trench coat, belted in the middle, black stockings, and black shoes.

After kneeling and sitting, she turned around and said. "So glad to see you, Larry. It's been too long. It's an unfortunate event that brings us together."

"Yes . . . Cornelius was a wonderful man."

"Yes. Maybe, we can talk afterwards."

James turned around and asked, "Where's Lauren?"

Larry saw Clare give James a "not the right moment" look and said, "She wasn't feeling well."

With a simple, unassuming smile, Clare said, "Tell her I said hello."

Larry looked around and saw Mark and Joan genuflect at the pew directly behind his.

He could have come alone.

Larry started to count the number of people in attendance until numbers turned blue. He had been diagnosed at age eleven as having the neurological condition of synesthesia. For him, it was seeing numbers in color. The numbers mattered less than the solemnity of the occasion.

Maureen Daley and her daughter, Megan, passed by the gray and white marble communion rail and followed the dark red carpet down the middle aisle. They took their seats behind Mark and Joan. Larry looked forward. Clare never turned her head, and James was looking down at the wooden floor beneath the kneelers.

Larry gazed at the Fourteenth Station of the Cross, Christ's Body Is Laid in the Tomb, and couldn't stop thinking about Cornelius until the second reading began:

"My sons, do not disdain the discipline of the Lord, nor lose heart when he reproves you; For whom the Lord loves, he disciplines; he scourges every son he received." Hebrews, 12, 5.

When Father Ralph raised the chalice, Larry felt the pain of his son's defiance.

Doesn't Mark know I must correct him?

Before Mass and before the call from the Situation Investigation Team, Larry had rung up Josh to be sure he would be at the funeral. He didn't sound like himself, but he showed up early, proving that Father Ralph's rigorous training was working, and their mutual respect was lasting.

Larry left by the side door and stood with a small crowd out on the expansive lawn. He saw James and Clare walking quickly to the back of the church. Larry wanted to say hello to Josh but seeing James and knowing that Father Ralph blamed Larry for failing to protect Cornelius caused him to change his mind.

He saw Mark's and Maureen's lips flapping, a stark contrast to the tranquility of Joan's crescent-shaped lips.

Time for me to leave.

During the drive to Central, he caressed a jumping leg muscle, and damp, gray streets added to his dismay over Mark's choices. No employees from the Greenwich came to the funeral, and Joe and Hieu didn't make an appearance.

•••

Joe sat behind his desk.

"Busy?" Larry asked

"Yes, I am," he said.

Larry stood squarely in front of Joe and said, "I heard the results of the autopsy and the ballistics test."

"Interesting results, aren't they?" he said, with a gleam in his eye that matched the stone in his Marine ring. "The gun that killed Cornelius is missing. We have to figure out who took it from the Greenwich Security office."

Fresh air from Joe's open window chilled Larry's ears. "How do you know it was the other Security office gun?"

Joe said, "I'm working on that assumption."

"I spoke to Gerald Smith."

"You did what?" Joe's voice shook.

"I interviewed Mr. Smith at his apartment. I took notes." He handed Joe the notes and said, "You can add them to the file."

Joe snatched the notes. Admiral-blue eyes glared over glasses resting on the tip of his nose. He pounded the desk, and the notes flew out of his hands and dispersed in every direction. "Why did you do that? Smith is scheduled for an interview. You may have compromised it. All the key employees of the Greenwich have appointments! All you've done is . . . pick up bits and pieces with paper tongs!" His glasses fell off and hung on the black cord against his white shirt. Procedures not followed caused his ruddy facial lines to contort.

The hotter Joe's temper got, the more citrus body splash Larry smelled.

"I can explain. I wanted to catch him off guard. I'm helping you out. It's all there in my notes. I didn't compromise anything."

As he stormed out, he heard Joe say, "Captain Dempsey will be informed."

Larry steamed down the hall to his office. He flung the black jacket past Hieu. "Dammit. Dammit." Larry paced, picked the jacket off the floor, and sat down, every inch of his body hot to the touch.

Hieu was silent.

"Over the weekend I visited Gerald Smith."

"Why didn't you call me?"

"It was an oversight. I gave Joe my notes on Smith, and Joe exploded. Is that for me?" Larry asked, looking at a bottled water on his desk.

"Thought you might need it. I ran to my office and back when I heard Joe."

Larry took a swig. His face cooled. "Maybe Joe is right, but investigations are like seeing through dark glass. You see people on the other side, but you don't know who." The phone rang. "Yes, sir, I'll be right in."

"You had better come along. You'll see me flagellated and turned upside down until I'm emptied of every drop of blood but chock it up to a 'learning' experience."

Varton sat in one of three chairs lined up opposite Dempsey's desk. The office occupied a corner of the building and looked out over more roofs and alleys. Through open blinds Larry could see clothes drying on a fire escape and a small, half-closed window.

Floor disinfectant rose in the heat.

Larry thought about his father's warning long ago, "Why make excuses?"

"Sit down, Leahy. Good morning, Inspector Trang." Larry gripped the smooth arms of the chair next to Varton's and looked straight ahead. Hieu took the chair on the other side of Larry, and all three faced Dempsey.

"You interviewed Smith at home. What is the damn problem, Leahy?"

Say as little as possible.

"Mea culpa. I should have informed Inspector Varton beforehand."

"I appreciate the apology. I'm not going to take disciplinary action, but you can bet your ass I will next time. You are too good and too experienced to let this happen again. Is there anything else to report?"

Larry's grip didn't loosen. "Yes. I also interviewed Maureen Daley at her home."

The only sound in the room came from outside when a neighbor slammed a window shut.

"I want Leahy taken off the case." Varton's complexion hadn't changed over the past several minutes, but now it was the color of fruit punch.

Dempsey ran his hands through black hair that reminded Larry of Father Ralph's. His seat sprang forward when he got up and walked to the window.

"I'll retire if taken off the case. Before I do, may I add one thing?"

Dempsey looked at the three inspectors and said, "I want this case solved in five days. What do you want to say, Leahy?"

"We should consider Smith a suspect, but he appeared to be telling me the truth. He wasn't lying. He told me he did go to Cornelius' apartment on the night in question but didn't go in. He ducked into a hiding spot when he heard someone else in the hall. Smith didn't see who it was, and the formal interview can pick up there." It had taken one breath to say what he had to say. Larry's vocal chords were taut when he wheezed out, "As you know better than any of us, Captain, interviewing a suspect at home has some advantages. When I accused Smith of killing Cornelius, he got agitated but gave reasonable answers to my questions."

Dempsey's blank look allowed Larry to state his case. "All I ask is I be allowed on as the second investigator in the case."

"Absolutely not," Varton interjected. "Leahy has already violated procedures. I object to any further involvement from him." Varton's neck then turned a deeper shade of punch, and Larry felt his own face heating up.

Dempsey sat back in his chair, which creaked in the silence. He leaned forward and placed both hands squarely on the desk. "You two have presented me with a tough choice. I can't let things remain as they are. There is too much ill will in the room."

"Fine, I'll retire. You can have the case to yourself, Joe."

Larry let go of the arms of the chair and walked out.

In his office, he gathered up what remained of the case, which wasn't much.

Hieu walked in. "Larry, what did you do that for?" His voice was filled with shock and disappointment.

"Sit down, Hieu. I have something to tell you."

Larry began to tell him the story of his dad.

"And Joe wants you as his trainee." Larry pushed his chair back and rolled it past Hieu toward the open window. He reached up, shut it, and left the chair where it was. Standing over his desk he handed Hieu the thin MacKenzie file and said, "I'm taking the rest of the day off." He grabbed his black jacket and walked out.

Larry drove to the AT&T Park box office and asked for two afternoon tickets. He splurged on the last two tickets in Row F, Section 107, six rows behind the Giants' dugout. It didn't matter who the opposing team was.

•••

Larry braced himself for Lauren's reaction as he walked up the inside staircase. She usually took her afternoon nap at one o'clock. In the kitchen he debated whether to slather on the contents of a small, yellow and white tube he found in a drawer. A day at the ballpark would require fortification for the main Irish fight, the endless battle against skin cancer.

Lauren pushed open the kitchen door, and, with her right hand still holding the door, scrunched up her face, licked her finger, and placed it on his lips. "You're a doll stick. What's that on your face?"

"I have two tickets for a one o'clock game. Want to go?"

"When did you buy these?" she asked, seeing the tickets on the counter next to the Jack Daniels.

"Today."

"I have a hair appointment." She walked past him and slid into the bench seat.

He turned and said, "I'm retiring. I have the day off. Would you mind cancelling the appointment?"

"You're doing what?"

She lit a cigarette, giving Larry time to prepare for the face-off.

"I'm off the MacKenzie case. They all wanted me to go. So, I'm retiring."

"That's a mistake. What are you going to do around the house all day? I don't want you in my hair."

"Please, Lauren, I'm very disappointed, and these tickets will get my mind off things."

She puffed once and snuffed the cigarette in the ashtray. "All right." She looked at the clock. "For Christ sake, we've got to go, or we'll be late, and you know how I hate being late. I'll be upstairs getting ready. Take the car out and wait for me."

Larry backed out the Chevy, jumped onto mowed grass, and waited on her side. She came down the drying steps. The wind was still blowing as he opened her door. Once they were inside, he tried looking in the rear-view mirror, but Lauren was adjusting her flowered scarf.

"Did you see Mark this morning?"

"Yes. Did you know he was coming?"

"I called him last night and told him to go to the funeral."

"He brought Joan."

"Who else was there?"

"What?"

"You need a hearing aid. Keep your eyes on the road. Was Maureen there?"

"Yes."

"I knew she would be."

Shortly after one o'clock, under a clear-blue sky, the park erupted over the first pitch.

After a call in the third inning, Lauren yelled, "Bum call, umpire. Larry, we need another umpire. This one's blind as a bat."

"Like the seats?"

"Uh-huh."

Larry took a sip of coke, and Lauren munched on a hot dog smothered in slippery, caramelized onions. The stadium began to empty in the seventh inning, but they stayed to the very end. It wasn't often that they enjoyed a game together.

As they headed out of the stadium parking lot, she pulled the scarf over her gray-blonde roots and looked in the mirror again. "How is Father Ralph taking all this?"

Larry wanted to forget about the case, but Father Ralph was her friend, too. He gripped the steering wheel as they passed Cristo Rey Monastery, but it was too late in the afternoon for Lauren to order him to stop for a consult.

"He seems to be okay."

"Just okay?"

As the Chevy turned at Forty-Third Avenue and Fulton, Lauren said, "Maureen. What a harmless, little butterfly she is. I see Clare O'Hara at the Franklin Street nail salon, and every time, she's parked right in front. I don't know how she manages that."

"She has a nice figure."

"I bet she was dressed all in black. She knows how to handle every situation. You would have to, to be married to James O'Hara. What's he got to say for himself? The murder occurred in his hotel. Two-bit joint."

Larry laughed for the first time all day.

"You know, I have a funny feeling that a woman killed Cornelius. Don't ask me why. I could be wrong. Larry, you should be solving the case. The rest of them are city bureaucrats. You're better than that. It's true."

Without looking, Larry leaned over to kiss her, but the door slammed shut.

It was five o'clock. Lauren stood at the sink peeling potatoes. "Maybe, Father Ralph needs a vacation."

"Priests don't take vacations."

"Then a retreat. Maybe, I should call him. Funny, me counseling a priest."

"You've got your own problems," Larry said.

She frowned and said, "Is there something I don't know about you and Father Ralph?"

Larry smelled pot roast and turned on the radio. Lauren dropped the plate in front of him. He said grace and slurped up the dark gravy. "Aren't you eating?"

"No. Shouldn't he talk to a counselor? I'm worried about Father Ralph. Aren't you?"

"Let God take care of Father Ralph."

"Like the situation with Mark? Is that what you mean?"

"If God didn't correct me, I would doubt He loved me."

"Do you love Mark?"

"Of course."

Larry settled into his living room chair and heard the torrent of water running over dishes.

The water stopped.

Lauren appeared under the wood beam of the entry hall. A dish towel lay in the bend of her arm, which rested on her hip. "Well, what about Ralph, should I call him?"

"Do whatever you think is best."

"Are you going to tell me what's going on between you and Ralph?"

"What are you going to say to him?"

"Nothing about Cornelius. People die. I'm going to talk to him about Joyce Contorado. How can any woman fall in love with a priest? She should be ashamed of herself, a married woman chasing a priest. I wish she were . . . Poor Ralph."

"Don't bring that up with Ralph."

"Sometimes you have your head under water. And call Captain Dempsey!"

The water onslaught resumed.

Chapter 12

Tuesday, July 9

Larry pushed mush around with a spoon. The hall phone rang.

"Can you get that, Larry?" Lauren called from upstairs. Her voice reminded him of the umpire's bad call the day before.

"Leahy, can you be here at nine?"

"Yes, of course, Captain."

Joe and Hieu didn't look in Larry's direction when he entered Dempsey's office.

Dempsey did.

He looks dumb and happy.

"Inspectors Varton and Trang had their say. They weren't very pleased with what happened yesterday, but that's over. You will continue as the second lead in the investigation and work in tandem with Varton and Trang. And Larry, do not deviate from procedure again. Is that understood?"

"Yes, sir, absolutely."

"Now, Varton, Trang, and Leahy, shake hands and let's get this done."

Hieu made the first move and shook hands with Larry. Varton and Larry reluctantly grabbed each other's hand.

Dempsey asked, "What are we going to do now?"

Hieu said, "Finish this investigation in five days."

"Correct. Joe?"

"We will do it."

"Leahy?"

"Do what Inspector Trang said."

They all exchanged face-saving smiles.

Varton was as broad as a church tower and seemed taller than usual. "Follow orders, Leahy, and we can work out our differences." He slapped Larry on the back.

Larry felt the sting.

That damn Marine ring.

"Be safe out there, boys," Dempsey said.

Varton led the way to his office. Once inside, he looked at Trang and said, "We have four interviews today: James O'Hara at ten o'clock, Gerald Smith at one, Pablo Morales at two, and Bud Fletcher at three. I have more questions for O'Hara."

Joe must have muffed the first interview with O'Hara.

"I'd like to be present during the Morales and Fletcher interviews."

"You, Trang?"

"All four interviews."

Hieu's eyes were on Joe.

Joe looked at his watch. "O'Hara will be here soon. You stay with me, Hieu."

Larry stared out the window of his office. He favored shade and dusk and drew the blinds closed. The clicking of keyboards and the distant hum of conversations began to sap his vitality, but it wasn't the noise. Varton had poached Hieu. Hieu wasn't for the taking.

How do I get Hieu back on my side?

An hour later, Joe walked in holding a single page. "O'Hara says he was at home on the night of July 4, all night. When I asked about his personal gun, he said it's a Smith and Wesson 345 and stays at home. An inventory occurs at the end of every month at the Greenwich, and the Security office guns are inventoried at that time. He said both guns were in the Security office at the end of June, so we know whoever took them did so after June 30 and on or before July 4."

Larry said, "Maureen Daley substantiates what O'Hara said. She said she was at O'Hara's home on July 4; he was there all night, and she left at two in the morning."

"Maybe, you should go home. Maybe, a trip to Russian River. Maybe, Ireland. Maybe, you should just quit this case and let me and Trang finish it. We will, you know, with or without you. That may come as surprise, but it's a fact. These folks you're so in love with are nothing special. Criminals never are. Stick to our agreement."

All the air in the room had been sucked out. Larry got up and opened the blinds with such force that the cord broke.

"Joe, these people you talk about are more than a pocketful of bed bugs, and I doubt if any one of them is a criminal." He turned and faced Varton.

"One of them is."

"What about Fletcher?"

"I'll be asking him if he made that phone call telling you to stay away from the Greenwich, and if he did, why. Smith is due. Want to stay and listen?"

"No. After the interview we can compare our reactions to Smith, and Joe, I'm sorry for everything."

"I know, and you should be."

Larry sat down with the cord in his hand and nothing to do but read O'Hara's statement. A feeling overwhelmed him as he threw the broken cord into the waste paper basket.

Something is there – O'Hara has charm and charisma, but did it get the better of him?

•••

Gerald leaned on one side of the seat and then the other.

Varton gazed over the desk and said, "Thank you for being on time. Our conversation will be recorded."

Gerald watched Varton lift the see-though box and flip a switch.

He ran both hands through his neatly combed hair and felt the rubber band. Dressed in a floppy-collared, blue and white plaid shirt and the same white sweatshirt he always wore, he had made himself more presentable with dark slacks, the only pair he owned. He looked at his medium-brown shoes that needed polish and felt "as if the dogs was after him."

"On Friday, Mr. Smith, you were interviewed by Inspector Leahy. He said that you left your apartment at four o'clock, got into a rental car, and drove off. Where did you go?"

"I was plannin' on goin' to Topaz Lake. That's Mr. MacKenzie's hideaway, but Inspector Leahy bummed me out. So, I drove around for a while, went to the Haight, didn't see anything there, and drove over to the Greenwich to see if Pepper was on duty."

"Fine. You gave a satisfactory answer. Let's hope the rest of the interview goes that way."

"You're from Waco. Do you have family there?" Hieu asked.

"Yes."

"Do you miss them?"

"No. I've been asked these questions before." His fed-up emotions permeated what he said next. "I have a daughter there. She lives with her mother. I'm not allowed to see her. That's all."

"I'm sure that's quite a disappointment."

Why's Trang asking me this crap?

Varton interrupted, "What is your relationship with Chase?"

"She's a good girl. That's all."

Gerald felt a mood coming on and resisted it. He wanted to go home, get into his sweat pants, and rework the fly. Varton got up, moved around the desk, and sat on its edge.

Gerald heard Varton's heavy breathing and smelled pineapple. Something warm instigated a look down at the whale's tooth dangling outside his sweatshirt. There was a red smudge on the ivory. A drop of blood on his right forefinger covered a small prick caused by the hook of a fly.

"You said you were outside Room 1212, MacKenzie's room. Is that correct?"

"Yes." Gerald slowly dropped his hand and pressed the drop of blood against his brown slacks.

"You told Inspector Leahy you were in the hall."

"Well, that came later. When I got out of the elevator . . ."

"Let's step back and discuss why you went to MacKenzie's room that night. You had been fired and went there to borrow some money. MacKenzie loaned you money before, and you just wanted a couple hundred dollars to help pay the rent. Right?"

"Yes."

"O'Hara fired you a couple of days before. It was unfair, and you thought Mr. MacKenzie would understand. You had a good record and should not have been fired for being late three times. MacKenzie was sympathetic."

"Yeah. The day I went to the accounting office to pick up my last paycheck, I saw Mr. MacKenzie. He said he was sorry I got fired and that if I ever needed help, just ask." The last word betrayed his drawl.

"Where did you see Mr. MacKenzie?" Hieu asked.

"The hall."

"On the first floor or the twelfth floor?"

"I saw him on the second floor outside the accounting office, next to O'Hara's. I wanted to have it out with O'Hara, but Cornelius was leaving O'Hara's office. We talked. Then I took the elevator back to the first floor."

"What time was that?"

"I don't remember."

Varton said, "You thought about MacKenzie's offer and returned the night of July 4, which is why you were on the twelfth floor. Correct?"

"That's all I wanted to do. Borrow a couple hundred dollars."

Varton stood up and walked to Gerald's chair. He stood behind it, out of Gerald's view, and said, "Had you ever been on the twelfth floor before?"

"Yeah. I went up there sometimes when me and Mr. MacKenzie left for the lake."

Varton's phone rang. "Yes, I see." He put the cell phone back in his pocket, "Inspector Trang, Leahy has some information about this case. Talk to him."

"Yes, sir."

God, what's that all about?

Gerald sat back and ran his hands through his hair. Both hands brushed up against Varton. The rubber band exacerbated the pain of the cut, and blank walls offered no relief. As Hieu got up, Gerald looked at him and valiantly said, "I can tell you're a swell guy."

Without warning, Varton had stepped out in front of Gerald and lowered his head, his face in Gerald's face. "I think you went into his room, MacKenzie said no, and you killed him."

Gerald backed up his chair, which would have tipped over, but Varton righted it with his left hand, and the pineapple smell swelled. Gerald grabbed the whale's tooth, the only gift his father had ever given him, and stuffed it and the black leather strap under his sweat shirt. He pictured his old man doing what Varton was doing and with the same pleasure in making others squirm.

"You were trespassing when you entered the hotel the night of July 4."

Hieu stood still.

"Trang, go see Leahy."

Hieu closed the door quietly.

"You had been fired. You snuck up to his room, knocked on his door, MacKenzie let you in, you asked for money, he said no, and you killed him."

"No. I didn't enter his room. I'm telling you, when I got to his door, I heard someone in the hall and ran to the stairs, walked down a few steps, and . . ."

"There's one flaw in your story." Without changing the angle of his face, Varton staked a position between Gerald and the desk and placed a hand on Gerald's right wrist. Varton had his foot up against Gerald's. Gerald thought he was about to be manacled.

Varton's hand and foot left him feeling immobilized, and he worried about what he had done. Escorted out of the hotel on his last day as an employee, he had ignored the consequences of returning. Now it was looking serious.

"Let's go back to your past. I checked your record. You had a child support warrant issued three months ago. I called the Waco sheriff's office. The warrant was cancelled because the amount owed was paid, and it was paid on the fifth," Varton yelled, "one day after the murder."

Gerald said nothing.

"Where did you get the money? Inspector Trang and Inspector Leahy are discussing plans to subpoena your bank account."

Guilt was pointing at him. He felt like a bug under foot, and he thought about what the Texas judge had said, "You are not to see your daughter except in the company of her mother," and the voice of a Texas Ranger ringing in his ear, "*Vamos.*" It was the last time he saw her. The urge to get drunk made him shiver. He wanted Leahy in the room but couldn't think why. Anyone but Varton.

"I got paid. I just told you. I used that to pay the child support."

"But you had rent due, didn't you? Well?"

"I asked Cornelius' help paying the rent."

"Then you still owe rent. I'll be talking to your landlord. Now, back to the night in question. You would have been seen by the person you heard in the hall. MacKenzie's room is at the end of the hall. There is no other way to get to the stairs or the elevators without being seen. I think your story is false . . . every word of it."

Gerald looked down at the floor. Should he tell the truth or lie? The room seemed to cave in around him. "All right, I did enter his room, but he was already dead."

I should apologize for being there.

"Because you killed him!"

"He loved me, like a son. I swear. It's the truth."

Hieu returned.

"Smith just admitted to being in MacKenzie's room. Is Leahy getting that subpoena?"

Gerald saw the stern look on Varton's face.

"Yes, sir."

"Smith, get up. No, just sit there. I'm disgusted with you. You lied about being in his room. If you lied once, you could be lying again. You needed the money. You didn't kill him in cold blood. You wouldn't have gone to his room, except for the money. You're not an axe murderer. It just happened . . . in the heat of the moment."

Gerald looked at Hieu. "Haven't you ever been short of money?" He placed both hands on the desk and decided not to say any more, fearful that the truth would come out. A spot of blood appeared on the gray desk.

Hieu didn't speak.

"Do you own a gun?" Varton asked.

"No. Leahy already asked me that."

"Have you ever fired a gun?"

"Sure. I'm from Texas."

"What does that mean?"

"Everyone from Texas has shot a gun. Cornelius had a lot of guns at Topaz Lake, but I never used them. He hunted small game with his other friends up there, not with me."

"Don't be flippant. Who did you see in the hall?" Varton pressed.

"The person I heard could have come out of one of the other rooms or around the corner."

Varton interrupted again, "You killed MacKenzie, and the rest is a made-up story to protect yourself."

Gerald's hands came off the desk and he sat back. "I told you the truth. I went to his room to borrow money, saw he was dead, and left. I heard someone in the hall and ran down the stairs. I have nothing more to say. I want a lawyer."

He didn't know why he said that but thought it was right.

"Why didn't you report the death?"

Gerald thought he was done for and couldn't think of what to say.

"I'm not arresting you, yet. Let's get back to your bank account." Varton lifted the potted desk daisy and walked around the room with it in his hand, his head down.

Gerald blurted, "I was scared. I was in his room for God's sake."

"Fine," Varton said as calmly as a psychiatrist. "I can arrest you for not reporting a dead body."

Varton and Gerald's eyes met. Gerald tried to figure out what was in his mind.

The prey is found when the hound dogs are on it.

He decided not to say another word.

Varton carefully placed the potted plant on the desk and said, "You're my number one suspect. We will be looking at your bank account. So, you better be telling the truth. I've given you the chance to tell your side of the story. Do you want to change anything?"

Gerald was silent.

"You'll be back in here if you're not telling the truth. Is that understood, Smith?" Varton asked, a little less calmly than before.

"Yes."

"You're free to go."

Hieu ushered Smith out. In the hall, Hieu put his hand on Gerald's shoulder and said, "Telling the truth is the best thing to do in these circumstances."

"I have, Inspector, I have. Have a nice day."

Joe bit into his pencil and looked at the calendar.

At half past two, he said, "It looks like Morales is a no show. Have him picked up."

"I think I have a plan, Joe," Hieu said.

"What is it?"

"Go to Morales's house and catch him off-guard by doing the interview on the spot."

"Okay. I'm confident you can get all the information needed, Hieu."

"Do you want me to get Larry?"

"If you do, don't let him direct the interview. You take charge."

•••

Larry looked up as Hieu entered the room. "How did it go?" he asked.

"Fine. Morales didn't show up. Joe gave his approval for an interview at Morales' home. Do you want to come?"

"I know what you're thinking. Morales is closer to your age. I can hit him with questions and . . ."

"I can be his friend."

"Sounds like you don't need my help anymore."

"Naw. You still have a sharp eye. My car, Larry?"

"Up to you."

The black Toyota Forerunner turned right on Quesada Street.

On the stairs Larry said, "I know the floorplan – it's a typical stucco, Junior Five house."

Hieu stepped over dark brown paint chips and tried peering through the window, but drab lace curtains obscured the view. He smelled wood-rot and heard a baby crying.

"Smell that? It hasn't rained since April," Larry said. He rang the doorbell when no one answered his knock. Hieu waited one step below and looked at his cell phone: five minutes to three.

Pablo opened the door. He wore a red, oversized shirt and a bright green t-shirt showing underneath at the collar line. His head was tilted back.

"Mr. Morales? I'm Inspector Leahy, and this is Inspector Trang. May we come in?"

"Man, what do you want?" Pablo stood his ground. Hieu watched Larry side-step Pablo.

"Excuse me, Mr. Morales," Hieu said. He trailed Larry, who was moving toward an archway. On the right, a girl painted her nails at a table in a kitchen with pale pink walls, and next to her, a baby rocked back and forth in a yellow and blue swinging chair.

"Let's get down to the questions. May we sit here?" Larry asked.

Pablo shrugged and slouched into the couch. Larry set aside baby toys and clothes, a cell phone, and a pair of Adidas, and made a space for himself.

Hieu asked for a chair.

"There's one in the kitchen." Pablo glanced in its direction.

Hieu walked into the kitchen. "May I take this one?"

"Yes, sir, of course," the girl answered.

"I'm Inspector Trang."

She stood. "I'm Larissa Rey."

"Very nice to meet you. How old is your baby?"

"Joaquin is eleven months."

"I hope my first one is as handsome as Joaquin."

"Thank you."

"Please sit down. We're here to talk to Pablo."

Hieu lifted the chair and accidentally hit the swing set. "Oh, I'm sorry," he said.

Larissa got up and knocked over her nail polish bottle. Drops of sparkle-filled, banana yellow polish dotted the flowered vinyl table cloth.

Her sloe eyes drew out Hieu's sympathies.

"I'll clean it up," he said.

She offered a nervous smile and answered, "This is a special nail polish from the manicurist at the Greenwich. It's called *Lemon Drops*."

"That's nice." Hieu walked over to the sink, clean but rusted, and picked up a sponge. He wiped up the polish and rinsed the sponge back at the sink. A milky concoction in a glass bottle marked by a frothy line half-way up brightened a dark corner of the counter.

He turned and faced her long hair, streaked with shiny, marigold highlights.

"Thank you for cleaning up the mess," she said with one eye on the baby, who started crying. She stroked the top of his head.

Hieu brought the chair into the living room and sat next to Larry.

Larry started the questioning. "You had an appointment with Inspector Varton at Central Station. Why weren't you there?"

I guess I will let Larry lead.

"No way to get there."

"You work as a bellhop at the Greenwich Hotel. For how long?"

"Year and a half."

Larissa spoke up, "No, almost two years."

"Shut up." Pablo stood up and stared in her direction. The baby started crying again. He lifted a box of Marlboros and shook one out.

Hieu wondered how far they would get in their interrogation if Pablo's interruptions continued, reminding everyone present that he was the man of the house. Pablo took hold of the arm rest and eased himself back into a slouch.

"Can you just ask your questions . . . do what you're here for?"

"You worked the night of July 4. What time was your shift that night?" Larry asked.

"5:00 p.m. to 1:30 a.m."

"Where were you from midnight to the end of your shift?"

"Yeah, I was there, wherever." Pablo shrugged, looked at his cell phone, and punched some numbers with his right hand. The cigarette was balanced on a small glass ashtray. His dimples materialized when he smiled at his phone.

Hieu recognized the La Raza-type colors of his shirt, undershirt, and pants and wondered if the phone was a Boost.

"Are you a member of a gang, Mr. Morales?"

Larry got that right.

"No," he said, without looking up from the phone.

Hieu took out his notepad.

"Don't lie to me. I know about Carlos Ortiz and the other fella, Vega. All three of you have had some run-ins with the police lately. Tell me about it," Larry said.

With hands in the air and the cell phone still in his right hand, he said, "So what! What you got against Latinos, dude?"

"You have any brothers or sisters?" Larry asked.

Pablo let out a sigh, dropped his hands, and punched in some numbers. It looked as if he were playing a game on the cell phone.

"When do you take your breaks: dinner break, coffee break, et cetera?" Hieu asked.

Pablo looked at Hieu for the first time and appeared, for a moment, to be assessing him. "We got assigned times. My dinner break was at ten, and I took a coffee break after that."

"Can you be more precise, Pablo?" Hieu asked with pen in hand.

"What? You take breaks as a cop, don't you? Do you remember every break you take? When's this gonna end?" He looked down at his cell phone. "You can check the records, man."

Larry said, "I will do that. So, you took a second coffee break around midnight."

"Where did you go?" Hieu asked.

"See a friend."

"Who was that?"

"Guy from housekeeping."

"What did you and your friend do?"

"Smoke a cigarette."

Larry interrupted Hieu's questioning. "I have spoken to other employees, and they tell me you have resumed your marijuana habit. Is that true?" Neither he, nor Larry, nor Varton had heard anything about Pablo's marijuana use.

"Nope."

"What else do you smoke besides cigarettes?"

"My old lady can hear."

His blasé look spoke loudly. When the doorbell rang, Hieu looked in the direction of a commotion. It could have been a parade of Las Vegas chorus girls for all the attention he gave, until he heard the voice. He jumped up.

Larry continued. "Now, you were on your second break. How long were you gone?"

"Check your records." Pablo looked forward and backward as if he were trying to decide to clean up the mess.

Hieu heard Larissa say, "Gloria, this way. Let's give these guys some space."

A woman of medium height, fortyish, olive skin, and jet-black hair peeked into the living room. She had a small nose like Pablo. A long, walnut-colored scarf covered her neck and a white blouse. She pulled her black jacket forward and smiled.

"Joaquin is here in the kitchen," Larissa said.

"Mom, what are you doing here?"

"*Vengo a ver al bebe*," she answered.

In that moment, it seemed to Hieu that Pablo had become the person he really was. He wondered if the presence of his mother coming to see the baby would change the dynamics of the interview and was hoping it would when he heard her speaking baby-talk.

"But you were on your coffee break and kept time," Larry said.

Pablo paused and sat down. "About twenty minutes, something like that." He dropped the phone on the couch, picked up his cigarette, and stared at Larry.

Hieu said, "You left for approximately twenty minutes to smoke a cigarette. Where did you go after that?"

"The can."

Pablo leaned forward and placed one hand on his crotch and the other under his chin, the tip of his cigarette filter just beyond his lips. Then he sat back and dropped both feet on the coffee table.

Larry resumed the questioning. "You returned to the front desk. Was Ms. Chase there when you returned?"

Pablo shifted slightly and said, "Yep."

"Can anyone verify that you were in the bathroom the entire time?"

Pablo bristled. "Hey, bro, I'm not gay." He dragged both feet off the coffee table, tossed the cigarette in the ashtray, and jumped up, waving his hands and pacing around the room. Hieu sat up straight. Larry didn't blink. "Shit, dude, just leave it alone." Pablo stopped in front of the arch, looked toward the kitchen, and swung around.

Larry spoke firmly, "Sit down, behave like a normal human being, and answer the questions."

Pablo sat on the couch. The cigarette in the ashtray continued its slow burn.

"During your absence, Mr. MacKenzie was killed, and Mr. Ready, your friend from housekeeping, says you told him you knew where to get some money. What do you have to say about that?" Larry asked.

Larry's leading him.

"What the shit? Ready don't know what he's talking about."

"Clean it up. Your mother's here. Did you plan on getting money from Mr. MacKenzie and when he refused, you killed him?"

The cigarette continued to burn.

"No way, no way." Pablo's voice trailed off after the first denial. "I ain't killed nobody. I'm not crazy, man."

"Do you own a gun?"

"No."

Hieu addressed Pablo directly. "Pablo, I know this is a lot to be going through, but a man was killed. We're trying to find out what happened. I don't think you're the type of person to kill anyone." The baby started crying. "I'm married. You have a baby, and I know it's important for you to be a good example, like I want to be for children I bring into the world. So, all you have to do is tell the truth."

"Shut up!" Pablo yelled over the baby's wails. "Hey man, I'm telling the truth. Larissa doesn't know about me smoking weed, and I don't want her to know. I don't own no gun."

"We have information that you bought a gun recently, then pawned it. What's the name of the guy who sold you the gun?"

Pablo looked surprised. He swiped his clipped brow and looked out the window. Hieu's chair tipped forward. "Just tell the truth, and we are done with the interview."

"Aight. I bought a gun," he whispered.

Hieu looked at Larry and said, "What kind of gun, Pablo?"

Larry moved his chair closer.

"Magnum 357. I got it from another dude. All I did was make the buy and sell it two days later."

"What were you going to do with it?"

"I changed my mind."

"Where did you get the Magnum?"

"Some dealer."

"Drug dealer?"

"Yeah."

"Where is he located?" Hieu asked.

"Don't know. We hooked up at Burton High School. I don't even know his name."

"Come on, Pablo, give me his name and this is at an end," Hieu said, his eyes never leaving Pablo, who looked back at him.

"Will I be in some sort of trouble?"

"We aren't sure, yet, Pablo. It helps just to tell us everything you know. We appreciate good information."

Pablo whispered, "His name is Marco Pate. I don't know where he lives, except it's in the Bayview. Look, can you help me out . . . if it's a stolen gun . . . or something? I need the help, man. I don't want to be in trouble."

"I'll see what I can do, Pablo."

Pablo nodded Hieu closer with a head gesture. "Man, I know some of you are okay, but I see racism everywhere. Just 'cuz I'm Latino doesn't mean what you think is true. I got things to do, and my mom's here. So . . ."

Larry interrupted, "Morales, I'm going to arrest you if you're telling me a lie. You have a good job. Your new baby needs a future. Don't plan on going anywhere."

Larry stood. Hieu placed the notepad back in his suit pocket, shook hands with Pablo, and noticed that his tattooed fingers were ice-cold. His mother stayed in the kitchen, and Larissa showed them out.

On the way back to Central, Larry said, "Wasn't it odd when I asked him about being in the bathroom and he said he isn't gay. There's conflict inside Pablo."

"Exactly. Say, Larry, what made you say Pablo told Ready where there was some money to be found?"

"Just a hunch. You'll get the knack."

Chapter 13

Tuesday, July 9

Varton stuck his head in Larry's office and said, "I postponed the Fletcher interview until four thirty, just for you. I vetoed his request to do the interview tomorrow. I said, 'I don't care if you're at work. Get yourself down here or I'll send a very sociable officer to the Greenwich.'"

"Thanks."

"Why are you in here, Trang?"

"I'm writing the report on Morales. It should be done in a few minutes. Larry said he would review it."

"No, bring it to me when you're finished. What about the trip to Ireland?"

"What about it?" Larry asked.

"Would be a nice trip."

"The case is unfinished. I'll think about the trip after we find the murderer."

"Never been to Ireland," Varton said.

"Me neither."

"I can picture you with the family on a sweet little picnic beside a green stream, and joining the little group, a nice treat, family guest, lips smothered in glitter and wiggling her assets."

Hieu stifled a laugh.

"When Fletcher shows up, Hieu, I'll ring. Bring that report in before he gets here."

Hieu looked up. "Morales purchased a gun and pawned it two days later, the day after the murder."

"Is that all you got, Leahy?"

"He smokes weed. We think he needs money to feed his habit," Larry answered.

"Well, does he use hard drugs? Did you at least find that out?"

Hieu spoke up. "He could be. He's a big kid and can hide it."

Varton looked out Larry's door when he heard footsteps. "He's early. I guess you want to be present, Leahy."

Varton exited Larry's office before he could answer, and Hieu hastily printed the report.

•••

Fletcher stood looking at the name plate on Varton's door.

"Mr. Fletcher, Inspector Varton." He turned and saw them coming down the hall. "This is Inspector Trang and, of course, Inspector Leahy. Come in and take a seat."

Fletcher sat down.

His green and brown tweed sports coat stretched across hunched shoulders. Varton looked at the man's black slacks, which were shiny at the knees. Old Spice filled the room. Varton slid his window open. A framed picture of his wife looked up at him.

Varton rearranged the paper mound on his desk.

"Inspector Varton, let me help with that," Hieu said.

"Leahy, please stand up. Put the paper on your chair. We won't need it."

Hieu struggled to get the papers all together, and Varton let the minutes pass while looking at the picture of his wife. He had rebuilt his peak-roofed Victorian home, and together they had decorated the interior to their tastes, green and floral. Bernal Heights, known as "nanny goat hill" for the sizable number of lesbians living there, had undergone a transformation, from middle class to all types, including: white-haired, Prius-driving liberals; ex-hippies; Marxists; middle-aged libertarians; new agers; hipsters; and an ex-priest who was now married.

Larry had informed him there was no such thing as an ex-priest.

Varton straightened up when he saw a post-it note on his blotter reminding him of the ballroom dancing lesson scheduled for seven o'clock. Whatever pleased his wife pleased him. Attached to the sticky note was another note:

Honey, please take the Prius in for an oil change.

His own vehicle, an older model, gray Chevrolet Silverado, sat in Central's garage. At night, it occupied the driveway while hers was in the garage.

"All right, let's go down to room two and begin the interview."

"Can't we do it here?" Fletcher asked.

"No."

They entered, and Fletcher eased himself into the chair in front of the desk.

Larry and Hieu took their places on the chairs below the two-way mirror.

Varton flipped the switch and asked, "Can you explain your role at the Greenwich, Mr. Fletcher?"

"I watch the comings and goings of employees and report back to Mr. O'Hara."

"On the night of July 4, did you see anything unusual?"

"No."

"Mr. Fletcher, please understand we are not accusing you of anything or assuming anything. We just ask for truthful answers.

What did you do before you began working as O'Hara's investigator?" Hieu asked politely.

"I was his chief accountant."

Varton watched Fletcher slump in his chair.

He pities himself.

"As an accountant, you know about facts and figures. You are familiar with the hotel's finances, payroll, bank deposits, cash, et cetera. Why did you change jobs? Wasn't it unusual to go from being chief accountant to being O'Hara's spy?" Larry asked.

"I'm not his spy," Fletcher said indignantly. "I made some mistakes and O'Hara told me I would be fired."

"What mistakes?" Varton asked.

"An account was short. I didn't know where the money went. One of my employees told O'Hara I stole the money. I knew she was angling for my job, and she got it."

Varton saw the surprise registering on Larry's face and asked, "How much money went missing?"

Fletcher compressed his hands. Beads of sweat the color of dishwater ringed his hairline. He had O'Hara's dark brown hair, but not the bravado.

"$50,000."

"And you never located the money?" Varton asked.

"No."

"How long ago did this happen?"

"Three months ago."

"Didn't O'Hara say anything to you about where the money went?"

"He's a hawk and reviews the accounts every month, but he didn't tell me anything about where it went."

"What happened next?"

"He demoted me. He said I would be fired unless I started working for him but in a different capacity. I had no choice."

"Did you check the vault?" Varton asked.

"For the missing money?"

Varton nodded.

Fletcher didn't answer.

"Are you part of hotel security?" Varton's chair squeaked.

"No, absolutely not. I answer solely to O'Hara."

"Anything else you can tell us? Any other irregularities?" Varton asked, looking past Fletcher at the wall behind him.

"No, I've told you what happened."

Varton stood behind his chair. Each time he passed the chair, he would pull it back and let it ease forward, "I'm sure your current job is very important to hotel management. But we're here to find out what you know. Did Pablo Morales ever mention owning a gun?"

"No. Why would he say that to me? I told you I'm not part of security. They would know the answer. Morales wouldn't be so stupid to bring it to work."

Varton watched Larry moved his chair far forward, its leg touching Fletcher's leg.

Fletcher didn't budge.

"Did you call Inspector Leahy and tell him to stay away from the Greenwich?" Varton asked.

Fletcher didn't answer.

"In that anonymous call, did you say anything about guns?"

"No!"

There it is.

Varton let go of his chair. It hit the desk, which moved a little closer to Fletcher.

"Back to Morales. What do you know about him?"

"He's a good-for-nothing beaner." Beads of sweat now clung to Fletcher's stubble.

"Tell me more."

"It's an opinion I've formed over the past year. He's a low-class, son-of-a-bitch and shouldn't be at the Greenwich. Our guests are well-to-do, and he's not the right fit."

Larry moved his chair up to Fletcher's leg. Fletcher tried to pull his leg away. Larry's lips withdrew into his face, and he said, "You *were* the anonymous caller."

"I suppose you'll find out eventually . . . yes, I was. O'Hara put me up to it."

Fletcher's lips looked crooked.

"Why would he do that?" Then Larry raised his voice. "Didn't he know you had an appointment with us?"

"You would have to ask him."

Varton calmly said, "Don't worry, we will. But this interview is about you, and I'm not sure we have the whole story, yet. Please proceed."

"I'm thirsty. Does anyone ever offer a person a drink?"

"Oh, I apologize for our rudeness. Inspector Trang, would you get a bottled water for Mr. Fletcher?"

"No, I mean a real drink."

Varton circled around and looked at the ceiling. "Do you have anything else to say?"

"No."

"Why not? You have a chance to talk about the activities of the other employees, and you don't want to? You have an opportunity to tell us about the outstanding job you're doing, and you don't want to? You have a moment to quell some doubts, and you don't want to? Leahy, move your chair. Our good man here needs some space."

Larry was staring at Fletcher.

"Now."

Varton watched Larry pick up his chair and bring it over to the two-way mirror.

"I know how good you are at observing. You patrol the Greenwich. You stick to the basement garage, the first floor, and the second floor and seldom go to the twelfth floor, if ever, but you're in a position to see everything that's going on. Do I have that right?"

Fletcher nodded.

"Please, tell me more."

Fletcher put his head in his hands.

"All right. I saw O'Hara enter the building."

"What time was that?"

"It was about ten after twelve."

"Where did he go?"

"The second floor."

"To his office?"

"Yes."

"Mr. Fletcher, look at me. Why did he go to his office?"

"I don't know. All I saw was the elevator stopped at the second floor."

"Very good. Thank you for the time. Be available for further questioning. You can leave."

Fletcher dragged his gimpy leg to the door.

Hieu asked, "Do you know the way out, Mr. Fletcher? Can I help you?"

"Of course, I do. Do you think I'm an idiot? I'll be okay if I can get to the bus stop quickly."

Hieu speedily opened the door.

"Of course, you know the way. If any pertinent information comes to your attention while carrying out your duties, give us a call."

Hieu watched him leave and shut the door.

"I appreciate those words, Hieu, but they came a little late . . . after the interview."

"Inspector Varton, I . . ."

Larry said, "He's an old fart."

Joe puckered his lips to conceal a smile. "Fletcher suffers from *cerebral rectumitus* – head up the ass."

Hieu sat down next to Larry and said, "What's behind O'Hara telling him to make an anonymous call?"

"O'Hara's a master manipulator. He runs his hotel like a maharajah."

"And Fletcher is his maharani."

Larry and Hieu started laughing, and Joe interrupted, "What's so funny? O'Hara needs a good kick in the ass. Larry, you talk to him. He's your best friend. Ask him why he had Fletcher make the call and what he was doing at the Greenwich before you called him down there and," and he raised his voice, "why he left that bit of essential information out. He didn't 'forget' where he was or when. You've got the statement. Read it again."

"O'Hara is a wily man. You interviewed him. I thought you had a favorable opinion. Now you've got a different opinion. He threatens Fletcher, has him on his knees begging for his job, and, for the coup de grâce, gets Fletcher to do his dirty work."

Joe shoved his pencil into the desk and slammed it shut. "Just do it."

Without looking back, he threw the key for the recorder on the desk and said, "I have a dancing date with my wife tonight. After that, I might return to the office and handle some things begging for attention. You know how it is, Leahy."

He left the door open on his way out.

Joe and Aioki drove out of the Bernal Center parking lot as the lights were turned off. Before he dropped her at home, they laughed at Joe's comment that all the dancers were "green terrorists," the name he had given native plant enthusiasts. She didn't complain when he said he had some work at the office.

He pried off the cowboy boots. The tango made his feet ache. After three hours, he filed everything in his drawer. A clean desk added to satisfaction over the interviews of Chase, Smith, and Fletcher and the Morales report Hieu had filed.

For all Leahy was supposed to know about the people involved, he wasn't doing much, and there were still plenty of unanswered questions about his playmate, O'Hara.

He shook his head, knowing that his desk wouldn't stay clean for long and gingerly stuck his feet back into the boots.

The night air renewed his depleted energy, and the nocturnal chill made him hungry.

One block ahead was Tosca Café.

It occupied a tiny spot on busy Columbus Street less than three hundred feet from the Broadway Street corner made famous by topless go-go dancer, Carol Doda. Joe took a window seat, washed down some hot-buttered French bread with warm, sugary red wine, and looked across the street at City Lights Bookstore.

A week before, he had read his poem to stony faces in the audience. It parodied the Board of Supervisors and got a mention in the *North Beach News.*

Joe had moved to the Tosca after a falling-out with the owners of a musical espresso house two blocks up the street. The Caffe Trieste's proprietors, Fabio and Sonia, had asked Joe to leave after he got into a fiery argument with Lawrence Ferlinghetti. After providing some light SFPD supervision for a scene from *Dawn of the Planet of the Apes* in front of Tosca, Joe's locus had changed. At the Tosca he found a more welcoming home.

His cell phone rested on the spoon. He sat back and felt stiff from the effects of a long day that was ending at half-past twelve. On the other side of the street, a thug-type ambled past a young man slumped against the book store. The man's head hung over his chest. He was coatless and wore a Hawaiian shirt, proving he must have lost his companions somewhere in the mix of live sex shows, Chinese kitchens, and Italian side-walk bistros.

Out-of-towner.

Consoled by the thought that alcohol would keep the young man warm, Joe set his wine glass next to the bill.

His glasses hung on his chest, and he squinted to get a clearer picture. Two ruffians in dark hoodies followed closely on the heels of their leader. Joe watched him flick a cigarette into the street, reverse direction, and walk past the drunk again. The other two stood watching, half-on and half-off the curb. Their leader made a signal and instantly all three pounced on the victim. They rifled through his pants. Joe watched a wallet yanked from a pocket. The leader thumbed through it quickly and passed it. Two charged toward Broadway and disappeared around the corner, and the leader ran in the opposite direction.

Joe stood up, throwing enough bills on the table to cover his meal. It looked as if his shift just got extended, but it didn't matter. He lived for spectacle, and crime was not going to get a pass on his time. He flung open the door, sailed off the curb, paved a way in and out of headlights, and called dispatch to report the robbery.

"I have a Code 33, Code 33. On view 211 in front of City Lights on Columbus. Suspects are three Latino males who split up and are running. Two are headed westbound on Broadway toward Grant. The other ran down Columbus, turned the corner at Pacific, and is headed westbound to Grant. 10/25. 10/25."

Their heading in opposite directions indicated to Joe that they were experienced. Pedestrians flooded the picturesque district. Automobile traffic and barkers in front of clubs kept everything at a fever pitch, making it difficult to hear the dispatcher's response.

"No! Three suspects." He rushed his words. "Suspect one is LMA, 20 to 25, 5'8, 170, dark hoodie, and jeans. Suspect two is LMA. 15 to 25, 5'9, 140, dark hoodie, and jeans."

Joe breathed deeply. "Suspect three is a Latino, 20 to 25, tall."

He pocketed his cell phone and sprinted up Broadway in the direction of suspects one and two. Number three was free. It didn't matter. Back-up was on the way. The enchantment of an evening of tango had worn off, but his boogie had been reborn.

At Grant, he saw his suspects at the Stockton corner. Soon they would be lost in the crowd, but the sound of his cowboy boots crushing sidewalk grit had a pleasing effect.

I'm still up to the challenge.

The service semi-automatic attached to his belt bounced up and down. When he reached Stockton, he stopped. Flashing lights one block ahead at the corner of Powell lit up a scuffle. Both suspects were down.

Joe looked down Stockton. He retraced his steps to Grant, Chinatown's busy main street, and hoped to see number three. He moved back and forth on his boot toes. Over tops of heads, he spotted a figure running for his life across Grant. Joe vaulted in the direction of the man he was sure was his. Midway down the street he felt as if the sidewalk were a conveyor belt. Slowing down was out of the question and, just when he needed it, a bolt of energy propelled him into fast-forward mode and supplied what was needed to catch a man half his age.

The sound of boots sent pedestrians whirling in opposite directions. Clubbers looking for a late-night tandoori bite looked up and scattered. At the corner, he caught a glimpse of his man running up the hill. The suspect suddenly switched direction. Joe raised his hand to stop a motorist, but it didn't matter, because the suspect tore down the street past him.

The smell of sweet and sour and saffron filled Joe' lungs.

At the next corner, the suspect turned right. In three more smelly and thirsty blocks, the foot chase had moved into the financial district beneath the Transamerica Building. Joe lunged forward and reached for his shoulders. In the roll, Joe recognized his man: Pablo Morales.

They flipped over, and Joe put his right knee on Morales' back, but Morales lifted him off in a single motion. Morales stood up straight. Joe looked up and watched as Pablo followed the glare of moving red lights.

Damn!

He had lost Morales. With pants torn at the knees, Joe stomped back to Central. As he got closer, he noticed one of the other suspects had happy feet in Central's wind-swept side alley.

Joe blocked his exit. Feeling so angry he could punch a baby in the face, he landed a fist on the suspect's nose. The man's knees buckled, and he dropped like a slug in a parking meter. The collapsing body of this jackal shielded drops of his own blood spilling on the asphalt.

The other officer picked up the man and dragged his fat legs back over the threshold of the side door. Joe looked up at a seagull eyeing the scene, flapping its wings, and squawking at the unexpected smash-up.

"Who tackled the suspects?" Joe asked, inside the holding area. He held out his other hand and withdrew a camouflage-colored handkerchief to wipe off the blood on his finger. "Great job. Do we know their names?" Joe looked down at his shoes and tried shedding himself of sticky asphalt.

"Yes, sir. Jorge Lopez Vega and Angel Ernesto Padilla Morales."

Joe pulled his head back. "Morales?"

"Yes, sir."

"Let me speak to him. I'll see him in room two." Joe asked the desk sergeant to issue an arrest warrant for Pablo Morales and entered the interrogation room. He sat on the edge of a table and waited under a single florescent light. Another officer led Angel into the room and sat him down in the only chair.

"I'm Inspector Varton. You're Angel Morales?"

"Yeah."

"How old are you?"

"Sixteen."

"Take the gum out of your mouth."

What a noob.

Angel looked around for a place to put the gum.

"Swallow it. Take the baseball cap off. Put it on the table."

Joe saw a pack of Marlboros in the pocket of his black t-shirt. "Where'd you get the welt?"

Angel raised a hand and rubbed his right cheek. "You know, playin' basketball at the rec center. My *mijo's*."

"Uh-huh. Pablo Morales, your brother?"

"Yeah. That cop hit me."

Joe got a whiff. "Were you smoking marijuana?"

"No, no way. If Jorge says I was smoking weed, *ese loco*."

"Guy's crazy, huh?"

"Yeah, crazy, dude."

"Do you smoke weed?"

"Sometimes, dude."

"Inspector Varton, to you. Comprende?"

"Uh-huh."

Joe watched him scratch a tiny beard on the edge of his chin. "What school?"

"Burton. Can I smoke a cigarette?"

"Why were you and your brother and Vega walking around North Beach?"

"Out for some fun."

"Get that phony immigrant grin off your face. You're in hot water, Mr. Morales. A wallet was stolen." He looked at the officer standing over Angel. "Where is it?"

"The desk sergeant has the wallet."

"Has the money been counted?"

"I think so," the officer answered.

"Make sure it is . . . and ask the victim if he knows how much he had." Joe thought the victim was probably too sozzled to remember.

"Hey, I had nothing to do with it. Jorge had the wallet. I never even touched it. I didn't know they was gonna steal a wallet." Angel leaned back and reached for the Oakland A's baseball cap.

"Leave it there. You're under arrest. A probation officer from Juvenile Probation will be assigned to you and, tomorrow, they'll determine if you should be held over or returned home. As for tonight, you're stuck here."

"Shiiiit. This ain't chill, bro. I wanna see my brother."

"He's not here, and you have your brother to thank for the trouble you're in, not me."

Joe left Angel in the care of the officer.

Jorge Vega was being questioned in the next interrogation room. The wallet lay on one end of a table. Vega sat at the other end and held a rag to his face. The toes of his Adidas shoes barely touched the floor. In an ashtray, a cigarette burned, imparting to the room the smell of hot blacktop.

Joe listened for a few minutes and asked, "So, you and Angel took a Muni bus to the Greenwich, and Pablo and you two took another bus and got off around Stockton. Is that correct?"

"Yeah, but Angel had nothing to do with this. He's a good kid. You can ask Pablo."

"How old are you, Vega?"

"Why you wanna know?"

"One more time. Age?"

"Twenty-three . . . pig."

"Why did you take Angel along? He's underage."

"He wanted to come. He ain't got nothin to do."

Vega sounds like all the rest.

"Hey, bro, what you got against me? Why your mother raised you this way? Racist pig."

"Outside." Vega followed Joe into the corridor. "I didn't see you in any family portraits, and here's for mentioning my mother, calling me a pig, and bringing Angel along." He punched Vega in the stomach, then walked to the desk sergeant and said, "Look after Vega. He fell down."

The man who had been robbed was sobering up with some coffee, and Joe heard him say, "I was plastered," when asked if he could identify the suspects.

Joe saw the arresting officer. "Nice pinch out there . . . did you have to run far to catch these jerk-offs?"

"No, Inspector, they fell into our laps."

"Call me Joe."

"Thanks, but I'm good with calling you Inspector. My dad spoke highly of you."

Joe recognized the cop. His grandfather was Francis Upland, a highly decorated and popular cop killed in the line of duty by a bank robber in 1958. Kevin was third generation SFPD, and his father, Charlie, had just retired.

"I worked with your father. Great cop and an even better man. How's your mother and sister?"

"They're good. Thanks for asking."

The six-foot red-head had a Cupid's bow and cheeks as red as a heart. The hue extended down both sides of his face to the chin, which gave him the permanent visage of a runner. He was fresh out of the Police Academy.

"Your dad told me you got drafted by the Cubs out of high school. Sacred Heart Cathedral, right?"

"Yes, sir, made it to Double A, and all I got was a cup of coffee . . . so I followed in my pop's footsteps."

"Like I said, great job on the arrest."

"Thanks. It's all about timing, right place, right time. Vega and Morales were pussy-cats once we got them on the ground. Vega whimpered, but the young kid acted tough and started to get up. Looked like he wanted to poke me in the teeth. So, I put a knee in his groin, and he flopped. Vega got as much. After that, I decided a little sweet talk on the way to the station would soften them up. I'm thinking this one will earn me a commendation."

"You did what?" Joe's face got redder than Elmo.

"I kneed him."

"Were they hand-cuffed before this happened?"

"Yeah, Inspector, but they were moving around."

"Get your ass in my office . . . right now."

"What did I do?"

"It's a little thing called police brutality."

Joe marched to his office.

The officer said under his breath, "Why's he so pissed?"

Joe heard the comment and turned around, yelling quietly, "I got rolled around the asphalt tonight and never had a chance to slap on some bangles." Joe's feet hurt and sitting down eased the pain as he prepared another reprimand. "Don't take me for a moron! Sit down and listen."

Officer Upland sat in his chair, both he and the chair awkwardly poised for some time on the instructions Joe gave and his thoughts on his very reputation. "I'm known as a 'Jack'. Argue with me, and you'll make a fool out of yourself."

The night came to an end, one officer had been chided, and Joe went home. He took a hot shower, washed off his Marine finger, got into bed, and wrapped his big arms around the wife.

She quietly said, "You feel good. Long night?"

"Some young kid is mixed up in this Greenwich murder. At least, I think he is."

They fell asleep.

Chapter 14

Wednesday, July 10

Larry saw a familiar name in the headline of the Matier and Ross column, "James O'Hara and Mortmain." Five minutes had passed since the entry hall clock chimed six times. Larry poured some orange juice into his glass and read the Chronicle column.

A mortmain transfer of land in Sonoma County to St. Francis Solano Church is underway. Mortmain is a land transfer to a non-profit for permanent ownership. Price of the land: $50,000. On one side of the vacant lot is the church, and on the other side is an adoption agency. The agency wants to sell the lot. Sources say the purchaser is James O'Hara, owner of the Greenwich Grand Hotel. According to court documents, Mr. O'Hara is the party suing the adoption agency. Purchase and transfer of the lot have been delayed. Attorneys for all sides blame legal difficulties. Just last week, a Greenwich employee from a wealthy family was killed. Is there a connection between the death and the delay? Calls to Mr. O'Hara have not been returned.

Larry coughed up his toast and his eyes fixated on the dollar figure, the same amount taken out of the Greenwich vault, the same amount Fletcher was accused of stealing. With one hand, he dumped the newspaper and a napkin holding bits of toast into the waste basket and, with the other, poured his juice into the sink.

Lauren walked in, pulling on an ear lobe, and stared at the orange sink. "What are you doing?"

"Good morning, dear."

"Morning. Move out of the way and let me clean it up."

"I'm in a hurry."

"I bet Father Ralph will be absent."

"I don't know. See you tonight."

Standing behind her passion pink bathrobe, Larry kissed her hairnet.

She shook her shoulders.

In her unique way of cooking up an excuse, she turned around and said, "Some people think I'm an odd duck, but I know I have you." She picked up the pack of Benson & Hedges and smiled, upper and lower lips fastened to the filter of a cigarette she had extracted.

He began plotting his approach to O'Hara as soon as he got the Chevy pointed in the right direction.

Visit or phone call?

Seven o'clock Mass at St. Ignatius interrupted his thoughts.

No sign of Father Ralph or Josh.

Just as he exited through the side door, his phone vibrated.

"Leahy."

"Have you talked to O'Hara, yet?"

"No, and a good thing, Joe. There's a Matier column about O'Hara and $50,000."

"I'll read it later. There's an arrest warrant for Pablo Morales. His sixteen-year-old brother, Angel Morales, and another idiot named Vega are being held for robbery pending action by the District Attorney's office."

"What happened?"

"Upland and two other officers made the arrest on Broadway and Powell. Kevin Upland. We'll talk about it after your little chat with

O'Hara. Do it before you come traipsing into the office. Understand me?"

Oh, yes.

The first reading at Mass had described the suffering in hell, where there's "weeping and gnashing of teeth," and Larry was feeling the heat, but before he could utter a word, he heard Varton's voice whispering in his ear.

Martin Flaherty.

It was Flaherty who had killed Kevin Upland's grandfather during the bank robbery, and Varton had purposely reminded Larry.

Larry hopped into the Chevy and would arrive at Central on time. After a few minutes had passed and the Stockton Tunnel was behind him, Larry loosened his grip on the steering wheel. He knew a city attorney he could call about the newspaper column. He pulled into the Central garage and walked to the sidewalk. Reception in the garage was poor.

"Hello, Mr. Crowley. This is Larry Leahy. Do you have a minute?"

"How are you, Larry. What's on your mind?"

"Did you read the Matier and Ross column in today's Chronicle?"

"Nope. What's it about?"

"Matier talked about a mortmain transfer. It's related to a homicide that I'm investigating: the MacKenzie case."

"That case has been in the newspaper more than once. Is it mortmain you want to understand, and you think I can help?"

"Can you?"

"I'll give it a try. During the Middle Ages, the Church acquired land that it kept in perpetuity. The land was never inherited by a descendant. The Church held onto it, which caused problems between Church and King. Mortmain statutes were enacted to prevent land from being transferred in perpetuity. Mortmain statutes were replaced by the modern rule against perpetuities. In what way is the word being used in the column?"

Larry said, "A land transfer to St. Francis Solano Church in Sonoma."

"One doesn't hear the word 'mortmain' these days. If land goes into a charitable trust for the promotion of religion, then mortmain, or, more apropos, the modern rule against perpetuities, would not apply. It is legal to donate land to the church in the form of a charitable trust."

"All right. So, the land can be donated legally. Thank you."

Larry pulled the newspaper out of his pocket. "Purchase and transfer of the lot have been delayed."

Something else was standing in the way.

Larry called Hieu. "Meet at the Greenwich. I'll tell you why when you get there."

Inside the lobby, at half-past eight, they sat down on the three-seater, and Larry began. "Today's Matier column said that O'Hara tried to purchase some land from the Solano County Catholic Adoption Agency for $50,000 and is now suing the agency. The amount is more than a coincidence . . . and there's an arrest warrant on Pablo Morales."

"Joe told me the story about the Morales clones when I arrived at Central," Hieu said.

"Let's have a friendly chat with O'Hara and ask him about being at the Greenwich at midnight on the night of the murder. I know he's here because I saw his Rolls in the basement. For all the interviews he's been through, he will complain like a whore who's not been paid in eight weeks."

It dawned on Larry that he had never heard a single vulgarity from his partner.

Hieu said, "Angel Morales was released to his mother. The assistant DA told Joe that Angel's a minor without a record and it would be hard to prove he touched the wallet."

"Let's take another walk around the building before we talk to O'Hara. You never know what we will see or find . . . like the last time when we found the fingernail."

In the back of the hotel, Larry had a richer view of the details of the employee entrance and the garage ingress. He looked up and thought he could see the bottoms of O'Hara's shoes resting on the window sill. A strip of decaying mortar hung below the window.

He looked down in time to avoid tripping over a homeless man who was passed out. "Get going." When the man failed to respond, Larry got closer and shouted, "Wake up!" Larry noticed small bits of broken mortar on either side of the sleeper.

Larry heard a tapping coming from above. James opened his window further and yelled down at the bum, "God dammit. Get out of here . . . for the last time, you bastard."

The man sat straight up and said, "That bastard doesn't know how to run his hotel."

It crossed Larry's mind that the vagrant might have some kind of inside knowledge on the Greenwich, but the man got up and staggered down the alleyway.

Ms. Keck sat sideways looking at her computer screen. Larry took several long strides and cleared his throat to get her attention. The hefty desk couldn't hide a florid face and bouncing bosom as she rose and stood erect in a pink lemonade, leather mini skirt with side ruffle, and asked, "Do you wish to see Mr. O'Hara?" Her silk stockings, which were stitched in a crisscross pattern, exhibited a lustrous sheen sufficient to mesmerize a snake charmer's cobra.

"He should be ready to see us."

The back of James' chair faced Larry and Hieu. The window was wide open. Larry could barely see the ornate, black-iron balcony outside the window. On a wall to the right, the television blared San Francisco crime statistics. A cut-glass decanter and set of five glasses sat on the credenza behind O'Hara. A sixth glass, which was half-filled with dark orange liquid, was next to James' blotter.

He swung around.

Larry and Hieu sat down.

"You know why we're here. You tried to buy a piece of property in Sonoma."

"You read the paper."

"I manage from time to time."

James swung around and put his feet back on the window sill. He puffed and, with the strong push from one foot, swung around again. "See that hotel across the street. It's killing me. We have a convention in September, and we're limping along, and we're in summer. That worries me." He took off his monogrammed glasses, rubbed his eyes, and stared at Larry.

"Back to the Chronicle column. You tried to buy a piece of property in Sonoma."

"I tried to buy the property, but some bozo objected."

"When did you start calling lawyers bozos?"

In a barely audible voice, he answered, "I tried to buy the land, which is worthless, and give it to the church. Anything wrong with that, Larry?"

"No, but why would you buy a worthless piece of land?"

"I had a problem that needed fixing."

"I think there is something else going on. Now, I'm speaking as a cop. An investigation is going on, and you are part of it. What you say is extremely important." To underscore his point, Larry lifted his chair off the carpet and set it down on the desk-side of the black and white fret print border, which left no extra room for his knees.

James swung around. "See those, Larry. Those are vertical exhaust vents to let out stale, hot air. We're covering the same ground."

Larry stood up and banged his hand on the desk, rattling the glass. "Answer me. What's going on?"

James spoke to the window. "I got someone pregnant and the adoption agency got involved. I wanted some retribution. I tried to buy the land and sued them. I may be an SOB, but then most people would do exactly what I did, if they could afford to."

"Maureen or Pepper? Which one is pregnant?"

Now facing Larry and Hieu, he said, "Don't be ridiculous. Maureen."

"Let me get this straight." Larry spoke slowly. He glanced at Hieu, who was sitting as straight as a totem pole, and back at O'Hara. "You planned on buying land for $50,000, the same amount that went missing from a hotel account. The deal fell through, and you placed the money in the vault, oh, forgetting to tell Fletcher, but he's as good as a galley slave. Next, you dreamt up a scheme involving Cornelius and Pepper. That brings us back to Pepper." He spoke more deliberately and slowly than before. "How is she involved?"

"That tramp thought she was in love with Cornelius. He confided to me that he had a gambling debt, and I got Pepper to bring him the money."

Larry had to refocus his eyes, the admission was so stunning. "You sent her the e-mail?"

"Mm."

"You had $50,000 on hand to buy the property, which, coincidentally, was the same amount as Cornelius' debt. You can't think anyone would believe that his debt was the same amount as the purchase price of the land. Now, give me all the truth."

"You think you know everything." He looked Larry in the eye, took a swig from the glass, and looked over the rim. "Cornelius was in debt up to his eyeballs . . . and he didn't want Ralph to know. I showed him some mercy. He promised to pay it back out of his salary, and the actual amount of his debt was a little less."

"He was your responsibility and mine. The debt didn't exist. The MacKenzie family has more money than it knows what to do with, and how would Cornelius gamble? He doesn't even drive."

"Online gambling."

"Ridiculous. There's something missing, something you don't want to talk about." He bent over, placed both hands on O'Hara's desk, and said calmly, "What is missing?"

"The land deal had already fallen through. I don't have to tell you anything else, or are you arresting me, Larry?"

"How did you do it? How did you send an e-mail to Pepper from Cornelius?" Hieu asked.

"Easy. Every employer monitors employee e-mails and passwords. Why are you two taking her side in all of this? She's not worth a free piss."

"Why would you ask her to bring the money and then accuse her of stealing it?" Larry asked, pleased with his partner's poise.

James got up, the back of his legs forcing the chair against the window sill. "Someday . . . I'd like to retire. I plan on leaving this empire to someone who has my trust, and it surely isn't that homely little desk clerk, though she did just as I told her. So far, I haven't found that person. I want to keep my marriage, have Clare join me in retirement, and leave all this behind, but for now, I'm done with you two. Good-bye." He walked in the direction of the double doors, unbolted a panel, spat into a wash basin, and slammed the panel shut.

He waited there and said, "Did you forget your father's role in that bank robbery?"

Larry bristled at the mention and said, "One more question. Your man, Fletcher, said you arrived at the Greenwich a few minutes after midnight on the night of the murder."

"Ten minutes after, to be exact," Hieu added.

"Not true."

Larry stood up and said, "There's video. This is a warning, James. Keep walking the wide path to hell and you might end up there."

"Don't worry about me. Your men have looked at the video. Didn't they? I've got a few more years running this place."

"Murder may be lying at the end of your destination. Remember this, God doesn't come when you want him to, or expect him to, but he's never late. Most of my trainees have asked me the question, 'What does a murderer look like?' My response is always the same, 'A murderer looks like you.'"

"What about this Morales kid? He hasn't shown up for work in days."

"Thinking of firing him, too?"

"What other choice have I got? His disappearance shows he's guilty."

"We're looking for him." Larry got up. At the door, standing in O'Hara's face, he asked, "Cornelius and Maureen were up to something. What was it?"

James' laughter filled the office. He walked back to his desk, pulled a ledger out of the top drawer, and picked up the phone without looking at Larry. "I'm not going to prison!"

"There's more than one prison. There's the prison that is your mind and keeps you locked in a room without windows and won't let you see truth."

Larry shut the oak doors on his way out and stopped to say good-bye to the secretary. She had the ear-phones around her neck. Her other attributes were in full view. Larry heard the buzzer on her desk as he carefully shut the outer door.

Hieu emerged unruffled and rode the elevator with him to the first-floor lobby.

"I think we need to talk to Pablo," Hieu said.

"First, we have to find him," Larry groused.

"Where to, Larry?"

"Well, we aren't going to find him having tea at the Press Club, the Metropolitan, or Pacific Union!"

Varton called Larry and Hieu into his office at half past eleven.

Larry's cell phone vibrated. He fumbled to get it out of his jacket.

"Are you there?" she asked.

He grabbed the phone off the floor. "Yes, I'm here. I'm busy, Lauren."

"I got an invitation from Maureen Daley. I was at the mailbox and rummaged through the flyers and junk-mail. I saw an envelope with a pale green, glued-on return address and her Palmer method script. I knew what it was."

Larry started to speak, but she kept talking.

"I opened it. Maude sees Maureen at St. Brendan's every Sunday. How can she go to church and be sleeping with James O'Hara? I left the mail on the floor. Gather it up when you get home. I'll read the note. 'Dear Lauren: You and Larry are invited for dinner and trivia games at my home Saturday, July 13, at seven o'clock. I'm expecting a small gathering of friends. We haven't seen each other in such a long time. I look forward to catching up. RSVP.' Can we go?"

"I thought you didn't like to go out on such short notice?"

"This is an exception, and the mail was late. What do you think she's up to?"

"I don't know."

"Larry! How can you be so dense?"

"I'm busy."

"It's at seven. You're home by that time."

"The answer is no."

The click at the other end made mincemeat of his ear drum.

"Domestic troubles, Larry?" Varton asked.

"I think Pablo is gay," Hieu announced.

Joe sat back in his chair.

Larry stuffed the phone in his jacket. "I don't like labels. They belong on cereal boxes."

Joe raised his eyebrows and said, "What makes you say that, Hieu?"

"Larissa told me that her boyfriend before Pablo was gay."

"When did you talk to her?" Larry asked.

"I spoke to her on the phone from my office. She is Pablo's first girlfriend. I asked where Pablo was on the day of the Pride parade, and she said he was gone all day. He's a gang member, but none of them may know about a secret life. We observed Pablo's rudeness toward Larissa. It's like the man who takes a bite out of an onion to disguise the alcohol on his breath."

Larry choked on his laughter, "And Larissa is the onion. But an onion doesn't attract anyone."

Hieu looked out Varton's window from where he was sitting and said, "Larissa is attractive. Pablo is an angry man and may have been driven to kill."

"That may be, but we need facts. What did you find out from O'Hara?"

Larry answered, "He denied being at the Greenwich at ten after twelve. He said that there was no coincidence that Cornelius' debt matched the amount of money taken from the vault by Pepper. He admitted that Maureen is pregnant with his baby." He turned to Hieu. "How can we be sure that what you claimed about Pablo is true?"

"I can call her and ask her if sexual relations have declined or ended, or if she's ever checked his text messages, or if she's even seen pictures of men on their home computer. We could have it examined forensically."

"Not yet, Hieu. We have no probable cause, but he is our number one suspect. His drug use may be a major factor." Joe stuck his straight finger up in the air. "All right. Find him. Bring Morales in."

"That's what I said before. Pablo needs money."

"Just do it."

•••

At half past two, two blocks from the Greenwich, Pablo texted Ready to be at the employee entrance.

Ready was there. Pablo told him to step back under the overhang and stick his foot between the door and the jam.

"Ready, I need some cash."

"I don't have any."

"Let me in. I wanna see O'Hara."

"No way. I ain't gonna lose my job for you."

"What, what? You my homie."

Ready moved his foot, and Pablo put his against the door.

"Hey, Ortiz said he saw you in the Castro. You weren't in our colors. Widdat?"

Pablo's back straightened. "I thought he was in jail."

"No. He got let go and has to be back in court next month. You been stayin' away from us past few days. Like I said, he saw you in the Castro."

"Why was he there?"

Ready made a hand sign and said, "You was in some tight pants in the Castro, dude."

Pablo looked over his shoulder and said, "Shut up."

"Sorry, bro, but I got news. You better hang low. Ortiz is already talkin' you up."

Pablo turned his back to Ready, took off his wife-beater, and wiped his face clean. He turned back around and said, "I never liked you anyway, Ready."

With a vengeance, Pablo pushed past Ready. He hurried down the hallway and took the stairs to the second floor. In less than a minute he stood in front of O'Hara's secretary.

"I wanna see O'Hara."

She buzzed O'Hara's phone.

Pablo could hear O'Hara's voice through the doors.

"I'm sorry, but Mr. O'Hara can't see you today."

Pablo barged in, and the doors hit the paneling.

O'Hara rolled backward. "What do you want?"

"Another $500."

"No. Get out."

"If you don't give me the money, I'll tell Leahy the whole story."

"He won't believe you."

"You bastard. You gave me $500 to buy a gun. Now, I'm busted."

Pablo started to move around the desk.

O'Hara pushed his chair to the other side. "Your fingerprints are on the gun, not mine. Now, get out or I'll call the cops."

"The hell with you." Pablo grabbed O'Hara and lifted him out of his chair. He didn't know what to do next, let go, and walked out, leaving all the doors wide open.

•••

Larry's phone rang.

"Morales was here," O'Hara said in a voice to be minded.

"Where is he now?"

"I don't know. He walked out. I'm looking out the window . . . wait a minute . . . he's in the alley behind the hotel."

"What direction is he going? Which end of the alley . . . Ellis or Eddy?"

"Eddy."

"I'm on the way. If he returns, try to keep him occupied and don't let him leave."

Larry informed Joe and asked for Hieu. They raced to Central's garage. Two squad cars followed and in five minutes they were in the alley. Larry parked outside the basement entrance. After telling the officers to wait there, he walked fast to O'Hara's office. Hieu ran behind.

"I'm here to see Mr. O'Hara." Larry's head rush warned him to slow down.

With a smudge of orange lipstick on her teeth and sweet-smelling knobs bouncing, Ms. Keck smiled as if someone had just excited her. "He's waiting for you, sir."

Larry opened the double doors.

O'Hara was standing and said, "Have a seat."

"We didn't see him on the street. So, exactly what did he say?" Larry dragged a chair on the plush carpet.

"Pablo demanded $500 and stomped out."

Larry paused and asked, "Why $500?"

O'Hara sat down hard. "How the hell should I know? He looked like he had the hell beat out of him."

"What?"

"He had a cut over his eye, a bruise on the side of his face, and was wringing wet."

"Who let him in?"

"I'd like to know that, too."

"What about his friend in housekeeping, Mr. Ready?" Hieu asked.

"I'll have him here in two minutes."

O'Hara buzzed Ms. Keck. "Get Ready in my office now."

"Let me do the talking, James."

Two minutes later, Ready walked in, the petrified expression on his face giving him away. Larry stood up and took a few paces toward Ready. "Mr. Ready, I'm Inspector Leahy and seated over there is Inspector Trang."

O'Hara stood up.

"I didn't let him in. He rushed past me. I couldn't stop him."

O'Hara took one step to the side of his desk and scrutinized Ready. "Stand up straight. Your white shirt has a coffee stain. That's one violation."

Larry interrupted, "You say he rushed past you. How did you know Morales would be at the back entrance?"

"He texted me."

"What did he say?"

"He needed money. I told him I don't have any."

Larry's fears were swelling like a balloon. "Did he say anything else?"

"Pablo said he wanted to see O'Hara . . . Mr. O'Hara. He rushed past me. I couldn't stop him."

"Did he touch you?" Larry asked.

"Sort of, sir. He came up against me hard and pushed me out of the way."

"Did he say he was going to rob anyone in the hotel?"

"Yeah."

"Who?"

"I dunno."

"All right. Don't let Morales back in the hotel. Is that understood?"

Ready turned around to leave, and O'Hara barked, "Is that understood?"

"Yes, sir."

"Stand still. Turn around. I'll be speaking to your supervisor about your attire."

Ready looked as if he were going to pee in his pants as he backed out of the office.

"Cornering Morales in a closed environment like the Greenwich is an easier way to catch him than on the streets, but he's a threat to all the Greenwich employees," Larry said. "What about the $500? What happened to it and who has it? I want an answer."

O'Hara sat down, leaned back in his chair, and rolled his eyes. He noticed a crack in the oak panel where the door had slammed against it. "Dammit, I have to get that wall repaired. That Morales kid is going to pay for it!" He walked over to the sink, looked at the damage, and soaked a wash cloth in hot water. From the sink he said, "I told you, I don't know anything about $500."

"I don't believe that. I'm taking a walk around and see what I can find out. That way I can be sure Morales is gone."

"Your choice, Larry." O'Hara laid the wash cloth on the back of his neck.

Ms. Keck withdrew a pencil from platinum curls piled high. She smiled as Larry and Hieu passed. Larry was tired of her, too.

At the back of the hotel, Larry and Hieu described Morales to the officers, directed one of the officers to the front door, and walked him down the employee hall.

Larry found Larissa at the switchboard. "Can we talk to you privately?"

"I have to tell Pepper. She can handle the switchboard or ask the other desk clerk to fill in for me."

Larry, Hieu, and Larissa sat down at the lunch room table.

"What's going on?" Larissa asked.

"Pablo was in the hotel about thirty minutes ago. Did you see him?"

Her face suddenly dropped, and Larry saw tears forming. He scrambled for the right words. "Don't get upset. All I want to know is, have you seen Pablo since Inspector Trang spoke to you?"

"No, I haven't seen him. I'm worried."

Hieu asked, "Have you heard from his mother, his friends, associates . . . did any of them say anything?"

"No, and I haven't seen him since Tuesday when you came to our house for the interview. What was he doing here?"

Larissa started to cry, and Larry said, "He came to see Mr. O'Hara. Can you recall anything that's happened that might help us find Pablo?"

"I got his uniform dry-cleaned yesterday and hoped he would come home and go back to work. When I picked up his uniform, the clerk handed me a knife and a fingernail. She found them in his jacket pocket. She thought the fingernail was mine. They're in my locker."

"Please bring them here."

She left the room.

"Wherever he is, he forgot his knife," Hieu said.

"I want to see the fingernail."

Larissa dropped the knife and broken fingernail on the table. "I was jealous when I saw the fingernail. . . Pablo is seeing another woman, isn't he?"

Larry examined the knife, handed it to Hieu, and turned the black, red, and blue fingernail over several times. It looked like the shiny object he had found outside the Security office.

"This isn't your fingernail?"

"No. I don't wear that color."

"We will keep these items."

Hieu looked it over and asked, "Who wears this color, Larissa?"

"I don't know. Do you think he's having an affair?"

"No. I don't think so. Have you read any of Pablo's text messages other than the messages he's sent you?" Hieu asked.

"No. He's protective of the phone, and mostly he texts Ortiz and Ready or plays games."

"Can you tell us any more about his past?" Larry asked.

"A little."

"Did he ever go to church? Does he believe in God?"

"I know his mother took him to church, but I don't think he believes in God."

"Does he ever talk about his father?"

"No. His father abandoned them when Gloria was pregnant with Angel. I think Pablo gets mixed up sometimes, but he's a good person. Do you think he's all right?"

"You have our promise to do whatever we can to find Pablo and bring him home safely."

Hieu then turned his attention to Larry, who placed the items in his jacket pocket. "We're looking for him. He's moving around quickly, and we're just a few steps behind."

"I know I can count on both of you," she said and wiped away her tears. "I'm worried about my baby and my Pablo."

Chapter 15

Wednesday, July 10

Immediately after his interview at the police station, Gerald had rushed to Topaz Lake for two days of communing with nature. It gave him plenty of time to think about Varton and O'Hara, his bullies. He had the house key in his pocket. As the sun set behind Monitor Pass, an owl hooted a single melody in the cottonwood trees hanging overhead on what could be his last night of staying at the lake house. Circumstances beyond his control might demand the key be returned.

The grandfather clock's iridescent dial let him know that it was just past eight. A bookcase stood in the corner of the living room, and the spine of Cornelius' Bible eyed him. He wished he had religion the way Cornelius spoke about it. He said the story of Adam and Eve wasn't about them. It was God saying, "I'm God, and you aren't." The way that Cornelius had explained things made sense.

Temptation had him remove the black and white Jack Daniels bottle from the liquor cabinet, but a partly open dining room window and a rustling noise, which left him wondering if a California quail had flown from Mono Lake, enticed him away from the bottle. The window was kept open an inch to keep the house free from musty odors during long absences, and it would remain that way out of respect for Cornelius and the meticulous way he kept house.

The moon threw a stream of light across the lake, and a duck, its feathers yellowed by a moon beam, slid onto the smooth surface. A clumsy landing sent ripples across the waters, disturbing the ageless reflection of a full moon, while crickets droned their love calls.

His cell phone rang.

"Hello."

"It's Pepper."

"How are you?"

"Fine. Did you hear what happened today?"

"I'm at Topaz Lake."

"What are you doing there?"

"Relaxing."

"Don't you get lonely up there?"

Gerald didn't know what to say. "So, tell me what happened."

"Well, Pablo came into the hotel, and he hasn't showed up for work for two days, and he pushed Ready aside, and he went to O'Hara's office." Gerald heard her take a breath. "And he demanded money from O'Hara, and now they're looking for him."

"That guy is crazy."

"Tell me! Well, anyway, I was hoping you would walk me home, but I guess you can't, because you're so far away, and, well, I'm a little lonely, too. Oh well. Good night and sleep tight."

"Wait, don't hang up."

"Yes?"

"I was plannin' on going back to the city tonight, anyway."

"Are you? Could you make it back in time?"

"Yeah, I could. You're off duty at one thirty, right?"

"Yes, but you don't have to rush home just for me. It would be dangerous driving fast on dark highways. Wouldn't it? Can you come home? No, I don't know. I'll just walk myself home tonight. Can you come?"

"Of course. If you want me to, just say so."

"I don't know. Were you planning on it?"

"Pepper, just tell me what you want."

"Well, were you planning to drive home?"

"Yes. See you at one thirty. I have to get going."

"Are you sure?"

"Yes. Good-bye, Pepper. See you later tonight."

Gerald now had a good reason to resist the urge to get drunk. If he did, it would be impossible to secure the vacation hideaway and take care of Pepper. The unbearable night heat was another reason to go.

He walked past the liquor cabinet again. Cornelius always had a drink before dinner, but whenever they were together, he drank milk. Gerald told himself to go to the back door and rest on the porch lounge, but he had to leave. He started crying as fatigue and respect for his buddy carried him around Cornelius' fly tying equipment spread out on the floor. He lay down on the lounge chair, and a tear trickled down a deep furrow of skin between his nose and cheek bone and reached the top of his upper lip.

What to do?

Return to Texas and the family that gave him so much pain and the one who seldom saw him? His little girl was turning eleven years old in two days. Her stamped birthday card sat in his Tenderloin apartment. How had life turned out this way? He looked down and wiped away sadness with a balled-up fist.

Distant thunder drowned out the sound of mating crickets, but the rain had stopped. Absence from his young daughter made him yearn to see her face again, but the menacing ogre of a lawman standing between father and daughter reminded him of the reason for his long absence. An alcoholic was an unfit father.

His allotment of women had been fair, and to many of them he had said, "I look like ten miles of bad road." Tonight, he felt like it. But those were not his kind. They tell an honest man one thing and mean another. Lately, he was having no luck with women, and chastity had entered through the back door as the new guest. His little girl was gone. He hoped that she would turn out differently, but, at the moment, he was powerless to do anything about it.

No headlights encroached on the mountain road, and the sky twinkled.

Back in the city, Gerald rushed into his apartment. It was one o'clock. He filled his cereal bowl and ended a three-second search for milk in an empty refrigerator. A walk to the corner liquor store didn't excite a single corpuscle in his body, and he was running out of time.

He stuck his head through a gray sweatshirt and looked in the mirror.

Pepper will be happy to see me.

His outlook improved even as he stepped over human trash on the sidewalk. Ignoring caution by returning to the place of his former employment, he entered through the front door, shook loose the cold, and made a bee-line to the front desk.

How excited and stupid I must look.

"I'm here," he said.

She was pitter-pattering behind the desk and looked up when she heard his voice.

"You made it. I was worried about you."

"Don't worry about me. You're looking good." He looked down at the whale's tooth hanging outside the sweatshirt and stuffed it inside.

"It's five more minutes before I go off duty. Can you wait outside?"

"Ugh, I guess so."

"I'll be quick."

Outside the lobby, he shivered inside the gray sweatshirt.

She grabbed his hand and pressed hard. They gave each other a "glad to have you with me" look.

I wonder if she will invite me in.

As they passed under a street light, he felt her hand holding on.

Seeing the apartment night clerk from outside the lobby, he said, "That guy watches everybody. He's creepy."

"Don't let him bother you. Sometimes, he dozes off."

She got the building key out of her red patent leather purse and unlocked the door.

"Come on. It's freezing outside."

Patel, the night clerk, got behind the upper part of his counter.

Pepper gave Gerald a nip on the cheek and caused him to jump.

She whispered, "That bald, pin-headed man always answers, 'You talk to the owner', whenever there's something broken, and never remembers the owner's phone number, and chatters in a never-ending argument with some family member on the other end."

Gerald started to laugh as Pepper put her building key in the purse and fished around for her apartment key.

Suddenly, Pablo jumped out from behind a pillar.

Gerald looked for Patel. He was hiding.

Pablo snatched Pepper's purse.

"What are you doing here?" she asked.

"Give her back that purse," Gerald said.

Pablo rummaged through it and found the other key. He rummaged some more, found two one-dollar bills, and placed them in his pocket.

"Where's the rest?"

"The rest?"

"I told you I wanted $200. Where is it?"

"I don't have any money."

"What money? What's this all about?" Gerald asked.

Pablo dropped the purse. A right fist hovered long enough for both to see it. The blow sent her backward.

Gerald immediately took a swing at Pablo and missed. They grappled with each other all the way to the floor. Gerald tasted the spicy sweat on Pablo's wrist and thrashed about to wriggle free of a headlock. He put Pablo in a scissor lock. When Pablo broke out, he smacked Gerald in the face, and Gerald hit the carpet. Sparks of light blurred his vision, but it cleared in time for him to see Pablo calmly walk to the front door and unlatch the lock, and he was gone.

"Mr. Patel, we need help."

Patel moved back into view, looking like a bank teller about to say, "Go to the next line."

"Mr. Patel!" she shouted.

He stood on his tippy-toes, leaned over the counter, and said, "Are you, all right?"

"No, we're not."

Slowly, Patel put his hand to his mouth.

Pepper got into a sitting position and looked for the apartment key.

From the floor, Gerald said, "Call 911, Patel."

"No," Pepper screamed, "Just help us up. We can manage once we're inside the apartment," she said in a strained voice. "C'mon, Gerald, get up. We'll be safe in my apartment."

"Patel, you make sure never to let that guy into this apartment building, never again. If you do, I'll see you hanged." Out had come his Texas drawl like a shotgun, and Patel scurried back to this counter.

"Let's get to your apartment real quick. I'm startin' to feel sick."

"Let me help you get up," Pepper said.

"No. I'm fine. Just lead the way. Get me out of here."

All he could see was the top of Patel's shiny head.

What a weasel.

They passed a broken-down couch and trudged up one flight. Pepper opened the front door and sat Gerald down on a kitchen chair. She came out of the bathroom with a pretty powder-blue hand towel, steaming hot.

"Let me wipe off the blood from your nose. How do you feel? Do you need to use the bathroom?"

"No. I'm startin' to feel better. Can you get me something to drink? Some milk?"

"Yes, of course."

When she returned to his side, he asked, "What happened?"

"Well, you saw what happened."

"No. I mean, why did he want $200?"

Pepper said, "It's not the first time he demanded money." She told him about the encounter in the employee lunch room. "He looked even scarier than that day."

"Why does he think you have money?"

"I don't know."

"Pepper, you have a bruise on your face. Let me take care of that."

"No. I'm fine. I'll wash it off once you're feeling better."

"I didn't know you were that tough."

Pepper smiled. "Ouch, that bruise does hurt."

"Go to the bathroom and get another towel."

"Yes, sir." She laughed. "Oh, that hurt even more. Gerald, do you want to stay the night?"

"Yes, please."

"I have an extra blanket. Is it okay if you sleep on the floor next to my bed?"

His head was splitting. All he wanted was something to eat.

"Are you hungry?"

"Starving."

"There's not much. I eat my meals at the Greenwich, but I'll find something."

"I ain't fussy."

"Go lie down on the bed while I throw something together. You'll feel better there."

Gerald did just that.

When he lifted his head, he could see Pepper heating a can of tomato soup and finding a half loaf of French bread in the fridge. She buttered it and put it under the broiler. After she poured milk into a yellow and white striped glass, Gerald dropped his head back on the bedspread.

"I heard you moan. What's wrong?" she said, kneeling by his side.

"It might be worse than I thought. When I closed my eyes, I saw Pablo in the room." It hurt just to say the words.

"Maybe, we should call 911?"

"No. All I need is some food, and I'll be right again."

"Are you sure?"

He nodded.

"The soup is ready."

"Get me up. It smells good."

He ate the entire loaf at her tiny kitchen table.

She handed him two aspirins, which he swallowed with the milk.

After her shower, she handed him another blanket and a pillow and said, "Are you sure everything is okay?"

"Yeah, but no coon from San Francisco is gonna get the best of me. Next time, I'll be ready."

"What's a coon?"

"Racoon. They got teeny-tiny hands, but, somehow, a one got hold of my nose and twisted it."

"You're my hero."

The furnace had warmed the studio apartment, and a country music station played softly. A husky male voice coming from the street below drew her first, and then Gerald, to the window. He stood behind her, up against her clean, cozy nighty. His headache was beginning to recede.

Pepper pulled the curtain back with one finger. Except for a vehicle stopped at an angle, the sidewalk was empty, and the only conversation they heard was the finalization of an easy street bargain.

They fell asleep.

•••

"What you want, Pablo? It's almost two o'clock. I just got home from work"

"Ready, I need some really bad."

"What you want? We been through this shit already. Hang low, bro."

"I just need one more favor. Just gimme a name."

"What you want? Weed?"

"A rock."

"Aight. Here's his cell." Ready recited the numbers. "An' don't call me again."

Pablo called, arranged a meet-up, and found the spot, the abandoned Hibernia Bank at Jones and McAllister.

This is nasty. Ready better be right.

He didn't know whether to stand on the bank steps or the sidewalk. He looked up and down the streets and saw a man walking toward him from Market Street. Pablo's hoodie didn't keep him from shivering, and he felt sick to his stomach.

The man passed and walked up the stairs. He turned and yelled down, "Yo, Pablo?"

"Yeah, you got something for me?" Pablo asked in a hollow, scared voice.

"Yeah, brutha."

"Twenty-five, right?"

"Come up here." The man used one finger to bring Pablo up the stairs. In the dark recesses of old colonnades, the odor of urine filled Pablo's nose. He stood on the top step and gave the man his price. They were face-to-face. Pablo saw scars and a blue tattoo teardrop. Even Pablo felt uneasy and beat it.

He walked to Seventh and Market, ate at a fast-food restaurant, dove into the bathroom, and smoked his buy in a stinking stall. He had spent everything.

It was late. He needed money to get home. Out of harm's way for now, he spotted a tall police officer walking Market next to a shorter cop who looked mean as nails. The cops stopped to shout at a drunk passed out on the sidewalk.

Glad I'm not him.

"Leave him alone. He just wants a place to stay," a passerby said.

The tall one answered the passerby in what could have become a loud shouting match, "You're right. Wanna take him home?"

Pablo kept his head down and was relieved the cop wasn't the one on Broadway.

The short one looked at Pablo and said, "You look like a spook."

Pablo kept going, thinking he could reach Ortiz's house.

•••

Gerald woke up the next morning at half past nine and called Inspector Varton. "I need to talk to you right away."

"What's this about?"

"Pablo Morales."

"Do you know where he is?"

"No, but I want to report a crime." His head started aching again.

"All right. When can you be here?"

"About an hour."

"Fine," Varton answered.

Pepper stood close by in her nighty. "Good-bye, Pepper, and thanks for everything."

"I heard what you said. I'd rather you didn't go."

"Sorry, but this has to be done."

"How are you feeling?"

"Lousy, but I got to run with the big dogs or stay on the porch."

•••

Gerald arrived a little late. The Muni bus was behind schedule. It was half past eleven.

Inspectors Leahy and Trang were waiting inside Inspector Varton's office.

Gerald glanced at the city calendar on Varton's wall. No job and it's Thursday, July 11. He brushed back his greasy hair with his hands. Dressed in the same gray sweatshirt, he said, "How y'all doin?"

"Mr. Smith, please have a seat. What's your business with us today?" Varton asked.

"I have some information about Pablo Morales. I want him arrested right away. Last night, he was inside Pepper's apartment building and attacked her. He said he wanted $200. She doesn't have $200."

"Were you a witness to this attack?"

"Look at my nose."

"Did anyone else witness the incident?" Hieu asked.

"Patel, the lobby clerk."

"Was Morales armed?"

Gerald looked at Larry and said, "I didn't see a gun, if that's what you mean."

Gerald belched and felt dizzy. "I'm worn out. Can't you just arrest this varmint?"

"Inspector Varton, it's almost lunch time." Larry whispered a few words to Varton.

Varton said, "All right. We'll break for lunch and see you after, Mr. Smith."

Gerald exited and could hear Leahy and Trang following right behind.

"We'll go to San Remo's, three blocks from here. Can you make it, Gerald?"

"Thanks, Inspector Leahy. You know when a guy's down on his luck."

"I'll pay for lunch. You need a decent meal."

At the Fior d'Italia, below a thirty-foot-long painting of the Tuscan countryside, Gerald slurped up hot, homemade minestrone soup served in a wild game soup tureen with a pearly swan top. A dark-haired, older waitress who didn't take any hell from anyone stood by. On the clean, white table cloth, a white ceramic plate was jammed full of prosciutto, salami, olives, anchovies, mushrooms, artichoke hearts, provolone cheese, and vegetables cooked in olive oil.

Gerald sampled each one and scarfed them down. He crunched on stiff French bread and washed every scrap down his gullet with fruity red wine.

Larry and Hieu nursed cokes through the meal.

"Mr. Smith, do you have something you wanted to tell Inspector Leahy?"

"Do you gamble?" Larry asked.

"Sometimes, when I went up to Topaz Lake with Cornelius."

"Did Cornelius gamble?"

"A little, never more than $120. What Cornelius liked most was fishing on the lake and hunting. He wanted to spend as much time there as he could. He told me that he wanted to retire there, but he changed his mind."

"Why?" they asked in one voice.

"The winters are cold. Topaz Lake is at 2,500 feet. He went up there in January only for the fishing contest." Gerald asked the waitress for more wine. "He said San Francisco is home."

After the waitress filled Gerald's glass a third time, Larry asked, "Did you see Cornelius lying dead on the floor?"

"If I tell you the truth, will you believe me?"

Larry answered, "Yes. Tell us everything."

"Yes. I went to Cornelius to borrow some money, just like I told you, because O'Hara fired me."

"How did you get in?"

Larry's expression had changed little. . . Gerald was beginning to sense a change.

Something is bothering Larry.

"Maybe, you should limit the amount of wine you're drinking, Gerald."

There it is.

Gerald sat back in his chair and grasped the seat with his hands. "The door to Cornelius' apartment was open slightly, and I pushed it the rest of the way."

"What did you see?"

"Nothing, at first."

"Did you go farther?" Larry asked.

"I saw light, so I thought Cornelius wasn't asleep. I called his name. There was no answer. I walked into the living room and saw him. I can't describe how bad I felt. I walked over to him and knelt. He wasn't breathing."

"Why didn't you call 911?"

"I backed out of the apartment. I didn't know what to do. Here I'm in his apartment, and he's dead."

Gerald saw Hieu's ears take off their little hats in excitement upon hearing him say he was in Cornelius' apartment.

"You had a gun."

"Absolutely not, Inspector Trang. I came there to borrow money. I thought about calling the police. That's when I heard someone coming. The dude came out of the stairwell. It was O'Hara."

Hieu sat forward. "What happened next?"

"I told him he was too late."

"What do you mean?"

Gerald placed both elbows on the table and said, "This is the part where you have to believe me. Both of you have to believe me."

"I believe you. Go on."

Larry accepted his cue. "We believe you. All you have to do is tell us the truth."

"Several days before Cornelius was killed, O'Hara told me he wanted Cornelius dead."

"After he fired you or before?" Larry asked.

"Before. When I told him he was crazy, he fired me. I got it, and he knew it. If I did his dirty work, I could keep my job."

"What do you mean?"

"At first, I didn't want to listen, but he kept talking, and I realized Cornelius was in danger. He was my friend, so I decided to listen. O'Hara said Cornelius was going to reveal information, and he couldn't let that happen. I got the feeling that if I didn't do what O'Hara said, he might kill me, too."

Larry stopped tapping his finger. "What happened next?"

"Well, when I left his apartment and saw O'Hara, I panicked, but I wasn't afraid of him. I was scared that I had been seen coming from Cornelius' apartment. I said, 'You're too late.' I punched him, and it knocked the wind out of him.

"That's when I saw it. There was a gun on the floor. I picked it up, cursed at him, got real close, and polished his face with it. Then I left."

"What happened to the gun?" Larry asked. He reached one hand over his bald head and the other hand followed. Then they came down on the table with a thud. "Where's the gun?"

"I can't remember. It probably fell on the floor. I was angrier than any man could be, and I needed to get away, so I rode the elevator down."

"Did anyone see you leave the building?" Larry asked.

"No, I don't think so."

"Didn't Pepper see you leave?" Hieu asked.

"I got off the elevator and went out the employee entrance in the back."

"What time was it?" they asked simultaneously.

"Around twelve thirty."

"Are you in love with Pepper and would she cover for you?" Hieu asked.

"She's a good girl, no ariana, but we see each other, and sometimes I walk her home."

Larry asked, "What's an ariana?"

Hieu answered, "That's a girly girl."

Larry pressed harder. "Is the rest of what you said true, all of it, Gerald?"

"I swear it on a stack of Bibles."

After a pause, Larry said, "All right."

"Thanks for the lunch and everything, Mr. Leahy."

"I think you and I can agree about one thing. Cornelius was a fine man."

"You're right there, and one more thing. Pablo asked me for money. I refused to give him anything."

"Before or after Cornelius was killed?"

"Before. I didn't ask why he wanted money. I wasn't going to be his man, and after he manhandled Pepper last night, I'm glad as hell I wasn't."

Gerald wondered if he was understood or gave too much information.

On the way back to Central, the sidewalk seemed to weave.

Just keep up with them.

He listened as Larry told the story to Varton.

"Fingerprint him," Varton said.

Gerald looked at Larry. "But . . . but I thought you were happy with me for coming forward. Now you want to fingerprint me. What's going on, man?"

Larry answered very calmly, "A formality. Inspector Trang will get you fingerprinted."

"I've got a job interview at two o'clock." Gerald's shoulders drew back.

"We'll try to get you there on time."

Hieu took Gerald by the arm.

•••

Varton held up a report and told them that Morales had been seen at Seventh and Market. "Take a look. Hieu, we need to review the entire case."

Larry took the report, read it quickly, and handed it to Hieu.

"We're always a few steps behind. What do you think, Larry?"

"I've been making notes on the case. Here."

Larry handed Joe a legal-size notepad.

Varton read aloud:

1) *O'Hara tried to buy land for $50,000 and kept the money in the vault.*
2) *O'Hara got Maureen Daley pregnant.*
3) *Fletcher said $50,000 went missing from a hotel account.*

4) *Chase took $50,000 to Cornelius.*
5) *Security reported two nine-millimeter guns missing.*
6) *The gun lying next to Cornelius is not the murder weapon.*
7) *Smith denied he was in possession of a gun.*
8) *Morales bought a gun and pawned it after the murder.*
9) *Two broken fingernails were found outside the Security office.*

Larry said, "I need to add number ten. Smith says he saw Cornelius dead in his apartment and O'Hara in the hall. Smith says he picked up the gun O'Hara had dropped and left behind. Now, can I have the notepad back?"

"What about these fingernails, Leahy?"

"One is in evidence, and the other I have in a baggie in my office. Larissa handed me the one I put in the baggie. It came out of Morales' pocket."

"Was it hers?"

"She said it wasn't."

"What's their significance?"

"I'm not sure," Larry answered.

"I got a call this morning. They finally got some fingerprints from the gun lying next to MacKenzie. They're Smith's," Varton said, pleased with himself.

"But that's not the gun that killed Cornelius. The gun that killed him is missing. You said so yourself. The fingernails may be the key to solving this. You heard Smith say O'Hara wanted Cornelius dead, but I don't believe O'Hara killed Cornelius either. The killer is somebody else. I just don't know who."

"All right. You have one more day."

"For what?"

"Before Smith is arrested. He admitted he was in Cornelius' apartment. He was the last person to see Cornelius alive."

"Smith doesn't paint his nails!"

When Larry got back to his office, he had difficulty adding number ten. The synesthesia was returning. The numbers weren't really blue.

He left Central at a few minutes before six o'clock.

Lauren stood at the stove. A Jack Daniels bottle had been pushed to the corner of the counter.

"You look tired," she said.

"Did you call Father Ralph?"

Lauren sat down at the table. "He's going on a retreat next Monday. He has a girlfriend. You know that, don't you?"

"That's not true." He looked out the window.

"Ask around. Everyone knows."

"I don't want to know. When I see or hear something I don't like, I keep going as if I didn't. Things work out much better that way."

Lauren showed him her hands. "They're as red as your face."

"Lauren, God sends us trials to make us better. We don't understand them. If we did, they wouldn't be trials. God asks us to have faith and trust in him. God might be testing Ralph. I don't know. Is dinner ready?"

Lauren walked back to the stove.

Larry followed her and continued into the entry hall. He grabbed his jacket off the bannister. Before sitting down, he extracted what was needed and placed it on the plate. Lauren sat down, pushed the jacket into the corner, and reached for a cigarette.

"What's that?" she asked.

Larry smiled. "What does it look like?"

She lifted her elbows, pulled the ashtray closer, and lit up. "Well?"

"I've got two fingernails that match. One I picked up outside the Security office the night of the murder, and the other was given to me by Larissa. She found it inside Pablo's uniform jacket pocket. What a stroke of luck!"

"Whose are they?"

"I signed out of evidence the fingernail I had picked up, so I could compare it with the one Larissa gave me. It proves that Pablo picked up the fingernail outside the Security office just like I did. Whoever lost these fingernails must have been at the Security office. The odds are that she went there and took the other gun, the missing gun."

"What's the difference?" Lauren puffed on her cigarette.

Chapter 16

Friday, July 12

"Larry, it's Hieu. Sorry to bother you at home."

"I'm in a rush to get to Mass. It's . . . a quarter to eight. What's up?"

"Larry, I think I can find Morales."

"How?"

"Larry, you hinted that O'Hara has a secret. It may be a bigger secret than we could imagine. I've got a hunch. You get hunches, and now I have one. I think Morales can tell us something. I've got the phone number for Vega, the kid who was arrested with Angel. I want to reach out to Vega to get to Morales."

"Call Joe. Ask him first."

"Of course."

"No. Let me. Hang on."

Hieu waited.

"All right, Joe says go for it. Good luck, Hieu, and be careful what you do and where you go. Keep it public. Understand?" Larry asked.

"Don't worry. I've been watching you for weeks."

"Very good."

Hieu punched some numbers without delay.

"Mr. Vega, this is Inspector Trang. How are you?"

"I was released, and my lawyer said not to talk to anyone."

"I'm not asking you about your case. We're worried about Pablo. He's a pretty good friend, isn't he?"

"No."

"Okay. I just thought you might be able to help me out." Hieu waited. "Is he with you?"

"Hell no. Call his house."

Hieu heard the click.

What happened between Vega and Pablo?

Hieu punched in the numbers for the Morales home.

A young voice answered, "Hello."

"May I speak to Pablo."

"He ain't here. Who's this?"

"Inspector Trang. Angel, please let me talk to him."

"What for?"

There it is.

"Just let me talk to him. I want to meet him somewhere and talk. Nothing will happen. I'm not going to arrest him."

Hieu could hear some muffled words.

"He said he'll meet with you, but only to talk."

"Good. I promise nothing will happen. Just some talk. Where does he want to meet?"

More muffled words.

"He said Bayview Park. He'll meet you there . . . at the top."

"All right. What time should I be there?" Hieu waited.

More muffled voices.

"Will you be alone?"

"Yes."

"He said in one hour."

"Thanks, man."

Hieu had been to the park before when he worked out of the Bayview Station. He had saved pictures on his phone. One showed a long road to the hilltop. It would take 30-45 minutes to get there. He changed into casual clothes, kissed his wife good-bye, and checked his service revolver.

At the end of Key Street, he found a swinging fence blocking the road and turned off his engine. He left his light brown leather jacket on the front seat and pulled back the sleeves of the cream-colored, slim-fit hoodie picked out by his wife. She had said his tanned forearms looked manly.

He skirted the locked fence, looked up the road, and gave himself ten minutes to reach the top and find Pablo. It was five minutes past nine.

Patches of dry grass ran down the slopes, and he could see a stand of trees at the top. Along the way, he sneezed. Several broom plants with yellow blooms dotted the hillsides, and, if it were not for the seriousness of his mission, he might have enjoyed the hike.

As he rounded a curve, he saw no one and began thinking he had been misled.

Pablo stepped out from behind a red, rocky outcropping. He stood smoking a cigarette, which he threw away. He said something to Angel.

"Hey, Pablo, I appreciate your coming."

"What you want from me?" Pablo stood against a bright blue sky.

"I came alone." Hieu looked over his shoulder down the road.

Pablo was off-balance when they shook hands. His hand felt clammy, not dry as it should have been in the cool morning sunshine.

Angel looked out at Highway 101 and toward San Bruno Mountain.

Above them, eucalyptus branches rasped in the wind.

"How have you been?" Hieu asked.

"Baked."

"What'd you say that for?" Angel asked.

"You should lay off the shit, Pablo," Hieu said. He smelled pungent sweat. "Can we talk for a while?" Hieu looked for some agreement in his face. "Can we walk up to the ridge?"

Pablo shrugged, and Angel followed.

When they got to the top, Hieu stood about five feet from the brothers.

"So, what's your involvement in MacKenzie's death?"

"I got nothing to say about it."

"Okay, no problem."

Hieu didn't like the way he was feeling, uncertain this was the right place or time. He thought about his own past snags, like his repeated efforts to explain his parents' foreign customs to childhood friends, but he didn't want the encounter to be a monologue.

Larry had said, "Murder is like a spinning top. It twirls perfectly in balance. Put too much pressure on one side, and it falls over." But Larry's trouble with his own son and the difficulty he had explaining his father's crime left Hieu questioning how much reliance he could put on anyone other than himself.

Despite the bright sun, he felt gloom surrounding Pablo and watched him looking out in the distance over brown water. His posture, head up, eyes staring out into the distance, gave Hieu the impression that he was searching, but the only noise and action was vehicle traffic and a jet flying overhead.

The three of them stood together without saying a word, and Hieu waited.

Another jet flew over them. Hieu decided the best way to engage Pablo was to talk about his family.

"So, Pablo, where's your father?"

"I don't know, man. I never knew him."

"What about that? Ever want to meet him?"

"No."

"Ever want to talk to him?"

"Yeah, sometimes."

Pablo's wife beater had remnants of small, weedy spurs stuck to it. He leaned against the red rock and pulled out his cigarette pack. Angel asked for one.

Hieu stood above them and, despite a dislike for cigarette smoke, took a couple steps closer. A few clumps of sod were all that was between them.

"Pablo, we can talk to each other. There's something you want to say, and no one will listen. So, let's talk."

"About what?" Pablo sucked on his cigarette. A nose jet blew away like a memory to be forgotten, and Hieu waited.

"Tell me about the problem eating you up."

"You won't think I'm sick. It won't make you sick . . . will it?"

"No." Hieu waited.

"I'm not what everyone thinks. It won't make you think I'm weird or something if I tell you?"

Angel said, "Don't say nothing. You can't trust him."

Pablo lit another cigarette, and his head rose slowly.

Hieu kept his balance on a single dirt clod.

Suddenly, Pablo took off.

Hieu gave chase down the road.

In seconds, Hieu had him by the arm.

Pablo tried to push him away and shrieked, "I'm not what you think, dude. Get your hands off me."

Hieu tightened his grip, ready to take a bigger man down, and shouted, "What the hell's wrong with you, Pablo?"

Pablo pulled up and swung at Hieu. Hieu caught his fist and pushed it up, grabbed him around his waist, and felled him on the weedy road. Hieu straddled Pablo and put a forearm across his neck.

Once he had been subdued and appeared to be wounded, Hieu slowly got up and took a few steps back.

"Now, get up and don't move."

Hieu's heartbeat was in his mouth, and he felt as if he were still astride Pablo and pinning him to the gravelly rubble. Hieu planted both feet firmly on the downward grade to keep himself from falling.

Pablo slowly stood up.

Hieu noticed a scrape on Pablo's face and reached into his pocket for a handkerchief. "Sorry about that."

Angel came running down the hill. His eyes were big and scared.

Pablo touched his cheekbone, and said, "Shiiiit, what'd you do that for, bro?"

"You gave me no choice." Hieu waited.

Pablo shook his head and stared at Hieu.

"Look, man, let's just be friends. I'm not here to arrest you or get inside your head."

Angel brushed off tiny specs of debris wherever he could find them on Pablo.

Pablo said, "Stop it."

His voice had changed. It was fraternal.

"You just owned me, and now you wanna talk. Leave me alone."

Hieu thought the encounter was finished, so he turned to Angel and said, "Your brother's okay. It's over." Hieu was about to leave when something inside himself changed. He heard his mother saying, "Church isn't out 'till they stop singing."

"Look, Pablo, I know you think I'm the enemy, but you've got to see things differently. Just let it out."

"No way."

Will he sing?

Angel repeated, "No way."

Pablo looked down at his feet, paced, and whispered, "I'm gay."

"What's you say that for, Pablo?" Angel pushed his brother on the arm.

Pablo pushed back, and regret appeared on his face, regret for not living right, regret for being a bad brother, regret for being a bad son. It was all there for Hieu to see.

"You don't look so good. What you go on and say that for, bro? Let's go."

Pablo put his arm around Angel and gave him a hug.

Hieu breathed deeply. "Right. I'm glad you told me."

Hieu was close enough to see Pablo's cracked lips and unclear eyes.

"I have friends who are gay. They're okay, just like my brother." Angel looked at Pablo and said, "You gotta accept what you are."

"It doesn't make you hate me?"

"No," Hieu pled.

"I don't like people."

"No one?"

"You don't know what it's like."

"Yes, I do." Hieu reached out a hand and said, "I get it. It's not that bad, Pablo. No one's going to hate you."

"That's right, Pablo."

"Yeah, they are, Larissa, my mother, everyone, except Angel. They hate my ass. I hate myself. Do you understand that?" Pablo asked angrily.

"I don't like myself sometimes. Everyone feels that way."

"No! You're a cop. You got it all going right. Not me."

"Why not stop? Stop running away. Find someone to run to?"

"Who? Who'd want me?"

"You need someone to talk to, someone who listens, someone who knows what you're going through . . . like me." The look of astonishment on Pablo's face confirmed that it must have been the right thing to say.

"You mean that?"

Hieu brushed off his pants and said, "Yes."

"Sorry, man, about your clothes."

"It's all right. So, what about it? Are we friends?"

Hieu stuck out his hand and waited.

"What do you want from me?"

Hieu spotted his notepad lying on the road and picked it up. A few feet further down the roadway was his pen. Pablo picked it for him.

"Here's my phone number." He scribbled the numbers and handed Pablo the page from his notepad. "Put it in your pocket. Call me when you want to talk. I'll always answer, no matter what."

"Thanks, man. No one ever did that for me. Why you doin' this for me? I mean, you're a cop."

Angel pulled on his brother's arm again.

"Let's just say, I think you need me . . . and maybe I need you, too. You can't run for the rest of your life."

"Aren't you going to arrest me?"

"What for? Did you kill MacKenzie?"

"No way."

"I just want you to stay out of trouble. Let's leave it at that."

"What? You're a cop. I did a whole bunch of shit lately."

"I'm also a man, and I want to help you out."

"So, you just gonna let me go?"

"Yep. Shake on it?"

"Sure."

Hieu shook hands with Pablo and then Angel.

Without looking back, he walked down the long road, pulled the light brown leather jacket from the car seat, carefully put it on over a sore shoulder, got into his vehicle, and looked up for the last time at Pablo and Angel standing next to each other. On the way to Central, he began framing a report for Larry. Pablo had stolen nothing, although he had made several attempts, so the most he could be charged with was attempted robbery by force.

Did I do the right thing, letting him go?

•••

Pablo stood at the corner of Eighteenth and Castro and spotted the same blond-haired panhandler.

The sun was directly above. No one would recognize him, because it wasn't Saturday.

He threw his cigarette into the street, but a slight breeze blew the butt to the edge of the panhandler's kaftan. He picked it up and asked Pablo for a light. The panhandler puffed a couple of times and stuffed the butt into his belongings. The dog lying next to him moved.

"Hey, bro, I need to make a buy. Whacha got?"

"What?"

"Any good shit?" Pablo felt like walloping him.

"Nah, I don't sell, bro."

Liar.

"Know anyone around here who does?"

"Sorry."

Pablo started walking down Eighteenth Street. His pace was slow, and he asked the same question of every person lying in a doorway. The same two cops he had seen before walked past. He noticed them talking to a man lying in one of the doorways. Pablo's thoughts were muddled, and he felt himself moving slowly.

The female cop caught up. "Whacha doing out here, today? It's not even lunch time."

Pablo stepped back. "Nothing." Words were slow in coming. "I was supposed to meet someone."

"Who?" she asked. "You're slurring your words."

"Just a friend . . . a girl."

Wish it was Saturday.

"You were asking if anyone had some meth. Weren't you?"

"No! I was just kidding." He wiped his brow and his mouth.

"Turn around."

Pablo snapped to. He knew what was coming next.

Dolores Park is close. It won't be crowded. I can outrun her.

He took off. When he got to the bottom of the park, he looked up. The view was enough to make him sick, but he knew he could make it.

The chain that clipped the wallet to his belt jingled on the grassy slope as he passed the children's playground. When he looked back, the bold, gold paint on an old church dome blurred his vision. The cops were at the bottom, and, at that moment, every sound, whether of man or nature, died.

He picked out a sunbathing couple sitting under a row of new palm trees. Their baby crawled around on the grass and chewed a pacifier. Dampened by warm sweat pouring down his face, he asked for some water. The woman was dressed in a blue tank top, and her husband had a long beard and a blue and yellow checkered shirt that made Pablo dizzier. The man adjusted his dark-framed glasses. She handed Pablo a bottled water. He drank half, poured the remainder over his head, took off his wife-beater off, and wiped his face.

He couldn't hear what she said. The cops were passing the dog-play area and getting closer. He threw the plastic bottle down and ran up the hill, veered to the right, and tripped over the shiny J Church streetcar tracks. He tried to focus on the big homes above a wall that divided the street into one-way traffic. Up he went on the stairs imbedded in the wall. The upper street made him invisible to the cops.

Outside a big house with a dark blue garage door, there was a black Lexus and a tall man about to get into the driver's seat. Pablo rushed to his side and, leaning with all his weight, pinned the man against the car door.

"Dude, can I have a ride? I . . . lost my friend, and I don't have any money to get home."

Cracker.

The man shook his head. Pablo put his hand into his pants pocket. "I have a knife. Now, get in the car." Pablo put his hand on top of the man's head, pushed down, and pushed him inside. He ran around to the other side and jumped in.

"What do you want?"

"Start driving and shut up." Pablo reached across and, with his right hand, clamped on the man's chin, jerked his face sharply and said, "Get going."

"You want money?" the man asked, his words nearly muted by Pablo's wet fingers.

Pablo let go and grabbed the outside of his pants pocket. "I have a knife."

The man backed out of his driveway and stammered, "Where to?"

"Just go."

Pablo rolled down the passenger window and felt the breeze cooling his bare chest and neck. They drove for ten minutes, Pablo directing the way. At Market and Van Ness, Pablo saw a parked taxi cab. "Give me a twenty, and I'll let you go."

The man pulled out his wallet.

Pablo opened it wide.

He grabbed bills.

He jumped out.

Chapter 17

Friday, July 12

Larry sat in his office and waited for Hieu's return.

He had picked up a new history book from a local book seller. The third chapter caught his notice.

Emperors Diocletian and Galerius shared power amicably. Under an order from Diocletian, St. Romanus of Caesarea had his tongue cut out. After Diocletian retired, Galerius issued the Edict of Toleration in 311AD, declaring publicly that the persecution of the Christians had failed.

He thought about Constantine, who would succeed and preside over the Catholic council that issued the Nicene Creed.

The phone rang.

Is it Mark?

"Inspector Leahy, we have a possible jumper at the Golden Gate Bridge. We believe the jumper is Pablo Morales."

"How do you know it's Morales?"

"The cab driver gave a description: Hispanic male, twenty to twenty-five, short dark hair, tattoos on hands, pierced eyebrow. Before the cabbie knew where they were headed, he asked his passenger what his name was."

"Has Inspector Varton been notified?"

"Affirmative. Inspector Varton has been notified."

"And the Negotiation Team?"

"Affirmative. The Negotiation Team is on the way."

"Thank you. I'm on my way."

Larry punched number five for Father Ralph.

"Ralph, I need you right away. We have a jumper on the Golden Gate Bridge. I can pick you up in ten minutes. Can you be ready?"

"Yes, of course."

The red Chevy siren blared.

Five minutes later, Larry reached across and pushed the door open. "It's Pablo Morales."

"Pablo Morales?"

"Employee at the Greenwich. We've been trying to find him. We think he may be involved in Cornelius' murder."

"I see."

Father Ralph opened his breviary and read the passage he had prepared.

Behold my servant, whom I uphold, my chosen, in whom my soul delights; I have put my Spirit upon him, he will bring forth justice to the nations. . . He will not fail or be discouraged till he has established justice in the earth; and the coastlands wait for his law.
Isaiah 42

"The coastlands on either side of the bridge are waiting. Let's do some good today."

"Pray God has mercy on this young man."

Pray God has mercy on us for our part in it.

When they arrived, the Negotiation Team was already on scene. Vehicles moved unimpeded in all lanes but the one next to the walkway. Spectators near the action huddled in small groups like mourners. Larry pulled up behind a police vehicle and turned off his engine. It was near the middle of the bridge. The ugly suicide prevention barrier was yet to be constructed.

Larry looked at his watch: a few minutes before one o'clock.

Both men leapt out and rushed to the waist-high, easily-scaled railing. Larry's coarse hands ran across the prickly surface, and they stood just a few feet from a set of cables securing the roadbed to the suspension cable. It was anything but peaceful.

Pablo was perched on a beam below and leaning outward. From above, he looked like a circus acrobat. Gusts of wind brought up the smell of salt and fish and mixed with engine exhaust. The sound of tires hitting sections of the pavement had the rhythm of a freight train rolling across tracks. The deck trembled.

The straps of Pablo's wife-beater clung to his shoulders, and he looked sweaty, weak, and cold in the fierce gale.

Father Ralph held onto his black fedora.

Larry's legs felt like mush. Leaning over the rail induced an unwanted memory of a family trip at age ten, when the Grand Canyon had gifted him with a fear of heights. The gale whipped off cold sweat beads that tried attaching to his forehead.

"Ralph, hold onto me. I get sick out here."

Larry turned in the other direction and shouted, "I know this young man. May we talk with him?" Larry could barely hear the answer. The cold wind howled and the ringing sound that came when he was in high places started.

"Has he spoken?" Larry asked.

The officer stepped toward Larry and shouted, "Very little. We got here about ten minutes ago. He's a wobbler."

Larry yelled, "Pablo, I didn't expect to find you here...what's wrong? It's Inspector Leahy. I have Father Ralph with me. Can we please talk?" Larry wasn't sure Pablo could hear. He felt Ralph's firm hand and smelled burning rubber.

"Hey, man, go away and leave me alone."

"Pablo, I know things are tough right now and everything's going wrong but think this through. Is this what you really want?"

"Back off!"

"Okay, okay, I'm here. I'll stay right here." Larry kept his eyes focused on Pablo's left hand gripping the cold, thick, steel cable.

"I didn't do it."

"Just give me your hand, and we can talk about it."

"No."

Larry looked down at the swirling whitecaps. He wanted to keep Pablo looking up at him, but he wasn't sure Pablo could see his face in the glare of the bright sun.

"You talk to him."

"Pablo, this is Father Ralph."

Now he may listen.

Pablo would not look up.

"Pablo, tell me how it went down," Larry shouted.

"I stole the gun from the office. O'Hara gave me $500 and I blew it. I can't get out of this now."

Larry turned to Father Ralph and asked, "What did he say?"

"He says he stole a gun from the Security office. Is that the gun that killed Cornelius?"

"No, I don't think so."

Larry's straining to hear voices was increasing. "Yes, you can get out of this. There's hope, Pablo. Just look up at me. Look at my face, Pablo."

"I saw Chase at the office. I didn't kill MacKenzie. I swear it."

"Look up at me. Tell me again what you just said, but this time, look at me."

Father Ralph pleaded, "Pablo, think about your family and how sad they will be. They need you. Think about your mother."

The wind blew so fiercely it hurt the backs of Larry's ears.

Larry yelled, "Your son needs a dad, Pablo, and Larissa needs a man to raise her son. Look at me. I spoke to your mom, and she told me you couldn't have killed that man. She knows you're in trouble but not capable of murder . . . she told me 'I didn't raise a killer!' She believes you, Pablo . . . and so do I . . . my job is to find the killer. . . I need your help to get you out of this mess . . . help me clear your name . . . for your mother . . . for you. . ."

"Look after my brother."

Larry gulped the wind and exhaust.

At that moment, Father Ralph's fedora blew off.

Pablo let go.

Larry said, "Shit."

Father Ralph made the sign of the cross.

The distant splash was inaudible.

The sun kept shining.

Time drifted.

Larry heard Varton's cowboy boots on the sidewalk. "Too bad. Troubled kid. Not surprising it ended this way."

Larry snapped to attention. "Shut up, Varton. C'mon Father, we've got nothing more to do here."

On the way to Loyola House, Larry said, "I wish we had done the job."

"Larry, death has a certain kind of logic. For Pablo, death was a release. We shouldn't despair over it. Pray God forgave him in that moment. Because of our own limitations, we cannot possibly understand, and God will take care of Pablo and bring him home."

Street signs passed by without notice or significance.

Father Ralph pulled a prayer card from his breviary and left it on the seat.

Larry joined in reciting a Hail Mary; Father Ralph read the prayer for the dead; they concluded with another Hail Mary.

Larry's left hand gripped the steering wheel. "Over and over I heard God saying, 'take my hand and come with me.' If only Pablo would have taken my hand."

"I know. God has his hand now." He slipped a small crucifix into Larry's and said, "You may need this."

•••

In Joe's office, a debriefing occurred.

Hieu listened quietly and somberly.

"I'm sorry for what I said, Joe."

"Like I said, I expected as much from this kid."

"Pablo said O'Hara gave him $500 to buy a gun."

"What!"

"Well, now we know where the missing $500 went. O'Hara wanted Pablo to kill Cornelius. He must have propositioned Pablo the same way he propositioned Gerald Smith, and Pablo agreed. He must have used the $500 O'Hara gave him and bought a gun at Burton High School for less. With the extra money and the money from pawning the gun, he could buy more dope. So, it looks like he stole the gun from the Security office and changed his mind, which is why O'Hara was there, to make sure Pablo did the deed. If Pablo didn't kill Cornelius, who did? Smith told us Cornelius was already dead, and that was before he saw O'Hara, so O'Hara couldn't have killed Cornelius."

Varton said, "The gun found next to Cornelius had Smith's fingerprints on it, but it wasn't the gun that killed Cornelius. It was the other gun from the Security office that killed Cornelius. We've got to find that gun." He stood up and said, "Right. Let's go to the Greenwich. I want to personally arrest O'Hara."

"Wait. Does Smith own a gun," Varton asked.

"No, I don't think he does," Larry answered.

"And he never stole a gun from the Greenwich?"

"No."

•••

After leaving Central, Larry called Father Ralph.

Larry felt his heart pounding, his vision blurring, and his neck hurting.

How do I tell Ralph our mutual friend had plotted to murder his Cornelius?

"Ralph, it's Larry."

"Any more news about Pablo?"

"No. The reason I called is James."

"I'm sure he is worried about the effects of the suicide on the hotel."

"No. James is going to be arrested."

"What? Why? Surely, he couldn't have had anything to do with Pablo's death."

Larry took a moment to find his courage before continuing.

"James solicited Pablo and Gerald Smith to kill Cornelius."

Silence met him at the other end.

"Ralph? Are you still there?"

"I don't believe you. James loved Cornelius."

"Talk to him yourself. Only you better do it quick and ask him why he was at the Greenwich on the night Cornelius died."

"I will. Good-bye, Larry."

"And do not tell him he will be arrested."

Larry heard the line go dead.

•••

Father Ralph's hands shook as he hung up the phone.

Why would Larry say such things?

James is like a brother.

Larry is lying. . . or he's crazy.

He's too old to be doing police work.

He doesn't know what he's talking about.

Father Ralph dialed his old friend's number.

"O'Hara."

Father Ralph's other hand hit his desk blotter when James answered.

"It's me," Father Ralph responded in a weakened voice. He wanted to leave his office and be alone.

"Oh. It's you, Ralph. How are you?"

Father Ralph slowly said, "Larry . . . Larry told me something I don't believe. I just wanted to check in with you. You know about the suicide?"

"That kid was nothing but trouble for me. I'm not surprised."

"James, Larry said something else. He said . . . he said you solicited Pablo to kill Cornelius."

Silence met him at the other end.

Father Ralph continued, "I know it's outlandish . . ."

"It is," O'Hara interrupted.

His denial brought Father Ralph a jolt of relief.

"So, what do you think happened to Cornelius? I'm so frustrated, James. I need answers."

"Larry is unable to solve the murder. He's grasping at straws to save himself from drowning in the investigation. I wouldn't believe a word he says. You don't believe him, do you?"

James sounds a little uncertain.

"I don't want to, but why would a man who was about to jump off a bridge say that?"

"You know people. In desperation, a man might say anything."

"I'm just after the truth . . . and so is Larry."

"So am I."

"Then why were you at the Greenwich before I found Cornelius? I thought you were at the party all night?"

"I was. Who said I was at the Greenwich?"

"Larry."

There was an unnerving silence, and Father Ralph sensed that a crossroad had been reached in the conversation. He got out of his chair and paced. The edge of his desk became a formidable adversary when he bumped into it. He sat down and stretched out his leg. It felt stiff.

I might have a heart attack.

"I've got to go – lots of work to do."

"I want an answer."

Father Ralph felt his heart rate rising.

"What if I said that Pablo wanted to kill Cornelius?" James quickly added.

"Why?"

"All I know is what Pablo told me."

"Then . . . it's true. You talked to Pablo about it."

"I may have, but it wasn't important."

"Why didn't you tell Larry or me?"

"It's Larry's investigation, not mine."

Father Ralph's anger was growing.

"That's no answer. You promised to protect Cornelius. You obviously didn't keep that promise. You're not as innocent as you pretend to be. And when's the last time you went to confession?"

"I don't need confession. Why should a man confess to another man?"

"Christ is present in the confessional. You want to come see me?"

"No. I have no need to see you and nothing to confess."

"I think you do. Tell me now what you did!"

"I'm busy. Good-bye, Ralph."

James had dropped the ball, and Father Ralph's confidence in him hit the floor.

Could Larry be right?

•••

Minutes later, at 2:45 p.m., Varton pushed open the double doors and walked past Ms. Keck into O'Hara's office. O'Hara swung around in his chair. Varton crossed the room.

"Stand up. You are under arrest for solicitation to commit murder."

"What? What's the idea of barging into my office?"

"Turn around."

"You have the right to remain silent. Anything you say can and will be used against you in a court of law. You have the right to an attorney. If you cannot afford an attorney, one will be provided for you. Do you understand the rights I have just read to you? With these rights in mind, do you wish to speak to me?"

"I pay your salary."

Varton reached into his pocket and said, "Here's your nickel," as he poked him in the eye with it. The cigar fell onto the plush rug. Varton pulled the handcuffs off his belt, and the sound of them clicking shut disturbed only one man, the man whose grand office was now witness to the odor of a hole burning into the carpet and a trail of smoke spiraling toward the chandelier.

O'Hara was led out.

Larry left Varton's triumphant side and entered the lobby.

Larissa saw Larry coming toward her and seemed to sense what was coming.

He rushed her down the hall to the lunch room.

"My baby will never know his father."

Larry reached inside his jacket pocket and placed the crucifix in front of her on the lunch room table, but sitting with her, there in the room, the heat was all wrong, the setting was all wrong, and the outcome was all wrong. He started to cry with Larissa. The unkindness of the world filled the room, and he hoped he had nothing to do with it.

Back in his office at Central, Larry read Hieu's report on Pablo.

Silence meant the seagull chicks were gone. The sky was gray, and Hieu was the only bright spot.

The desk phone rang, and Larry toyed with the idea of not answering it. He smelled dust and sneezed.

"Sir, I have something for you. A fisherman turned in a black hat drifting near Pier 47. He turned it over to the coast guard, and a courier brought it in."

"Thanks. Any news on Pablo Morales?"

"The body of Mr. Morales was found at 1530 hours and is with the Medical Examiner."

The service aide walked in and handed Hieu the black fedora.

Larry reached over and took the hat from Hieu.

He quickly pushed it into a bottom drawer.

"I'll call Father Ralph and let him know."

"I'm sorry about what happened."

Larry cleared his throat. "Thanks, Hieu. You did the best you could. Let's talk to Joe."

Hieu followed Larry into Joe's office.

Through a glittering smile, Joe said, "I re-interviewed O'Hara in his jail cell. I was surprised he was willing to talk. He admitted to entering MacKenzie's room. He repeated the claim that Smith killed MacKenzie. I asked him if he knew where the missing gun was, and he said no. Are you any closer to finding the gun?"

"No. I'd like to visit Larissa at home."

Varton said, "She was informed, Larry."

"I'm hoping we can find out something more from her."

"Doubt it. The kid committed suicide. Smith and O'Hara were in the apartment. We know the kid wasn't and that he bought a gun and pawned it the day after the murder. What can Larissa add?"

"Remember the fingernails? Maybe, she can tell us more."

"Well, it can't hurt. Go for it."

Larry called Larissa from his own office phone.

She had been excused from work and agreed to a meeting at her home.

"Should we bring something?" Hieu asked.

"What can we bring?"

"Fresh flowers from my mom's garden. Would she like them?"

"Sure. My plan is to tell her we want to clear Pablo's name."

Father Ralph answered his phone and agreed to come along.

Hieu's mother walked quickly to Central and gave him a bunch of English lavender with the bottoms of the stems wrapped in dampened paper towels covered by tin foil and purple wrapping paper with white polka dots.

They drove to Quesada and waited at Larissa's door.

"Hello, Mr. Leahy. Please come in. The baby is with my mother."

"Larissa, this is Father Ralph MacKenzie."

"Nice to meet you, Father. Please come this way."

They sat down in the living room as if they were waiting for someone else to arrive.

Father Ralph said a Hail Mary, and Larry joined in.

"Larissa, I have a few questions I'd like to ask. It will take just a few minutes. Okay?" Larry said.

"Yes. I know Pablo is innocent."

"You gave me a fingernail that was in Pablo's jacket pocket." He pulled out his baggie and emptied its contents onto the coffee table. Larissa picked up a baby rattle and held it. "Please take another look. You'll see that the fingernails match. One is the fingernail you gave me, and the other is a fingernail I picked up outside the Security office."

Everyone looked at the evidence.

"On the night of the incident, I remember Pepper's fingernails were broken. Did you talk to Pepper at any time during the night?"

"Yes. You know I sit close to the front desk. We talk to each other when neither of us is busy."

"How did Pepper appear to you? Was there anything that had upset her?"

"What I remember is that she passed the switchboard and talked about breaking a nail."

That's what I saw.

"Did you see the nail polish Pepper was wearing?"

"Yes. We talked about it earlier. Pepper had her nails done the day before and was so happy with them." Larissa held back the tears.

"What color were her fingernails?"

"Glittery black with red and blue stripes, the same as those."

"It wasn't red or another color?"

"No. The next day she had her nails redone in red."

Larry placed the nails back inside the baggie and said, "Inspector Trang, Father Ralph, and I will be at Pablo's funeral."

"Thank you so much. The memorial is Sunday."

Back in Joe's office, the aide came in and told Larry he had a phone call. He rushed to his office. "Hello. I'll see you at . . . five o'clock."

Hieu walked in and asked, "Who was that?"

"Gerald. I asked him to call me. First, let's have a chat with Pepper Chase."

"Joe said he wanted Smith arrested. He doesn't believe his story."

"I know. I'll stall him."

Larry came back from Joe's office and said, "We have one more day until Smith is arrested. We've got an interview to do."

"Larry, let me question Pepper. We gotta put the squeeze on this girl."

Larry and Hieu arrived at the Greenwich at just after four o'clock and were told that Pepper was a no-show for two days.

"Let's go to her apartment," Larry said.

They entered her apartment building and climbed the stairs to the second floor. He put his finger to his lips and listened at her door. He knocked. No one answered. They walked back to the lobby and asked Patel if he had seen Pepper that morning, and he said no.

Larry's phone call to her went to voice mail.

"Call my number, Patel, as soon as she arrives. Hieu, wait for me at the Greenwich. I'm going to pay a visit to Gerald Smith."

Larry patted Hieu on the arm and headed on foot for Gerald's apartment.

Outside, a transaction moved to the edge of the sidewalk.

Inside, the lobby was desolate. It was half past four.

Gerald answered. "Come on in, Inspector."

"I'm early. How did the job interview go?"

"It didn't work out. I was late."

"Sorry about that Gerald."

"It's okay. I'll get a job sooner or later. There are a lot of jobs out there."

"Gerald, did Cornelius keep fire arms at Topaz Lake?'

"His rifles."

"Anything else?"

"No."

"Where did he hunt?"

"Sweetwater Mountains. Mostly ducks, birds, and rabbits." Gerald smoothed the back his hair and asked, "Why?"

Larry walked around the room and looked in the closet.

"What are you doing?"

"Just making sure there are no guns in your apartment."

"I told you I don't own a gun. When are you going to start trusting me?"

"It's habit."

"I'm not real educated, but I think you're trying to figure me out . . . or is it something else?"

"What do you mean?" Larry stopped looking.

"Remember you told me about your son?"

"Did I?" Larry stopped at the fishing rod and sat down on the kitchen chair.

"Well, something's eatin' you up. Is it about Trang?"

"What about him?"

"I think you like him . . . something about him and your son."

"You don't know what you're talking about."

"Okay."

"Ever heard of Ansel Adams?"

There aren't any pictures in his apartment.

"No."

"You like the Sierras. Adams took photographs of Yosemite and the Sierras. Black and white pictures with shadows as his focus."

"You a photographer?"

"Amateur photographer. I like old San Francisco. Some pictures hang in my office."

"Any of the family?"

Larry closed his eyes for a moment. "Yes."

"Your son and you don't see eye-to-eye? Right?"

"Sometimes."

"How come?" Gerald asked.

"He's living with a woman. That's not the way I raised him." Larry saw Gerald looking at him intently from the sofa.

"Maybe he'll make an honest woman of her." Gerald picked up a fly and admired it. "If I had a dad like you, I'd do my best to make him happy."

"What about Pepper?" Larry asked.

"I'm pretty ornery. She needs someone really, really stable." Gerald opened his fly-tying box. "So, what is it you really want to know?"

"Have you dated her?"

"Nope." Gerald looked at Larry.

"Tell me more about her."

"Say what you wanna say."

"Has she ever . . . well, let me put it this way . . . were you ever suspicious of her?"

"No."

"Would you have given her a gun if she asked?"

"Not on your life. Besides, she's happier than a tick on a stray dog. If you're thinking she shot Cornelius, I would say you have the wrong person. Besides, she told me she loved him."

"Okay. Thanks. I appreciate it."

"Any time."

That confirms it – she stole the gun.

Larry stood up and said, "Gerald, you may be arrested."

Gerald dropped a fly and jumped up. "What? You waited all this time to tell me. You're my friend, aren't you?"

"Hang on a minute. Let me explain. Morales is dead."

"I know."

"O'Hara was arrested for soliciting a murder."

"See. I told you."

"Varton has no other suspects. That's about all I can tell you for now. I have a plan, but I need your help. No one else knows about it, and I can tell you only some of it."

"What's my part?" he said in that Texas drawl.

"We can't find Pepper. Call her. If she answers, ask to meet for dinner. If she doesn't answer, leave a voicemail asking her to return the call."

"No problem there." He picked up his cell phone and punched in her number.

They waited.

"Hi. This is Gerald. I been looking for you. Call me. I want to see you." He looked at Larry. "Now what?"

"Perfect. Just wait for her call. Try to find out where she is. Say you want to invite her to dinner, and you will pay for it, and ask where she is. Do you think she will say 'yes'?"

"I don't know, but I'll think of something."

"Good. I'll ask Varton for another day, maybe two."

Chapter 18

Saturday, July 13

Gerald moped around his apartment.

Check her apartment and then the Greenwich.

No one answered his knock at Pepper's door. Four o'clock.

Fearful now of being seen in the Greenwich, he stayed close to the walls of the buildings on the same side of the street as the hotel and entered through the garage.

He heard a man and a boy and some scuffling at the other end, but they were too far away to be recognized.

The man shoved the boy against a car. It sounded like a clunk. He stuck his finger in the boy's face.

Gerald ran in their direction and yelled, "Back off, dude."

When he was close enough, he issued a warning. "Leave him alone or I'll knock the inlays out of your mouth. Oh, it's you, Ready. I seen you do this before. You on duty?"

Ready nodded.

"Then, get yur ass upstairs."

Ready slinked away.

"Is that you, Josh?"

"Yeah. Thanks for helping me."

"He ever done that to you before?"

"He's a gangbanger and tries it on all the guys."

"Are you okay?"

"Yeah, I'm fine."

"He on drugs or something?"

"I don't think so."

"He was a friend of Pablo's, wasn't he?" Gerald knew he was.

"Yep."

"Well, we don't have to worry about Pablo anymore."

"Why?"

"He killed himself – jumped off a bridge. That dumb Mexican is no loss to anyone."

"Yeah, I know what you mean."

"Are we good?"

"Yeah."

"All right, you don't have to worry. Ready will stay out of your way 'till all this crazy shit is over."

Gerald shook hands with Josh and watched him go up the stairs into the hotel. He wanted to follow but knew that was a bad idea and gave up the search for Pepper.

•••

Father Ralph soberly entered St. Ignatius Church for the 4:00 p.m. start of confessions. He looked up at the mahogany confessional's ornate wood trim and avoided eye contact with those standing in line, opened the middle door, turned on the green light, sat down, and slid his screen to the right.

He heard the other door open and close and the weight of a person pressing down on the kneeler. The grill on the penitent's side allowed him to see only a lattice pattern superimposed on a shadowy face.

"Bless me, Father, for I have sinned. It's been one month since my last confession."

The grill failed to suppress a strong dose of pikake, and the aroma left him feeling wedged in the corner of the box.

She needn't have said more, but she did.

"How are you, Ralph?"

"Tell me your sins."

"I had a terrible argument with him."

"Who and how many times?"

"Ronny. Once. It was last night."

"Are there any other sins?"

"I'm unable to stop thinking about you. Ronny angrily reminded me of our wedding day and the vows we took. Am I entertaining impure thoughts when I think of you?"

At this moment, a screen and a grill could not protect him from the release of double-barreled words.

Is it the time and place to tell her?

He knew this could not be done in the confessional and pressed on.

"Any other sins?"

"No, but have I sinned every time I think about you, every time I see you and when we kiss?"

"Joyce, don't," Father Ralph warned. "We can't talk about this here. Do you have any other sins to confess?"

"No, I guess not."

"Say the Act of Contrition."

"I . . . can't."

"You must."

"Stop hurting me," she pleaded.

"Say the Act of Contrition." When she didn't, he spoke in a stern voice, "Go outside. Wait at the communion rail. I will see you there."

"What about the others in line?"

"Please do what I say."

The moment of absolution, which brings the golden sound of peace, never came.

He heard her get up off the kneeler.

One of his hands removed his stole, and the other turned the knob.

Outside the confessional, he said to those standing in line, "Please go over to the other priest. I'm very sorry. I have an emergency."

Their reaction was astonishment, sighs, and disappointed looks.

At the communion rail, Father Ralph led her to the sacristy and sat her down in the red velvet chair.

"Why did you come to me for confession, Joyce?"

"Did I do something wrong? You're a priest."

"I told you before to see the other priest. There are two on duty every Saturday. Now, listen to me."

She silently obeyed.

Father Ralph ran his hands through his black hair. She wore the same black overcoat, but the yellow scarf was missing. "We cannot see each other anymore."

"Why? What's happened? Is it about your brother?"

"Yes. I've realized that I must be true to myself, to Cornelius and Anne, and my mother, and, above all, to my Jesuit brothers. You can cheat them, but you can't cheat yourself. I'm sorry to disappoint you. I can't say more."

She jumped up, plucked the stole out of his hand, and threw it to the floor. "You led me down this path. How can you just cut me off? No concern for me or my feelings. I should slap you."

"Go ahead. I deserve it."

She started to cry. "No, I'm still in love with you. I can't believe this is happening." She held up both hands and asked, "What did I do wrong?" but before he could answer, she turned away.

He spoke to her back. "Please, Joyce, go to the other priest for confession. Do not try to contact me."

From behind he watched as she raised a hand to her face.

Then, she left without uttering another word.

He hoped he wouldn't see her again, but, for one moment, he allowed himself to grieve over a lost future together.

Then, he pulled himself together and returned to the box.

Chapter 19

Sunday, July 14

At Holy Cross Cemetery in Colma, on the other side of San Francisco's only land boundary, a bitter wind blew around marble crypts and wide, wet slopes, below the colossal, rounded sandcastle known as San Bruno Mountain. Bundled-up mourners gathered in small groups. A purple stole weighed down the presiding priest's surplice.

Father Ralph sat in the front passenger seat and looked at Larry. "O'Hara betrayed me."

"So, now you believe."

"I was in denial. Somehow, I always knew that O'Hara was capable of something like this, but friendship and pride got in the way of seeing the depth of his fear. I apologize for doubting you."

"I know. It took me time to get past memories to reach the truth about O'Hara and his evil scheme to have Cornelius killed. Our friendship is unbroken. Isn't it?"

"Of course."

Larry paused. "Ralph, I explained to you who Angel is. Now, I want you to pay for his education."

"But I hardly know the boy."

Hieu sat in the back seat and poked Larry in the shoulder. "Tell him, Larry."

"You heard Pablo ask us to take care of his brother. After that, I started thinking, how can I help? I thought of you." Larry looked out at the mourners and back at Father Ralph. "I'm sorry to have to bring this up, but it's necessary. You've been seeing a woman." He cleared his throat. "She has bragged about gifts, like a diamond studded clip, the foolish woman. You reoutfitted the family boat, and you've been seen taking her out on the bay. Secrets have a way of . . . spanking us. Yours is a secret no more. Do I need to go on?"

"Frankly, Larry, you and I love and support each other, but this sounds like blackmail."

"That's putting it the wrong way. I would never broadcast your relationship. That would be breaking the Eighth Commandment. You often hear me say, 'Let's do some good today'. I'm giving you the chance to do just that."

Father Ralph looked down at his hands and out the window.

He's thinking.

"What's this got to do with Angel?"

"Pablo. We can do something for Angel that we didn't do for Pablo."

He's thinking some more.

"Angel is a student at Burton. Not where he should be. I want him accepted at Riordan. It has a residential program, which would take him out of the Bayview and his environment. If you agree to pay his tuition, I'll get Mark to work on a quick acceptance, and we can write out a recommendation."

Father Ralph looked at the crowd.

"What are you thinking?" Larry asked.

"How many years of tuition?"

"Just two years."

"Okay. I'll do it in memory of Cornelius."

From the back seat, Hieu pinched both of Father Ralph's shoulders.

Larry looked in the rear-view mirror at his own smile and Hieu's.

They were about to do some good.

"I have another idea. After Angel graduates, I can start a memorial scholarship in memory of Cornelius."

"I like that, Ralph. Don't you, Hieu?"

"I do."

As they approached the crowd, Larry overheard Father Ralph enlightening Hieu. "God sanctifies everything, even wealth, and it can be used for good. Larry knows me pretty well. He's turned my mess into something good."

Larry looked for Larissa. Groups seemed to be gathered according to age or type of dress. She stood next to Mrs. Gloria Padilla. A long, chestnut-colored scarf around her neck lifted in the wind, and a graphite-gray coat was buttoned up over a black skirt.

"Mrs. Padilla?"

"Yes, sir."

"I'm Inspector Leahy. This is Inspector Trang and Father Ralph MacKenzie."

"I'm pleased to meet you."

"My condolences for your loss," Father Ralph said and stood still.

"My condolences, Mrs. Padilla. I just want to tell you what a fine man Pablo was." Larry stood still, too, but knew it was the right thing to say.

"Thank you for coming." She wrapped her hands around Larry's.

Hieu stepped forward and said, "I'm very sorry for what happened."

"Thank you. I'm so glad two police officers have come. Pablo was a good boy. I wanted a better life for both my sons. If I had stayed in Mexico, they would have been better behaved, but there are few opportunities in Mexico, and coming here could give them a better life. I blame myself."

Pools of water gathered in her brown eyes.

Hieu knew what was required. He put his arm around her and held on.

Angel stood by her side. Larry introduced himself and watched Angel take a step back. He was shorter and thinner than Pablo. His mother told him to shake hands.

Hieu reached his arm around Mrs. Padilla, took Angel's hand, and said, "Angel is a fine young man, Mrs. Padilla. Perhaps, Inspector Leahy and I can help him."

The presider began. The wind blotted out some of his words, and Larry felt himself drifting, people beginning to blend in with the gray background. The service revolver rubbed against his hip, and his neck got chilled. Not far off he could see a bright white statue of Lacrimosa. Large black letters were printed beneath the doleful figure reclining on her pedestal.

Lacrimosa dies illa (Full of tears will be that day).

Forgetting is the last stage of forgiveness. He wanted to forget the past and the transgressions of others and wondered if Pablo was at peace inside the polished white coffin under the gold crucifix. The chrome fender of a parakeet-blue Chevrolet Impala blocked the road by the gravesite, and an over-rotated axel squeaked.

With an exaggerated vibrato, the priest sang the final song. To Larry, he resembled a hard-snouted swine, burying himself by day in the paper slop of a parish office and never seeing the light. The lack of color in his face had come from spending too much time in his office, not from listening to a poor sinner's admissions in the dark confessional.

On a day such as this, the fog was strong enough to spread a burn over the pale face of this Irish priest.

Get rid of those thoughts. This day is for the dead.

Larissa threw a handful of dirt on Pablo's coffin.

Larry felt sympathy for her stab him deeply. Now, he understood that Pablo had used Larissa. He had stripped away her self-esteem to boost his own.

Drizzle swept over the gravestones, and a new wind whipped up dresses, baggy pants, and scarves. Larry's wet eyelids were closed, and he swayed back and forth, when there was a tap on his shoulder.

"The crowd is breaking up. Should we talk to her now?" Hieu asked.

"Okay."

Larry, Hieu, and Father Ralph took their places at the end of a line. Larissa and Angel stood on either side of Mrs. Padilla, and the rumble of Impalas started. Larry saw no sign of Pablo's father and thought Mrs. Padilla must be divorced.

"Mrs. Padilla. We would like to speak to you privately. Can we take a short walk?" On the other side of the grave, Larry said, "There's a residential program at Riordan High School. We'd like to get Angel admitted and finish the rest of high school there. If you are concerned about cost, we think we can take care of that."

She embraced Larry immediately. His hands touched the back of her shoulders lightly, and she released him. "How wonderful you are. I don't know what to say." She hugged him again and stood back. "Would Angel be able to come home on weekends?"

"He could come home for Thanksgiving, Christmas, and Easter. You could arrange to visit him on weekends."

"I'd miss him, but if you think it's a good program, I would agree to it. We have to talk to Angel."

"We have to be firm with him. Give him no other option. Either he accepts, or he will continue to be monitored by his juvenile probation officer. That was part of the agreement you and the Assistant DA worked out."

Hieu heard his cue and said, "Let me talk to Angel."

Larry and Mrs. Padilla watched as Hieu and Angel sat down on a marble bench a short distance away. Larissa stood over the grave, and Larry put his hands in his pockets.

"How would this be paid for, Mr. Leahy?"

"We can get him a full scholarship, but we wanted to get your approval first. Father Ralph will make the arrangements." Father Ralph nodded.

Mrs. Padilla looked worried. "Angel is a poor student."

"Don't worry. Riordan can turn things around. What kind of work do you do, Mrs. Padilla?"

"I have a house cleaning business. Two women work for me. I own a home, but there's little left over."

She kissed Larissa on the cheek when she rejoined them.

The presiding priest and the cars had departed.

Hieu and Angel returned.

"Inspector Trang, have you told Angel about the plan?" Larry asked.

"Yes." Hieu looked at Angel, who looked at his mother.

"Angel, it's up to you, but this is what I want," she said.

Angel put his hands in his back pockets. "Yeah, I guess so."

"Mr. Leahy, thank you so much." She kissed Larry.

Hieu, Larry, and Father Ralph shook hands with Angel before the sad, little group of three, Angel, Mrs. Padilla, and Larissa, departed.

Larry thought Hieu should get some sort of reward.

"So, Hieu, Ralph, I'm going to call Mark next – get Angel admitted. We have a lot in front of us. What did Angel have to say?"

"He listened to me, Larry. I talked about Pablo first. I told him we could arrange for his probation to end if he accepted. He didn't want to leave his friends, but I told him there wasn't any other choice, and he didn't say much after that."

"Good. I'm going to call Maureen Daley. Knowing James has been arrested may help her tell me what she knows. But, first, a call to Mark."

Hieu had a small smile on his face. "He'll agree, Larry. Trust me."

Larry punched in number three.

"How are you, Mark?"

"Dad?"

"Listen carefully. I'm trying to get a young man into Riordan's residential program. His name is Angel Morales. His brother, Pablo Morales . . . killed himself, and I just left his funeral. Angel is a student at Burton High School. Go to Riordan and get his application process started. Father Ralph and I will send in recommendations, and Father Ralph will pay the tuition."

"What? I don't even know this kid. What should I say?" Mark asked.

"Just vouch for him . . . on my word. We'll write the necessary recommendations."

"When is all this happening?"

"Right away. I'll fill you in later. I need your help. Please join us in looking after this boy. He needs us."

He's thinking.

"I guess so. Yes, I'll do it."

"Thank you, son."

Hieu smiled.

•••

Father Ralph looked at his cell phone: 2:30 p.m. The funeral and college applications had left him worn-out. On his desk was his mother's letter, which was several years old. He had received his brother's possessions and was organizing them when he found the letter.

It contained an account of Cornelius' first attempt at piloting a new 1967 Chris Craft 46' vessel.

Cornelius took hold of the steering wheel and gunned the engine. Dad had to jump to the controls and turn off the engine before we hit the shoreline. What a sight it would have been had we run up onto the Marina Green. Cornelius had such a self-satisfied look on his face. Remember, we all started laughing. How old was he?

Cornelius was nine. Father Ralph couldn't remember how the letter wound up in Cornelius' possessions.

Dad let Cornelius take charge of the boat. Dad was still in denial.

He came to the place in the letter where his mother reminded him to look after Cornelius. She wrote about his attempt to become an altar boy.

Sister Mary Clement pleaded with the pastor to let him be an altar boy. He refused, claiming Cornelius could not retain the lengthy Latin responses. Sister confided to me that before he ran home, she used the black serge sleeve of her habit to wipe away his tears.

Father Ralph opened his office door with the letter in hand. He looked at his assistant and said, "Please send this to my sister. She can keep it. I don't have a place for it. Thanks."

He looked across the room at a wall plaque given to him by a former student. The shellacked wooden plaque hung on a wall to the right of his large desk.

Fathers, do not anger your children. Bring them up with the training and instruction befitting the Lord. Ephesians, 6:4.

He crossed campus and saw Josh walking alone and stepping over green puddles.

"Josh! Aren't you supposed to be at work?"

"I have time, and I have some things to say to you."

They walked like two strangers through the back door and into the sacristy.

Father Ralph said, "Please sit down."

Josh stared at him. "I want to come back to Mass. Before I do, I have to know some things about you."

"I understand. However, my personal life is not going to be the subject of our conversation. I want you to come back, and I have someone I'd like you to consider training."

"As my replacement?" Josh yelled and walked out.

Father Ralph rushed after him.

On the mud, under a cypress tree, Josh turned and said, "Leave me alone."

"I apologize for what happened. You're not old enough to understand all this, but I want you to reconsider. What brought you back?"

"I don't know. Who is that woman? And what are you going to do? I'm not a baby and don't treat me like one."

"You're too young to understand. I know I'm not what you thought I was, but I'm going to make some changes. I can't say more."

"And neither can I."

"Wait."

"Why should I?" Josh said, without looking back.

"I promise things will be better."

"How do I know?" he asked, looking at the campus.

"Things will be better."

Father Ralph looked up as the bell tolled.

"How can I know that for sure?"

"You've served Mass with me these three years. You know I wouldn't make a promise unless I meant it. There's something else I want to ask. I want you to train a new altar server. Uncle Larry is working on a plan for Angel Morales."

"What! Pablo Morales was a thug, and so is his brother."

Father Ralph thought of the words Larry had spoken to Mark.

"Trust me on this. Angel needs someone like you to help him. You know what to do. You're the best person for this."

He's thinking.

"What's it got to do with me?"

"Your uncle is trying to get Angel into Riordan and turn his life around."

Josh turned around, and his hands dropped. "If Uncle Larry agrees to this, then I will, too."

"Thank you. Be here at half past six Monday morning. I'll introduce you to Angel, and you can show him what to do."

Josh pulled down hard on his baseball cap, and Father Ralph pulled down hard on his Roman collar.

•••

"Maureen, this is Larry Leahy. I'm coming over to speak to you. I should be there at four o'clock."

He rang her doorbell.

Let's do some more good.

Maureen ushered him into the living room.

"Maureen, James was arrested for solicitation to commit murder. I want to ask you about your relationship with him. Are you pregnant with his child?"

She sank into the chesterfield next to him. "Did James tell you that?" She reached for her wine glass and stopped. With a hand pressed down on the coffee table, she leaned forward, swept a magazine onto the floor, and sank back into the cushions. "James and I decided to put the baby up for adoption. I refused an abortion."

"What connection is there between the adoption agency and the land?"

"I had to find a reputable adoption agency, so I visited Cornelius. His sister had adopted two children, and we decided to use the same agency." She took a deep breath. "Cornelius and I discovered accidentally we were using the same agency James' parents had used."

She picked at her nails.

"I don't get it. Why did James want to purchase the land?"

"I told James what we did. He was furious. I told him it didn't matter, but he said it did matter. He was worried about Clare finding out. I told him she wouldn't."

"Mr. Smith told me that James wanted Cornelius killed."

"That's nonsense. James never said anything of the sort."

"He did, to Gerald Smith."

"Who is he?"

"An ex-bellboy."

"That explains it. A disgruntled employee."

"No, I'm afraid not. James told him there was some damaging information. Mr. Smith didn't know what it was, but we know. Now, you were at James' house the night of the murder. Were you there the entire time?"

"Yes, I was. James was furious that Cornelius knew about the baby. James planned to buy that land and give it to the church. I asked him why. He said it made him feel better. Maybe, it was a way to redeem himself for straying from marriage. Anyway, he gets it into his head to sue the agency for agreeing to meet us. He said they should have told us to go elsewhere."

Wow.

"He got angry and told me not to tell anyone else about the baby. He was mixed up. I feel sorry that I got him into this mess."

Larry's face darkened. Thinking about the past made his head heavy. His father and James' father had given their sons a horrible legacy of deceit and crime. The police notepad fell into the crease of the chair.

"All right. Is there anything else you need to tell me?"

"No."

Larry let go of the silky armrest.

"Back to the night of the murder . . . just for a minute. Were you with James the entire night?"

"Yes, until two in the morning, when I went home."

Why is she lying?

"Did you drive yourself home or did James offer to take you home?"

She didn't answer.

"Has he been good to you?"

"I didn't know all this would happen. James told me to find another agency. I'm still looking."

"Has James helped you with that?"

"No." Her eyes roamed the room. "Can you?"

"I will do whatever I can to help you, but please tell the truth."

"James gave me a gun. He said it belonged to Cornelius. I told him to give it to the police. He said no."

She grabbed the wine glass from the coffee table, walked to the liquor cabinet, and nervously pointed her forefinger down. "I don't want to see it. Just take it."

Her hand dropped, and she stepped away.

"One more question. Did James leave during the night . . . before midnight?"

"I didn't see him for a while, but there were so many guests, I couldn't really be sure."

"I called James that night at about two. Did he take you home?"

She didn't answer.

Larry placed the police notepad in his breast pocket. His rough hand rubbed against the armrest's fabric as he pushed himself up.

Maureen looked deflated.

He turned the cloth-covered cabinet knob, its yellow and gold tassel becoming entwined in his fingers, and pulled the door open.

There it is.

"Thank you, Maureen, for being honest. I'll take care of this."

He stuck the police pen inside the trigger and lifted the gun.

"Do you have a paper bag, Maureen?"

"Yes, I'll get one."

Larry followed her to the kitchen and said, "I'm finished with the questions." The gun rocked back and forth. "Did you happen to go with James to the Greenwich on the night Cornelius was found dead?"

"Yes. I wasn't honest about that. I'm sorry."

They stood face-to-face. He dropped the gun into the bag. "Did you go into the hotel with him?"

"No. I stayed in the car in the garage."

"What time was it?"

"About midnight."

"How long was he in the hotel?"

"About an hour, maybe less."

"When he returned, did he say anything?"

"We drove home in silence."

"Whose home?"

"Mine."

"And did he leave you after that?"

"We said good-bye in the car."

"Did you see the gun?"

"When he came back to the garage, he handed it to me. I told him I didn't want it. After kissing me, he said he would tell me more about the gun at another time. I knew he owned a gun, but the one he gave me didn't look like his. I was upset the whole way home and couldn't get to sleep, so I took a sleeping pill, against doctor's orders."

"Thank you. Tomorrow, give Lauren a call, and we'll help find a good adoption agency. Maureen, you've got the future in your hands. Funny, me giving comfort to someone who's had six children, but it might help. When St. Theresa of Calcutta was asked why God hadn't given the world a cure for AIDS, she said, 'You aborted the future.' You did the best you could."

She kissed him on the lips, and he felt a little embarrassed.

Only one cloud lingered, and it was on a different lady.

Larry needed to clear his head. A walk on the Mt. Davidson foot path would give him some fresh air and some time to think about what had happened and what would come next. The trailhead was a few yards from Maureen's home.

A light drizzle had soaked the path and stairs, which coiled in a loop that would take him to the top of the city's highest hill. His black jacket brushed against hanging vines of elderberry and blackberry, leaving traces of dark green, sapphire, and yellow. He kept his hands in his pockets to avoid the sting of their branches. He spotted a garter snake, but didn't see a single coyote, and the ground felt hallowed when the sound of chirping, resident white-crowned sparrows reached his ears.

Mud and eucalyptus leaves stuck to shoes that got him to the base of the 103-foot cross. On the side of the cross was an old bolt ladder. The first bolt was missing, and most of the ladder rested on rusted hangers. Dusk was approaching. He walked to a knoll and looked out over the city. Two women, Maureen and Clare, in love with the same man, confirmed that love often leads to results unintended.

It wasn't unlike Father Ralph's dilemma. He loved two women but was committed to just one, the Church.

He slid on the last step of the loop, and the forest's spell was broken.

•••

Lauren's cigarette balanced in the groove of a pink ashtray adorned with tiny yellow and blue flowers. Larry took off his jacket.

Lauren grabbed it and looked it over. "How did you get these?"

"Mt. Davidson." Larry smelled pot roast and trail stains. "It's okay. They'll come out in the wash."

He slid into the bench seat.

"What were you doing there?"

"Thinking."

Her eyes stared fearlessly back at him. Two hissing burners warmed the smell of whiskey and tea, and seven chimes in the entry hall signaled the end of another day.

"I don't see the point of helping that boy. He's like his brother. No good." She stood fixed in place, toes riveted to her slippers, hands dripping suds onto the kitchen floor.

"How did you know?"

"Mark was here."

"I'm going by my instincts, Lauren . . . trust me."

Lauren dried her hands on the passion pink bathrobe as she walked from the stove to the bench seat, slid in, and pushed up her eyeglasses. When a few bits of gravel hit the window panes, she looked out. Larry could hear sparrows chittering on the roof gutter.

I wish I was outside with them.

"You never helped Mark."

"Mark agreed."

"To what? You still haven't come to terms with him, and here you are helping someone else, a total stranger. You don't need any more excuses. Helping a stranger over your own son. What kind of father are you?"

"I can't help that Mark has forgotten about sin, but he agreed to support Angel."

"That's no answer. You're his father. Tell him to stop living with her. Put your foot down." She reached across the table with a free hand. He pulled it down to the cold tablecloth. One of her eyelids flickered when he let go. He slid off the seat, crossed the floor, and poured the Jack Daniels in the sink.

After dinner had ended, he sat in his favorite chair, moved his son's pipe from one side of the end table to the other, and cleared away everything else. "Was Mark sitting in my chair?"

The clanging of pots made it impossible to hear anything.

Something shattered.

"Dammit."

The closet door banged against the swinging door, followed by scratching and swishing sounds.

Chapter 20

Monday, July 15

While Father Ralph was vesting, Angel sat on a chair on the other side of the room. Angel's white socks showed below tan trousers. Josh appeared and said nothing to Father Ralph.

"I'm Josh. Father likes polished black shoes. The tan Dockers need to go. He likes black slacks. Do you have a pair?"

"Yeah, whatever."

"Just follow me and do what I do." Josh walked over to the closets, three in a row, and opened one. Out came a black cassock and white surplice. "Put these on."

"What the . . ." Angel looked at Father Ralph. "I don't wear dresses."

"They aren't dresses. They're called cassocks. Try it on. Take your jacket off first."

To Father Ralph's surprise and elation, Angel obediently did what he was told. Josh took off his baseball cap, smoothed down his cowlick, and pulled the black cassock over his head.

"Good. Guys, we are ready to start. Angel, when you get into the sanctuary, stay on the kneeler. Josh will show you where and watch what Josh does. He's an expert." Josh glanced quickly at Father Ralph and motioned to Angel to get behind him. Father Ralph looked at the back of the heads of two boys and wondered how it would go.

After Mass, back in the sacristy, Father Ralph listened to their conversation.

"How long you been doin' this?" Angel asked, as he took off the surplice and cassock. "Where do I put these?

"About three years. I'll hang them up for you."

"Where you go to school?"

"St. Ignatius," Josh said without turning around. "I hear you'll be going to Riordan."

"Yeah, that's what all of them want. Me, I don't know about it. I'm leaving all my homies."

"Yeah, I can understand that, but Riordan is a pretty good school, and you'll make new friends."

He faced Angel, who looked back at him.

"You got many friends?" Angel asked.

"Yeah, I do."

"Girlfriend?"

"What . . . no."

Josh stepped back against the closet door.

Father Ralph had removed the last of his vestments, watched, and listened.

I know where this is going. Josh doesn't.

"I knew about Pablo," Angel said.

"What?"

"I knew he was gay."

"What are you talking about? He had a girlfriend, Larissa."

"So. Don't make no difference. He was gay. I got no problem with it. My friends are against gays, but I'm not. Pablo was the best thing in my life. So, uh, I got no problem with your being gay, either."

"But I'm not."

"Sure."

Josh quickly put the baseball cap on. "Do you like the Giants?"

"No. I'm an Oakland A's fan. I bet you're a runner."

"How do you know that?"

"You're lean . . . leaner than me. Can we go outside and have a smoke?"

"We can go outside, but I don't smoke. I serve Mass on Mondays, Wednesdays, and Fridays. Can you be here on Wednesday?"

"Yeah sure, bro. You got a ride? My mom is parked across the street."

"I walk home. Does your mom know you smoke?"

"Yeah, listen, bro, you can be honest with me." Angel looked at Father Ralph. "I think it's better we start off . . . well, you know what I'm sayin'?"

"No. See you at quarter to seven, Wednesday."

•••

At half past nine, Larry received a call from Father Ralph, who gave a good report on Angel and Josh.

Larry asked Varton for the phone call record on the night of the murder, all incoming and outgoing calls. Varton retrieved the logs. Back in his office, Larry sifted through the calls, disqualified irrelevant ones, and made a list on his large yellow notepad.

1) *Last call from Smith to the lobby, 2345 hours, answered*
2) *Page from lobby desk to Cornelius room at 2355 hours, unanswered*
3) *Page from lobby desk to Cornelius room at 2356 hours, unanswered*
4) *Call from O'Hara to lobby 2358 hours, sent to Cornelius, answered*

Larry jotted down all calls from O'Hara's cell phone.

1) *O'Hara calls the lobby desk at 2358 hours, answered*

2) O'Hara calls Pablo's phone at 2400 hours, answered.

Numbers started turning blue, but the color faded, and Larry concluded that Cornelius was in his room at the time O'Hara's call was passed through because Cornelius knew who it was and answered, but Cornelius didn't want to reply to the other pages, because he was tired. Who paged Cornelius? Larry concluded that O'Hara called Pablo at 2400 hours to be sure Pablo had the gun. Who was in Cornelius' room after midnight? He thought he knew.

At half past ten, Hieu walked in.

"I spoke to Joe on my way in, Larry. The fingerprint tests just arrived. It's conclusive. The fingerprints on the gun from Mrs. Daley belong to her, Gerald Smith, and Pepper Chase. Joe has issued an arrest warrant for Chase."

"All we have to do now is find her. I have a plan, and I'm right in the middle of it."

Larry picked up the receiver. "Joe, I'm using Smith as bait to find Chase. I know this will work. Thanks." Larry looked at Hieu and said, "I hope Smith comes through."

The morning passed without a word from Gerald. Hieu and Larry drove to Pepper's apartment building after lunch and asked the desk clerk if he had seen Pepper.

"No, sir."

"Have any of the other clerks said anything about her? Has anyone seen her?"

"No, sir."

The afternoon passed by as if something were about to happen.

At five o'clock, Hieu and Joe went home.

In the dark of his office, Larry started thinking. He had confirmed Father Ralph's affair, and O'Hara sat in jail. It seemed as if the world had come crashing down. What had happened to them? He tried to understand Father Ralph's desires. He tried to understand O'Hara's desires. Neither one had self-control. Could he ever forgive them?

If I didn't believe in God and His guidance, I might have lost my way.

The love between a father and his son, or between a husband and his wife, joins them, the way the Holy Spirit joins Father and Son.

Why don't people understand?

The phone rang just before his eyes closed, and he leapt in his chair.

"Hello, Gerald. Yes. Excellent. Where? I'll pick you up in . . . ten minutes. Be waiting outside." The receiver hit the cradle.

Larry slapped his police light on the roof before backing out. His radio sputtered and sparked to life, and the dispatcher repeated the code for a female suspect and her location. A mix of pity and indignation kept his thoughts moving, and his siren kept pedestrians plugging their ears.

This isn't looking good.

A vermillion sunset lit the streets and buildings. His call to Father Ralph went to voicemail. A fire engine came out of nowhere, and its siren invaded the interior of the Chevy. He rolled up the window. The fire engine's bright red lights swept the streets and signaled a race to keep someone alive.

Gerald hopped in, dressed in a heavy, navy pea coat.

"Be prepared for anything," Larry said.

"I'm ready."

A sparkling Venus shown through layered colors of dusty orange and purple above Fort Point.

Larry saw her sitting on the seawall.

Gerald left Larry's side, rushed forward, and put his arm around her. Waves rolled, and seagulls circled for a late catch on white wings that turned and dipped. The salty smell and the structure of the bridge above reminded him of Pablo and imparted a sense of urgency and the purpose for being there.

In the damp air, Larry took off his stained jacket and threw it on the driver's seat. Now he was short-sleeved and ready to go. He walked quickly to the seawall.

"Hello, Pepper."

"Hello."

"I'm glad you're here. Where have you been?"

In a weak voice, she said, "I needed some time off. I talked to my aunt. She told me to be truthful."

"You know I want to ask you a few more questions and get this over with. Can we move over there under the light?" He gestured toward the fort. She didn't move. "The waves are very loud." She was sitting sideways, looking down at the water. Larry found a spot and sat down close to her.

Larry looked at each successive wave, the upper curls lit by the fort's spotlight.

They sat there under a single street light that allowed shadows to fill every layer of the fort's brick façade. Two sides of the square fortress disappeared into the dark.

It's warm, and my sadness is almost, almost gone.

She raised herself off the seawall's barnacles and sat down facing Gerald with both of her arms clasped together, each dressed in red. "Gerald bought me a new red sweater a few weeks ago to replace the one I lost."

Larry could barely hear Pepper. "Can you answer one or two questions?"

She looked at Gerald and said, "Yes, I think so."

"On the night Cornelius died, there were two pages to him. Both came from the lobby desk phone. Did you page Cornelius?" Larry hoped Gerald's gentle presence would cajole an answer.

"Yes, Gerald asked me to page Cornelius."

"That's right, Inspector, I wanted to talk to Cornelius."

Larry leaned forward, and his back cracked. He raised his voice, saying, "Gerald, you wanted to speak to Cornelius about borrowing money. Isn't that right?"

"Yes."

"Gerald, I would have loaned you some money. Why didn't you ask?"

Larry couldn't see her face and tried to move, but back pain kept him stationary.

Gerald said, "Pepper, you're barely managing. I would never ask for money."

"Pepper, did you page Cornelius a second time?"

She turned toward Larry and said, "No."

"Who did the page come from? Can you help me?"

Her voice gained strength as she said, "It could have come from Doris."

"Why would she page Cornelius?"

In a quiver, she responded, "I . . . I'm not sure."

She turned away and faced the thrashing waves. Her dress caught on the barnacles. She lifted herself again and sat down. Barnacles picked at her dress with the slightest movement.

"Pepper, tell us what happened. Were you at the Security office that night?"

"I can't remember."

"Did you go there to get a gun?"

"I went there during my break. I was angry at Cornelius for having an affair with that woman."

All eyes scanned the foam.

"Pepper, Cornelius did not have an affair with Maureen Daley. She was pregnant by another man and went to Cornelius for help. They searched for an adoption agency . . . and found one. That's all."

"But there was the e-mail. He said he was in debt and needed money. I knew he was spending too much money on her."

"Did you go to the Security office before or after you brought him the money?"

"Is that important?" she asked. The air was heavy, and she dropped her head.

Gerald reached around and cradled her face. He let go, lifted her hand to his lips, and kissed trembling fingers.

Pepper weaved before wrenching her hand free.

Larry saw the red fingernail polish. "What color nail polish were you wearing that night?"

Suddenly, Pepper's face brightened. "It was a special nail color. Quan said it was perfect for the night. Black, red, and blue, a shimmery black. I forget the name. I'm confused."

"Did you go to the Security office that night?"

"Yes."

Pepper raised her head and looked at Gerald.

"After or before you brought Cornelius the money?"

"After."

"What time?"

"After midnight. Gerald had left, I wasn't sure, but the time was right."

"Did you see anyone at the Security office?"

"No."

"Did anyone see you there?"

"No. Did someone say they saw me? That must be it! Someone saw me. That's why you're asking me all these questions."

Larry began to panic. She might stop talking.

"You're doing really great, Pepper. Just one or two more questions, and we're done. How long were you there?"

She answered quickly, "A few minutes."

"Did you take a gun?"

"Yes."

There it is.

In the bright reflection of the foam, Pepper's face grew pale.

"What did you do next?"

Pepper took a breath and then another.

Gerald looked around Pepper and said, "Inspector, Pepper looks really sick."

"Are you comfortable? Do you want to move somewhere? We can talk in the car."

She stared ahead.

"Pepper, did you get a call from Mr. O'Hara?" Larry asked.

"Yes. I forgot to tell you that. I sent the call to Cornelius."

"What did O'Hara say?"

"He asked if Cornelius was in the lobby."

"And you told him Cornelius was in his apartment?"

"Yes."

"So, you went to the Security office and took the gun. You were angry. What happened next?"

"Gerald will hate me." She averted her eyes and stared at the foam.

"He will love you more if you tell the truth. Remember what your aunt said."

"I loved Cornelius."

"Which is why you did . . . what . . . ." Gerald said, and then he was silent.

"You took the gun and went to his room. You meant to confront him about his affair with Maureen. You didn't mean to do anything else. Is that right?" Larry asked.

A seagull swooped down. Pepper leaned back sharply and flailed at the bird as if she could strike it dead. A silver bangle slid down to her elbow, and she gave in. "Yes, Inspector. You understand. Cornelius understood, but that night I was . . ."

A barnacle pulled on her dress.

"You were terribly upset, and you wanted to tell Cornelius that you loved him."

"Yes. That's all I wanted to do."

Her breaths gradually slowed.

Her face reflected the rose-gold glow of the bridge.

Larry paused before asking, "How did the gun go off?"

"I don't know. I can't remember what happened next."

There it is.

She had confessed.

Larry leaned slightly forward.

The back pain was gone.

Sirens pierced the night.

Larry raised his voice, rushing to ask one final question. "What time did you get back to the front desk?"

"I don't remember. Pablo was there, but Gerald was gone." She looked at Gerald. "Why didn't you take me away?"

He started to say something, and Larry said, "After you paged Cornelius for Gerald, you paged Cornelius a second time. He didn't answer. You needed an answer. So, you got the gun and went to his apartment. Did you let yourself in or ring the doorbell?"

"I rang the doorbell."

"And the first time you saw O'Hara that night was when he came to the Greenwich and spoke to us. Do I have that right?"

"Yes. Am I in trouble?"

Larry reached into his jacket and felt for the voice recorder. He hoped that their voices had been audible over the waves, birds, and sirens.

"Inspector, I want to do everything possible to help Pepper."

"Yes, of course." Larry walked toward the sweeping lights. After a brief conversation with the officers, he walked to his car and tossed the soiled jacket from the front seat to the back seat. A somber and pale-looking Gerald joined him on the front seat.

Their long journey had ended with a handcuffed girl sitting in the back of a squad car beneath a landmark.

Epilogue

Tuesday, July 16

"I called Mark and Joan this morning. Your shirt is downstairs." Lauren removed her house dress in front of Larry, put on a spruce-blue dress, adjusted new frames, and draped a brand new flowered scarf over her shoulders, which blew back in Larry's face as she danced down the stairs. A hanger holding his starched, white shirt hung on the kitchen closet doorknob. She checked the corned beef roasting in the oven.

The setting sun brightened the steamed-up windows and gave the kitchen walls a golden glow. The neighborhood crow was roosting elsewhere. A new, unopened Jack Daniels bottle was sitting on the counter. Larry inhaled the aroma of mustard and brown sugar, and Lauren gave the kitchen a once-over before handing him his shirt.

"What did she say when you called?" he asked.

"She was thrilled. I think she's nervous. Be good, and don't go on and on at the table. Have you ordered the hearing aid, yet?"

"No time. I hear they don't work very well."

"They will for you, dear."

Lauren kissed Larry on the lips.

He put his fingertips on her eyeglasses. "I like these. Are they new?" He hugged her and felt her stomach against his. "Have you gained weight?"

"No."

Larry put on the white shirt, and Lauren knotted a new, blue silk tie.

"When did you buy this?"

"Never mind." She patted his chest. "That looks nice."

He kissed her.

Joan complimented Lauren on her crab hors d'oeuvres and cheese puffs and offered to make margaritas. A few minutes later, Larry watched her crescent lips rise as he licked the salt on the rim.

Before Lauren served dinner, the phone rang. Larry sprang to his feet, saluted the framed picture of the pope, and noticed a never-seen-before, medium gray, suit jacket with white pin stripes. It hung on the coat rack. He checked the tag on the inside label. Half-price.

"Yes. How are you Gerald?" During the conversation, he kept his eyes focused on Mark, who was looking down at his stomach. Larry knew another diet was in the making.

Larry hung up and walked back into living room. "That was Gerald Smith."

"Who's he, Dad?"

"Very nice young man. He worked at the Greenwich and got mixed up with all this. Anyway, he told me he accepted a new job. The Topaz Lake Lodge wants him to rent boats and fishing equipment and manage the fishing contests. He told me that Cornelius recommended him for the job before he died."

"How did the case turn out?"

"Well, it's a long story." With a glint in his eye, Larry sat down in his green chair opposite Mark and began.

"Pepper Chase, one of the front desk clerks, killed Cornelius. The gun she used was one of two nine-millimeter guns stolen from the Greenwich Security office. She took one, and Pablo Morales took the other. Two guns, the Pepper gun and the Morales gun, confused the hell out of me.

"James O'Hara wanted Cornelius dead and asked Morales to do the deed. O'Hara thought that Morales bought a gun with the $500 he gave Morales. O'Hara must have carefully extracted five one-hundred-dollar bills from one of the bundles of $10,000, but he didn't know that the gun Morales gave him was the one Morales had stolen from the Security office.

"Morales used the $500 to buy a gun from a drug dealer, but he needed money and probably kept the gun at home. He planned to pawn it, which he did the day after the murder. He went to the Security office and stole the nine-millimeter gun. Morales had a conscience, and I think he was the one who called Cornelius and warned him that his life was in danger. He decided not to kill Cornelius and gave O'Hara the stolen gun on the night of the murder. More?"

"Yes. This sounds exciting."

Larry polished off his margarita.

"Murder is never exciting. Gerald Smith found Cornelius dead. Gerald picked up the gun that O'Hara got from Morales. The gun had fallen out of O'Hara's pocket onto the floor in the hallway. Gerald picked it up and rubbed it in O'Hara's face. Then he must have dropped it and rushed out of the building. O'Hara ran into Cornelius' apartment and found him dead. At that point, O'Hara didn't know who killed Cornelius. It was looking bad for him. He had solicited a murder, but the gun he held in a handkerchief had Smith's fingerprints on it. He placed the gun next to Cornelius' body. That was the Morales gun. He took the gun that was there, the Pepper gun, which she had used to kill Cornelius.

"O'Hara wanted people to believe that Smith had killed Cornelius. He gave the Pepper gun to Maureen Daley for safekeeping. Maureen turned it over to me, and Pepper confessed."

"Why did Pepper kill Cornelius?"

"She was in love with him and thought he was having an affair with Maureen Daley. Pepper killed him in a fit of jealousy."

"Why did O'Hara want to kill Cornelius?'

"Ah, that was the question that had me stumped for a long time. It's the most important aspect of the case . . . and the most damning. O'Hara got Maureen pregnant. O'Hara is married. Cornelius' sister had adopted several children, which Maureen knew about, so Maureen went to Cornelius for help finding an adoption agency. They went to the same agency that adopted O'Hara to his parents. What a coincidence!

"Maureen told O'Hara what they had done. He was scared that Cornelius might tell his brother, and he threatened to fire Cornelius. Whether he would have told Father Ralph or not, or what he would have said we'll never know."

Mark raised his eyebrows with a look of surprise.

"I know. It sounds crazy and irrational, but O'Hara felt threatened by the loss of two of the most important things in his life: his fortune and his marriage. O'Hara had himself convinced that Clare would have demanded a divorce if she found out he was the father of another woman's baby. Whether she would have, we'll never know.

"When you think about it, O'Hara had a lot to lose. In the end, O'Hara didn't need to do anything. Pepper took care of his problem.

"O'Hara was arrested for soliciting a murder, first with Gerald Smith and then with Pablo Morales.

"Now all the secrets have been revealed. As for Pepper Chase, it will be up to the DA to determine the charge and up to a jury to determine guilt."

"Cornelius didn't deserve to die," Lauren said. She and Joan sat next to each other on the soft, green sofa.

"You must be glad it's over, Dad."

"It's all in a day's work. As Mom would say, it wouldn't be called 'work' if it was easy. Work can be compared to the making of a fine sword. A blade, pounded again and again at the foundry, involves effort, but it cuts clean.

"This is one murder I'll never forget."

The foursome sat down for dinner.

Before apple pie was served, Mark said, "Mom, Dad, I have some good news. Joan is pregnant, and we've decided to get married."

Larry saw the look of surprise on Lauren's face.

"Mark, Joan, I'm so happy for you," Lauren roared.

"Did I hear right? You're getting married?"

"Yes, Dad."

Larry started clapping and in the middle of their smiles, he said. "I'd like to propose a toast. Raise your glasses, please. To Joan, may she make Mark a wonderful, loving wife, and to Mark, may he make Joan a wonderful, obedient husband." Everyone laughed. "Best news I've heard all year. Would you like Father Ralph to officiate, or have you decided on someone else?"

"We haven't reached a decision about that. I don't know how he would feel about her pregnancy."

"Yes, yes," Joan said. "It's a wonderful idea. Your father is right. Father Ralph is the perfect priest to marry us." She leaned over and kissed Mark. For the first time in weeks, the house smelled good.

After the joy had subsided, an unseen force moved Larry to say, "Let's not give in to indifference and become smug. The Greenwich will never be the same. We lost two wonderful human beings. Cornelius MacKenzie and Pablo Morales. Pablo was a troubled soul and needed help. We didn't give it."

"What could you have done, Dad?"

"Well, look at Angel. He's with you and Father Ralph. Angel will straighten out. We could have brought Pablo to Father Ralph."

"I doubt that would have helped."

"I think it could have. When you have your own problems, you understand someone else's problems better. Father Ralph told me he would have worked with Pablo and taken him to *Courage*."

"I doubt it would have helped, Dad. If you're gay, you should be happy with it and accept it."

"It's not that simple. Your identity comes from God, not from other people or any community, and others can get you confused about your identity. Believing in God and His providence gives you hope, and no person or community can do that . . . not hope that will take you into eternity. The real problem was that Pablo felt rejected by God, and that isn't reality. No one reached into the fog in his mind and cleared it away, not me, not anybody. Let's say an Our Father for him."

When Larry began, Joan joined in.

"Well, I think it's time for another announcement. I got the promotion to Chief Inspector."

Lauren blew a kiss from her seat. "You deserved it, dear."

Mark and Joan congratulated him in perfect unison.

Larry rubbed his face and put his hands down on the tablecloth. "Go down to the basement and get one of those wines . . . from Europe." Larry thought for a minute. "Bring the one from last summer."

Mark started to get up and said, "No, I know just the one."

When Mark returned, he walked through the kitchen, pulled a corkscrew out of the drawer, which rattled with knick-knacks and coins, and slammed it shut.

Lauren smiled at Joan and said, "I've got to clean it out."

As Mark poured the musky Portuguese wine into his father's glass, Larry asked, "Did you get Angel accepted?"

"Conditionally. Father Ralph sent in his recommendation. Can you send yours?"

"Tomorrow."

"How was your meeting with Angel?"

"I gave him a short diagnostic test, and he's far behind the other students. Phil Marks, an English teacher, and I will set up a schedule. I'll have him for basic math two days a week, and Phil will tutor him in English one day a week."

"Can you help him?"

"I think so. How do I talk to him? He has an attitude."

"Talk to him about his mother and Pablo. They're the only people he loves. He's serving Mass with Josh, and Father Ralph tells me they're getting along. Josh is coming up to Russian River next weekend."

"Maybe, we should invite Angel?"

Larry thought for a minute and said, "I'll have Josh ask Angel."

"I'm coming, too."

"You, Mom?"

"Can I go?"

"Yes, Joan, we'll all go."

Lauren had spoken definitively for everyone.

"I'm going to make a novena . . . for Cornelius and Pablo," Larry said.

At eleven o'clock, Mark and Joan left.

Lauren shuffled up the stairs, and Larry went downstairs. Inside the garbage can, he saw Mark's letter. Lauren must have tossed it out.

Next to the garbage can was Mark's childhood bike, illuminated by a slice of moon light coming through the open door from the backyard. The blue bike lay flush against the wall. The opportunity to help a young man like Angel made him feel good, and Pablo could have been forgiven in the moments before he hit the water, too.

Back upstairs in the bedroom, he read one page of *History of the Roman Empire*, put it down, kissed Lauren, turned over, said an Act of Contrition for the first time in weeks, and wondered if Father Ralph would be the best priest to marry Mark and Joan.

In the middle of the night, he awoke, needing some fresh air. On his nightstand lay reading glasses and a note to buy a hearing aid. To relieve the stuffiness, he walked down two flights of stairs to the basement and out into the back yard.

The sky was unusually clear, and a full moon lit up the back of the house a bright gray. Something brushed against his leg. A ranunculus lay demolished on the grass. Larry tossed it into the garbage can on top of Mark's letter. The Leahy family had crushed one problem, but there are always more to come.

Rise up in splendor! Your light has come, the glory of the Lord shines upon you. See, the darkness covers the earth, and thick clouds cover the peoples; But upon you the Lord shines, and over you appears his glory. Nations shall walk by your light, and kings by your shining radiance. Raise your eyes and look about; they all gather and come to you: Your sons come from afar, and your daughters in the arms of their nurses.

Isaiah 60:1-4

The End

Thank you for reading *Pretty City Murder*. If you enjoyed it, please consider leaving a review at Amazon.com or Goodreads.com.

To keep updated on news from Robert E Dunn Publishing, including the latest books, exclusive discounts, and contests to win books and prizes, please sign up for our newsletter at www.robertedunn.com.

Lightning Source UK Ltd.
Milton Keynes UK
UKHW01n1423050718
325277UK00002B/23/P